Out of the Sand

Out of the Sand

Mummies, Pyramids, and Egyptology in Classic Science Fiction and Fantasy

Chad Arment, Editor

Coachwhip Publications
Landisville, Pennsylvania

Out of the Sand
2008, Coachwhip Publications
Coachwhipbooks.com

ISBN 1-930585-58-6
ISBN-13 978-1-930585-58-4

Front cover images: Sand (AlexanderTheGreat, Fotolia);
Frieze of Thoth (Franck Camhi)
Back cover image: Jackal (Goce Risteski)

Contents

Out of the Sand

He told me, however, of an actual occurrence which may not have been heretofore published. It was to the effect that when the mummies of the kings were being taken away from Luxor some of the natives pretended to be affected with great grief at the carrying away of their ancient kings, and ran along the shore, after the boat, wailing, shrieking and throwing sand into their hair, when suddenly a strange and weird spectacle presented itself; a number of the mummies of the kings, which were spread out on the deck of the boat, and which had been lying motionless and serene for thousands of years, gradually raised their heads as though in recognition of the tribute of respect which the natives were paying, and as though they desired to take a last look at their ancient resting place.

If I said nothing more about this story the sanity of both the professor and myself might seriously be brought into question, and Rider Haggard might also use the incident in a coming story of "He," to illustrate the weird and perpetual power of the early Egyptian sorcerers. As a matter, however, of cold, scientific fact, the apparent miraculous movements were nothing more than the expansion and contraction of the skin, caused by the intense rays of a Luxor sun beating down upon the exposed bodies.

—Finley Acker
Pen Sketches (1899)

The Mummy's Foot

Théophile Gautier

I had entered, in an idle mood, the shop of one of those curiosity-venders, who are called *marchands de bric-à-brac* in that Parisian argot which is so perfectly unintelligible elsewhere in France.

You have doubtless glanced occasionally through the windows of some of these shops, which have become so numerous now that it is fashionable to buy antiquated furniture, and that every petty stock-broker thinks he must have his *chambre au moyen âge.*

There is one thing there which clings alike to the shop of the dealer in old iron, the wareroom of the tapestry-maker, the laboratory of the chemist, and the studio of the painter:—in all those gloomy dens where a furtive daylight filters in through the window-shutters, the most manifestly ancient thing is dust;—the cobwebs are more authentic than the guimp laces; and the old pear-tree furniture on exhibition is actually younger than the mahogany which arrived but yesterday from America.

The warehouse of my *bric-à-brac* dealer was a veritable Capharnaum; all ages and all nations seemed to have made their rendezvous there; an Etruscan lamp of red clay stood upon a Boule cabinet, with ebony panels, brightly striped by lines of inlaid brass; a duchess of the court of Louis XV nonchalantly extended her fawn-like feet under a massive table of the time of Louis XIII with heavy spiral supports of oak, and carven designs of chimeras and foliage intermingled.

Upon the denticulated shelves of several sideboards glittered immense Japanese dishes with red and blue designs relieved by gilded hatching; side by side with enameled works by Bernard Palissy, representing serpents, frogs, and lizards in relief.

From disemboweled cabinets escaped cascades of silver-lustrous Chinese silks and waves of tinsel, which an oblique sunbeam shot through with luminous beads; while portraits of every era, in frames more or less tarnished, smiled through their yellow varnish.

The striped breastplate of a damascened suit of Milanese armor glittered in one corner; Loves and Nymphs of porcelain; Chinese Grotesques, vases of *céladon* and crackle-ware; Saxon and old Souvres cups encumbered the shelves and nooks of the apartment.

The dealer followed me closely through the tortuous way contrived between the piles of furniture; warding off with his hands the hazardous sweep of my coat-skirts; watching my elbows with the uneasy attention of an antiquarian and a usurer.

It was a singular face that of the merchant:—an immense skull, polished like a knee, and surrounded by a thin aureole of white hair, which brought out the clear salmon tint of his complexion all the more strikingly, lent him a false aspect of patriarchal *bonhomie*, counteracted, however, by the scintillation of two little yellow eyes which trembled in their orbits like two louis-d'or upon quicksilver. The curve of his nose presented an aquiline silhouette, which suggested the Oriental or Jewish type. His hands—thin, slender, full of nerves which projected like strings upon the finger-board of a violin, and armed with claws like those on the terminations of bats' wings—shook with senile trembling; but those convulsively agitated hands became firmer than steel pincers or lobsters' claws when they lifted any precious article—an onyx cup, a Venetian glass, or a dish of Bohemian crystal. This strange old man had an aspect so thoroughly rabbinical and cabalistic that he would have been burnt on the mere testimony of his face three centuries ago.

"Will you not buy something from me to-day, sir? Here is a Malay kreese with a blade undulating like flame: look at those grooves contrived for the blood to run along, those teeth set backwards so as to tear out the entrails in withdrawing the weapon—it is a fine character of ferocious arm, and will look well in your collection: this two-handed sword is very beautiful—it is the work of Josepe de la Hera; and this *coliche-marde*, with its fenestrated guard—what a superb specimen of handicraft!"

"No; I have quite enough weapons and instruments of carnage;—I want a small figure, something which will suit me as a paper-weight; for I cannot endure those trumpery bronzes which the stationers sell, and which may be found on everybody's desk."

The old gnome foraged among his ancient wares, and finally arranged before me some antique bronzes—so-called, at least; fragments of malachite; little Hindoo or Chinese idols—a kind of poussah toys in jadestone, representing the incarnations of Brahma or Vishnoo, and wonderfully appro-priate to the very undivine office of holding papers and letters in place.

I was hesitating between a porcelain dragon, all constellated with warts—its mouth formidable with bristling tusks and ranges of teeth—and an abominable little Mexican fetish, representing the god Vitziliputzili *au naturel*, when I caught sight of a charming foot, which I at first took for a fragment of some antique Venus.

It had those beautiful ruddy and tawny tints that lend to Florentine bronze that warm living look so much preferable to the gray-green aspect of common bronzes, which might easily be mistaken for statues in a state of putrefaction: satiny gleams played over its rounded forms, doubtless polished by the amorous kisses of twenty centuries; for it seemed a Corinthian bronze, a work of the best era of art—perhaps molded by Lysippus himself.

"That foot will be my choice," I said to the merchant, who regarded me with an ironical and saturnine air, and held out the object desired that I might examine it more fully.

I was surprised at its lightness; it was not a foot of metal, but in sooth a foot of flesh—an embalmed foot—a mummy's foot: on examining it still more closely the very grain of the skin, and the almost imperceptible lines impressed upon it by the texture of the bandages, became perceptible. The toes were slender and delicate, and terminated by perfectly formed nails, pure and transparent as agates; the great toe, slightly separated from the rest, afforded a happy contrast, in the antique style, to the position of the other toes, and lent it an aerial lightness—the grace of a bird's foot;—the sole, scarcely streaked by a few almost imperceptible cross lines, afforded evidence that it had never touched the bare ground, and had only come in contact with the finest matting of Nile rushes, and the softest carpets of panther skin.

"Ha, ha!—you want the foot of the Princess Hermonthis,"—exclaimed the merchant, with a strange giggle, fixing his owlish eyes upon me— "ha, ha, ha!—for a paper-weight!—an original idea!—artistic idea! Old Pharaoh would certainly have been surprised had some one told him that the foot of his adored daughter would be used for a paper-weight after he had had a mountain of granite hollowed out as a receptacle for the triple coffin, painted and gilded—covered with hieroglyphics and beautiful paintings of the Judgment of Souls,"—continued the queer little merchant, half audibly, as though talking to himself!

"How much will you charge me for this mummy fragment?"

"Ah, the highest price I can get; for it is a superb piece: if I had the match of it you could not have it for less than five hundred francs;—the daughter of a Pharaoh! nothing is more rare."

"Assuredly that is not a common article; but, still, how much do you want? In the first place let me warn you that all my wealth consists of just five louis: I can buy anything that costs five louis, but nothing dearer;—you might search my vest pockets and most secret drawers without even finding one poor—five-franc piece more."

"Five louis for the foot of the Princess Hermonthis! that is very little, very little indeed; 'tis an authentic foot," muttered the merchant, shaking his head, and imparting a peculiar rotary motion to his eyes.

"Well, take it, and I will give you the bandages into the bargain," he added, wrapping the foot in an ancient damask rag— "very fine! real damask—Indian damask which has never been redyed; it is strong, and yet it is soft," he mumbled, stroking the frayed tissue with his fingers, through the trade-acquired habit which moved him to praise even an object of so little value that he himself deemed it only worth the giving away.

He poured the gold coins into a sort of mediaeval alms-purse hanging at his belt, repeating:

"The foot of the Princess Hermonthis, to be used for a paper-weight!"

Then turning his phosphorescent eyes upon me, he exclaimed in a voice strident as the crying of a cat which has swallowed a fish-bone:

"Old Pharaoh will not be well pleased; he loved his daughter—the dear man!"

"You speak as if you were a contemporary of his: you are old enough, goodness knows! but you do not date back to the Pyramids of Egypt," I answered, laughingly, from the threshold. I went home, delighted with my acquisition.

With the idea of putting it to profitable use as soon as possible, I placed the foot of the divine Princess Hermonthis upon a heap of papers scribbled over with verses, in themselves an undecipherable mosaic work of erasures; articles freshly begun; letters forgotten, and posted in the table drawer instead of the letter-box—an error to which absent-minded people are peculiarly liable. The effect was charming, *bizarre*, and romantic.

Well satisfied with this embellishment, I went out with the gravity and price becoming one who feels that he has the ineffable advantage over all the passers-by whom he elbows, of possessing a piece of the Princess Hermonthis, daughter of Pharaoh.

I looked upon all who did not possess, like myself, a paper-weight so authentically Egyptian, as very ridiculous people; and it seemed to me that the proper occupation of every sensible man should consist in the mere fact of having a mummy's foot upon his desk.

Happily I met some friends, whose presence distracted me in my infatuation with this new acquisition: I went to dinner with them; for I could not very well have dined with myself.

When I came back that evening, with my brain slightly confused by a few glasses of wine, a vague whiff of Oriental perfume delicately titillated my olfactory nerves: the heat of the room had warmed the natron, bitumen, and myrrh in which the *paraschistes*, who cut open the bodies of the dead, had bathed the corpse of the princess;—it was a perfume at once sweet and penetrating—a perfume that four thousand years had not been able to dissipate.

The Dream of Egypt was Eternity: her odors have the solidity of granite, and endure as long.

I soon drank deeply from the black cup of sleep: for a few hours all remained opaque to me; Oblivion and Nothingness inundated me with their somber waves.

Yet light gradually dawned upon the darkness of my mind; dreams commenced to touch me softly in their silent flight.

The eyes of my soul were opened; and I beheld my chamber as it actually was; I might have believed myself awake, but for a vague consciousness which assured me that I slept, and that something fantastic was about to take place.

The odor of the myrrh had augmented in intensity; and I felt a slight headache, which I very naturally attributed to several glasses of champagne that we had drunk to the unknown gods and our future fortunes.

I peered through my room with a feeling of expectation which I saw nothing to justify: every article of furniture was in its proper place; the lamp, softly shaded by its globe of ground crystal, burned upon its bracket; the water-color sketches shone under their Bohemian glass; the curtains hung down languidly; everything wore an aspect of tranquil slumber.

After a few moments, however, all this calm interior appeared to become disturbed; the woodwork cracked stealthily; the ash-covered log suddenly emitted a jet of blue flame; and the disks of the pateras seemed like great metallic eyes, watching, like myself, for the things which were about to happen.

My eyes accidentally fell upon the desk where I had placed the foot of the Princess Hermonthis.

Instead of remaining quiet—as behooved a foot which had been embalmed for four thousand years—it commenced to act in a nervous manner; contracted itself, and leaped over the papers like a startled frog;—one would have imagined that it had suddenly been brought into contact with a galvanic battery: I could distinctly hear the dry sound made by its little heel, hard as the hoof of a gazelle.

I became rather discontented with my acquisition, inasmuch as I wished my paper-weights to be of a sedentary disposition, and thought it very unnatural that feet should walk about without legs; and I commenced to experience a feeling closely akin to fear.

Suddenly I saw the folds of my bed-curtain stir; and heard a bumping sound, like that caused by some person hopping on one foot across the floor. I must confess I became alternately hot and cold; that I felt a strange wind chill my back; and that my suddenly rising hair caused my nightcap to execute a leap of several yards.

The bed-curtains opened and I beheld the strangest figure imaginable before me.

It was a young girl of a very deep coffee-brown complexion, like the bayadere Amani, and possessing the purest Egyptian type of perfect beauty: her eyes were almond-shaped and oblique, with eyebrows so black that they seemed blue; her nose was exquisitely chiseled, almost Greek in its delicacy of outline; and she might indeed have been taken for a Corinthian statue of bronze, but for the prominence of her cheek-bones and the slightly African fullness of her lips, which compelled one to recognize her as belonging beyond all doubt to the hieroglyphic race which dwelt upon the banks of the Nile.

Her arms, slender and spindle-shaped, like those of very young girls, were encircled by a peculiar kind of metal bands and bracelets of glass beads; her hair was all twisted into little cords; and she wore upon her bosom a little idol-figure of green paste, bearing a whip with seven lashes, which proved it to be an image of Isis: her brow was adorned with a shining plate of gold; and a few traces of paint relieved the coppery tint of her cheeks.

As for her costume, it was very odd indeed. Fancy a *pagne* or skirt all formed of little strips of material bedizened with red and black hieroglyphics, stiffened with bitumen, and apparently belonging to a freshly unbandaged mummy.

In one of those sudden flights of thought so common in dreams I heard the hoarse falsetto of the *bric-à-brac* dealer, repeating like a monotonous refrain the phrase he had uttered in his shop with so enigmatical an intonation:

"Old Pharaoh will not be well pleased: he loved his daughter, the dear man!"

One strange circumstance, which was not at all calculated to restore my equanimity, was that the apparition had but one foot; the other was broken off at the ankle!

She approached the table where the foot was starting and fidgeting about more than ever, and there supported herself upon the edge of the desk. I saw her eyes fill with pearly-gleaming tears.

Although she had not as yet spoken, I fully comprehended the thoughts which agitated her: she looked at her foot—it was indeed her own—with an exquisitely graceful expression of coquettish sadness; but the foot leaped and ran hither and thither, as though impelled on steel springs.

Twice or thrice she extended her hand to seize it, but could not succeed.

Then commenced between the Princess Hermonthis and her foot—which appeared to be endowed with a special life of its own—a very fantastic dialogue in a most ancient Coptic tongue, such as might have been spoken thirty centuries ago in the syrinxes of the land of Ser: luckily, I understood Coptic perfectly well that night.

The Princess Hermonthis cried, in a voice sweet and vibrant as the tones of a crystal bell:

"Well, my dear little foot, you always flee from me; yet I always took good care of you. I bathed you with perfumed water in a bowl of alabaster; I smoothed your heel with pumice-stone mixed with palm oil; your nails were cut with golden scissors and polished with a hippopotamus tooth; I was careful to select *tatbebs* for you, painted and embroidered and turned up at the toes, which were the envy of all the young girls in Egypt: you wore on your great toe rings bearing the device of the sacred Scarabaeus; and you supported one of the lightest bodies that a lazy foot could sustain."

The foot replied, in a pouting and chagrined tone:

"You know well that I do not belong to myself any longer;—I have been bought and paid for; the old merchant knew what he was about; he bore you a grudge for having refused to espouse him;—this is an ill turn which he has done you. The Arab who violated your royal coffin in the subterranean pit of the necropolis of Thebes was sent thither by him: he desired to prevent you from being present at the reunion of the shadowy nations in the cities below. Have you five pieces of gold for my ransom?"

"Alas, no!—my jewels, my rings, my purses of gold and silver, they were all stolen from me," answered the Princess Hermonthis, with a sob.

"Princess," I then exclaimed, "I never retained anybody's foot unjustly;—even though you have not got the five louis which it cost me, I present it to you gladly: I should feel unutterably wretched to think that I were the cause of so amiable a person as the Princess Hermonthis being lame."

I delivered this discourse in a royally gallant, troubadour tone, which must have astonished the beautiful Egyptian girl.

She turned a look of deepest gratitude upon me; and her eyes shone with bluish gleams of light.

She took her foot—which surrendered itself willingly this time—like a woman about to put on her little shoe, and adjusted it to her leg with much skill.

This operation over, she took a few steps about the room, as though to assure herself that she was really no longer lame.

"Ah, how pleased my father will be!—he who was so unhappy because of my mutilation, and who from the moment of my birth set a whole nation at work to hollow me out a tomb so deep that he might preserve me intact until that last day, when souls must be weighed in the balance of Amenthi! Come with me to my father;—he will receive you kindly; for you have given me back my foot."

I thought this proposition natural enough. I arrayed myself in a dressing-gown of large-flowered pattern, which lent me a very Pharaonic aspect; hurriedly put on a pair of Turkish slippers, and informed the Princess Hermonthis that I was ready to follow her.

Before starting, Hermonthis took from her neck the little idol of green paste, and laid it on the scattered sheets of paper which covered the table.

"It is only fair," she observed smilingly, "that I should replace your paper-weight."

She gave me her hand, which felt soft and cold, like the skin of a serpent; and we departed.

We passed for some time with the velocity of an arrow through a fluid and grayish expanse, in which half-formed silhouettes flitted swiftly by us, to right and left.

For an instant we saw only sky and sea.

A few moments later obelisks commenced to tower in the distance: pylons and vast flights of steps guarded by sphinxes became clearly outlined against the horizon.

We had reached our destination.

The princess conducted me to the mountain of rose-colored granite, in the face of which appeared an opening so narrow and low that it would have been difficult to distinguish it from the fissures in the rock, had not its location been marked by two stelae wrought with sculptures.

Hermonthis kindled a torch, and led the way before me.

We traversed corridors hewn through the living rock: their walls, covered with hieroglyphics and paintings of allegorical processions, might well have occupied thousands of arms for thousands of years in their formation;—these corridors, of interminable length, opened into square chambers, in the midst of which pits had been contrived, through which we descended by cramp-irons or spiral stairways;—these pits again conducted us into other chambers, opening into other corridors, likewise decorated with painted sparrow-hawks, serpents coiled in circles, the symbols of the *tau* and *pedum*—prodigious works of art which no living eye can ever examine—interminable legends of granite which only the dead have time to read through all eternity.

At last we found ourselves in a hall so vast, so enormous, so immeasurable, that the eye could not reach its limits; files of monstrous columns streatched far out of sight on every side, between which twinkled livid stars of yellowish flame;—points of light which revealed further depths incalculable in the darkness beyond.

The Princess Hermonthis still held my hand, and graciously saluted the mummies of her acquaintance.

My eyes became accustomed to the dim twilight, and objects became discernible.

I beheld the kings of the subterranean races seated upon thrones—grand old men, though dry, withered, wrinkled like parchment, and blackened with naphtha and bitumen—all wearing *pshents* of gold, and breastplaces and gorgets glittering with precious stones; their eyes immovably fixed like the eyes of sphinxes, and their long beards whitened by the snow of centuries. Behind them stood their peoples, in the stiff and constrained posture enjoined by Egyptian art, all eternally preserving the attitude prescribed by the hieratic code. Behind these nations, the cats, ibises, and crocodiles contemporary with them—rendered monstrous of aspect by their swathing bands—mewed, flapped their wings, or extended their jaws in a saurian giggle.

All the Pharaohs were there—Cheops, Chephrenes, Psammetichus, Sesostris, Amenotaph—all the dark rulers of the pyramids and syrinxes—on yet higher thrones sat Chronos and Xixouthros—who was contemporary with the deluge; and Tubal Cain, who reigned before it.

The beard of King Xixouthros had grown seven times around the granite table, upon which he leaned, lost in deep reverie—and buried in dreams.

Further back, through a dusty cloud, I beheld dimly the seventy-two pre-Adamite Kings, with their seventy-two peoples—forever passed away.

After permitting me to gaze upon this bewildering spectacle a few moments, the Princess Hermonthis presented me to her father Pharaoh, who favored me with a most gracious nod.

"I have found my foot again!—I have found my foot!" cried the Princess, clapping her little hands together with every sign of frantic joy: "it was this gentleman who restored it to me."

The races of Kemi, the races of Nahasi—all the black, bronzed, and copper-colored nations repeated in chorus:

"The Princess Hermonthis has found her foot again!"

Even Xixouthros himself was visibly affected.

He raised his heavy eyelids, stroked his mustache with his fingers, and turned upon me a glance weighty with centuries.

"By Oms, the dog of Hell, and Tmei, daughter of the Sun and of Truth! this is a brave and worthy lad!" exclaimed Pharaoh, pointing to me with his scepter, which was terminated with a lotus-flower.

"What recompense do you desire?"

Filled with that daring inspired by dreams in which nothing seems impossible, I asked him for the hand of the Princess Hermonthis;—the hand seemed to me a very proper antithetic recompense for the foot.

Pharaoh opened wide his great eyes of glass in astonishment at my witty request.

"What country do you come from? and what is your age?"

"I am a Frenchman; and I am twenty-seven years old, venerable Pharaoh."

"—Twenty-seven years old! and he wishes to espouse the Princess Hermonthis, who is thirty centuries old!" cried out at once all the Thrones and all the Circles of Nations.

Only Hermonthis herself did not seem to think my request unreasonable.

"If you were even only two thousand years old," replied the ancient King, "I would willingly give you the Princess; but the disproportion is too great; and, besides, we must give our daughters husbands who will last well: you do not know how to preserve yourselves any longer; even those who died only fifteen centuries ago are already no more than a handful of dust;—behold! my flesh is solid as basalt; my bones are bars of steel!

"I shall be present on the last day of the world, with the same body and the same features which I had during my lifetime: my daughter Hermonthis will last longer than a statue of bronze.

"Then the last particles of your dust will have been scattered abroad by the winds; and even Isis herself, who was able to find the atoms of Osiris, would scarce be able to recompose your being.

"See how vigorous I yet remain, and how mighty is my grasp," he added, shaking my hand in the English fashion with a strength that buried my rings in the flesh of my fingers.

He squeezed me so hard that I awoke, and found my friend Alfred shaking me by the arm to make me get up.

"O you everlasting sleeper!—must I have you carried out into the middle of the street, and fireworks exploded in your ears? It is after noon; don't you recollect your promise to take me with you to see M. Aguado's Spanish pictures?"

"God! I forgot all, all about it," I answered, dressing myself hurriedly; "we will go there at once; I have the permit lying on my desk."

I started to find it;—but fancy my astonishment when I beheld, instead of the mummy's foot I had purchased the evening before, the little green paste idol left in its place by the Princess Hermonthis!

Some Words with a Mummy

Edgar Allen Poe

The *symposium* of the preceding evening had been a little too much for my nerves. I had a wretched headache, and was desperately drowsy. Instead of going out therefore to spend the evening as I had proposed, it occurred to me that I could not do a wiser thing than just eat a mouthful of supper and go immediately to bed.

A *light* supper of course. I am exceedingly fond of Welsh rabbit. More than a pound at once, however, may not at all times be advisable. Still, there can be no material objection to two. And really between two and three, there is merely a single unit of difference. I ventured, perhaps, upon four. My wife will have it five;—but, clearly, she has confounded two very distinct affairs. The abstract number, five, I am willing to admit; but, concretely, it has reference to bottles of Brown Stout, without which, in the way of condiment, Welsh rabbit is to be eschewed.

Having thus concluded a frugal meal, and donned my nightcap, with the serene hope of enjoying it till noon the next day, I placed my head upon the pillow, and, through the aid of a capital conscience, fell into a profound slumber forthwith.

But when were the hopes of humanity fulfilled? I could not have completed my third snore when there came a furious ringing at the street-door bell, and then an impatient thumping at the knocker, which awakened me at once. In a minute afterward, and while I was still rubbing my eyes, my wife thrust in my face a note, from my old friend, Doctor Ponnonner. It ran thus:

"Come to me, by all means, my dear good friend, as soon as you receive this. Come and help us to rejoice. At last, by long persevering diplomacy, I have gained the assent of the Directors of the City Museum, to my examination of the Mummy—you know the one I mean. I have permission to unswathe it and open it, if desirable. A few friends only will be present—you, of course. The Mummy is now at my house, and we shall begin to unroll it at eleven to-night.

"Yours, ever,
Ponnonner.

By the time I had reached the "Ponnonner," it struck me that I was as wide awake as a man need be. I leaped out of bed in an ecstacy, overthrowing all in my way; dressed myself with a rapidity truly marvellous; and set off, at the top of my speed, for the doctor's.

There I found a very eager company assembled. They had been awaiting me with much impatience; the Mummy was extended upon the dining-table; and the moment I entered its examination was commenced.

It was one of a pair brought, several years previously, by Captain Arthur Sabretash, a cousin of Ponnonner's from a tomb near Eleithias, in the Lybian mountains, a considerable distance above Thebes on the Nile. The grottoes at this point, although less magnificent than the Theban sepulchres, are of higher interest, on account of affording more numerous illustrations of the private life of the Egyptians. The chamber from which our specimen was taken, was said to be very rich in such illustrations; the walls being completely covered with fresco paintings and bas-reliefs, while statues, vases, and Mosaic work of rich patterns, indicated the vast wealth of the deceased.

The treasure had been deposited in the Museum precisely in the same condition in which Captain Sabretash had found it;—that is to say, the coffin had not been disturbed. For eight years it had thus stood, subject only externally to public inspection. We had now, therefore, the complete Mummy at our disposal; and to those who are aware how very rarely the unransacked antique reaches our shores, it will be evident, at once that we had great reason to congratulate ourselves upon our good fortune.

Approaching the table, I saw on it a large box, or case, nearly seven feet long, and perhaps three feet wide, by two feet and a half deep. It was oblong—not coffin-shaped. The material was at first supposed to be the wood of the sycamore (*platanus*), but, upon cutting into it, we found it to be pasteboard, or, more properly, *papier maché*, composed of papyrus. It was thickly ornamented with paintings, representing funeral scenes, and other mournful subjects—interspersed among which, in every variety of position, were certain series of hieroglyphical characters, intended, no doubt, for the name of the departed. By good luck, Mr. Gliddon formed one of our party; and he had no difficulty in translating the letters, which were simply phonetic, and represented the word *Allamistakeo*.

We had some difficulty in getting this case open without injury; but having at length accomplished the task, we came to a second, coffin-shaped, and very considerably less in size than the exterior one, but resembling it precisely in every other respect. The interval between the two was filled with resin, which had, in some degree, defaced the colors of the interior box.

Upon opening this latter (which we did quite easily), we arrived at a third case, also coffin-shaped, and varying from the second one in no particular, except in that of its material, which was cedar, and still emitted the peculiar and highly aromatic odor of that wood. Between the second and the third case there was no interval—the one fitting accurately within the other.

Removing the third case, we discovered and took out the body itself. We had expected to find it, as usual, enveloped in frequent rolls, or bandages, of linen; but, in place of these, we found a sort of sheath, made of papyrus, and coated with a layer of plaster, thickly gilt and painted. The paintings represented subjects connected with the various supposed duties of the soul, and its presentation to different divinities, with numerous identical human figures, intended, very probably, as portraits of the persons embalmed. Extending from head to foot was a columnar, or perpendicular, inscription, in phonetic hieroglyphics, giving again his name and titles, and the names and titles of his relations.

Around the neck thus ensheathed, was a collar of cylindrical glass beads, diverse in color, and so arranged as to form images of deities, of the scarabaeus, etc, with the winged globe. Around the small of the waist was a similar collar or belt.

Stripping off the papyrus, we found the flesh in excellent preservation, with no perceptible odor. The color was reddish. The skin was hard, smooth, and glossy. The teeth and hair were in good condition. The eyes (it seemed) had been removed, and glass ones substituted, which were very beautiful and wonderfully life-like, with the exception of somewhat too determined a stare. The fingers and the nails were brilliantly gilded.

Mr. Gliddon was of opinion, from the redness of the epidermis, that the embalmment had been effected altogether by asphaltum; but, on scraping the surface with a steel instrument, and throwing into the fire some of the powder thus obtained, the flavor of camphor and other sweet-scented gums became apparent.

We searched the corpse very carefully for the usual openings through which the entrails are extracted, but, to our surprise, we could discover none. No member of the party was at that period aware that entire or unopened mummies are not infrequently met. The brain it was customary to withdraw through the nose; the intestines through an incision in the side; the body was then shaved, washed, and salted; then laid aside for several weeks, when the operation of embalming, properly so called, began.

As no trace of an opening could be found, Doctor Ponnonner was preparing his instruments for dissection, when I observed that it was then past two o'clock. Hereupon it was agreed to postpone the internal examination until the next evening; and we were about to separate for the present, when some one suggested an experiment or two with the Voltaic pile.

The application of electricity to a mummy three or four thousand years old at the least, was an idea, if not very sage, still sufficiently original, and we all caught it at once. About one-tenth in earnest and nine-tenths in jest, we arranged a battery in the Doctor's study, and conveyed thither the Egyptian.

It was only after much trouble that we succeeded in laying bare some portions of the temporal muscle which appeared of less stony rigidity than other parts of the frame, but which, as we had anticipated, of course, gave no indication of galvanic susceptibility when brought in contact with the wire. This, the first trial, indeed, seemed decisive, and, with a hearty laugh at our own absurdity, we were bidding each other good night, when my eyes, happening to fall upon those of the Mummy, were there immediately riveted in amazement. My brief glance, in fact, had sufficed to assure me that the orbs which we had all supposed to be glass, and which were originally noticeable for a certain wild stare, were now so far covered by the lids, that only a small portion of the *tunica albuginea* remained visible.

With a shout I called attention to the fact, and it became immediately obvious to all.

I cannot say that I was *alarmed* at the phenomenon, because "alarmed" is, in my case, not exactly the word. It is possible, however, that, but for the Brown Stout, I might have been a little nervous. As for the rest of the company, they really made no attempt at concealing the downright fright which possessed them. Doctor Ponnonner was a man to be pitied. Mr. Gliddon, by some peculiar process, rendered himself invisible. Mr. Silk Buckingham, I fancy, will scarcely be so bold as to deny that he made his way, upon all fours, under the table.

After the first shock of astonishment, however, we resolved, as a matter of course, upon further experiment forthwith. Our operations were now directed against the great toe of the right foot. We made an incision over the outside of the exterior *os sesamoideum pollicis pedis*, and thus got at the root of the *abductor* muscle. Readjusting the battery, we now applied the fluid to the bisected nerves—when, with a movement of exceeding life-likeness, the Mummy first drew up its right knee so as to bring it nearly in contact with the abdomen, and then, straightening the limb with inconceivable force, bestowed a kick upon Doctor Ponnonner, which had the effect of discharging that gentleman, like an arrow from a catapult, through a window into the street below.

We rushed out *en masse* to bring in the mangled remains of the victim, but had the happiness to meet him upon the staircase, coming up in an unaccountable hurry, brimful of the most ardent philosophy, and more than ever impressed with the necessity of prosecuting our experiment with vigor and with zeal.

It was by his advice, accordingly, that we made, upon the spot, a profound incision into the tip of the subject's nose, while the Doctor himself, laying violent hands upon it, pulled it into vehement contact with the wire.

Morally and physically—figuratively and literally—was the effect electric. In the first place, the corpse opened its eyes and winked very rapidly for several minutes, as does Mr. Barnes in the pantomime, in the second place, it sneezed; in the third, it sat upon end;

in the fourth, it shook its fist in Doctor Ponnonner's face; in the fifth, turning to Messieurs Gliddon and Buckingham, it addressed them, in very capital Egyptian, thus:

"I must say, gentlemen, that I am as much surprised as I am mortified at your behavior. Of Doctor Ponnonner nothing better was to be expected. He is a poor little fat fool who *knows* no better. I pity and forgive him. But you, Mr. Gliddon—and you, Silk—who have travelled and resided in Egypt until one might imagine you to the manner born—you, I say who have been so much among us that you speak Egyptian fully as well, I think, as you write your mother tongue—you, whom I have always been led to regard as the firm friend of the mummies—I really did anticipate more gentlemanly conduct from you. What am I to think of your standing quietly by and seeing me thus unhandsomely used? What am I to suppose by your permitting Tom, Dick, and Harry to strip me of my coffins, and my clothes, in this wretchedly cold climate? In what light (to come to the point) am I to regard your aiding and abetting that miserable little villain, Doctor Ponnonner, in pulling me by the nose?"

It will be taken for granted, no doubt, that upon hearing this speech under the circumstances, we all either made for the door, or fell into violent hysterics, or went off in a general swoon. One of these three things was, I say, to be expected. Indeed each and all of these lines of conduct might have been very plausibly pursued. And, upon my word, I am at a loss to know how or why it was that we pursued neither the one nor the other. But, perhaps, the true reason is to be sought in the spirit of the age, which proceeds by the rule of contraries altogether, and is now usually admitted as the solution of every thing in the way of paradox and impossibility. Or, perhaps, after all, it was only the Mummy's exceedingly natural and matter-of-course air that divested his words of the terrible. However this may be, the facts are clear, and no member of our party betrayed any very particular trepidation, or seemed to consider that any thing had gone very especially wrong.

For my part I was convinced it was all right, and merely stepped aside, out of the range of the Egyptian's fist. Doctor Ponnonner thrust his hands into his breeches' pockets, looked hard at the Mummy, and grew excessively red in the face. Mr. Glidden stroked his whiskers and drew up the collar of his shirt. Mr. Buckingham hung down his head, and put his right thumb into the left corner of his mouth.

The Egyptian regarded him with a severe countenance for some minutes and at length, with a sneer, said:

"Why don't you speak, Mr. Buckingham? Did you hear what I asked you, or not? *Do* take your thumb out of your mouth!"

Mr. Buckingham, hereupon, gave a slight start, took his right thumb out of the left corner of his mouth, and, by way of indemnification inserted his left thumb in the right corner of the aperture above-mentioned.

Not being able to get an answer from Mr. B., the figure turned peevishly to Mr. Gliddon, and, in a peremptory tone, demanded in general terms what we all meant.

Mr. Gliddon replied at great length, in phonetics; and but for the deficiency of American printing-offices in hieroglyphical type, it would afford me much pleasure to record here, in the original, the whole of his very excellent speech.

I may as well take this occasion to remark, that all the subsequent conversation in which the Mummy took a part, was carried on in primitive Egyptian, through the medium (so far as concerned myself and other untravelled members of the company)—through the medium, I say, of Messieurs Gliddon and Buckingham, as interpreters. These gentlemen spoke the mother tongue of the Mummy with inimitable fluency and grace; but I could not help observing that (owing, no doubt, to the introduction of images entirely modern, and, of course, entirely novel to the stranger) the two travellers were reduced, occasionally, to the employment of sensible forms for the purpose of conveying a particular meaning. Mr. Gliddon, at one period, for example, could not make the Egyptian comprehend the term "politics," until he sketched upon the wall, with a bit of charcoal a little carbuncle-nosed gentleman, out at elbows, standing upon a stump, with his left leg drawn back, right arm thrown forward, with his fist shut, the eyes rolled up toward Heaven, and the mouth open at an angle of ninety degrees. Just in the same way Mr. Buckingham failed to convey the absolutely modern idea "wig," until (at Doctor Ponnonner's suggestion) he grew very pale in the face, and consented to take off his own.

It will be readily understood that Mr. Gliddon's discourse turned chiefly upon the vast benefits accruing to science from the unrolling and disembowelling of mummies; apologizing, upon this score, for any disturbance that might have been occasioned him, in particular, the individual Mummy called Allamistakeo; and concluding with a mere hint (for it could scarcely be considered more) that, as these little matters were now explained, it might be as well to proceed with the investigation intended. Here Doctor Ponnonner made ready his instruments.

In regard to the latter suggestions of the orator, it appears that Allamistakeo had certain scruples of conscience, the nature of which I did not distinctly learn; but he expressed himself satisfied with the apologies tendered, and, getting down from the table, shook hands with the company all round.

When this ceremony was at an end, we immediately busied ourselves in repairing the damages which our subject had sustained from the scalpel. We sewed up the wound in his temple, bandaged his foot, and applied a square inch of black plaster to the tip of his nose.

It was now observed that the Count (this was the title, it seems, of Allamistakeo) had a slight fit of shivering—no doubt from the cold. The Doctor immediately repaired to his wardrobe, and soon returned with a black dress coat, made in Jennings' best manner, a pair of sky-blue plaid pantaloons with straps, a pink gingham *chemise*, a flapped vest of brocade, a white sack overcoat, a walking cane with a hook, a hat with no brim, patent-leather boots, straw-colored kid gloves, an eye-glass, a pair of whiskers, and a waterfall cravat. Owing to the disparity of size between the Count and the doctor (the proportion being as two to one), there was some little difficulty in adjusting these habiliments upon the person of the Egyptian; but when all was arranged, he might have been said to be dressed. Mr. Gliddon, therefore, gave him his arm, and led him to a comfortable chair by the fire, while the Doctor rang the bell upon the spot and ordered a supply of cigars and wine.

The conversation soon grew animated. Much curiosity was, of course, expressed in regard to the somewhat remarkable fact of Allamistakeo's still remaining alive.

"I should have thought," observed Mr. Buckingham, "that it is high time you were dead."

"Why," replied the Count, very much astonished, "I am little more than seven hundred years old! My father lived a thousand, and was by no means in his dotage when he died."

Here ensued a brisk series of questions and computations, by means of which it became evident that the antiquity of the Mummy had been grossly misjudged. It had been five thousand and fifty years and some months since he had been consigned to the catacombs at Eleithias.

"But my remark," resumed Mr. Buckingham, "had no reference to your age at the period of interment (I am willing to grant, in fact, that you are still a young man), and my illusion was to the immensity of time during which, by your own showing, you must have been done up in asphaltum."

"In what?" said the Count.

"In asphaltum," persisted Mr. B.

"Ah, yes; I have some faint notion of what you mean; it might be made to answer, no doubt—but in my time we employed scarcely any thing else than the Bichloride of Mercury."

"But what we are especially at a loss to understand," said Doctor Ponnonner, "is how it happens that, having been dead and buried in Egypt five thousand years ago, you are here to-day all alive and looking so delightfully well."

"Had I been, as you say, *dead*," replied the Count, "it is more than probable that dead, I should still be; for I perceive you are yet in the infancy of Calvanism, and cannot accomplish with it what was a common thing among us in the old days. But the fact is, I fell into catalepsy, and it was considered by my best friends that I was either dead or should be; they accordingly embalmed me at once—I presume you are aware of the chief principle of the embalming process?"

"Why not altogether."

"Ah, I perceive;—a deplorable condition of ignorance! Well I cannot enter into details just now: but it is necessary to explain that to embalm (properly speaking), in Egypt, was to arrest indefinitely *all* the animal functions subjected to the process. I use the word 'animal' in its widest sense, as including the physical not more than the moral and *vital* being. I repeat that the leading principle of embalmment consisted, with us, in the immediately arresting, and holding in perpetual abeyance, all the animal functions subjected to the process. To be brief, in whatever condition the individual was, at the period of embalmment, in that condition he remained. Now, as it is my good fortune to be of the blood of the Scarabaeus, I was embalmed alive, as you see me at present."

"The blood of the Scarabaeus!" exclaimed Doctor Ponnonner.

"Yes. The Scarabaeus was the *insignium* or the 'arms,' of a very distinguished and very rare patrician family. To be 'of the blood of the Scarabaeus,' is merely to be one of that family of which the Scarabaeus is the *insignium*. I speak figuratively."

"But what has this to do with you being alive?"

"Why, it is the general custom in Egypt to deprive a corpse, before embalmment, of its bowels and brains; the race of the Scarabaei alone did not coincide with the custom. Had I not been a Scarabeus, therefore, I should have been without bowels and brains; and without either it is inconvenient to live."

"I perceive that," said Mr. Buckingham, "and I presume that all the *entire* mummies that come to hand are of the race of Scarabaei."

"Beyond doubt."

"I thought," said Mr. Gliddon, very meekly, "that the Scarabaeus was one of the Egyptian gods."

"One of the Egyptian *what?*" exclaimed the Mummy, starting to its feet.

"Gods!" repeated the traveller.

"Mr. Gliddon, I really am astonished to hear you talk in this style," said the Count, resuming his chair. "No nation upon the face of the earth has ever acknowledged more than one god. The Scarabaeus, the Ibis, etc., were with us (as similar creatures have been with others) the symbols, or *media*, through which we offered worship to the Creator too august to be more directly approached."

There was here a pause. At length the colloquy was renewed by Doctor Ponnonner.

"It is not improbable, then, from what you have explained," said he, "that among the catacombs near the Nile there may exist other mummies of the Scarabaeus tribe, in a condition of vitality?"

"There can be no question of it," replied the Count; "all the Scarabaei embalmed accidentally while alive, are alive now. Even some of those *purposely* so embalmed, may have been overlooked by their executors, and still remain in the tomb."

"Will you be kind enough to explain," I said, "what you mean by 'purposely so embalmed'?"

"With great pleasure!" answered the Mummy, after surveying me leisurely through his eye-glass—for it was the first time I had ventured to address him a direct question.

"With great pleasure," he said. "The usual duration of man's life, in my time, was about eight hundred years. Few men died, unless by most extraordinary accident, before the age of six hundred; few lived longer than a decade of centuries; but eight were considered the natural term. After the discovery of the embalming principle, as I have already described it to you, it occurred to our philosophers that a laudable curiosity might be gratified, and, at the same time, the interests of science much advanced, by living this natural term in installments. In the case of history, indeed, experience demonstrated that something of this kind was indispensable. An historian, for example, having attained the age of five hundred, would write a book with great labor and then get himself carefully embalmed; leaving instructions to his executors *pro tem.*, that they should cause him to be revivified after the lapse of a certain period—say five or six hundred years. Resuming existence at the expiration of this time, he would invariably find his great work converted into a species of hap-hazard note-book—that is to say, into a kind of literary arena for the conflicting guesses, riddles, and personal squabbles of whole herds of exasperated commentators. These guesses, etc., which passed under the name of annotations, or emendations, were found so completely to have enveloped, distorted, and overwhelmed the text, that the author had to go about with a lantern to discover his own book. When discovered, it was never worth the trouble of the search. After re-writing it throughout, it was regarded as the bounden duty of the historian to set himself to work immediately in correcting, from his own private knowledge and experience, the traditions of the day concerning the epoch at which he had originally lived. Now this process of rescription and personal rectification, pursued by various individual sages from time to time, had the effect of preventing our history from degenerating into absolute fable."

"I beg your pardon," said Doctor Ponnonner at this point, laying his hand gently upon the arm of the Egyptian— "I beg your pardon, sir, but may I presume to interrupt you for one moment?"

"By all means, *sir*," replied the Count, drawing up.

"I merely wished to ask you a question," said the Doctor. "You mentioned the historian's personal correction of *traditions* respecting his own epoch. Pray, sir, upon an average what proportion of these Kabbala were usually found to be right?"

"The Kabbala, as you properly term them, sir, were generally discovered to be precisely on a par with the facts recorded in the un-re-written histories themselves;—that is to say, not one individual iota of either was ever known, under any circumstances, to be not totally and radically wrong."

"But since it is quite clear," resumed the Doctor, "that at least five thousand years have elapsed since your entombment, I take it for granted that your histories at that period, if not your traditions were sufficiently explicit on that one topic of universal interest, the Creation, which took place, as I presume you are aware, only about ten centuries before."

"Sir!" said the Count Allamistakeo.

The Doctor repeated his remarks, but it was only after much additional explanation that the foreigner could be made to comprehend them. The latter at length said, hesitatingly:

"The ideas you have suggested are to me, I confess, utterly novel. During my time I never knew any one to entertain so singular a fancy as that the universe (or this world if you will have it so) ever had a beginning at all. I remember once, and once only, hearing something remotely hinted, by a man of many speculations, concerning the origin *of the human race*; and by this individual, the very word *Adam* (or Red Earth), which you make use of, was employed. He employed it, however, in a generical sense, with reference to the spontaneous germination from rank soil (just as a thousand of the lower *genera* of creatures are germinated)—the spontaneous germination, I say, of five vast hordes of men, simultaneously upspringing in five distinct and nearly equal divisions of the globe."

Here, in general, the company shrugged their shoulders, and one or two of us touched our foreheads with a very significant air. Mr. Silk Buckingham, first glancing slightly at the occiput and then at the sinciput of Allamistakeo, spoke as follows:

"The long duration of human life in your time, together with the occasional practice of passing it, as you have explained, in installments, must have had, indeed, a strong tendency to the general development and conglomeration of knowledge. I presume, therefore, that we are to attribute the marked inferiority of the old Egyptians in all particulars of science, when compared with the moderns, and more especially with the Yankees, altogether to the superior solidity of the Egyptian skull."

"I confess again," replied the Count, with much suavity, "that I am somewhat at a loss to comprehend you; pray, to what particulars of science do you allude?"

Here our whole party, joining voices, detailed, at great length, the assumptions of phrenology and the marvels of animal magnetism.

Having heard us to an end, the Count proceeded to relate a few anecdotes, which rendered it evident that prototypes of Gall and Spurzheim had flourished and faded in Egypt so long ago as to have been nearly forgotten, and that the manoeuvres of Mesmer were really very contemptible tricks when put in collation with the positive miracles of the Theban savans, who created lice and a great many other similar things.

I here asked the Count if his people were able to calculate eclipses. He smiled rather contemptuously, and said they were.

This put me a little out, but I began to make other inquiries in regard to his astronomical knowledge, when a member of the company, who had never as yet opened his mouth, whispered in my ear, that for information on this head, I had better consult Ptolemy (whoever Ptolemy is), as well as one Plutarch *de facie lunae*.

I then questioned the Mummy about burning-glasses and lenses, and, in general, about the manufacture of glass; but I had not made an end of my queries before the silent member again touched me quietly on the elbow, and begged me for God's sake to take a peep at Diodorus Siculus. As for the Count, he merely asked me, in the way of reply, if we moderns possessed any such microscopes as would enable us to cut cameos in the style of the Egyptians. While I was thinking how I should answer this question, little Doctor Ponnonner committed himself in a very extraordinary way.

"Look at our architecture!" he exclaimed, greatly to the indignation of both the travellers, who pinched him black and blue to no purpose.

"Look," he cried with enthusiasm, "at the Bowling-Green Fountain in New York! or if this be too vast a contemplation, regard for a moment the Capitol at Washington, D. C.!" —and the good little medical man went on to detail very minutely, the proportions of the fabric to which he referred. He explained that the portico alone was adorned with no less than four and twenty columns, five feet in diameter, and ten feet apart.

The Count said that he regretted not being able to remember, just at that moment, the precise dimensions of any one of the principal buildings of the city of Aznac, whose foundations were laid in the night of Time, but the ruins of which were still standing, at the epoch of his entombment, in a vast plain of sand to the westward of Thebes. He recollected, however, (talking of the porticoes,) that one affixed to an inferior palace in a kind of suburb called

Carnac, consisted of a hundred and forty-four columns, thirty-seven feet in circumference, and twenty-five feet apart. The approach to this portico, from the Nile, was through an avenue two miles long, composed of sphynxes, statues, and obelisks, twenty, sixty, and a hundred feet in height. The palace itself (as well as he could remember) was, in one direction, two miles long, and might have been altogether about seven in circuit. Its walls were richly painted all over, within and without, with hieroglyphics. He would not pretend to *assert* that even fifty or sixty of the Doctor's Capitols might have been built within these walls, but he was by no means sure that two or three hundred of them might not have been squeezed in with some trouble. That palace at Carnac was an insignificant little building after all. He (the Count), however, could not conscientiously refuse to admit the ingenuity, magnificence, and superiority of the Fountain at the Bowling Green, as described by the Doctor. Nothing like it, he was forced to allow, had ever been seen in Egypt or elsewhere.

I here asked the Count what he had to say to our railroads.

"Nothing," he replied, "in particular." They were rather slight, rather ill-conceived, and clumsily put together. They could not be compared, of course, with the vast, level, direct, iron-grooved causeways upon which the Egyptians conveyed entire temples and solid obelisks of a hundred and fifty feet in altitude.

I spoke of our gigantic mechanical forces.

He agreed that we knew something in that way, but inquired how I should have gone to work in getting up the imposts on the lintels of even the little palace at Carnac.

This question I concluded not to hear, and demanded if he had any idea of Artesian wells; but he simply raised his eyebrows; while Mr. Gliddon winked at me very hard and said, in a low tone, that one had been recently discovered by the engineers employed to bore for water in the Great Oasis.

I then mentioned our steel; but the foreigner elevated his nose, and asked me if our steel could have executed the sharp carved work seen on the obelisks, and which was wrought altogether by edge-tools of copper.

This disconcerted us so greatly that we thought it advisable to vary the attack to Metaphysics. We sent for a copy of a book called the "Dial," and read out of it a chapter or two about something that is not very clear, but which the Bostonians call the Great Movement of Progress.

The Count merely said that Great Movements were awfully common things in his day, and as for Progress, it was at one time quite a nuisance, but it never progressed.

We then spoke of the great beauty and importance of Democracy, and were at much trouble in impressing the Count with a due sense of the advantages we enjoyed in living where there was suffrage *ad libitum*, and no king.

He listened with marked interest, and in fact seemed not a little amused. When we had done, he said that, a great while ago, there had occurred something of a very similar sort. Thirteen Egyptian provinces determined all at once to be free, and to set a magnificent example to the rest of mankind. They assembled their wise men, and concocted the most ingenious constitution it is possible to conceive. For a while they managed remarkably well; only their habit of bragging was prodigious. The thing ended, however, in the consolidation of the thirteen states, with some fifteen or twenty others, in the most odious and insupportable despotism that was ever heard of upon the face of the Earth.

I asked what was the name of the usurping tyrant.

As well as the Count could recollect, it was *Mob*.

Not knowing what to say to this, I raised my voice, and deplored the Egyptian ignorance of steam.

The Count looked at me with much astonishment, but made no answer. The silent gentleman, however, gave me a violent nudge in the ribs with his elbows—told me I had sufficiently exposed myself for once—and demanded if I was really such a fool as not to know that the modern steam-engine is derived from the invention of Hero, through Solomon de Caus.

We were now in imminent danger of being discomfited; but, as good luck would have it, Doctor Ponnonner, having rallied, returned to our rescue, and inquired if the people of Egypt would seriously pretend to rival the moderns in the all- important particular of dress.

The Count, at this, glanced downward to the straps of his pantaloons, and then taking hold of the end of one of his coat-tails, held it up close to his eyes for some minutes. Letting it fall, at last, his mouth extended itself very gradually from ear to ear; but I do not remember that he said any thing in the way of reply.

Hereupon we recovered our spirits, and the Doctor, approaching the Mummy with great dignity, desired it to say candidly, upon its honor as a gentleman, if the Egyptians had comprehended, at *any* period, the manufacture of either Ponnonner's lozenges or Brandreth's pills.

We looked, with profound anxiety, for an answer—but in vain. It was not forthcoming. The Egyptian blushed and hung down his head. Never was triumph more consummate; never was defeat borne with so ill a grace. Indeed, I could not endure the spectacle of the poor Mummy's mortification. I reached my hat, bowed to him stiffly, and took leave.

Upon getting home I found it past four o'clock, and went immediately to bed. It is now ten A.M. I have been up since seven, penning these memoranda for the benefit of my family and of mankind. The former I shall behold no more. My wife is a shrew. The truth is, I am heartily sick of this life and of the nineteenth century in general. I am convinced that every thing is going wrong. Besides, I am anxious to know who will be President in 2045. As soon, therefore, as I shave and swallow a cup of coffee, I shall just step over to Ponnonner's and get embalmed for a couple of hundred years.

Lost in a Pyramid, or the Mummy's Curse

Louisa May Alcott

I

"And what are these, Paul?" asked Evelyn, opening a tarnished gold box and examining its contents curiously.

"Seeds of some unknown Egyptian plant," replied Forsyth, with a sudden shadow on his dark face, as he looked down at the three scarlet grains lying in the white hand lifted to him.

"Where did you get them?" asked the girl.

"That is a weird story, which will only haunt you if I tell it," said Forsyth, with an absent expression that strongly excited the girl's curiosity.

"Please tell it, I like weird tales, and they never trouble me. Ah, do tell it; your stories are always so interesting," she cried, looking up with such a pretty blending of entreaty and command in her charming face, that refusal was impossible.

"You'll be sorry for it, and so shall I, perhaps; I warn you beforehand, that harm is foretold to the possessor of those mysterious seeds," said Forsyth, smiling, even while he knit his black brows, and regarded the blooming creature before him with a fond yet foreboding glance.

"Tell on, I'm not afraid of these pretty atoms," she answered, with an imperious nod.

"To hear is to obey. Let me read the facts, and then I will begin," returned Forsyth, pacing to and fro with the far-off look of one who turns the pages of the past.

Evelyn watched him a moment, and then returned to her work, or play, rather, for the task seemed well suited to the vivacious little creature, half-child, half-woman.

"While in Egypt," commenced Forsyth, slowly, "I went one day with my guide and Professor Niles, to explore the Cheops. Niles had a mania for antiquities of all sorts, and forgot time, danger and fatigue in the ardor of his pursuit. We rummaged up and down the narrow passages, half choked with dust and close air; reading inscriptions on the walls, stumbling over shattered mummy-cases, or coming face to face with some shriveled specimen perched like a hobgoblin on the little shelves where the dead used to be stowed away for ages. I was desperately tired after a few hours of it, and begged the professor to return. But he was bent on exploring certain places, and would not desist. We had but one guide, so I was forced to stay; but Jumal, my man, seeing how weary I was, proposed to us to rest in one of the larger passages, while he went to procure another guide for Niles. We consented, and assuring us that we were perfectly safe, if we did not quit the spot, Jumal left us, promising to return speedily. The professor sat down to take notes of his researches, and stretching my self on the soft sand, I fell asleep.

"I was roused by that indescribable thrill which instinctively warns us of danger, and springing up, I found myself alone. One torch burned faintly where Jumal had struck it, but Niles and the other light were gone. A dreadful sense of loneliness oppressed me for a moment; then I collected myself and looked well about me. A bit of paper was pinned to my hat, which lay near me, and on it, in the professor's writing were these words:

> "'I've gone back a little to refresh my memory on certain points. Don't follow me till Jumal comes. I can find my way back to you, for I have a clue. Sleep well, and dream gloriously of the Pharaohs. N N.'

"I laughed at first over the old enthusiast, then felt anxious then restless, and finally resolved to follow him, for I discovered a strong cord fastened to a fallen stone, and knew that this was the clue he spoke of. Leaving a line for Jumal, I took my torch and retraced my steps, following the cord along the winding ways. I often shouted, but received no reply, and pressed on, hoping at each turn to see the old man poring over some musty relic of antiquity. Suddenly the cord ended, and lowering my torch, I saw that the footsteps had gone on.

"'Rash fellow, he'll lose himself, to a certainty,' I thought, really alarmed now.

"As I paused, a faint call reached me, and I answered it, waited, shouted again, and a still fainter echo replied.

"Niles was evidently going on, misled by the reverberations of the low passages. No time was to be lost, and, forgetting myself, I stuck my torch in the deep sand to guide me back to the clue, and ran down the straight path before me, whooping like a madman as I went. I did not mean to lose sight of the light, but in my eagerness to find Niles I turned from the main passage, and, guided by his voice, hastened on. His torch soon gladdened my eyes, and the clutch of his trembling hands told me what agony he had suffered.

"'Let us get out of this horrible place at once,' he said, wiping the great drops off his forehead.

"'Come, we're not far from the clue. I can soon reach it, and then we are safe'; but as I spoke, a chill passed over me, for a perfect labyrinth of narrow paths lay before us.

"Trying to guide myself by such land-marks as I had observed in my hasty passage, I followed the tracks in the sand till I fancied we must be near my light. No glimmer appeared, however, and kneeling down to examine the footprints nearer, I discovered, to my dismay, that I had been following the wrong ones, for among those marked by a deep boot-heel, were prints of bare feet; we had had no guide there, and Jumal wore sandals.

"Rising, I confronted Niles, with the one despairing word, 'Lost!' as I pointed from the treacherous sand to the fast-waning light.

"I thought the old man would be overwhelmed but, to my surprise, he grew quite calm and steady, thought a moment, and then went on, saying, quietly:

"'Other men have passed here before us; let us follow their steps, for, if I do not greatly err, they lead toward great passages, where one's way is easily found.'

"On we went, bravely, till a misstep threw the professor violently to the ground with a broken leg, and nearly extinguished the torch. It was a horrible predicament, and I gave up all hope as I sat beside the poor fellow, who lay exhausted with fatigue, remorse and pain, for I would not leave him.

"'Paul,' he said suddenly, 'if you will not go on, there is one more effort we can make. I remember hearing that a party lost as we are, saved themselves by building a fire. The smoke penetrated further than sound or light, and the guide's quick wit understood the unusual mist; he followed it, and rescued the party. Make a fire and trust to Jumal.'

"'A fire without wood?' I began; but he pointed to a shelf behind me, which had escaped me in the gloom; and on it I saw a slender mummy-case. I understood him, for these dry cases, which lie about in hundreds, are freely used as firewood. Reaching up, I pulled it down, believing it to be empty, but as it fell, it burst open, and out rolled a mummy. Accustomed as I was to such sights, it startled me a little, for danger had unstrung my nerves. Laying the little brown chrysalis aside, I smashed the case, lit the pile with my torch, and soon a light cloud of smoke drifted down the three passages which diverged from the cell-like place where we had paused.

"While busied with the fire, Niles, forgetful of pain and peril, had dragged the mummy nearer, and was examining it with the interest of a man whose ruling passion was strong even in death.

"'Come and help me unroll this. I have always longed to be the first to see and secure the curious treasures put away among the folds of these uncanny winding-sheets. This is a woman, and we may find something rare and precious here,' he said, beginning to unfold the outer coverings, from which a strange aromatic odor came.

"Reluctantly I obeyed, for to me there was something sacred in the bones of this unknown woman. But to beguile the time and amuse the poor fellow, I lent a hand, wondering as I worked, if this dark, ugly thing had ever been a lovely, soft-eyed Egyptian girl.

"From the fibrous folds of the wrappings dropped precious gums and spices, which half intoxicated us with their potent breath, antique coins, and a curious jewel or two, which Niles eagerly examined.

"All the bandages but one were cut off at last, and a small head laid bare, round which still hung great plaits of what had once been luxuriant hair. The shriveled hands were folded on the breast, and clasped in them lay that gold box."

"Ah!" cried Evelyn, dropping it from her rosy palm with a shudder.

"Nay; don't reject the poor little mummy's treasure. I never have quite forgiven myself for stealing it, or for burning her," said Forsyth, painting rapidly, as if the recollection of that experience lent energy to his hand.

"Burning her! Oh, Paul, what do you mean?" asked the girl, sitting up with a face full of excitement.

"I'll tell you. While busied with Madame la Momie, our fire had burned low, for the dry case went like tinder. A faint, far-off sound made our hearts leap, and Niles cried out: 'Pile on the wood; Jumal is tracking us; don't let the smoke fail now or we are lost!'

"'There is no more wood; the case was very small, and is all gone,' I answered, tearing off such of my garments as would burn readily, and piling them upon the embers.

"Niles did the same, but the light fabrics were quickly consumed, and made no smoke.

"'Burn that!' commanded the professor, pointing to the mummy.

"I hesitated a moment. Again came the faint echo of a horn. Life was dear to me. A few dry bones might save us, and I obeyed him in silence.

"A dull blaze sprung up, and a heavy smoke rose from the burning mummy, rolling in volumes through the low passages, and threatening to suffocate us with its fragrant mist. My brain grew dizzy, the light danced before my eyes, strange phantoms seemed to people the air, and, in the act of asking Niles why he gasped and looked so pale, I lost consciousness."

Evelyn drew a long breath, and put away the scented toys from her lap as if their odor oppressed her.

Forsyth's swarthy face was all aglow with the excitement of his story, and his black eyes glittered as he added, with a quick laugh:

"That's all; Jumal found and got us out, and we both forswore pyramids for the rest of our days."

"But the box: how came you to keep it?" asked Evelyn, eyeing it askance as it lay gleaming in a streak of sunshine.

"Oh, I brought it away as a souvenir, and Niles kept the other trinkets."

"But you said harm was foretold to the possessor of those scarlet seeds," persisted the girl, whose fancy was excited by the tale, and who fancied all was not told.

"Among his spoils, Niles found a bit of parchment, which he deciphered, and this inscription said that the mummy we had so ungallantly burned was that of a famous sorceress who bequeathed her curse to whoever should disturb her rest. Of course I don't believe that curse has anything to do with it, but it's a fact that

Niles never prospered from that day. He says it's because he has never recovered from the fall and fright and I dare say it is so; but I sometimes wonder if I am to share the curse, for I've a vein of superstition in me, and that poor little mummy haunts my dreams still."

A long silence followed these words. Paul painted mechanically and Evelyn lay regarding him with a thoughtful face. But gloomy fancies were as foreign to her nature as shadows are to noonday, and presently she laughed a cheery laugh, saying as she took up the box again:

"Why don't you plant them, and see what wondrous flower they will bear?"

"I doubt if they would bear anything after lying in a mummy's hand for centuries," replied Forsyth, gravely.

"Let me plant them and try. You know wheat has sprouted and grown that was taken from a mummy's coffin; why should not these pretty seeds? I should so like to watch them grow; may I, Paul?"

"No, I'd rather leave that experiment untried. I have a queer feeling about the matter, and don't want to meddle myself or let anyone I love meddle with these seeds. They may be some horrible poison, or possess some evil power, for the sorceress evidently valued them, since she clutched them fast even in her tomb."

"Now, you are foolishly superstitious, and I laugh at you. Be generous; give me one seed, just to learn if it will grow. See I'll pay for it," and Evelyn, who now stood beside him, dropped a kiss on his forehead as she made her request, with the most engaging air.

But Forsyth would not yield. He smiled and returned the embrace with lover-like warmth, then flung the seeds into the fire, and gave her back the golden box, saying, tenderly:

"My darling, I'll fill it with diamonds or bonbons, if you please, but I will not let you play with that witch's spells. You've enough of your own, so forget the 'pretty seeds' and see what a Light of the Harem I've made of you."

Evelyn frowned, and smiled, and presently the lovers were out in the spring sunshine reveling in their own happy hopes, untroubled by one foreboding fear.

II

"I have a little surprise for you, love," said Forsyth, as he greeted his cousin three months later on the morning of his wedding day.

"And I have one for you," she answered, smiling faintly.

"How pale you are, and how thin you grow! All this bridal bustle is too much for you, Evelyn." he said, with fond anxiety, as he watched the strange pallor of her face, and pressed the wasted little hand in his.

"I am so tired," she said, and leaned her head wearily on her lover's breast. "Neither sleep, food, nor air gives me strength, and a curious mist seems to cloud my mind at times. Mamma says it is the heat, but I shiver even in the sun, while at night I burn with fever. Paul, dear, I'm glad you are going to take me away to lead a quiet, happy life with you, but I'm afraid it will be a very short one."

"My fanciful little wife! You are tired and nervous with all this worry, but a few weeks of rest in the country will give us back our blooming Eve again. Have you no curiosity to learn my surprise?" he asked, to change her thoughts.

The vacant look stealing over the girl's face gave place to one of interest, but as she listened it seemed to require an effort to fix her mind on her lover's words.

"You remember the day we rummaged in the old cabinet?"

"Yes," and a smile touched her lips for a moment.

"And how you wanted to plant those queer red seeds I stole from the mummy?"

"I remember," and her eyes kindled with sudden fire.

"Well, I tossed them into the fire, as I thought, and gave you the box. But when I went back to cover up my picture, and found one of those seeds on the rug, a sudden fancy to gratify your whim led me to send it to Niles and ask him to plant and report on its progress. Today I hear from him for the first time, and he reports that the seed has grown marvelously, has budded, and that he intends to take the first flower, if it blooms in time, to a meeting of famous scientific men, after which he will send me its true name and the plant itself. From his description, it must be very curious, and I'm impatient to see it."

"You need not wait; I can show you the flower in its bloom," and Evelyn beckoned with the *mechanté* smile so long a stranger to her lips.

Much amazed, Forsyth followed her to her own little boudoir, and there, standing in the sunshine, was the unknown plant. Almost rank in their luxuriance were the vivid green leaves on the slender purple stems, and rising from the midst, one ghostly-white flower, shaped like the head of a hooded snake, with scarlet stamens like forked tongues, and on the petals glittered spots like dew.

"A strange, uncanny flower! Has it any odor?" asked Forsyth, bending to examine it, and forgetting, in his interest, to ask how it came there.

"None, and that disappoints me, I am so fond of perfumes," answered the girl, caressing the green leaves which trembled at her touch, while the purple stems deepened their tint.

"Now tell me about it," said Forsyth, after standing silent for several minutes.

"I had been before you, and secured one of the seeds, for two fell on the rug. I planted it under a glass in the richest soil I could find, watered it faithfully, and was amazed at the rapidity with which it grew when once it appeared above the earth. I told no-one, for I meant to surprise you with it; but this bud has been so long in blooming, I have had to wait. It is a good omen that it blossoms today, and as it is nearly white, I mean to wear it, for I've learned to love it, having been my pet for so long."

"I would not wear it, for, in spite of its innocent color, it is an evil-looking plant, with its adder's tongue and unnatural dew. Wait till Niles tells us what it is, then pet it if it is harmless."

"Perhaps my sorceress cherished it for some symbolic beauty—those old Egyptians were full of fancies. It was very sly of you to turn the tables on me in this way. But I forgive you, since in a few hours, I shall chain this mysterious hand forever. How cold it is! Come out into the garden and get some warmth and color for tonight, my love."

But when night came, no-one could reproach the girl with her pallor, for she glowed like a pomegranate-flower, her eyes were full of fire, her lips scarlet, and all her old vivacity seemed to have returned. A more brilliant bride never blushed under a misty veil, and when her lover saw her, he was absolutely startled by the almost unearthly beauty which transformed the pale, languid creature of the morning into this radiant woman.

They were married, and if love, many blessings, and all good gifts lavishly showered upon them could make them happy, then this young pair were truly blest. But even in the rapture of the moment that made her his, Forsyth observed how icy cold was the little hand he held, how feverish the deep color on the soft cheek he kissed, and what a strange fire burned in the tender eyes that looked so wistfully at him.

Blithe and beautiful as a spirit, the smiling bride played her part in all the festivities of that long evening, and when at last light, life and color began to fade, the loving eyes that watched her thought it but the natural weariness of the hour. As the last guest departed, Forsyth was met by a servant, who gave him a letter marked "Haste." Tearing it open, he read these lines, from a friend of the professor's:

> "Dear Sir—Poor Niles died suddenly two days ago, while at the Scientific Club, and his last words were: 'Tell Paul Forsyth to beware of the Mummy's Curse, for this fatal flower has killed me.' The circumstances of his death were so peculiar, that I add them as a sequel to this message. For several months, as he told us, he had been watching an unknown plant, and that evening he brought us the flower to examine. Other matters of interest absorbed us till a late hour, and the plant was forgotten. The professor wore it in his buttonhole—a strange white, serpent-headed blossom, with pale glittering spots, which slowly changed to a glittering scarlet, till the leaves looked as if sprinkled with blood. It was observed that instead of the pallor and feebleness which had recently come over him, that the professor was unusually animated, and seemed in an almost unnatural state of high spirits. Near the close of the meeting, in the midst of a lively discussion, he suddenly dropped, as if smitten with apoplexy. He was conveyed home insensible, and after one lucid interval, in which he gave me the message I have recorded above, he died in great agony, raving of mummies, pyramids, serpents, and some fatal curse which had fallen upon him.
>
> "After his death, livid scarlet spots, like those on the flower, appeared upon his skin, and he shriveled like a withered leaf. At my desire, the mysterious plant was examined, and pronounced by the best authority one of the most deadly poisons known to the Egyptian sorceresses. The plant slowly absorbs the vitality of whoever cultivates it, and the blossom, worn for two or three hours, produces either madness or death."

Down dropped the paper from Forsyth's hand; he read no further, but hurried back into the room where he had left his young wife. As if worn out with fatigue, she had thrown herself upon a couch, and lay there motionless, her face half-hidden by the light folds of the veil, which had blown over it.

"Evelyn, my dearest! Wake up and answer me. Did you wear that strange flower today?" whispered Forsyth, putting the misty screen away.

There was no need for her to answer, for there, gleaming spectrally on her bosom, was the evil blossom, its white petals spotted now with flecks of scarlet, vivid as drops of newly spilt blood.

But the unhappy bridegroom scarcely saw it, for the face above it appalled him by its utter vacancy. Drawn and pallid, as if with some wasting malady, the young face, so lovely an hour ago, lay before him aged and blighted by the baleful influence of the plant which had drunk up her life. No recognition in the eyes, no word upon the lips, no motion of the hand—only the faint breath, the fluttering pulse, and wide-opened eyes, betrayed that she was alive.

Alas for the young wife! The superstitious fear at which she had smiled had proved true: the curse that had bided its time for ages was fulfilled at last, and her own hand wrecked her happiness forever. Death in life was her doom, and for years Forsyth secluded himself to tend with pathetic devotion the pale ghost, who never, by word or look, could thank him for the love that outlived even such a fate as this.

My New Year's Eve Among the Mummies

Grant Allen

I have been a wanderer and a vagabond on the face of the earth for a good many years now, and I have certainly had some odd adventures in my time; but I can assure you, I never spent twenty-four queerer hours than those which I passed some twelve months since in the great unopened Pyramid of Abu Yilla.

The way I got there was itself a very strange one. I had come to Egypt for a winter tour with the Fitz-Simkinses, to whose daughter Editha I was at that precise moment engaged. You will probably remember that old Fitz-Simkins belonged originally to the wealthy firm of Simkinson and Stokoe, worshipful vintners; but when the senior partner retired from the business and got his knighthood, the College of Heralds opportunely discovered that his ancestors had changed their fine old Norman name for its English equivalent some time about the reign of King Richard I; and they immediately authorized the old gentleman to resume the patronymic and the armorial bearings of his distinguished forefathers. It's really quite astonishing how often these curious coincidences crop up at the College of Heralds.

Of course it was a great catch for a landless and briefless barrister like myself—dependent on a small fortune in South American securities, and my precarious earnings as a writer of burlesque—to secure such a valuable prospective property as Editha Fitz-Simkins. To be sure, the girl was undeniably plain; but I have known plainer girls than she was, whom forty thousand pounds converted into My Ladies: and if Editha hadn't really fallen over head and ears in love with me, I suppose old Fitz-Simkins would never have consented to such a match. As it was, however, we had flirted so openly and so desperately during the Scarborough season, that it would have been difficult for Sir Peter to break it off: and so I had come to Egypt on a tour of insurance to secure my prize, following in the wake of my future mother-in-law, whose lungs were supposed to require a genial climate though in my private opinion they were really as creditable a pair of pulmonary appendages as ever drew breath.

Nevertheless, the course of true love did not run so smoothly as might have been expected. Editha found me less ardent than a devoted squire should be; and on the very last night of the old year she got up a regulation lovers' quarrel, because I had sneaked away from the boat that afternoon under the guidance of our dragoman, to witness the seductive performances of some fair Ghawázi, the dancing girls of a neighbouring town. How she found it out heaven only knows, for I gave that rascal Dimitri five piastres to hold his tongue: but she did find it out somehow, and chose to regard it as an offence of the first magnitude: a mortal sin only to be expiated by three days of penance and humiliation.

I went to bed that night, in my hammock on deck, with feelings far from satisfactory. We were moored against the bank at Abu Yilla, the most pestiferous hole between the cataracts and the Delta. The mosquitoes were worse than the ordinary mosquitoes of Egypt, and that is saying a great deal. The heat was oppressive even at night, and the malaria from the lotus beds rose like a palpable mist before my eyes. Above all, I was getting doubtful whether Editha Fitz-Simkins might not after all slip between my fingers. I felt wretched and feverish: and yet I had delightful interlusive recollections, in between, of that lovely little Gháziyah, who danced that exquisite, marvellous, entrancing, delicious, and awfully oriental dance that I saw in the afternoon.

By Jove, she *was* a beautiful creature. Eyes like two full moons; hair like Milton's Penseroso; movements like a poem of Swinburne's set to action. If Editha was only a faint picture of that girl now! Upon my word, I was falling in love with a Gháziyah!

Then the mosquitoes came again. Buzz—buzz—buzz. I make a lunge at the loudest and biggest, a sort of prima donna in their infernal opera. I kill the prima donna, but ten more shrill performers come in its place. The frogs croak dismally in the reedy shallows. The night grows hotter and hotter still. At last, I can stand it no longer. I rise up, dress myself lightly, and jump ashore to find some way of passing the time.

Yonder, across the flat, lies the great unopened Pyramid of Abu Yilla. We are going to-morrow to climb to the top; but I will take a turn to reconnoitre in that direction now. I walk across the moon-lit fields, my soul still divided between Editha and the Gháziyah, and approach the solemn mass of huge, antiquated granite blocks standing out so grimly against the pale horizon. I feel half awake, half asleep, and altogether feverish: but I poke about the base in an aimless sort of way, with a vague idea that I may perhaps discover by chance the secret of its sealed entrance, which has ere now baffled so many pertinacious explorers and learned Egyptologists.

As I walk along the base, I remember old Herodotus's story, like a page from the 'Arabian Nights', of how King Rhampsinitus built himself a treasury, wherein one stone turned on a pivot like a door; and how the builder availed himself of this his cunning device to steal gold from the king's storehouse. Suppose the entrance to the unopened Pyramid should be by such a door. It would be curious if I should chance to light upon the very spot.

I stood in the broad moonlight, near the north-east angle of the great pile, at the twelfth stone from the corner. A random fancy struck me, that I might turn this stone by pushing it inward on the left side. I leant against it with all my weight, and tried to move it on the imaginary pivot. Did it give way a fraction of an inch? No, it must have been mere fancy. Let me try again. Surely it is yielding! Gracious Osiris, it has moved an inch or more! My heart beats fast, either with fever or excitement, and I try a third time. The rust of centuries on the pivot wears slowly off, and the stone turned ponderously round, giving access to a low dark passage.

It must have been madness which led me to enter the forgotten corridor, alone, without torch or match, at that hour of the evening; but at any rate I entered. The passage was tall enough for a man to walk erect, and I could feel, as I groped slowly along, that the wall was composed of smooth polished granite, while the floor sloped away downward with a slight but regular descent. I walked with trembling heart and faltering feet for some forty or fifty yards down the mysterious vestibule: and then I felt myself brought suddenly to a standstill by a block of stone placed right across the pathway. I had had nearly enough for one evening, and I was preparing to return to the boat, agog with my new discovery, when my attention was suddenly arrested by an incredible, a perfectly miraculous fact.

The block of stone which barred the passage was faintly visible as a square, by means of a struggling belt of light streaming through the seams. There must be a lamp or other flame burning within. What if this were a door like the outer one, leading into a chamber perhaps inhabited by some dangerous band of outcasts? The light was a sure evidence of human occupation: and yet the outer door swung rustily on its pivot as though it had never been opened for ages. I paused a moment in fear before I ventured to try the stone: and then, urged on once more by some insane impulse, I turned the massive block with all my might to the left. It gave way slowly like its neighbour, and finally opened into the central hall.

Never as long as I live shall I forget the ecstasy of terror, astonishment, and blank dismay which seized upon me when I stepped into that seemingly enchanted chamber. A blaze of light first burst upon my eyes, from jets of gas arranged in regular rows tier above tier, upon the columns and walls of the vast apartment. Huge pillars, richly painted with red, yellow, blue and green decorations, stretched in endless succession down the dazzling aisles. A floor of polished syenite reflected the splendour of the lamps, and afforded a base for red granite sphinxes and dark purple images in porphyry of the cat-faced goddess Pasht, whose form I knew so well at the Louvre and the British Museum. But I had no eyes for any of these lesser marvels, being wholly absorbed in the greatest marvel of all: for there, in royal state and with mitred head, a living Egyptian king, surrounded by his coiffured court, was banqueting in the flesh upon a real throne, before a table laden with Memphian delicacies!

I stood transfixed with awe and amazement, my tongue and my feet alike forgetting their office, and my brain whirling round and round, as I remember it used to whirl when my health broke down utterly at Cambridge after the Classical Tripos. I gazed fixedly at the strange picture before me, taking in all its details in a confused way, yet quite incapable of understanding or realizing any part of its true import. I saw the king in the centre of the hall, raised on a throne of granite inlaid with gold and ivory; his head crowned with the peaked cap of Rameses, and his curled hair flowing down his shoulders in a set and formal frizz. I saw priests and warriors on either side, dressed in the costumes which I had often carefully noted in our great collections; while bronze-skinned maids, with light garments round their waists, and limbs displayed in graceful picturesqueness, waited upon them, half nude, as in the wall paintings which we had lately examined at Karnak and Syene. I saw the ladies, clothed from head to foot in dyed linen garments, sitting apart in the background, banqueting by themselves at a separate table; while dancing girls, like older representatives of my yesternoon friends, the Ghawázi, tumbled before them in strange attitudes, to the music of four-stringed harps and long straight pipes. In short, I beheld as in a dream the whole drama of everyday Egyptian royal life, playing itself out anew under my eyes, in its real original properties and personages.

Gradually, as I looked, I became aware that my hosts were no less surprised at the appearance of their anachronistic guest than was the guest himself at the strange living panorama which met his eyes. In a moment music and dancing ceased; the banquet paused in its course, and the king and his nobles stood up in undisguised astonishment to survey the strange intruder.

Some minutes passed before any one moved forward on either side. At last a young girl of royal appearance, yet strangely resembling the Gháziyah of Abu Yilla, and recalling in part the laughing maiden in the foreground of Mr. Long's great canvas at the previous Academy, stepped out before the throng.

"May I ask you," she said in Ancient Egyptian, "who you are, and why you come hither to disturb us?"

I was never aware before that I spoke or understood the language of the hieroglyphics: yet I found I had not the slightest difficulty in comprehending or answering her question. To say the truth, Ancient Egyptian, though an extremely tough tongue to decipher in its written form, becomes as easy as love-making when spoken by a pair of lips like that Pharaonic princess's. It is really very much the same as English, pronounced in a rapid and somewhat indefinite whisper, and with all the vowels left out.

"I beg ten thousand pardons for my intrusion," I answered apologetically: "but I did not know that this Pyramid was inhabited, or I should not have entered your residence so rudely. As for the points you wish to know, I am an English tourist, and you will find my name upon this card;" saying which I handed her one from the case which I had fortunately put into my pocket, with conciliatory politeness. The princess examined it closely, but evidently did not understand its import.

"In return," I continued, "may I ask you in what august presence I now find myself by accident?"

A court official stood forth from the throng, and answered in a set heraldic tone: "In the presence of the illustrious monarch, Brother of the Sun, Thothmes the Twenty-seventh, king of the Eighteenth Dynasty."

"Salute the Lord of the World," put in another official in the same regulation drone.

I bowed low to his Majesty, and stepped out into the hall. Apparently my obeisance did not come up to Egyptian standards of courtesy, for a suppressed titter broke audibly from the ranks of bronze-skinned waiting-women. But the king graciously smiled at my attempt, and turning to the nearest nobleman, observed in a voice of great sweetness and self-contained majesty: "This stranger, Ombos, is certainly a very curious person. His appearance does not at all resemble that of an Ethiopian or other savage, nor does he look like the pale-faced sailors who come to us from the Achaian land beyond the sea. His features, to be sure, are not very different from theirs; but his extraordinary and singularly inartistic dress shows him to belong to some other barbaric race."

I glanced down at my waistcoat, and saw that I was wearing my tourist's check suit, of grey and mud colour, with which a Bond Street tailor had supplied me just before leaving town, as the latest thing out in fancy tweeds. Evidently these Egyptians must have a very curious standard of taste not to admire our pretty and graceful style of male attire.

"If the dust beneath your Majesty's feet may venture upon a suggestion," put in the officer whom the king had addressed, "I would hint that this young man is probably a stray visitor from the utterly uncivilized lands of the North. The headgear which he carries in his hand obviously betrays an Arctic habitat."

I had instinctively taken off my round felt hat in the first moment of surprise, when I found myself in the midst of this strange throng, and I was standing now in a somewhat embarrassed posture, holding it awkwardly before me like a shield to protect my chest.

"Let the stranger cover himself," said the king.

"Barbarian intruder, cover yourself," cried the herald. I noticed throughout that the king never directly addressed anybody save the higher officials around him.

I put on my hat as desired. "A most uncomfortable and silly form of tiara indeed," said the great Thothmes.

"Very unlike your noble and awe-spiring mitre, Lion of Egypt," answered Ombos.

"Ask the stranger his name," the king continued.

It was useless to offer another card, so I mentioned it in a clear voice.

"An uncouth and almost unpronounceable designation truly," commented his Majesty to the Grand Chamberlain beside him. "These savages speak strange languages, widely different from the flowing tongue of Memnon and Sesostris."

The chamberlain bowed his assent with three low genuflexions. I began to feel a little abashed at these personal remarks, and I *almost* think (though I shouldn't like it to be mentioned in the Temple) that a blush rose to my cheek.

The beautiful princess, who had been standing near me meanwhile in an attitude of statuesque repose, now appeared anxious to change the current of the conversation. "Dear father," she said with a respectful inclination, "surely the stranger, barbarian though he be, cannot relish such pointed allusions to his person and costume. We must let him feel the grace and delicacy of Egyptian refinement. Then he may perhaps carry back with him some faint echo of its cultured beauty to his northern wilds."

"Nonsense, Hatasou," replied Thothmes XXVII testily. "Savages have no feelings, and they are as incapable of appreciating Egyptian sensibility as the chattering crow is incapable of attaining the dignified reserve of the sacred crocodile."

"Your Majesty is mistaken," I said, recovering my self-possession gradually and realizing my position as a freeborn Englishman before the court of a foreign despot—though I must allow that I felt rather less confident than usual, owing to the fact that we were not represented in the Pyramid by a British Consul— "I am an English tourist, a visitor from a modern land whose civilization far surpasses the rude culture of early Egypt; and I am accustomed to respectful treatment from all other nationalities, as becomes a citizen of the First Naval Power in the World."

My answer created a profound impression. "He has spoken to the Brother of the Sun," cried Ombos in evident perturbation. "He must be of the Blood Royal in his own tribe, or he would never have dared to do so!"

"Otherwise," added a person whose dress I recognized as that of a priest, "he must be offered up in expiation to Amon-Ra immediately."

As a rule I am a decent truthful person, but under these alarming circumstances I ventured to tell a slight fib with an air of nonchalant boldness. "I am a younger brother of our reigning king," I said without a moment's hesitation; for there was nobody present to gainsay me, and I tried to salve my conscience by reflecting that at any rate I was only claiming consanguinity with an imaginary personage.

"In that case," said King Thothmes, with more geniality in his tone, "there can be no impropriety in my addressing you personally. Will you take a place at our table next to myself, and we can converse together without interrupting a banquet which must be brief enough in any circumstances? Hatasou, my dear, you may seat yourself next to the barbarian prince."

I felt a visible swelling to the proper dimensions of a Royal Highness as I sat down by the king's right hand. The nobles resumed their places, the bronze-skinned waitresses left off standing like soldiers in a row and staring straight at my humble self, the goblets went round once more, and a comely maid soon brought me meat, bread, fruits and date wine.

All this time I was naturally burning with curiosity to inquire who my strange host might be, and how they had preserved their existence for so many centuries in this undiscovered hall; but I was obliged to wait until I had satisfied his Majesty of my own nationality, the means by which I had entered the Pyramid, the general state of affairs throughout the world at the present moment, and fifty thousand other matters of a similar sort. Thothmes utterly refused to believe my reiterated assertion that our existing civilization was far superior to the Egyptian; "because," he said, "I see from your dress that your nation is utterly devoid of taste or invention;" but he listened with great interest to my account of modern society, the steam-engine, the Permissive Prohibitory Bill, the telegraph, the House of Commons, Home Rule, and other blessings of our advanced era, as well as to a brief resume of European history from the rise of the Greek culture to the Russo-Turkish war. At last his questions were nearly exhausted, and I got a chance of making a few counter inquiries on my own account.

"And now," I said, turning to the charming Hatasou, whom I thought a more pleasing informant than her august papa, "I should like to know who you are."

"What, don't you know?" she cried with unaffected surprise. "Why, we're mummies."

She made this astonishing statement with just the same quiet unconsciousness as if she had said, "we're French," or "we're Americans." I glanced round the walls, and observed behind the columns, what I had not noticed till then—a large number of empty mummy-cases, with their lids placed carelessly by their sides.

"But what are you doing here?" I asked in a bewildered way.

"Is it possible," said Hatasou, "that you don't really know the object of embalming? Though your manners show you to be an agreeable and well-bred young man, you must excuse my saying that you are shockingly ignorant. We are made into mummies in order to preserve our immortality. Once in every thousand years we wake up for twenty-four hours, recover our flesh and blood, and banquet once more upon the mummied dishes and other good things laid by for us in the Pyramid. To-day is the first day of a millennium, and so we have waked up for the sixth time since we were first embalmed."

"The *sixth* time?" I inquired incredulously. "Then you must have been dead six thousand years."

"Exactly so."

"But the world has not yet existed so long," I cried, in a fervour of orthodox horror.

"Excuse me, barbarian prince. This is the first day of the three hundred and twenty-seven thousandth millennium."

My orthodoxy received a severe shock. However, I had been accustomed to geological calculations, and was somewhat inclined to accept the antiquity of man; so I swallowed the statement without more ado. Besides, if such a charming girl as Hatasou had asked me at that moment to turn Mohammedan, or to worship Oysteries, I believe I should incontinently have done so.

"You wake up only for a single day and night, then?" I said.

"Only for a single day and night. After that, we go to sleep for another millennium."

"Unless you are meanwhile burned as fuel on the Cairo Railway," I added mentally. "But how," I continued aloud, "do you get these lights?"

"The Pyramid is built above a spring of inflammable gas. We have a reservoir in one of the side chambers in which it collects during the thousand years. As soon as we awake, we turn it on at once from the tap, and light it with a lucifer match."

"Upon my word," I interposed, "I had no notion you Ancient Egyptians were acquainted with the use of matches."

"Very likely not. 'There are more things in heaven and earth, Cephrenes, than are dreamt of in your philosophy,' as the bard of Philae puts it."

Further inquiries brought out all the secrets of that strange tomb-house, and kept me fully interested till the close of the banquet. Then the chief priest solemnly rose, offered a small fragment of meat to a deified crocodile, who sat in a meditative manner by the side of his deserted mummy-case, and declared the feast concluded for the night. All rose from their places, wandered away into the long corridors or side-aisles, and formed little groups of talkers under the brilliant gas-lamps.

For my part, I strolled off with Hatasou down the least illuminated of the colonnades, and took my seat beside a marble fountain, where several fish (gods of great sanctity, Hatasou assured me) were disporting themselves in a porphyry basin. How long we sat there I cannot tell, but I know that we talked a good deal about fish, and gods, and Egyptian habits, and Egyptian philosophy, and, above all, Egyptian love-making. The last-named subject we found very interesting, and when once we got fully started upon it, no diversion afterwards occurred to break the even tenour of the conversation. Hatasou was a lovely figure, tall, queenly, with smooth dark arms and neck of polished bronze: her big black eyes full of tenderness, and her long hair bound up into a bright Egyptian head-dress, that harmonized to a tone with her complexion and her robe. The more we talked, the more desperately did I fall in love, and the more utterly oblivious did I become of my duty to Editha Fitz-Simkins. The mere ugly daughter of a rich and vulgar brand-new knight, forsooth, to show off her airs before me, when here was a Princess of the Blood Royal of Egypt, obviously sensible to the attentions which I was paying her, and not unwilling to receive them with a coy and modest grace.

Well, I went on saying pretty things to Hatasou, and Hatasou went on deprecating them in a pretty little way, as who should say, "I don't mean what I pretend to mean one bit;" until at last I may confess that we were both evidently as far gone in the disease of the heart called love as it is possible for two young people on first acquaintance to become. Therefore, when Hatasou pulled forth her watch—another piece of mechanism with which antiquaries used never to credit the Egyptian people—and declared that she had only three more hours to live, at least for the next thousand years, I fairly broke down, took out my handkerchief, and began to sob like a child of five years old.

Hatasou was deeply moved. Decorum forbade that she should console me with too much *empressement*; but she ventured to remove the handkerchief gently from my face, and suggested that there was yet one course open by which we might enjoy a little more of one another's society. "Suppose," she said quietly, "you were to become a mummy. You would then wake up, as we do, every thousand years; and after you have tried it once, you will find it just as natural to sleep for a millennium as for eight hours. Of course," she added with a slight blush, "during the next three or four solar cycles there would be plenty of time to conclude any other arrangements you might possibly contemplate, before the occurrence of another glacial epoch."

This mode of regarding time was certainly novel and somewhat bewildering to people who ordinarily reckon its lapse by weeks and months; and I had a vague consciousness that my relations with Editha imposed upon me a moral necessity of returning to the outer world, instead of becoming a millennial mummy. Besides, there was the awkward chance of being converted into fuel and dissipated into space before the arrival of the next waking day. But I took one look at Hatasou, whose eyes were filling in turn with sympathetic tears, and that look decided me. I flung Editha, life, and duty to the dogs, and resolved at once to become a mummy.

There was no time to be lost. Only three hours remained to us, and the process of embalming, even in the most hasty manner, would take up fully two. We rushed off to the chief priest, who had charge of the particular department in question. He at once acceded to my wishes, and briefly explained the mode in which they usually treated the corpse.

That word suddenly aroused me. "The corpse!" I cried; "but I am alive. You can't embalm me living."

"We can," replied the priest, "under chloroform."

"Chloroform!" I echoed, growing more and more astonished: "I had no idea you Egyptians knew anything about it."

"Ignorant barbarian!" he answered with a curl of the lip; "you imagine yourself much wiser than the teachers of the world. If you were versed in all the wisdom of the Egyptians, you would know that chloroform is one of our simplest and commonest anaesthetics."

I put myself at once under the hands of the priest. He brought out the chloroform, and placed it beneath my nostrils, as I lay on a soft couch under the central court. Hatasou held my hand in hers, and watched my breathing with an anxious eye. I saw the priest leaning over me, with a clouded phial in his hand, and I experienced a vague sensation of smelling myrrh and spikenard. Next, I lost myself for a few moments, and when I again recovered my senses in a temporary break, the priest was holding a small greenstone knife, dabbled with blood, and I felt that a gash had been made across my breast. Then they applied the chloroform once more; I felt Hatasou give my hand a gentle squeeze; the whole panorama faded finally from my view; and I went to sleep for a seemingly endless time.

When I awoke again, my first impression led me to believe that the thousand years were over, and that I had come to life once more to feast with Hatasou and Thothmes in the Pyramid of Abu Yilla. But second thoughts, combined with closer observation of the surroundings, convinced me that I was really lying in a bedroom of Shepheard's Hotel at Cairo. An hospital nurse leant over me, instead of a chief priest; and I noticed no tokens of Editha Fitz-Simkins's presence. But when I endeavoured to make inquiries upon the subject of my whereabouts, I was peremptorily informed that I mustn't speak, as I was only just recovering from a severe fever, and might endanger my life by talking.

Some weeks later I learned the sequel of my night's adventure. The Fitz-Simkinses, missing me from the boat in the morning, at first imagined that I might have gone ashore for an early stroll. But after breakfast time, lunch time, and dinner time had gone past, they began to grow alarmed, and sent to look for me in all directions. One of their scouts, happening to pass the Pyramid, noticed that one of the stones near the north-east angle had been displaced, so as to give access to a dark passage, hitherto unknown. Calling several of his friends, for he was afraid to venture in alone, he passed down the corridor, and through a second gateway into the central hall. There the Fellahin found me, lying on the ground, bleeding profusely from a wound on the breast, and in an advanced stage of malarious fever. They brought me back to the boat, and the Fitz-Simkinses conveyed me at once to Cairo, for medical attendance and proper nursing.

Editha was at first convinced that I had attempted to commit suicide because I could not endure having caused her pain, and she accordingly resolved to tend me with the utmost care through my illness. But she found that my delirious remarks, besides bearing frequent reference to a princess, with whom I appeared to have been on unexpectedly intimate terms, also related very largely to our *casus belli* itself, the dancing girls of Abu Yilla. Even this trial she might have borne, setting down the moral degeneracy which led me to patronize so degrading an exhibition as a first symptom of my approaching malady: but certain unfortunate observations, containing pointed and by no means flattering allusions to her personal appearance—which I contrasted, much to her disadvantage, with that of the unknown princess—these, I say, were things which she could not forgive; and she left Cairo abruptly with her parents for the Riviera, leaving behind a stinging note, in which she denounced my perfidy and empty-heartedness with all the flowers of feminine eloquence. From that day to this I have never seen her.

When I returned to London and proposed to lay this account before the Society of Antiquaries, all my friends dissuaded me on the grounds of its apparent incredibility. They declare that I must have gone to the Pyramid already in a state of delirium, discovered the entrance by accident, and sunk exhausted when I reached the inner chamber. In answer, I would point out three facts. In the first place, I undoubtedly found my way into the unknown passage—for which achievement I afterwards received the gold medal of the Société Khédiviale, and of which I retain a clear recollection, differing in no way from my recollection of the subsequent events. In the second place, I had in my pocket, when found, a ring of Hatasou's, which I drew from her finger just before I took the chloroform, and put into my pocket as a keepsake. And in the third place, I had on my breast the wound which I saw the priest inflict with a knife of greenstone, and the scar may be seen on the spot to the present day. The absurd hypothesis of my medical friends, that I was wounded by falling against a sharp edge of rock, I must at once reject as unworthy of a moment's consideration.

My own theory is either that the priest had not time to complete the operation, or else that the arrival of the Fitz-Simkins' scouts frightened back the mummies to their cases an hour or so too soon. At any rate, there they all were, ranged around the walls undisturbed, the moment the Fellahin entered.

Unfortunately, the truth of my account cannot be tested for another thousand years. But as a copy of this book will be preserved for the benefit of posterity in the British Museum, I hereby solemnly call upon Collective Humanity to try the veracity of this history by sending a deputation of archaeologists to the Pyramid of Abu Yilla, on the last day of December, Two thousand eight hundred and seventy-seven. If they do not then find Thothmes and Hatasou feasting in the central hall exactly as I have described, I shall willingly admit that the story of my New Year's Eve among the Mummies is a vain hallucination, unworthy of credence at the hands of the scientific world.

The Ring of Thoth

Arthur Conan Doyle

Mr. John Vansittart Smith, F.R.S., of 147A Gower Street, was a man whose energy of purpose and clearness of thought might have placed him in the very first rank of scientific observers. He was the victim, however, of a universal ambition which prompted him to aim at distinction in many subjects rather than pre-eminence in one. In his early days he had shown aptitude for zoology and for botany which caused his friends to look upon him as a second Darwin, but when a professorship was almost within his reach he had suddenly discontinued his studies and turned his whole attention to chemistry. Here his researches upon the spectra of the metals had won him his fellowship in the Royal Society; but again he played the coquette with his subject, and after a year's absence from the laboratory he joined the Oriental Society, and delivered a paper on the Hieroglyphic and Demotic inscriptions of El Kab, thus giving a crowning example both of the versatility and of the inconstancy of his talents.

The most fickle of wooers, however, is apt to be caught at last, and so it was with John Vansittart Smith. The more he burrowed his way into Egyptology the more impressed he became by the vast field which it opened to the inquirer, and by the extreme importance of a subject which promised to throw a light upon the first germs of human civilisation and the origin of the greater part of our arts and sciences. So struck was Mr. Smith that he straightway married an Egyptological young lady who had written upon the sixth dynasty, and having thus secured a sound base of operations he set himself to collect materials for a work which should unite the research of Lepsius and the ingenuity of Champollion. The preparation of his *magnum opus* entailed many hurried visits to the magnificent Egyptian collections of the Louvre, upon the last of which, no longer ago than the middle of last October, he became involved in a most strange and noteworthy adventure.

The trains had been slow and the Channel had been rough, so that the student arrived in Paris in a somewhat befogged and feverish condition. On reaching the Hotel de France, in the Rue Laffitte, he had thrown himself upon a sofa for a couple of hours, but finding that he was unable to sleep, he determined, in spite of his fatigue, to make his way to the Louvre, settle the point which he had come to decide, and take the evening train back to Dieppe. Having come to his conclusion, he donned his greatcoat, for it was a raw rainy day, and made his way across the Boulevard des Italiens and down the Avenue de l'Opera. Once in the Louvre he was on familiar ground, and he speedily made his way to the collection of papyri which it was his intention to consult.

The warmest admirers of John Vansittart Smith could hardly claim for him that he was a handsome man. His high-beaked nose and prominent chin had something of the same acute and incisive character which distinguished his intellect. He held his head in a birdlike fashion, and birdlike, too, was the pecking motion with which, in conversation, he threw out his objections and retorts. As he stood, with the high collar of his greatcoat raised to his ears, he might have seen from the reflection in the glass-case before him that his appearance was a singular one. Yet it came upon him as a sudden jar when an English voice behind him exclaimed in very audible tones, "What a queer-looking mortal!"

The student had a large amount of petty vanity in his composition which manifested itself by an ostentatious and overdone disregard of all personal considerations. He straightened his lips and looked rigidly at the roll of papyrus, while his heart filled with bitterness against the whole race of travelling Britons.

"Yes," said another voice, "he really is an extraordinary fellow."

"Do you know," said the first speaker, "one could almost believe that by the continual contemplation of mummies the chap has become half a mummy himself?"

"He has certainly an Egyptian cast of countenance," said the other.

John Vansittart Smith spun round upon his heel with the intention of shaming his countrymen by a corrosive remark or two.

To his surprise and relief, the two young fellows who had been conversing had their shoulders turned towards him, and were gazing at one of the Louvre attendants who was polishing some brass-work at the other side of the room.

"Carter will be waiting for us at the Palais Royal," said one tourist to the other, glancing at his watch, and they clattered away, leaving the student to his labours.

"I wonder what these chatterers call an Egyptian cast of countenance," thought John Vansittart Smith, and he moved his position slightly in order to catch a glimpse of the man's face. He started as his eyes fell upon it. It was indeed the very face with which his studies had made him familiar. The regular statuesque features, broad brow, well-rounded chin, and dusky complexion were the exact counterpart of the innumerable statues, mummy-cases, and pictures which adorned the walls of the apartment. The thing was beyond all coincidence. The man must be an Egyptian. The national angularity of the shoulders and narrowness of the hips were alone sufficient to identify him.

John Vansittart Smith shuffled towards the attendant with some intention of addressing him. He was not light of touch in conversation, and found it difficult to strike the happy mean between the brusqueness of the superior and the geniality of the equal. As he came nearer, the man presented his side face to him, but kept his gaze still bent upon his work. Vansittart Smith, fixing his eyes upon the fellow's skin, was conscious of a sudden impression that there was something inhuman and preternatural about its appearance. Over the temple and cheek-bone it was as glazed and as shiny as varnished parchment. There was no suggestion of pores. One could not fancy a drop of moisture upon that arid surface. From brow to chin, however, it was cross-hatched by a million delicate wrinkles, which shot and interlaced as though Nature in some Maori mood had tried how wild and intricate a pattern she could devise.

"Où est la collection de Memphis?" asked the student, with the awkward air of a man who is devising a question merely for the purpose of opening a conversation.

"C'est là," replied the man brusquely, nodding his head at the other side of the room.

"Vous êtes un Egyptien, n'est-ce pas?" asked the Englishman.

The attendant looked up and turned his strange dark eyes upon his questioner. They were vitreous, with a misty dry shininess, such as Smith had never seen in a human head before. As he gazed into them he saw some strong emotion gather in their depths, which rose and deepened until it broke into a look of something akin both to horror and to hatred.

"Non, monsieur; je suis francais." The man turned abruptly and bent low over his polishing. The student gazed at him for a moment in astonishment, one of the doors he proceeded to make notes of his researches among the papyri. This thoughts, however refused to return into their natural groove. They would run upon the enigmatical attendant with the sphinx-like face and the parchment skin.

"Where have I seen such eyes?" said Vansittart Smith to himself. "There is something saurian about them, something reptilian. There's the membrana nictitans of the snakes," he mused, bethinking himself of his zoological studies. "It gives a shiny effect. But there was something more here. There was a sense of power, of wisdom—so I read them—and of weariness, utter weariness, and ineffable despair. It may be all imagination, but I never had so strong an impression. By Jove, I must have another look at them!" He rose and paced round the Egyptian rooms, but the man who had excited his curiosity had disappeared.

The student sat down again in his quiet corner, and continued to work at his notes. He had gained the information which he required from the papyri, and it only remained to write it down while it was still fresh in his memory. For a time his pencil travelled rapidly over the paper, but soon the lines became less level, the words more blurred, and finally the pencil tinkled down upon the floor, and the head of the student dropped heavily forward upon his chest. Tired out by his journey, he slept so soundly in his lonely post behind the door that neither the clanking civil guard, nor the footsteps of sightseers, nor even the loud hoarse bell which gives the signal for closing, were sufficient to arouse him.

Twilight deepened into darkness, the bustle from the Rue de Rivoli waxed and then waned, distant Notre Dame clanged out the hour of midnight, and still the dark and lonely figure sat silently in the shadow. It was not until close upon one in the morning that, with a sudden gasp and an intaking of the breath, Vansittart Smith returned to consciousness. For a moment it flashed upon him that he had dropped asleep in his studychair at home. The moon was shining fitfully through the unshuttered window, however, and as his eye ran along the lines of mummies and the endless array of polished cases, he remembered clearly where he was and how he came there. The student was not a nervous man. He possessed that love of a novel situation which is peculiar to his race. Stretching out his cramped limbs, he looked at his watch, and burst into a chuckle as he observed the hour. The episode would make an admirable anecdote to be introduced into his next paper as a relief to the graver and heavier speculations. He was a little cold, but wide awake and much refreshed. It was no wonder that the guardians had overlooked him, for the door threw its heavy black shadow right across him.

The complete silence was impressive. Neither outside nor inside was there a creak or a murmur. He was alone with the dead men of a dead civilisation. What though the outer city reeked of the garish nineteenth century! In all this chamber there was scarce an article, from the shrivelled ear of wheat to the pigment-box of the painter, which had not held its own against four thousand years. Here was the flotsam and jetsam washed up by the great ocean of time from that far-off empire. From stately Thebes, from lordly Luxor, from the great temples of Heliopolis, from a hundred rifled tombs, these relics had been brought. The student glanced around at the long-silent figures who flickered vaguely up through the gloom, at the busy toilers who were now so restful, and he fell into a reverent and thoughtful mood. An unwonted sense of his own youth and insignificance came over him. Leaning back in his chair, he gazed dreamily down the long vista of rooms, all silvery with the moonshine, which extend through the whole wing of the widespread building. His eyes fell upon the yellow glare of a distant lamp.

John Vansittart Smith sat up on his chair with his nerves all on edge. The light was advancing slowly towards him, pausing from time to time, and then coming jerkily onwards. The bearer moved noiselessly. In the utter silence there was no suspicion of the pat of a footfall. An idea of robbers entered the Englishman's head. He snuggled up farther into the corner. The light was two rooms off. Now it was in the next chamber, and still there was no sound. With something approaching to a thrill of fear the student observed a face, floating in the air as it were, behind the flare of the lamp. The figure was wrapped in shadow, but the light fell full upon a strange, eager face. There was no mistaking the metallic, glistening eyes and the cadaverous skin. It was the attendant with whom he had conversed.

Vansittart Smith's first impulse was to come forward and address him. A few words of explanation would set the matter clear, and lead doubtless to his being conducted to some side-door from which he might make his way to his hotel. As the man entered the chamber, however, there was something so stealthy in his movements, and so furtive in his expression, that the Englishman altered his intention. This was clearly no ordinary official walking the rounds. The fellow wore felt-soled slippers, stepped with a rising chest, and glanced quickly from left to right, while his hurried, gasping breathing thrilled the flame of his lamp. Vansittart Smith crouched silently back into the corner and watched him keenly, convinced that his errand was one of secret and probably sinister import.

There was no hesitation in the other's movements. He stepped lightly and swiftly across to one of the great cases, and, drawing a key from his pocket, he unlocked it. From the upper shelf he pulled down a mummy, which he bore away with him, and laid it with much care and solicitude upon the ground. By it he placed his lamp, and then squatting down beside it in Eastern fashion he began with long, quivering fingers to undo the cerecloths and bandages which girt it round. As the crackling rolls of linen peeled off one after the other, a strong aromatic odour filled the chamber, and fragments of scented wood and of spices pattered down upon the marble floor.

It was clear to John Vansittart Smith that this mummy had never been unswathed before. The operation interested him keenly. He thrilled all over with curiosity, and his bird-like head protruded farther and farther from behind the door. When, however, the last roll had been removed from the four-thousand-year-old head, it was all that he could do to stifle an outcry of amazement. First, a cascade of long, black, glossy tresses poured over the workman's hands and arms. A second turn of the bandage revealed a low, white forehead, with a pair of delicately arched eyebrows. A third uncovered a pair of bright, deeply fringed eyes, and a straight, well-cut nose, while a fourth and last showed a sweet, full, sensitive mouth, and a beautifully curved chin. The whole face was one of extraordinary loveliness, save for the one blemish that in the centre of the forehead there was a single irregular, coffee-coloured splotch. It was a triumph of the embalmer's art. Vansittart Smith's eyes grew larger and larger as he gazed upon it, and he chirruped in his throat with satisfaction.

Its effect upon the Egyptologist was as nothing, however, compared with that which it produced upon the strange attendant. He threw his hands up into the air, burst into a harsh clatter of words, and then, hurling himself down upon the ground beside the mummy, he threw his arms round her, and kissed her repeatedly upon the lips and brow. "Ma petite!" he groaned in French. "Ma pauvre petite!" His voice broke with emotion, and his innumerable wrinkles quivered and writhed, but the student observed in the lamplight that his shining eyes were still dry and tearless as two beads of steel. For some minutes he lay, with a twitching face, crooning and moaning over the beautiful head. Then he broke into a sudden smile, said some words in an unknown tongue, and sprang to his feet with the vigorous air of one who has braced himself for an effort.

In the centre of the room there was a large, circular case which contained, as the student had frequently remarked, a magnificent collection of early Egyptian rings and precious stones. To this the attendant strode, and, unlocking it, threw it open. On the ledge at the side he placed his lamp, and beside it a small, earthenware jar which he had drawn from his pocket. He then took a handful of rings from the case, and with a most serious and anxious face he proceeded to smear each in turn with some liquid substance from the earthen pot, holding them to the light as he did so. He was clearly disappointed with the first lot, for he threw them petulantly back into the case and drew out some more. One of these, a massive ring with a large crystal set in it, he seized and eagerly tested with the contents of the jar.

Instantly he uttered a cry of joy, and threw out his arms in a wild gesture which upset the pot and set the liquid streaming across the floor to the very feet of the Englishman. The attendant drew a red handkerchief from his bosom, and, mopping up the mess, he followed it into the corner, where in a moment he found himself face to face with his observer.

"Excuse me," said John Vansittart Smith, with all imaginable politeness; "I have been unfortunate enough to fall asleep behind this door."

"And you have been watching me?" the other asked in English, with a most venomous look on his corpselike face.

The student was a man of veracity. "I confess," said he, "that I have noticed your movements, and that they have aroused my curiosity and interest in the highest degree."

The man drew a long, flamboyant-bladed knife from his bosom. "You have had a very narrow escape," he said; "had I seen you ten minutes ago, I should have driven this through your heart. As it is, if you touch me or interfere with me in any way you are a dead man."

"I have no wish to interfere with you," the student answered. "My presence here is entirely accidental. All I ask is that you will have the extreme kindness to show me out through some side-door." He spoke with great suavity, for the man was still pressing the tip of his dagger against the palm of his left hand, as though to assure himself of its sharpness, while his face preserved its malignant expression.

"If I thought—" said he. "But no, perhaps it is as well. What is your name?" The Englishman gave it.

"Vansittart Smith," the other repeated. "Are you the same Vansittart Smith who gave a paper in London upon El Kab? I saw a report of it. Your knowledge of the subject is contemptible."

"Sir!" cried the Egyptologist.

"Yet it is superior to that of many who make even greater pretensions. The whole keystone of our old life in Egypt was not the inscriptions or monuments of which you make so much, but was our hermetic philosophy and mystic knowledge of which you say little or nothing."

"Our old life!" repeated the scholar, wide-eyed; and then suddenly, "Good God, look at the mummy's face!"

The strange man turned and flashed his light upon the dead woman, uttering a long, doleful cry as he did so. The action of the air had already undone all the art of the embalmer. The skin had fallen away, the eyes had sunk inwards, the discoloured lips had writhed away from the yellow teeth, and the brown mark upon the forehead alone showed that it was indeed the same face which had shown such youth and beauty a few short minutes before.

The man flapped his hands together in grief and horror. Then mastering himself by a strong effort he turned his hard eyes once more upon the Englishman.

"It does not matter," he said, in a shaking voice. "It really does not matter. I came here to-night with the fixed determination to do something. It is now done. All else us as nothing. I have found my quest. The old curse is broken. I can rejoin her. What matter about her inanimate shell so long as her spirit is awaiting me at the other side of the veil!"

"These are wild words," said Vansittart Smith. He was becoming more and more convinced that he had to do with a madman.

"Time presses, and I must go," continued the other. "The moment is at hand for which I have waited this weary time. But I must show you out first. Come with me."

Taking up the lamp, he turned from the disordered chamber, and led the student swiftly through the long series of the Egyptian, Assyrian, and Persian apartments. At the end of the latter he pushed open a small door let into the wall and descended a winding, stone stair. The Englishman felt the cold, fresh air of the night upon his brow. There was a door opposite him which appeared to communicate with the street. To the right of this another door stood ajar, throwing a spurt of yellow light across the passage. "Come in here!" said the attendant shortly.

Vansittart Smith hesitated. He had hoped that he had come to the end of his adventure. Yet his curiosity was strong within him. He could not leave the matter unsolved, so he followed his strange companion into the lighted chamber.

It was a small room, such as is devoted to a concierge. A wood fire sparkled in the grate. At one side stood a truckle bed, and at the other a coarse, wooden chair, with a round table in the centre, which bore the remains of a meal. As the visitor's eye glanced round he could not but remark with an ever-recurring thrill that all the small details of the room were of the most quaint design and antique workmanship. The candlesticks, the vases upon the chimney-piece, the fire-irons, the ornaments upon the walls, were all such as he had been wont to associate with the remote past. The gnarled, heavy-eyed man sat himself down upon the edge of the bed, and motioned his guest into the chair.

"There may be design in this," he said, still speaking excellent English. "It may be decreed that I should leave some account behind as a warning to all rash mortals who would set their wits up against workings of Nature. I leave it with you. Make such use as you will of it. I speak to you now with my feet upon the threshold of the other world.

"I am, as you surmised, an Egyptian—not one of the down-trodden race of slaves who now inhabit the Delta of the Nile, but a survivor of that fiercer and harder people who tamed the Hebrew, drove the Ethiopian back into the southern deserts, and built those mighty works which have been the envy and the wonder of all after generations. It was in the reign of Tuthmosis, sixteen hundred years before the birth of Christ, that I first saw the light. You shrink away from me. Wait, and you will see that I am more to be pitied than to be feared.

"My name was Sosra. My father had been the chief priest of Osiris in the great temple of abaris, which stood in those days upon the Bubastic branch of the Nile. I was brought up in the temple and was trained in all those mystic arts which are spoken of in your own Bible. I was an apt pupil. Before I was sixteen I had learned all which the wisest priest could teach me. From that time on I studied Nature's secrets for myself, and shared my knowledge with no man.

"Of all the questions which attracted me there were none over which I laboured so long as over those which concern themselves with the nature of life. I probed deeply into the vital principle. The aim of medicine had been to drive away disease when it appeared. It seemed to me that a method might be devised which should so fortify the body as to prevent weakness or death from ever taking hold of it. It is useless that I should recount my researches. You would scarce comprehend them if I did. They were carried out partly upon animals, partly upon slaves, and partly on myself. Suffice it that their result was to furnish me with a substance which, when injected into the blood, would endow the body with strength to resist the effects of time, of violence, or of disease;. It would not indeed confer immortality, but its potency would endure for many thousands of years. I used it upon a cat, and afterwards drugged the creature with the most deadly poisons. That cat is alive in Lower Egypt at the present moment. There was nothing of mystery or magic in the matter. It was simply a chemical discovery, which may well be made again.

"Love of life runs high in the young. It seemed to me that I had broken away from all human care now that I had abolished pain and driven death to such a distance. With a light heart I poured the accursed stuff into my veins. Then I looked round for someone whom I could benefit. There was a young priest of Thoth, Parmes by name, who had won my goodwill by his earnest nature and his devotion to his studies. To him I whispered my secret, and at his request I injected him with my elixir. I should now, I reflected, never be with out a companion of the same age as myself.

"After this grand discovery I relaxed my studies to some extent, but Parmes continued his with redoubled energy. Every day I could see him working with his flasks and his distiller in the Temple of

Thoth, but he said little to me as to the result of his labours. For my own part, I used to walk through the city and look around me with exultation as I reflected that all this was destined to pass away, and that only I should remain. The people would bow to me as they passed me, for the fame of my knowledge had gone abroad.

"There was war at this time, and the Great King had sent down his soldiers to the eastern boundary to drive away the Hyksos. A Governor, too, was sent to Abaris, that he might hold it for the King. I had heard much of the beauty of the daughter of this Governor, but one day as I walked out with Parmes we met her, borne upon the shoulders of her slaves. I was struck with love as with lightning. My heart went out from me. I could have thrown myself beneath the feet of her bearers. This was my woman. Life without her was impossible. I swore by the head of Horus that she should be mine. I swore it to the Priest of Thoth. He turned away from me with a brow which was as black as midnight.

"There is no need to tell you of our wooing. She came to love me even as I loved her. I learned that Parmes had seen her before I did, and had shown her that he, too, lover her, but I could smile at his passion, for I knew that her heart was mine. The white plague had come upon the city and many were stricken, but I laid my hands upon the sick and nursed them without fear or scathe. She marvelled at my daring. Then I told her my secret, and begged her that she would let me use my art upon her.

"'Your flower shall then be unwithered, Atma,' I said. 'Other things may pass away, but you and I, and our great love for each other, shall outlive the tomb of King Chefru.'

"But she was full of timid, maidenly objections. 'Was it right?' she asked, 'was it not a thwarting of the will of the gods? If the great Osiris had wished that our years should be so long, would he not himself have brought it about?'

"With fond and loving words I overcame her doubts, and yet she hesitated. It was a great question, she said. She would think it over for this one night. In the morning I should know of her resolution. Surely one night was not too much to ask.

"She wished to pray to Isis for help in her decision.

"With a sinking heart and a sad foreboding of evil I left her with her tirewomen. In the morning, when the early sacrifice was over, I hurried to her house. A rightened slave met me upon the steps. Her mistress was ill, she said, very ill. In a frenzy I broke my way through the attendants, and rushed through hall and corridor to my Atma's chamber. She lay upon her couch, her head high upon the pillow, with a pallid face and glazed eye. On her forehead there blazed a single angry, purple patch. I knew that hell-mark of old. It was the scar of the white plague, the sign-manual of death.

"Why should I speak of that terrible time? For months I was mad, fevered, delirious, and yet I could not die. Never did an Arab thirst after the sweet wells as I longed after death. Could poison or steel have shortened the thread of my existence, I should soon have rejoined my love in the land with the narrow portal. I tried, but it was of no avail. The accursed influence was too strong upon me. One night as I lay upon my couch, weak and weary, Parmes, the priest of Thoth, came to my chamber. He stood in the circle of the lamp-light, and he looked down upon me with eyes which were bright with a mad joy.

"'Why did you let the maiden die?' he asked; 'why did you not strengthen her as you strengthened me?'

"'I was too late,' I answered. 'But I had forgot. You also loved her. You are my fellow in misfortune. Is it not terrible to think of the centuries which must pass ere we look upon her again. Fools, fools, that we were to take death to be our enemy!'

"'You may say that,' he cried with a wild laugh; 'The words come well from your lips. For me they have no meaning.'

"'What mean you? I cried, raising myself upon my elbow. 'Surely, friend, this grief has turned your brain.' His face was aflame with joy, and he writhed and shook like one who hath a devil.

"'Do you know whither I go?' he asked.

"'Nay,' I answered, 'I cannot tell.'

"'I go to her,' said he. 'She lies embalmed in the farther tomb by the double palm-tree beyond the city wall.'

"'Why do you go there?' I cried.

"'To die!' he shrieked, 'to die! I am not bound by earthen fetters.'

"'But the elixir is in your blood,' I cried.

"'I can defy it,' said he; 'I have found a stronger principle which will destroy it. It is working in my veins at this moment, and in an hour I shall be a dead man. I shall join her, and you shall remain behind.'

"As I looked upon him I could see that he spoke words of truth. The light in his eye told me that he was indeed beyond the power of the elixir.

"'You will teach me!' I cried.

"'Never!' he answered.

"'I implore you, by the wisdom of Thoth, by the majesty of Anubis!'

"'It is useless,' he said coldly.

"'Then I will find it out,' I cried.

"'You cannot,' he answered; 'it came to me by chance. There is one ingredient which you can never get. Save that which is in the ring of Thoth, none will ever more be made.'

"'In the ring of Thoth!' I repeated, 'where then is the ring of Thoth?'

"'That also you shall never know,' he answered. 'You won her love. Who has won in the end? I leave you to your sordid earth life. My chains are broken. I must go!' He turned upon his heel and fled from the chamber. In the morning came the news that the Priest of Thoth was dead.

"My days after that were spent in study. I must find this subtle poison which was strong enough to undo the elixir. From early dawn to midnight I bent over the test-tube and the furnace. Above all, I collected the papyri and the chemical flasks of the Priest of Thoth. Alas! they taught me little. Here and there some hint or stray expression would raise hope in my bosom, but no good ever came of it. Still month after month, I struggled on. When my heart grew faint I would make my way to the tomb by the palm-trees. There, standing by the dead casket from which the jewel had been rifled, I would feel her sweet presence, and would whisper to her that I would rejoin her if mortal wit could solve the riddle.

"Parmes had said that his discovery was connected with the ring of Thoth. I had some remembrance of the trinket. It was a large and weighty circlet, made, not of gold, but of a rarer and heavier metal brought from the mines of Mount Harbal. Platinum, you call it. The ring had, I remembered, a hollow crystal set in it, in which some few drops of liquid might be stored. Now, the secret of Parmes could not have to do with the metal alone, for there were many rings of that metal in the Temple. Was it not more likely that he had stored his precious poison within the cavity of the crystal? I had scarce come to this conclusion before, in hunting through his papers, I came upon one which told me that it was indeed so, and that there was still some of the liquid unused.

"But how to find the ring? It was not upon him when he was stripped for the embalmer. Of that I made sure. Neither was it among his private effects. In vain I searched every room that he had entered, every box and vase and chattel that he had owned. I sifted the very sand of the desert in places where he had been wont to walk; but, do what I would, I could come upon no traces of the ring of Thoth. Yet it may be that my lab ours would have overcome all obstacles had it not been for a new and unlooked-for misfortune.

"A great war had been waged against the Hyksos, and the Captains of the Great King had been cut off in the desert, with all their bowmen and horsemen. The shepherd tribes were upon us like the locusts in a dry year. From the wilderness of Shur to the great, bitter lake there was blood by day and fire by night. Abaris was the bulwark of Egypt, but we could not keep the savages back. The city fell. The Governor and the soldiers were put to the sword, and I, with many more was led away into captivity.

"For years and years I tended cattle in the great plains by the Euphrates. My master died, and his son grew old, but I was still as far from death as ever. At last I escaped upon a swift camel, and made my way back to Egypt. The Hyksos had settled in the land which they had conquered, and their own King ruled over the country. Abaris had been torn down, the city had been burned, and the great Temple there was nothing left save an unsightly mound. Everywhere the tombs had been rifled and the monuments destroyed. Of my Atma's grave no sign was left. It was buried in the sands of the desert, and the palm-trees which marked the spot had long disappeared. The papers of Parmes and the remains of the Temple of Thoth were either destroyed or scattered far and wide over the deserts of Syria. All search after them was vain.

"From that time I gave up all hope of ever finding the ring or discovering the subtle drug. I set myself to live as patiently as might be until the effect of the elixir should wear away. How can you understand how terrible a thing time is, you who have experience only of the narrow course which lies between the cradle and the grave! I know it to my cost, I who have floated down the whole stream of history. I was old when Ilium fell. I was very old when Herodotus came to Memphis. I was bowed down with years when the new gospel came upon earth. Yet you see me much as other men are, with the cursed elixir still sweetening my blood, and guarding me against that which I would court. Now, at last, at last I have come to the end of it!

"I have travelled in all lands and I have dwelt with all nations. Every tongue is the same to me. I learned them all to help pass the weary time. I need not tell you how slowly they drifted by, the long dawn of modern civilization, the dreary middle years, the dark times of barbarism. They are all behind me now. I have never looked with the eyes of love upon another woman. Atma knows that I have been constant to her.

"It was my custom to read all that the scholars had to say upon Ancient Egypt. I have been in many positions, sometimes affluent, sometimes poor, but I have always found enough to enable me to buy the journals which deal with such matters. Some nine months ago I was in San Francisco, when I read an account of some discoveries made in the neighbourhood of Abaris. My heart leapt into my mouth as I read it. It said that the excavator had busied himself in exploring some tombs recently unearth. In one there had been found an unopened mummy with an inscription upon the outer case setting forth that it contained the body of the daughter of the Governor of the city in the days of Tuthmosis. It added that on removing the outer case there had been exposed a large platinum ring set with a crystal, which had been laid upon the breast of the embalmed woman. This, then, was where Parmes had hid the ring of Thoth. He might well say that it was safe, for no Egyptian would ever stain his soul by moving even the outer case of a buried friend.

"That very night I set off from San Francisco, and in a few weeks I found myself once more at Abaris, if a few sand-heaps and crumbling walls may retain the name of the great city. I hurried to the Frenchmen who were digging there and asked them for the ring. They replied that both the ring and the mummy had been sent to the Boulak Museum at Cairo. To Boulak I went, but only to be told that Mariette Bey had claimed them and had shipped them to the Louvre. I followed them, and there, at last, in the Egyptian chamber, I came, after close upon four thousand years, upon the remains of my Atma, and upon the ring for which I had sought so long.

"But how was I to lay hands upon them? How was I to have them for my very own? It chanced that the office of attendant was vacant. I went to the Director. I convinced him that I knew much about Egypt. In my eagerness I said too much. He remarked that a Professor's chair would suit me better than a seat in the Conciergerie. I knew more, he said, than he did. It was only by blundering, and letting him think that he had over-estimated my knowledge, that I prevailed upon him to let me move the few effects which I have retained into this chamber. It is my first and my last night here.

"Such is my story, Mr. Vansittart Smith. I need not say more to a man of your perception. By a strange chance you have this night looked upon the face of the woman whom I loved in those far-off days. There were many rings with crystals in the case, and I had to test for the platinum to be sure of the one which I wanted. A glance at the crystal has shown me that the liquid is indeed within it, and that I shall at last be able to shake off that accursed health which has been worse to me than the foulest disease. I have nothing more to say to you. I have unburdened myself. You may tell my story or you may withhold it at your pleasure. The choice rests with you. I owe you some amends, for you have had a narrow escape of your life this night. I was a desperate man, and not to be balked in my purpose. Had I seen you before the thing was done, I might have put it beyond your power to oppose me or to raise an alarm. This is the door. It leads into the Rue de Rivoli. Good night."

The Englishman glanced back. For a moment the lean figure of Sosra the Egyptian stood framed in the narrow doorway. The next the door had slammed, and the heavy rasping of the bolt broke on the silent night.

It was on the second day after his return to London that Mr. John Vansittart Smith saw the following concise narrative in the Paris correspondence of The Times:— "*Curious Occurrence in the Louvre.*—Yesterday morning a strange discovery was made in the principal Eastern chamber. The *ouvriers* who are employed to clean out the rooms in the morning round one of the attendants laying dead upon the floor with his arms found one of the mummies. So close was his embrace that it was only with the utmost difficulty that they were separated. One of the cases containing valuable rings had been opened and rifled. The authorities are of opinion that the man was bearing away the mummy with some idea of selling it to a private collector, but that he was struck down in the very act by long-standing disease of the heart. It is said that he was a man of uncertain age and eccentric habits, without any living relations to mourn over his dramatic and untimely end."

Lot No. 249

Arthur Conan Doyle

Of the dealings of Edward Bellingham with William Monkhouse Lee, and of the cause of the great terror of Abercrombie Smith, it may be that no absolute and final judgment will ever be delivered. It is true that we have the full and clear narrative of Smith himself, and such corroboration as he could look for from Thomas Styles the servant, from the Reverend Plumptree Peterson, Fellow of Old's, and from such other people as chanced to gain some passing glance at this or that incident in a singular chain of events. Yet, in the main, the story must rest upon Smith alone, and the most will think that it is more likely that one brain, however outwardly sane, has some subtle warp in its texture, some strange flaw in its workings, than that the path of Nature has been overstepped in open day in so famed a centre of learning and light as the University of Oxford. Yet when we think how narrow and how devious this path of Nature is, how dimly we can trace it, for all our lamps of science, and how from the darkness which girds it round great and terrible possibilities loom ever shadowly upwards, it is a bold and confident man who will put a limit to the strange by-paths into which the human spirit may wander.

In a certain wing of what we will call Old College in Oxford there is a corner turret of an exceeding great age. The heavy arch which spans the open door has bent downwards in the centre under the weight of its years, and the grey, lichen-blotched blocks of stone are, bound and knitted together with withes and strands of ivy, as though the old mother had set herself to brace them up against wind and weather. From the door a stone stair curves upward spirally, passing two landings, and terminating in a third one, its steps all shapeless and hollowed by the tread of so many generations of the seekers after knowledge. Life has flowed like water down this winding stair, and, waterlike, has left these smooth- worn grooves behind it. From the long-gowned, pedantic scholars of Plantagenet days down to the young bloods of a later age, how full and strong had been that tide of young English life. And what was left now of all those hopes, those strivings, those fiery energies, save here and there in some old-world churchyard a few scratches upon a stone, and perchance a handful of dust in a mouldering coffin? Yet here were the silent stair and the grey old wall, with bend and saltire and many another heraldic device still to be read upon its surface, like grotesque shadows thrown back from the days that had passed.

In the month of May, in the year 1884, three young men occupied the sets of rooms which opened on to the separate landings of the old stair. Each set consisted simply of a sitting-room and of a bedroom, while the two corresponding rooms upon the ground-floor were used, the one as a coal-cellar, and the other as the living-room of the servant, or gyp, Thomas Styles, whose duty it was to wait upon the three men above him. To right and to left was a line of lecture-rooms and of offices, so that the dwellers in the old turret enjoyed a certain seclusion, which made the chambers popular among the more studious undergraduates. Such were the three who occupied them now—Abercrombie Smith above, Edward Bellingham beneath him, and William Monkhouse Lee upon the lowest storey.

It was ten o'clock on a bright spring night, and Abercrombie Smith lay back in his arm-chair, his feet upon the fender, and his briar-root pipe between his lips. In a similar chair, and equally at his ease, there lounged on the other side of the fireplace his old school friend Jephro Hastie. Both men were in flannels, for they had spent their evening upon the river, but apart from their dress no one could look at their hard-cut, alert faces without seeing that they were open-air men—men whose minds and tastes turned naturally to all that was manly and robust. Hastie, indeed, was stroke of his college boat, and Smith was an even better oar, but a coming examination had already cast its shadow over him and held him to his work, save for the few hours a week which health demanded. A litter of medical books upon the table, with scattered bones, models and anatomical plates, pointed to the extent as well as the nature of his studies, while a couple of single- sticks and a set of boxing-gloves above the mantelpiece hinted at the means by which, with Hastie's help, he might take his exercise in its most compressed and least distant form. They knew each other very well—so well that they could sit now in that soothing silence which is the very highest development of companionship.

"Have some whisky," said Abercrombie Smith at last between two cloudbursts. "Scotch in the jug and Irish in the bottle."

"No, thanks. I'm in for the sculls. I don't liquor when I'm training. How about you?"

"I'm reading hard. I think it best to leave it alone."

Hastie nodded, and they relapsed into a contented silence.

"By-the-way, Smith," asked Hastie, presently, have you made the acquaintance of either of the fellows on your stair yet?"

"Just a nod when we pass. Nothing more."

"Hum! I should be inclined to let it stand at that. I know something of them both. Not much, but as much as I want. I don't think I should take them to my bosom if I were you. Not that there's much amiss with Monkhouse Lee."

"Meaning the thin one?"

"Precisely. He is a gentlemanly little fellow. I don't think there is any vice in him. But then you can't know him without knowing Bellingham."

"Meaning the fat one?"

"Yes, the fat one. And he's a man whom I, for one, would rather not know."

Abercrombie Smith raised his eyebrows and glanced across at his companion.

"What's up, then?" he asked. "Drink? Cards? Cad? You used not to be censorious."

"Ah! you evidently don't know the man, or you wouldn't ask. There's something damnable about him—something reptilian. My gorge always rises at him. I should put him down as a man with secret vices—an evil liver. He's no fool, though. They say that he is one of the best men in his line that they have ever had in the college."

"Medicine or classics?"

"Eastern languages. He's a demon at them. Chillingworth met him somewhere above the second cataract last long, and he told me that he just prattled to the Arabs as if he had been born and nursed and weaned among them. He talked Coptic to the Copts, and Hebrew to the Jews, and Arabic to the Bedouins, and they were all ready to kiss the hem of his frock-coat. There are some old hermit Johnnies up in those parts who sit on rocks and scowl and spit at the casual stranger. Well, when they saw this chap Bellingham, before he had said five words they just lay down on their bellies and wriggled. Chillingworth said that he never saw anything like it. Bellingham seemed to take it as his right, too, and strutted about among them and talked down to them like a Dutch uncle. Pretty good for an undergrad. of Old's, wasn't it?"

"Why do you say you can't know Lee without knowing Bellingham?"

"Because Bellingham is engaged to his sister Eveline. Such a bright little girl, Smith! I know the whole family well. It's disgusting to see that brute with her. A toad and a dove, that's what they always remind me of."

Abercrombie Smith grinned and knocked his ashes out against the side of the grate.

"You show every card in your hand, old chap," said he. "What a prejudiced, green-eyed, evil-thinking old man it is! You have really nothing against the fellow except that."

"Well, I've known her ever since she was as long as that cherry-wood pipe, and I don't like to see her taking risks. And it is a risk. He looks beastly. And he has a beastly temper, a venomous temper. You remember his row with Long Norton?"

"No; you always forget that I am a freshman."

"Ah, it was last winter. Of course. Well, you know the towpath along by the river. There were several fellows going along it, Bellingham in front, when they came on an old market-woman coming the other way. It had been raining—you know what those fields are like when it has rained—and the path ran between the river and a great puddle that was nearly as broad. Well, what does this swine do but keep the path, and push the old girl into the mud, where she and her marketings came to terrible grief. It was a blackguard thing to do, and Long Norton, who is as gentle a fellow as ever stepped, told him what he thought of it. One word led to another, and it ended in Norton laying his stick across the fellow's shoulders. There was the deuce of a fuss about it, and it's a treat to see the way in which Bellingham looks at Norton when they meet now. By Jove, Smith, it's nearly eleven o'clock!"

"No hurry. Light your pipe again."

"Not I. I'm supposed to be in training. Here I've been sitting gossiping when I ought to have been safely tucked up. I'll borrow your skull, if you can share it. Williams has had mine for a month. I'll take the little bones of your ear, too, if you are sure you won't need them. Thanks very much. Never mind a bag, I can carry them very well under my arm. Good-night, my son, and take my tip as to your neighbour."

When Hastie, bearing his anatomical plunder, had clattered off down the winding stair, Abercrombie Smith hurled his pipe into the wastepaper basket, and drawing his chair nearer to the lamp, plunged into a formidable green-covered volume, adorned with great colored maps of that strange internal kingdom of which we are the hapless and helpless monarchs. Though a freshman at Oxford, the student was not so in medicine, for he had worked for four years at Glasgow and at Berlin, and this coming examination would place him finally as a member of his profession. With his firm mouth, broad forehead, and clear-cut, somewhat hard-featured face, he was a man who, if he had no brilliant talent, was yet so dogged, so patient, and so strong that he might in the end overtop a more showy genius. A man who can hold his own among Scotchmen and North Germans is not a man to be easily set back. Smith had left a name at Glasgow and at Berlin, and he was bent now upon doing as much at Oxford, if hard work and devotion could accomplish it.

He had sat reading for about an hour, and the hands of the noisy carriage clock upon the side table were rapidly closing together upon the twelve, when a sudden sound fell upon the student's ear—a sharp, rather shrill sound, like the hissing intake of a man's breath who gasps under some strong emotion. Smith laid down his book and slanted his ear to listen. There was no one on either side or above him, so that the interruption came certainly from the neighbour beneath—the same neighbour of whom Hastie had given so unsavoury an account. Smith knew him only as a flabby, pale-faced man of silent and studious habits, a man, whose lamp threw a golden bar from the old turret even after he had extinguished his own. This community in lateness had formed a certain silent bond between them. It was soothing to Smith when the hours stole on towards dawning to feel that there was another so close who set as small a value upon his sleep as he did. Even now, as his thoughts turned towards him, Smith's feelings were kindly. Hastie was a good fellow, but he was rough, strong-fibred, with no imagination or sympathy. He could not tolerate departures from what he looked upon as the model type of manliness. If a man could not be measured by a public-school standard, then he was beyond the pale with Hastie. Like so many who are themselves robust, he was apt to confuse the constitution with the character, to ascribe to want of principle what was really a want of circulation. Smith, with his stronger mind, knew his friend's habit, and made allowance for it now as his thoughts turned towards the man beneath him.

There was no return of the singular sound, and Smith was about to turn to his work once more, when suddenly there broke out in the silence of the night a hoarse cry, a positive scream—the call of a man who is moved and shaken beyond all control. Smith sprang out of his chair and dropped his book. He was a man of fairly firm fibre, but there was something in this sudden, uncontrollable shriek of horror which chilled his blood and pringled in his skin. Coming in such a place and at such an hour, it brought a thousand fantastic possibilities into his head. Should he rush down, or was it better to wait? He had all the national hatred of making a scene, and he knew so little of his neighbour that he would not lightly intrude upon his affairs. For a moment he stood in doubt and even as he balanced the matter there was a quick rattle of footsteps upon the stairs, and young Monkhouse Lee, half dressed and as white as ashes, burst into his room.

"Come down!" he gasped. "Bellingham's ill."

Abercrombie Smith followed him closely down stairs into the sitting-room which was beneath his own, and intent as he was upon the matter in hand, he could not but take an amazed glance around him as he crossed the threshold. It was such a chamber as he had never seen before—a museum rather than a study. Walls and ceiling were thickly covered with a thousand strange relics from Egypt and the East. Tall, angular figures bearing burdens or weapons stalked in an uncouth frieze round the apartments. Above were bull-headed, stork-headed, cat-headed, owl-headed statues, with viper-crowned, almond-eyed monarchs, and strange, beetle-like deities cut out of the blue Egyptian lapis lazuli. Horus and Isis and Osiris peeped down from every niche and shelf, while across the ceiling a true son of Old Nile, a great, hanging-jawed crocodile, was slung in a double noose.

In the centre of this singular chamber was a large, square table, littered with papers, bottles, and the dried leaves of some graceful, palm-like plant. These varied objects had all been heaped together in order to make room for a mummy case, which had been conveyed from the wall, as was evident from the gap there, and laid across the front of the table. The mummy itself, a horrid, black, withered thing, like a charred head on a gnarled bush, was lying half out of the case, with its clawlike hand and bony forearm resting upon the table. Propped up against the sarcophagus was an old yellow scroll of papyrus, and in front of it, in a wooden armchair, sat the owner of the room, his head thrown back, his widely-opened eyes directed in a horrified stare to the crocodile above him, and his blue, thick lips puffing loudly with every expiration.

"My God! he's dying!" cried Monkhouse Lee distractedly.

He was a slim, handsome young fellow, olive- skinned and dark-eyed, of a Spanish rather than of an English type, with a Celtic intensity of manner which contrasted with the Saxon phlegm of Abercombie Smith.

"Only a faint, I think," said the medical student. "Just give me a hand with him. You take his feet. Now on to the sofa. Can you kick all those little wooden devils off? What a litter it is! Now he will be all right if we undo his collar and give him some water. What has he been up to at all?"

"I don't know. I heard him cry out. I ran up. I know him pretty well, you know. It is very good of you to come down."

"His heart is going like a pair of castanets," said Smith, laying his hand on the breast of the unconscious man. "He seems to me to be frightened all to pieces. Chuck the water over him! What a face he has got on him!"

It was indeed a strange and most repellent face, for colour and outline were equally unnatural. It was white, not with the ordinary pallor of fear but with an absolutely bloodless white, like the under side of a sole. He was very fat, but gave the impression of having at some time been considerably fatter, for his skin hung loosely in creases and folds, and was shot with a meshwork of wrinkles. Short, stubbly brown hair bristled up from his scalp, with a pair of thick, wrinkled ears protruding on either side. His light grey eyes were still open, the pupils dilated and the balls projecting in a fixed and horrid stare. It seemed to Smith as he looked down upon him that he had never seen nature's danger signals flying so plainly upon a man's countenance, and his thoughts turned more seriously to the warning which Hastie had given him an hour before.

"What the deuce can have frightened him so?" he asked.

"It's the mummy."

"The mummy? How, then?"

"I don't know. It's beastly and morbid. I wish he would drop it. It's the second fright he has given me. It was the same last winter. I found him just like this, with that horrid thing in front of him."

"What does he want with the mummy, then?"

"Oh, he's a crank, you know. It's his hobby. He knows more about these things than any man in England. But I wish he wouldn't! Ah, he's beginning to come to."

A faint tinge of colour had begun to steal back into Bellingham's ghastly cheeks, and his eyelids shivered like a sail after a calm. He clasped and unclasped his hands, drew a long, thin breath between his teeth, and suddenly jerking up his head, threw a glance of recognition around him. As his eyes fell upon the mummy, he sprang off the sofa, seized the roll of papyrus, thrust it into a drawer, turned the key, and then staggered back on to the sofa.

"What's up?" he asked. "What do you chaps want?"

"You've been shrieking out and making no end of a fuss," said Monkhouse Lee. "If our neighbour here from above hadn't come down, I'm sure I don't know what I should have done with you."

"Ah, it's Abercrombie Smith," said Bellingham, glancing up at him. "How very good of you to come in! What a fool I am! Oh, my God, what a fool I am!"

He sunk his head on to his hands, and burst into peal after peal of hysterical laughter.

"Look here! Drop it!" cried Smith, shaking him roughly by the shoulder.

"Your nerves are all in a jangle. You must drop these little midnight games with mummies, or you'll be going off your chump. You're all on wires now."

"I wonder," said Bellingham, "whether you would be as cool as I am if you had seen—"

"What then?"

"Oh, nothing. I meant that I wonder if you could sit up at night with a mummy without trying your nerves. I have no doubt that you are quite right. I dare say that I have been taking it out of myself too much lately. But I am all right now. Please don't go, though. Just wait for a few minutes until I am quite myself."

"The room is very close," remarked Lee, throwing open the window and letting in the cool night air.

"It's balsamic resin," said Bellingham. He lifted up one of the dried palmate leaves from the table and frizzled it over the chimney of the lamp. It broke away into heavy smoke wreaths, and a pungent, biting odour filled the chamber. "It's the sacred plant—the plant of the priests," he remarked. "Do you know anything of Eastern languages, Smith?"

"Nothing at all. Not a word."

The answer seemed to lift a weight from the Egyptologist's mind.

"By-the-way," he continued, "how long was it from the time that you ran down, until I came to my senses?"

"Not long. Some four or five minutes."

"I thought it could not be very long," said he, drawing a long breath. "But what a strange thing unconsciousness is! There is no measurement to it. I could not tell from my own sensations if it were seconds or weeks. Now that gentleman on the table was packed up in the days of the eleventh dynasty, some forty centuries ago, and yet if he could find his tongue he would tell us that this lapse of time has been but a closing of the eyes and a reopening of them. He is a singularly fine mummy, Smith."

Smith stepped over to the table and looked down with a professional eye at the black and twisted form in front of him. The features, though horribly discoloured, were perfect, and two little nut-like eyes still lurked in the depths of the black, hollow sockets. The blotched skin was drawn tightly from bone to bone, and a tangled wrap of black coarse hair fell over the ears. Two thin teeth, like those of a rat, overlay the shrivelled lower lip. In its crouching position, with bent joints and craned head, there was a suggestion of energy about the horrid thing which made Smith's gorge rise. The gaunt ribs, with their parchment-like covering, were exposed, and the sunken, leaden-hued abdomen, with the long slit where the embalmer had left his mark; but the lower limbs were wrapt round with coarse yellow bandages. A number of little clove-like pieces of myrrh and of cassia were sprinkled over the body, and lay scattered on the inside of the case.

"I don't know his name," said Bellingham, passing his hand over the shrivelled head. "You see the outer sarcophagus with the inscriptions is missing. Lot 249 is all the title he has now. You see it printed on his case. That was his number in the auction at which I picked him up."

"He has been a very pretty sort of fellow in his day," remarked Abercrombie Smith.

"He has been a giant. His mummy is six feet seven in length, and that would be a giant over there, for they were never a very robust race. Feel these great knotted bones, too. He would be a nasty fellow to tackle."

"Perhaps these very hands helped to build the stones into the pyramids," suggested Monkhouse Lee, looking down with disgust in his eyes at the crooked, unclean talons.

"No fear. This fellow has been pickled in natron, and looked after in the most approved style. They did not serve hodsmen in that fashion. Salt or bitumen was enough for them. It has been calculated that this sort of thing cost about seven hundred and thirty pounds in our money. Our friend was a noble at the least. What do you make of that small inscription near his feet, Smith?"

"I told you that I know no Eastern tongue."

"Ah, so you did. It is the name of the embalmer, I take it. A very conscientious worker he must have been. I wonder how many modern works will survive four thousand years?"

He kept on speaking lightly and rapidly, but it was evident to Abercrombie Smith that he was still palpitating with fear. His hands shook, his lower lip trembled, and look where he would, his eye always came sliding round to his gruesome companion. Through all his fear, however, there was a suspicion of triumph in his tone and manner. His eye shone, and his footstep, as he paced the room, was brisk and jaunty. He gave the impression of a man who has gone through an ordeal, the marks of which he still bears upon him, but which has helped him to his end.

"You're not going yet?" he cried, as Smith rose from the sofa.

At the prospect of solitude, his fears seemed to crowd back upon him, and he stretched out a hand to detain him.

"Yes, I must go. I have my work to do. You are all right now. I think that with your nervous system you should take up some less morbid study."

"Oh, I am not nervous as a rule; and I have unwrapped mummies before."

"You fainted last time," observed Monkhouse Lee.

"Ah, yes, so I did. Well, I must have a nerve tonic or a course of electricity. You are not going, Lee?"

"I'll do whatever you wish, Ned."

"Then I'll come down with you and have a shake- down on your sofa. Good-night, Smith. I am so sorry to have disturbed you with my foolishness."

They shook hands, and as the medical student stumbled up the spiral and irregular stair he heard a key turn in a door, and the steps of his two new acquaintances as they descended to the lower floor.

In this strange way began the acquaintance between Edward Bellingham and Abercrombie Smith, an acquaintance which the latter, at least, had no desire to push further. Bellingham, however, appeared to have taken a fancy to his rough-spoken neighbour, and made his advances in such a way that he could hardly be repulsed without absolute brutality. Twice he called to thank Smith for his assistance, and many times afterwards he looked in with books, papers, and such other civilities as two bachelor neighbours can offer each other. He was, as Smith soon found, a man of wide reading, with catholic tastes and an extraordinary memory. His manner, too, was so pleasing and suave that one came, after a time, to overlook his repellent appearance. For a jaded and wearied man he was no unpleasant companion, and Smith found himself, after a time, looking forward to his visits, and even returning them.

Clever as he undoubtedly was, however, the medical student seemed to detect a dash of insanity in the man. He broke out at times into a high, inflated style of talk which was in contrast with the simplicity of his life.

"It is a wonderful thing," he cried, "to feel that one can command powers of good and of evil—a ministering angel or a demon of vengeance." And again, of Monkhouse Lee, he said,— "Lee is a good fellow, an honest fellow, but he is without strength or ambition. He would not make a fit partner for a man with a great enterprise. He would not make a fit partner for me."

At such hints and innuendoes stolid Smith, puffing solemnly at his pipe, would simply raise his eyebrows and shake his head, with little interjections of medical wisdom as to earlier hours and fresher air.

One habit Bellingham had developed of late which Smith knew to be a frequent herald of a weakening mind. He appeared to be forever talking to himself. At late hours of the night, when there could be no visitor with him, Smith could still hear his voice beneath him in a low, muffled monologue, sunk almost to a whisper, and yet very audible in the silence. This solitary babbling annoyed and distracted the student, so that he spoke more than once to his neighbour about it. Bellingham, however, flushed up at the charge, and denied curtly that he had uttered a sound; indeed, he showed more annoyance over the matter than the occasion seemed to demand.

Had Abercrombie Smith had any doubt as to his own ears he had not to go far to find corroboration. Tom Styles, the little wrinkled man-servant who had attended to the wants of the lodgers in the turret for a longer time than any man's memory could carry him, was sorely put to it over the same matter.

"If you please, sir," said he, as he tidied down the top chamber one morning, "do you think Mr. Bellingham is all right, sir?"

"All right, Styles?"

"Yes sir. Right in his head, sir."

"Why should he not be, then?"

"Well, I don't know, sir. His habits has changed of late. He's not the same man he used to be, though I make free to say that he was never quite one of my gentlemen, like Mr. Hastie or yourself, sir. He's took to talkin' to himself something awful. I wonder it don't disturb you. I don't know what to make of him, sir."

"I don't know what business it is of yours, Styles."

"Well, I takes an interest, Mr. Smith. It may be forward of me, but I can't help it. I feel sometimes as if I was mother and father to my young gentlemen. It all falls on me when things go wrong and the relations come. But Mr. Bellingham, sir. I want to know what it is that walks about his room sometimes when he's out and when the door's locked on the outside."

"Eh! you're talking nonsense, Styles."

"Maybe so, sir; but I heard it more'n once with my own ears."

"Rubbish, Styles."

"Very good, sir. You'll ring the bell if you want me."

Abercrombie Smith gave little heed to the gossip of the old man-servant, but a small incident occurred a few days later which left an unpleasant effect upon his mind, and brought the words of Styles forcibly to his memory.

Bellingham had come up to see him late one night, and was entertaining him with an interesting account of the rock tombs of Beni Hassan in Upper Egypt, when Smith, whose hearing was remarkably acute, distinctly heard the sound of a door opening on the landing below.

"There's some fellow gone in or out of your room," he remarked.

Bellingham sprang up and stood helpless for a moment, with the expression of a man who is half incredulous and half afraid.

"I surely locked it. I am almost positive that I locked it," he stammered. "No one could have opened it."

"Why, I hear someone coming up the steps now," said Smith.

Bellingham rushed out through the door, slammed it loudly behind him, and hurried down the stairs. About half-way down Smith heard him stop, and thought he caught the sound of whispering. A moment later the door beneath him shut, a key creaked in a lock, and Bellingham, with beads of moisture upon his pale face, ascended the stairs once more, and re-entered the room.

"It's all right," he said, throwing himself down in a chair. "It was that fool of a dog. He had pushed the door open. I don't know how I came to forget to lock it."

"I didn't know you kept a dog," said Smith, looking very thoughtfully at the disturbed face of his companion.

"Yes, I haven't had him long. I must get rid of him. He's a great nuisance."

"He must be, if you find it so hard to shut him up. I should have thought that shutting the door would have been enough, without locking it."

"I want to prevent old Styles from letting him out. He's of some value, you know, and it would be awkward to lose him."

"I am a bit of a dog-fancier myself," said Smith, still gazing hard at his companion from the corner of his eyes. "Perhaps you'll let me have a look at it."

"Certainly. But I am afraid it cannot be to-night; I have an appointment. Is that clock right? Then I am a quarter of an hour late already. You'll excuse me, I am sure."

He picked up his cap and hurried from the room. In spite of his appointment, Smith heard him re-enter his own chamber and lock his door upon the inside.

This interview left a disagreeable impression upon the medical student's mind. Bellingham had lied to him, and lied so clumsily that it looked as if he had desperate reasons for concealing the truth. Smith knew that his neighbour had no dog. He knew, also, that the step which he had heard upon the stairs was not the step of an animal. But if it were not, then what could it be? There was old Styles's statement about the something which used to pace the room at times when the owner was absent. Could it be a woman? Smith rather inclined to the view. If so, it would mean disgrace and expulsion to Bellingham if it were discovered by the authorities, so that his anxiety and falsehoods might be accounted for. And yet it was inconceivable that an undergraduate could keep a woman in his rooms without being instantly detected. Be the explanation what it might, there was something ugly about it, and Smith determined, as he turned to his books, to discourage all further attempts at intimacy on the part of his soft-spoken and ill-favoured neighbour.

But his work was destined to interruption that night. He had hardly caught tip the broken threads when a firm, heavy footfall came three steps at a time from below, and Hastie, in blazer and flannels, burst into the room.

"Still at it!" said he, plumping down into his wonted arm-chair. "What a chap you are to stew! I believe an earthquake might come and knock Oxford into a cocked hat, and you would sit perfectly placid with your books among the rains. However, I won't bore you long. Three whiffs of baccy, and I am off."

"What's the news, then?" asked Smith, cramming a plug of bird's-eye into his briar with his forefinger.

"Nothing very much. Wilson made 70 for the freshmen against the eleven. They say that they will play him instead of Buddicomb, for Buddicomb is clean off colour. He used to be able to bowl a little, but it's nothing but half-vollies and long hops now."

"Medium right," suggested Smith, with the intense gravity which comes upon a 'varsity man when he speaks of athletics.

"Inclining to fast, with a work from leg. Comes with the arm about three inches or so. He used to be nasty on a wet wicket. Oh, by-the-way, have you heard about Long Norton?"

"What's that?"

"He's been attacked."

"Attacked?"

"Yes, just as he was turning out of the High Street, and within a hundred yards of the gate of Old's."

"But who—"

"Ah, that's the rub! If you said 'what,' you would be more grammatical. Norton swears that it was not human, and, indeed, from the scratches on his throat, I should be inclined to agree with him."

"What, then? Have we come down to spooks?"

Abercrombie Smith puffed his scientific contempt.

"Well, no; I don't think that is quite the idea, either. I am inclined to think that if any showman has lost a great ape lately, and the brute is in these parts, a jury would find a true bill against it. Norton passes that way every night, you know, about the same hour. There's a tree that hangs low over the path—the big elm from Rainy's garden. Norton thinks the thing dropped on him out of the tree. Anyhow, he was nearly strangled by two arms, which, he says, were as strong and as thin as steel bands. He saw nothing; only those beastly arms that tightened and tightened on him. He yelled his head nearly off, and a couple of chaps came running, and the thing went over the wall like a cat. He never got a fair sight of it the whole time. It gave Norton a shake up, I can tell you. I tell him it has been as good as a change at the sea-side for him."

"A garrotter, most likely," said Smith.

"Very possibly. Norton says not; but we don't mind what he says. The garrotter had long nails, and was pretty smart at swinging himself over walls. By-the-way, your beautiful neighbour would be pleased if he heard about it. He had a grudge against Norton, and he's not a man, from what I know of him, to forget his little debts. But hallo, old chap, what have you got in your noddle?"

"Nothing," Smith answered curtly.

He had started in his chair, and the look had flashed over his face which comes upon a man who is struck suddenly by some unpleasant idea.

"You looked as if something I had said had taken you on the raw. By-the-way, you have made the acquaintance of Master B. since I looked in last, have you not? Young Monkhouse Lee told me something to that effect."

"Yes; I know him slightly. He has been up here once or twice."

"Well, you're big enough and ugly enough to take care of yourself. He's not what I should call exactly a healthy sort of Johnny, though, no doubt, he's very clever, and all that. But you'll soon find out for yourself. Lee is all right; he's a very decent little fellow. Well, so long, old chap! I row Mullins for the Vice-Chancellor's pot on Wednesday week, so mind you come down, in case I don't see you before."

Bovine Smith laid down his pipe and turned stolidly to his books once more. But with all the will in the world, he found it very hard to keep his mind upon his work. It would slip away to brood upon the man beneath him, and upon the little mystery which hung round his chambers. Then his thoughts turned to this singular attack of which Hastie had spoken, and to the grudge which Bellingham was said to owe the object of it. The two ideas would persist in rising together in his mind, as though there were some close and intimate connection between them. And yet the suspicion was so dim and vague that it could not be put down in words.

"Confound the chap!" cried Smith, as he shied his book on pathology across the room. "He has spoiled my night's reading, and that's reason enough, if there were no other, why I should steer clear of him in the future."

For ten days the medical student confined himself so closely to his studies that he neither saw nor heard anything of either of the men beneath him. At the hours when Bellingham had been accustomed to visit him, he took care to sport his oak, and though he more than once heard a knocking at his outer door, he resolutely refused to answer it. One afternoon, however, he was descending the stairs when, just as he was passing it, Bellingham's door flew open, and young Monkhouse Lee came out with his eyes sparkling and a dark flush of anger upon his olive cheeks. Close at his heels followed Bellingham, his fat, unhealthy face all quivering with malignant passion.

"You fool!" he hissed. "You'll be sorry."

"Very likely," cried the other. "Mind what I say. It's off! I won't hear of it!"

"You've promised, anyhow."

"Oh, I'll keep that! I won't speak. But I'd rather little Eva was in her grave. Once for all, it's off. She'll do what I say. We don't want to see you again."

So much Smith could not avoid hearing, but he hurried on, for he had no wish to be involved in their dispute. There had been a serious breach between them, that was clear enough, and Lee was going to cause the engagement with his sister to be broken off. Smith thought of Hastie's comparison of the toad and the dove, and was glad to think that the matter was at an end. Bellingham's face when he was in a passion was not pleasant to look upon. He was not a man to whom an innocent girl could be trusted for life. As he walked, Smith wondered languidly what could have caused the quarrel, and what the promise might be which Bellingham had been so anxious that Monkhouse Lee should keep.

It was the day of the sculling match between Hastie and Mullins, and a stream of men were making their way down to the banks of the Isis. A May sun was shining brightly, and the yellow path was barred with the black shadows of the tall elm-trees. On either side the grey colleges lay back from the road, the hoary old mothers of minds looking out from their high, mullioned windows at the tide of young life which swept so merrily past them. Black-clad tutors, prim officials, pale reading men, brown- faced, straw-hatted young athletes in white sweaters or many-coloured blazers, all were hurrying towards the blue winding river which curves through the Oxford meadows.

Abercrombie Smith, with the intuition of an old oarsman, chose his position at the point where he knew that the struggle, if there were a struggle, would come. Far off he heard the hum which announced the start, the gathering roar of the approach, the thunder of running feet, and the shouts of the men in the boats beneath him. A spray of half-clad, deep- breathing runners shot past him, and craning over their shoulders, he saw Hastie pulling a steady thirty-six, while his opponent, with a jerky forty, was a good boat's length behind him. Smith gave a cheer for his friend, and pulling out his watch, was starting off again for his chambers, when he felt a touch upon his shoulder, and found that young Monkhouse Lee was beside him.

"I saw you there," he said, in a timid, deprecating way. "I wanted to speak to you, if you could spare me a half-hour. This cottage is mine. I share it with Harrington of King's. Come in and have a cup of tea."

"I must be back presently," said Smith. "I am hard on the grind at present. But I'll come in for a few minutes with pleasure. I wouldn't have come out only Hastie is a friend of mine."

"So he is of mine. Hasn't he a beautiful style? Mullins wasn't in it. But come into the cottage. It's a little den of a place, but it is pleasant to work in during the summer months."

It was a small, square, white building, with green doors and shutters, and a rustic trellis-work porch, standing back some fifty yards from the river's bank. Inside, the main room was roughly fitted up as a study—deal table, unpainted shelves with books, and a few cheap oleographs upon the wall. A kettle sang upon a spirit-stove, and there were tea things upon a tray on the table.

"Try that chair and have a cigarette," said Lee. "Let me pour you out a cup of tea. It's so good of you to come in, for I know that your time is a good deal taken up. I wanted to say to you that, if I were you, I should change my rooms at once."

"Eh?"

Smith sat staring with a lighted match in one hand and his unlit cigarette in the other.

"Yes; it must seem very extraordinary, and the worst of it is that I cannot give my reasons, for I am under a solemn promise—a very solemn promise. But I may go so far as to say that I don't think Bellingham is a very safe man to live near. I intend to camp out here as much as I can for a time."

"Not safe! What do you mean?"

"Ah, that's what I mustn't say. But do take my advice, and move your rooms. We had a grand row to- day. You must have heard us, for you came down the stairs."

"I saw that you had fallen out."

"He's a horrible chap, Smith. That is the only word for him. I have had doubts about him ever since that night when he fainted—you remember, when you came down. I taxed him to-day, and he told me things that made my hair rise, and wanted me to stand in with him. I'm not strait-laced, but I am a clergyman's son, you know, and I think there are some things which are quite beyond the pale. I only thank God that I found him out before it was too late, for he was to have married into my family."

"This is all very fine, Lee," said Abercrombie Smith curtly. "But either you are saying a great deal too much or a great deal too little."

"I give you a warning."

"If there is real reason for warning, no promise can bind you. If I see a rascal about to blow a place up with dynamite no pledge will stand in my way of preventing him."

"Ah, but I cannot prevent him, and I can do nothing but warn you."

"Without saying what you warn me against."

"Against Bellingham."

"But that is childish. Why should I fear him, or any man?"

"I can't tell you. I can only entreat you to change your rooms. You are in danger where you are. I don't even say that Bellingham would wish to injure you. But it might happen, for he is a dangerous neighbour just now."

"Perhaps I know more than you think," said Smith, looking keenly at the young man's boyish, earnest face. "Suppose I tell you that some one else shares Bellingham's rooms."

Monkhouse Lee sprang from his chair in uncontrollable excitement.

"You know, then?" he gasped.

"A woman."

Lee dropped back again with a groan.

"My lips are sealed," he said. "I must not speak."

"Well, anyhow," said Smith, rising, "it is not likely that I should allow myself to be frightened out of rooms which suit me very nicely. It would be a little too feeble for me to move out all my goods and chattels because you say that Bellingham might in some unexplained way do me an injury. I think that I'll just take my chance, and stay where I am, and as I see that it's nearly five o'clock, I must ask you to excuse me."

He bade the young student adieu in a few curt words, and made his way homeward through the sweet spring evening feeling half-ruffled, half-amused, as any other strong, unimaginative man might who has been menaced by a vague and shadowy danger.

There was one little indulgence which Abercrombie Smith always allowed himself, however closely his work might press upon him. Twice a week, on the Tuesday and the Friday, it was his invariable custom to walk over to Farlingford, the residence of Dr. Plumptree Peterson, situated about a mile and a half out of Oxford. Peterson had been a close friend of Smith's elder brother Francis, and as he was a bachelor, fairly well-to-do, with a good cellar and a better library, his house was a pleasant goal for a man who was in need of a brisk walk. Twice a week, then, the medical student would swing out there along the dark country roads, and spend a pleasant hour in Peterson's comfortable study, discussing, over a glass of old port, the gossip of the 'varsity or the latest developments of medicine or of surgery.

On the day which followed his interview with Monkhouse Lee, Smith shut up his books at a quarter past eight, the hour when he usually started for his friend's house. As he was leaving his room, however, his eyes chanced to fall upon one of the books which Bellingham had lent him, and his conscience pricked him for not having returned it. However repellent the man might be, he should not be treated with discourtesy. Taking the book, he walked downstairs and knocked at his neighbour's door. There was no answer; but on turning the handle he found that it was unlocked. Pleased at the thought of avoiding an interview, he stepped inside, and placed the book with his card upon the table.

The lamp was turned half down, but Smith could see the details of the room plainly enough. It was all much as he had seen it before—the frieze, the animal-headed gods, the banging crocodile, and the table littered over with papers and dried leaves. The mummy case stood upright against the wall, but the mummy itself was missing. There was no sign of any second occupant of the room, and he felt as he withdrew that he had probably done Bellingham an injustice. Had he a guilty secret to preserve, he would hardly leave his door open so that all the world might enter.

The spiral stair was as black as pitch, and Smith was slowly making his way down its irregular steps, when he was suddenly conscious that something had passed him in the darkness. There was a faint sound, a whiff of air, a light brushing past his elbow, but so slight that he could scarcely be certain of it. He stopped and listened, but the wind was rustling among the ivy outside, and he could hear nothing else.

"Is that you, Styles?" he shouted.

There was no answer, and all was still behind him. It must have been a sudden gust of air, for there were crannies and cracks in the old turret. And yet he could almost have sworn that be heard a footfall by his very side. He had emerged into the quadrangle, still turning the matter over in his head, when a man came running swiftly across the smooth-cropped lawn.

"Is that you, Smith?"

"Hullo, Hastie!"

"For God's sake come at once! Young Lee is drowned! Here's Harrington of King's with the news. The doctor is out. You'll do, but come along at once. There may be life in him."

"Have you brandy?"

"No."

"I'll bring some. There's a flask on my table."

Smith bounded up the stairs, taking three at a time, seized the flask, and was rushing down with it, when, as he passed Bellingham's room, his eyes fell upon something which left him gasping and staring upon the landing.

The door, which he had closed behind him, was now open, and right in front of him, with the lamp-light shining upon it, was the mummy case. Three minutes ago it had been empty. He could swear to that. Now it framed the lank body of its horrible occupant, who stood, grim and stark, with his black shrivelled face towards the door. The form was lifeless and inert, but it seemed to Smith as he gazed that there still lingered a lurid spark of vitality, some faint sign of consciousness in the little eyes which lurked in the depths of the hollow sockets. So astounded and shaken was he that he had forgotten his errand, and was still staring at the lean, sunken figure when the voice of his friend below recalled him to himself.

"Come on, Smith!" he shouted. "It's life and death, you know. Hurry up! Now, then," he added, as the medical student reappeared, "let us do a sprint. It is well under a mile, and we should do it in five minutes. A human life is better worth running for than a pot."

Neck and neck they dashed through the darkness, and did not pull up until, panting and spent, they had reached the little cottage by the river. Young Lee, limp and dripping like a broken water- plant, was stretched upon the sofa, the green scum of the river upon his black hair, and a fringe of white foam upon his leaden-hued lips. Beside him knelt his fellow-student Harrington, endeavouring to chafe some warmth back into his rigid limbs.

"I think there's life in him," said Smith, with his hand to the lad's side. "Put your watch glass to his lips. Yes, there's dimming on it. You take one arm, Hastie. Now work it as I do, and we'll soon pull him round."

For ten minutes they worked in silence, inflating and depressing the chest of the unconscious man. At the end of that time a shiver ran through his body, his lips trembled, and he opened his eyes. The three students burst out into an irrepressible cheer.

"Wake up, old chap. You've frightened us quite enough."

"Have some brandy. Take a sip from the flask."

"He's all right now," said his companion Harrington. "Heavens, what a fright I got! I was reading here, and he had gone for a stroll as far as the river, when I heard a scream and a splash. Out I ran, and by the time that I could find him and fish him out, all life seemed to have gone. Then Simpson couldn't get a doctor, for he has a game-leg, and I had to run, and I don't know what I'd have done without you fellows. That's right, old chap. Sit up."

Monkhouse Lee had raised himself on his hands, and looked wildly about him.

"What's up?" he asked. "I've been in the water. Ah, yes; I remember."

A look of fear came into his eyes, and he sank his face into his hands.

"How did you fall in?"

"I didn't fall in."

"How, then?"

"I was thrown in. I was standing by the bank, and something from behind picked me up like a feather and hurled me in. I heard nothing, and I saw nothing. But I know what it was, for all that."

"And so do I, " whispered Smith.

Lee looked up with a quick glance of surprise. "You've learned, then!" he said. "You remember the advice I gave you?"

"Yes, and I begin to think that I shall take it."

"I don't know what the deuce you fellows are talking about," said Hastie, "but I think, if I were you, Harrington, I should get Lee to bed at once. It will be time enough to discuss the why and the wherefore when he is a little stronger. I think, Smith, you and I can leave him alone now. I am walking back to college; if you are coming in that direction, we can have a chat."

But it was little chat that they had upon their homeward path. Smith's mind was too full of the incidents of the evening, the absence of the mummy from his neighbour's rooms, the step that passed him on the stair, the reappearance—the extraordinary, inexplicable reappearance of the grisly thing—and then this attack upon Lee, corresponding so closely to the previous outrage upon another man against whom Bellingham bore a grudge. All this settled in his thoughts, together with the many little incidents which had previously turned him against his neighbour, and the singular circumstances under which he was first called in to him. What had been a dim suspicion, a vague, fantastic conjecture, had suddenly taken form, and stood out in his mind as a grim fact, a thing not to be denied. And yet, how monstrous it was! how unheard of! how entirely beyond all bounds of human experience. An impartial judge, or even the friend who walked by his side, would simply tell him that his eyes had deceived him, that the mummy had been there all the time, that young Lee had tumbled into the river as any other man tumbles into a river, and that a blue pill was the best thing for a disordered liver. He felt that he would have said as much if the positions had been reversed. And yet he could swear that Bellingham was a murderer at heart, and that he wielded a weapon such as no man had ever used in all the grim history of crime.

Hastie had branched off to his rooms with a few crisp and emphatic comments upon his friend's unsociability, and Abercrombie

Smith crossed the quadrangle to his corner turret with a strong feeling of repulsion for his chambers and their associations. He would take Lee's advice, and move his quarters as soon as possible, for how could a man study when his ear was ever straining for every murmur or footstep in the room below? He observed, as he crossed over the lawn, that the light was still shining in Bellingham's window, and as he passed up the staircase the door opened, and the man himself looked out at him. With his fat, evil face he was like some bloated spider fresh from the weaving of his poisonous web.

"Good-evening," said he. "Won't you come in?"

"No," cried Smith, fiercely.

"No? You are busy as ever? I wanted to ask you about Lee. I was sorry to hear that there was a rumour that something was amiss with him."

His features were grave, but there was the gleam of a hidden laugh in his eyes as he spoke. Smith saw it, and he could have knocked him down for it.

"You'll be sorrier still to hear that Monkhouse Lee is doing very well, and is out of all danger," he answered. "Your hellish tricks have not come off this time. Oh, you needn't try to brazen it out. I know all about it."

Bellingham took a step back from the angry student, and half-closed the door as if to protect himself.

"You are mad," he said. "What do you mean? Do you assert that I had anything to do with Lee's accident?"

"Yes," thundered Smith. "You and that bag of bones behind you; you worked it between you. I tell you what it is, Master B., they have given up burning folk like you, but we still keep a hangman, and, by George! if any man in this college meets his death while you are here, I'll have you up, and if you don't swing for it, it won't be my fault. You'll find that your filthy Egyptian tricks won't answer in England."

"You're a raving lunatic," said Bellingham.

"All right. You just remember what I say, for you'll find that I'll be better than my word." The door slammed, and Smith went fuming up to his chamber, where he locked the door upon the inside, and spent half the night in smoking his old briar and brooding over the strange events of the evening.

Next morning Abercrombie Smith heard nothing of his neighbour, but Harrington called upon him in the afternoon to say that Lee was almost himself again. All day Smith stuck fast to his work, but in the evening he determined to pay the visit to his friend Dr. Peterson upon which he had started upon the night before. A good walk and a friendly chat would be welcome to his jangled nerves.

Bellingham's door was shut as he passed, but glancing back when he was some distance from the turret, he saw his neighbour's head at the window outlined against the lamp-light, his face pressed apparently against the glass as he gazed out into the darkness. It was a blessing to be away from all contact with him, but if for a few hours, and Smith stepped out briskly, and breathed the soft spring air into his lungs. The half-moon lay in the west between two Gothic pinnacles, and threw upon the silvered street a dark tracery from the stone-work above. There was a brisk breeze, and light, fleecy clouds drifted swiftly across the sky. Old's was on the very border of the town, and in five minutes Smith found himself beyond the houses and between the hedges of a May-scented Oxfordshire lane.

It was a lonely and little frequented road which led to his friend's house. Early as it was, Smith did not meet a single soul upon his way. He walked briskly along until he came to the avenue gate, which opened into the long gravel drive leading up to Farlingford. In front of him he could see the cosy red light of the windows glimmering through the foliage. He stood with his hand upon the iron latch of the swinging gate, and he glanced back at the road along which he had come. Something was coming swiftly down it.

It moved in the shadow of the hedge, silently and furtively, a dark, crouching figure, dimly visible against the black background. Even as he gazed back at it, it had lessened its distance by twenty paces, and was fast closing upon him. Out of the darkness he had a glimpse of a scraggy neck, and of two eyes that will ever haunt him in his dreams. He turned, and with a cry of terror he ran for his life up the avenue. There were the red lights, the signals of safety, almost within a stone's throw of him. He was a famous runner, but never had he run as he ran that night.

The heavy gate had swung into place behind him, but he heard it dash open again before his pursuer. As he rushed madly and wildly through the night, he could hear a swift, dry patter behind him, and could see, as he threw back a glance, that this horror was bounding like a tiger at his heels, with blazing eyes and one stringy arm outthrown. Thank God, the door was ajar. He could see the thin bar of light which shot from the lamp in the hall. Nearer yet sounded the clatter from behind. He heard a hoarse gurgling at his very shoulder. With a shriek he flung himself against the door, slammed and bolted it behind him, and sank half-fainting on to the hall chair.

"My goodness, Smith, what's the matter?" asked Peterson, appearing at the door of his study.

"Give me some brandy!"

Peterson disappeared, and came rushing out again with a glass and a decanter.

"You need it," he said, as his visitor drank off what he poured out for him. "Why, man, you are as white as a cheese."

Smith laid down his glass, rose up, and took a deep breath.

"I am my own man again now," said he. "I was never so unmanned before. But, with your leave, Peterson, I will sleep here to-night, for I don't think I could face that road again except by daylight. It's weak, I know, but I can't help it."

Peterson looked at his visitor with a very questioning eye.

"Of course you shall sleep here if you wish. I'll tell Mrs. Burney to make up the spare bed. Where are you off to now?"

"Come up with me to the window that overlooks the door. I want you to see what I have seen."

They went up to the window of the upper hall whence they could look down upon the approach to the house. The drive and the fields on either side lay quiet and still, bathed in the peaceful moonlight.

"Well, really, Smith," remarked Peterson, "it is well that I know you to be an abstemious man. What in the world can have frightened you?"

"I'll tell you presently. But where can it have gone? Ah, now look, look! See the curve of the road just beyond your gate."

"Yes, I see; you needn't pinch my arm off. I saw someone pass. I should say a man, rather thin, apparently, and tall, very tall. But what of him? And what of yourself? You are still shaking like an aspen leaf."

"I have been within hand-grip of the devil, that's all. But come down to your study, and I shall tell you the whole story."

He did so. Under the cheery lamplight, with a glass of wine on the table beside him, and the portly form and florid face of his friend in front, he narrated, in their order, all the events, great and small, which had formed so singular a chain, from the night on which he had found Bellingham fainting in front of the mummy case until his horrid experience of an hour ago.

"There now," he said as he concluded, "that's the whole black business. It is monstrous and incredible, but it is true."

Dr. Plumptree Peterson sat for some time in silence with a very puzzled expression upon his face.

"I never heard of such a thing in my life, never!" he said at last. "You have told me the facts. Now tell me your inferences."

"You can draw your own."

"But I should like to hear yours. You have thought over the matter, and I have not."

"Well, it must be a little vague in detail, but the main points seem to me to be clear enough. This fellow Bellingham, in his Eastern studies, has got hold of some infernal secret by which a mummy—or possibly only this particular mummy—can be temporarily brought to life. He was trying this disgusting business on the night when he fainted. No doubt the sight of the creature moving had shaken his nerve, even though he had expected it. You remember that almost the first words he said were to call out upon himself as a fool. Well, he got more hardened afterwards, and carried the matter through without fainting. The vitality which he could put into it was evidently only a passing thing, for I have seen it continually in its case as dead as this table. He has some elaborate process, I fancy, by which he brings the thing to pass. Having done it, he naturally bethought him that he might use the creature as an agent. It has intelligence and it has strength. For some purpose he took Lee into his confidence; but Lee, like a decent Christian, would have nothing to do with such a business. Then they had a row, and Lee vowed that he would tell his sister of Bellingham's true character. Bellingham's game was to prevent him, and he nearly managed it, by setting this creature of his on his track. He had already tried its powers upon another man—Norton—towards whom he had a grudge. It is the merest chance that he has not two murders upon his soul. Then, when I taxed him with the matter, he had the strongest reasons for wishing to get me out of the way before I could convey my knowledge to anyone else. He got his chance when I went out, for he knew my habits, and where I was bound for. I have had a narrow shave, Peterson, and it is mere luck you didn't find me on your doorstep in the morning. I'm not a nervous man as a rule, and I never thought to have the fear of death put upon me as it was to-night."

"My dear boy, you take the matter too seriously," said his companion. "Your nerves are out of order with your work, and you make too much of it. How could such a thing as this stride about the streets of Oxford, even at night, without being seen?"

"It has been seen. There is quite a scare in the town about an escaped ape, as they imagine the creature to be. It is the talk of the place."

"Well, it's a striking chain of events. And yet, my dear fellow, you must allow that each incident in itself is capable of a more natural explanation."

"What! even my adventure of to-night?"

"Certainly. You come out with your nerves all unstrung, and your head full of this theory of yours. Some gaunt, half-famished tramp steals after you, and seeing you run, is emboldened to pursue you. Your fears and imagination do the rest."

"It won't do, Peterson; it won't do."

"And again, in the instance of your finding the mummy case empty, and then a few moments later with an occupant, you know that it was lamplight, that the lamp was half turned down, and that you had no special reason to look hard at the case. It is quite possible that you may have overlooked the creature in the first instance."

"No, no; it is out of the question."

"And then Lee may have fallen into the river, and Norton been garrotted. It is certainly a formidable indictment that you have against Bellingham; but if you were to place it before a police magistrate, he would simply laugh in your face."

"I know he would. That is why I mean to take the matter into my own hands."

"Eh?"

"Yes; I feel that a public duty rests upon me, and, besides, I must do it for my own safety, unless I choose to allow myself to be hunted by this beast out of the college, and that would be a little too feeble. I have quite made up my mind what I shall do. And first of all, may I use your paper and pens for an hour?"

"Most certainly. You will find all that you want upon that side table."

Abercrombie Smith sat down before a sheet of foolscap, and for an hour, and then for a second hour his pen travelled swiftly over it. Page after page was finished and tossed aside while his friend leaned back in his arm-chair, looking across at him with patient curiosity. At last, with an exclamation of satisfaction, Smith sprang to his feet, gathered his papers up into order, and laid the last one upon Peterson's desk.

"Kindly sign this as a witness," he said.

"A witness? Of what?"

"Of my signature, and of the date. The date is the most important. Why, Peterson, my life might hang upon it."

"My dear Smith, you are talking wildly. Let me beg you to go to bed."

"On the contrary, I never spoke so deliberately in my life. And I will promise to go to bed the moment you have signed it."

"But what is it?"

"It is a statement of all that I have been telling you to-night. I wish you to witness it."

"Certainly," said Peterson, signing his name under that of his companion. "There you are! But what is the idea?"

"You will kindly retain it, and produce it in case I am arrested."

"Arrested? For what?"

"For murder. It is quite on the cards. I wish to be ready for every event. There is only one course open to me, and I am determined to take it."

"For Heaven's sake, don't do anything rash!"

"Believe me, it would be far more rash to adopt any other course. I hope that we won't need to bother you, but it will ease my mind to know that you have this statement of my motives. And now I am ready to take your advice and to go to roost, for I want to be at my best in the morning."

Abercrombie Smith was not an entirely pleasant man to have as an enemy. Slow and easy-tempered, he was formidable when driven to action. He brought to every purpose in life the same deliberate resoluteness which had distinguished him as a scientific student. He had laid his studies aside for a day, but he intended that the day should not be wasted. Not a word did he say to his host as to his plans, but by nine o'clock he was well on his way to Oxford.

In the High Street he stopped at Clifford's, the gun-maker's, and bought a heavy revolver, with a box of central-fire cartridges.

Six of them he slipped into the chambers, and half-cocking the weapon, placed it in the pocket of his coat. He then made his way to Hastie's rooms, where the big oarsman was lounging over his breakfast, with the Sporting Times propped up against the coffeepot.

"Hullo! What's up?" he asked. "Have some coffee?"

"No, thank you. I want you to come with me, Hastie, and do what I ask you."

"Certainly, my boy."

"And bring a heavy stick with you."

"Hullo!" Hastie stared. "Here's a hunting-crop that would fell an ox."

"One other thing. You have a box of amputating knives. Give me the longest of them."

"There you are. You seem to be fairly on the war trail. Anything else?"

"No; that will do." Smith placed the knife inside his coat, and led the way to the quadrangle. "We are neither of us chickens, Hastie," said he. "I think I can do this job alone, but I take you as a precaution. I am going to have a little talk with Bellingham. If I have only him to deal with, I won't, of course, need you. If I shout, however, up you come, and lam out with your whip as hard as you can lick. Do you understand?"

"All right. I'll come if I hear you bellow."

"Stay here, then. It may be a little time, but don't budge until I come down."

"I'm a fixture."

Smith ascended the stairs, opened Bellingham's door and stepped in. Bellingham was seated behind his table, writing. Beside him, among his litter of strange possessions, towered the mummy case, with its sale number 249 still stuck upon its front, and its hideous occupant stiff and stark within it. Smith looked very deliberately round him, closed the door, locked it, took the key from the inside, and then stepping across to the fireplace, struck a match and set the fire alight. Bellingham sat staring, with amazement and rage upon his bloated face.

"Well, really now, you make yourself at home," he gasped.

Smith sat himself deliberately down, placing his watch upon the table, drew out his pistol, cocked it, and laid it in his lap. Then he took the long amputating knife from his bosom, and threw it down in front of Bellingham.

"Now, then," said he, "just get to work and cut up that mummy."

"Oh, is that it?" said Bellingham with a sneer.

"Yes, that is it. They tell me that the law can't touch you. But I have a law that will set matters straight. If in five minutes you have not set to work, I swear by the God who made me that I will put a bullet through your brain!"

"You would murder me?"

Bellingham had half risen, and his face was the colour of putty.

"Yes."

"And for what?"

"To stop your mischief. One minute has gone."

"But what have I done?"

"I know and you know."

"This is mere bullying."

"Two minutes are gone."

"But you must give reasons. You are a madman—a dangerous madman. Why should I destroy my own property? It is a valuable mummy."

"You must cut it up, and you must burn it."

"I will do no such thing."

"Four minutes are gone."

Smith took up the pistol and he looked towards Bellingham with an inexorable face. As the second- hand stole round, he raised his hand, and the finger twitched upon the trigger.

"There! there! I'll do it!" screamed Bellingham.

In frantic haste he caught up the knife and hacked at the figure of the mummy, ever glancing round to see the eye and the weapon of his terrible visitor bent upon him. The creature crackled and snapped under every stab of the keen blade. A thick yellow dust rose up from it. Spices and dried essences rained down upon the floor. Suddenly, with a rending crack, its backbone snapped asunder, and it fell, a brown heap of sprawling limbs, upon the floor.

"Now into the fire!" said Smith.

The flames leaped and roared as the dried and tinderlike debris was piled upon it. The little room was like the stoke-hole of a steamer and the sweat ran down the faces of the two men; but still the one stooped and worked, while the other sat watching him with a set face. A thick, fat smoke oozed out from the fire, and a heavy smell of burned rosin and singed hair filled the air. In a quarter of an hour a few charred and brittle sticks were all that was left of Lot No. 249.

"Perhaps that will satisfy you," snarled Bellingham, with hate and fear in his little grey eyes as he glanced back at his tormenter.

"No; I must make a clean sweep of all your materials. We must have no more devil's tricks. In with all these leaves! They may have something to do with it."

"And what now?" asked Bellingham, when the leaves also had been added to the blaze.

"Now the roll of papyrus which you had on the table that night. It is in that drawer, I think."

"No, no," shouted Bellingham. "Don't burn that! Why, man, you don't know what you do. It is unique; it contains wisdom which is nowhere else to be found."

"Out with it!"

"But look here, Smith, you can't really mean it. I'll share the knowledge with you. I'll teach you all that is in it. Or, stay, let me only copy it before you burn it!"

Smith stepped forward and turned the key in the drawer. Taking out the yellow, curled roll of paper, he threw it into the fire, and pressed it down with his heel. Bellingham screamed, and grabbed at it; but Smith pushed him back, and stood over it until it was reduced to a formless grey ash.

"Now, Master B.," said he, "I think I have pretty well drawn your teeth. You'll hear from me again, if you return to your old tricks. And now good-morning, for I must go back to my studies."

And such is the narrative of Abercrombie Smith as to the singular events which occurred in Old College, Oxford, in the spring of '84. As Bellingham left the university immediately afterwards, and was last heard of in the Soudan, there is no one who can contradict his statement. But the wisdom of men is small, and the ways of nature are strange, and who shall put a bound to the dark things which may be found by those who seek for them?

A Professor of Egyptology

Guy Boothby

From seven o'clock in the evening until half past, that is to say for the half-hour preceding dinner, the Grand Hall of the Hotel Occidental, throughout the season, is practically a lounge, and is crowded with the most fashionable folk wintering in Cairo. The evening I am anxious to describe was certainly no exception to the rule. At the foot of the fine marble staircase—the pride of its owner—a well-known member of the French Ministry was chatting with an English Duchess whose pretty, but somewhat delicate, daughter was flirting mildly with one of the Sirdar's Bimbashis, on leave from the Soudan. On the right-hand lounge of the Hall an Italian Countess, whose antecedents were as doubtful as her diamonds, was apparently listening to a story a handsome Greek attaché was telling her; in reality, however, she was endeavouring to catch scraps of a conversation being carried on, a few feet away, between a witty Russian and an equally clever daughter of the United States. Almost every nationality was represented there, but unfortunately for our prestige, the majority were English. The scene was a brilliant one, and the sprinkling of military and diplomatic uniforms (there was a Reception at the Khedivial Palace later) lent an additional touch of colour to the picture. Taken altogether, and regarded from a political point of view, the gathering had a significance of its own.

At the end of the Hall, near the large glass doors, a handsome, elderly lady, with grey hair, was conversing with one of the leading English doctors of the place—a grey-haired, clever-looking man, who possessed the happy faculty of being able to impress everyone with whom he talked with the idea that he infinitely preferred his or her society to that of any other member of the world's population. They were discussing the question of the most suitable clothing for a Nile voyage, and as the lady's daughter, who was seated next her, had been conversant with her mother's ideas on the subject ever since their first visit to Egypt (as indeed had been the Doctor), she preferred to lie back on the divan and watch the people about her. She had large, dark, contemplative eyes. Like her mother she took life seriously, but in a somewhat different fashion.

One who has been bracketed third in the Mathematical Tripos can scarcely be expected to bestow very much thought on the comparative merits of Jaeger, as opposed to dresses of the Common or Garden flannel. From this, however, it must not be inferred that she was in any way a blue stocking, that is, of course, in the vulgar acceptation of the word. She was thorough in all she undertook, and for the reason that mathematics interested her very much the same way that Wagner, chess, and, shall we say, croquet, interest other people, she made it her hobby, and it must be confessed she certainly succeeded in it. At other times she rode, drove, played tennis and hockey, and looked upon her world with calm, observant eyes that were more disposed to find good than evil in it. Contradictions that we are, even to ourselves, it was only those who knew her intimately, and they were few and far between, who realised that, under that apparently sober, matter-of-fact personality, there existed a strong leaning towards the mysterious, or, more properly speaking, the occult. Possibly she herself would have been the first to deny this—but that I am right in my surmise this story will surely be sufficient proof.

Mrs.. Westmoreland and her daughter had left their comfortable Yorkshire home in September, and, after a little dawdling on the Continent, had reached Cairo in November—the best month to arrive, in my opinion, for then the rush has not set in, the hotel servants have not had sufficient time to become weary of their duties, and what is better still, all the best rooms have not been bespoken. It was now the middle of December, and the fashionable caravanserai, upon which they had for many years bestowed their patronage, was crowded from roof to cellar. Every day people were being turned away, and the manager's continual lament was that he had not another hundred rooms wherein to place more guests. He was a Swiss, and for that reason regarded hotel-keeping in the light of a profession.

On this particular evening Mrs.. Westmoreland and her daughter Cecilia had arranged to dine with Dr. Forsyth—that is to say, they were to eat their meal at his table in order that they might meet a man of whom they had heard much, but whose acquaintance they had not as yet made.

The individual in question was a certain Professor Constanides—reputed one of the most advanced Egyptologists, and the author of several well-known works. Mrs. Westmoreland was not of an exacting nature, and so long as she dined in agreeable company did not trouble herself very much whether it was with an English earl or a distinguished foreign savant.

"It really does not matter, my dear," she was wont to observe to her daughter. "So long as the cooking is good and the wine above reproach, there is absolutely nothing to choose between them. A Prime Minister and a country vicar are, after all, only men. Feed them well and they'll lie down and purr like tame cats. They don't want conversation." From this it will be seen that Mrs. Westmoreland was well acquainted with her world. Whether Miss Cecilia shared her opinions is another matter. At any rate, she had been looking forward for nearly a fortnight to meeting Constanides, who was popularly supposed to possess an extraordinary intuitive knowledge—instinct, perhaps, it should be called—concerning the localities of tombs of the Pharaohs of the Eleventh, Twelfth and Thirteenth Dynasties.

"I am afraid Constanides is going to be late," said the Doctor, who had consulted his watch more than once. "I hope, in that case, as his friend and your host, you will permit me to offer you my apologies."

The Doctor at no time objected to the sound of his own voice, and on this occasion he was even less inclined to do so. Mrs. Westmoreland was a widow with an ample income, and Cecilia, he felt sure, would marry ere long.

"He has still three minutes in which to put in an appearance," observed that young lady, quietly.

And then she added in the same tone, "Perhaps we ought to be thankful if he comes at all."

Both Mrs. Westmoreland and her friend the Doctor regarded her with mildly reproachful eyes.

The former could not understand anyone refusing a dinner such as she felt sure the Doctor had arranged for them; while the latter found it impossible to imagine a man who would dare to disappoint the famous Dr. Forsyth, who, having failed in Harley Street, was nevertheless coining a fortune in the land of the Pharaohs.

"My good friend Constanides will not disappoint us, I feel sure," he said, consulting his watch for the fourth time. "Possibly I am a little fast, at any rate I have never known him to be unpunctual. A remarkable—a very remarkable man is Constanides. I cannot remember ever to have met another like him. And such a scholar!"

Having thus bestowed his approval upon him the worthy Doctor pulled down his cuffs, straightened his tie, adjusted his pince-nez in his best professional manner, and looked round the hall as if searching for someone bold enough to contradict the assertion he had just made.

"You have, of course, read his *Mythological Egypt*," observed Miss Cecilia, demurely, speaking as if the matter were beyond doubt.

The Doctor looked a little confused.

"Ahem! Well, let me see," he stammered, trying to find a way out of the difficulty. "Well, to tell the truth, my dear young lady, I'm not quite sure that I have studied that particular work. As a matter of fact, you see, I have so little leisure at my disposal for any reading that is not intimately connected with my profession. That, of course, must necessarily come before everything else."

Miss Cecilia's mouth twitched as if she were endeavouring to keep back a smile. At the same moment the glass doors of the vestibule opened and a man entered. So remarkable was he that everyone turned to look at him—a fact which did not appear to disconcert him in the least.

He was tall, well shaped, and carried himself with the air of one accustomed to command. His face was oval, his eyes large and set somewhat wide apart. It was only when they were directed fairly at one that one became aware of the power they possessed. The cheek bones were a trifle high, and the forehead possibly retreated towards the jet-black hair more than is customary in Greeks. He wore neither beard nor moustache, thus enabling one to see the wide, firm mouth, the compression of the lips which spoke for the determination of their possessor. Those who had an eye for such things noted the fact that he was faultlessly dressed, while Miss Cecilia, who had the precious gift of observation largely developed, noted that, with the exception of a single ring and a magnificent pearl stud, the latter strangely set, he wore no jewellery of any sort. He looked about him for Dr. Forsyth, and, when he had located him, hastened forward. "My dear friend," he said in English, which he spoke with scarcely a trace of foreign accent, "I must crave your pardon a thousand times if I have kept you waiting."

"On the contrary," replied the Doctor, effusively, "you are punctuality itself. Permit me to have the pleasure—the very great pleasure—of introducing you to my friends, Mrs. Westmoreland and her daughter, Miss Cecilia, of whom you have often heard me speak." Professor Constanides bowed and expressed the pleasure he experienced in making their acquaintance. Though she could not have told you why, Miss Cecilia found herself undergoing very much the same sensation as she had done when she had passed up the Throne Room at her presentation. A moment later the gong sounded, and, with much rustling of skirts and fluttering of fans, a general movement was made towards the dining-room.

As host, Dr. Forsyth gave his arm to Mrs. Westmoreland, Constanides following with Miss Cecilia. The latter was conscious of a vague feeling of irritation; she admired the man and his work, but she wished his name had been anything rather than what it was. (It should be here remarked that the last Constanides she had encountered had swindled her abominably in the matter of a turquoise brooch, and in consequence the name had been an offence to her ever since.) Dr. Forsyth's table was situated at the further end, in the window, and from it a good view of the room could be obtained. The scene was an animated one, and one of the party, at least, I fancy, will never forget it—try how she may.

During the first two or three courses the conversation was practically limited to Cecilia and Constanides; the Doctor and Mrs. Westmoreland being too busy to waste time on idle chatter.

Later, they became more amenable to the discipline of the table—or, in other words, they found time to pay attention to their neighbours.

Since then I have often wondered with what feelings Cecilia looks back upon that evening. In order, perhaps, to punish me for my curiosity, she has admitted to me since that she had never known, up to that time, what it was to converse with a really clever man. I submitted to the humiliation for the reason that we are, if not lovers, at least old friends, and, after all, Mrs. Westmoreland's cook is one in a thousand.

From that evening forward, scarcely a day passed in which Constanides did not enjoy some portion of Miss Westmoreland's society. They met at the polo ground, drove in the Gezireh, shopped in the Muski, or listened to the band, over afternoon tea, on the balcony of Shepheard's Hotel. Constanides was always unobtrusive, always picturesque and invariably interesting. What was more to the point, he never failed to command attention whenever or wherever he might appear. In the Native Quarter he was apparently better known than in the European. Cecilia noticed that there he was treated with a deference such as one would only expect to be shown to a king. She marvelled, but said nothing. Personally, I can only wonder that her mother did not caution her before it was too late. Surely she must have seen how dangerous the intimacy was likely to become. It was old Colonel Bettenham who sounded the first note of warning. In some fashion or another he was connected with the Westmorelands, and therefore had more or less right to speak his mind.

"Who the man is, I am not in a position to say," he remarked to the mother; "but if I were in your place I should be very careful. Cairo at this time of year is full of adventurers."

"But, my dear Colonel," answered Mrs. Westmoreland, "you surely do not mean to insinuate that the Professor is an adventurer. He was introduced to us by Dr. Forsyth, and he has written so many clever books."

"Books, my dear madam, are not everything," the other replied judicially, and with that fine impartiality which marks a man who does not read. "As a matter of fact I am bound to confess that Phipps—one of my captains—wrote a novel some years ago, but only one. The mess pointed out to him that it wasn't good form, don't you know, so he never tried the experiment again. But as for this man, Constanides, as they call him, I should certainly be more than careful." I have been told since that this conversation worried poor Mrs. Westmoreland more than she cared to admit, even to herself. To a very large extent she, like her daughter, had fallen under the spell of the Professor's fascination. Had she been asked, point blank, she would doubtless have declared that she preferred the Greek to the Englishman—though, of course, it would have seemed flat heresy to say so. And yet—well, doubtless you can understand what I mean without my explaining further. I am inclined to believe that I was the first to notice that there was serious trouble brewing. I could see a strained look in the girl's eyes for which I found if difficult to account. Then the truth dawned upon me, and I am ashamed to say that I began to watch her systematically. We have few secrets from each other now, and she has told me a good deal of what happened during that extraordinary time—for extraordinary it certainly was. Perhaps none of us realised what a unique drama we were watching—one of the strangest, I am tempted to believe, that this world of ours has ever seen. Christmas was just past and the New Year was fairly under way when the beginning of the end came. I think by that time even Mrs. Westmoreland had arrived at some sort of knowledge of the case. But it was then too late to interfere. I am as sure that Cecilia was not in love with Constanides as I am of anything. She was merely fascinated by him, and to a degree that, happily for the peace of the world, is as rare as the reason for it is perplexing. To be precise, it was on Tuesday, January the 3rd, that the crisis came. On the evening of that day, accompanied by her daughter and escorted by Dr. Forsyth, Mrs. Westmoreland attended a reception at the palace of a certain Pasha, whose name I am obviously compelled to keep to myself. For the purposes of my story it is sufficient, however, that he is a man who prides himself on being up-to-date in most things, and for that and other reasons invitations to his receptions are eagerly sought after. In his drawing-room one may meet some of the most distinguished men in Europe, and on occasion it is even possible to obtain an insight into certain political intrigues that, to put it mildly, afford one an opportunity of reflecting on the instability of mundane affairs and of politics in particular.

The evening was well advanced before Constanides made his appearance. When he did, it was observed that he was more than usually quiet. Later, Cecilia permitted him to conduct her into the balcony, whence, since it was a perfect moonlight night, a fine view of the Nile could be obtained. Exactly what he said to her I have never been able to discover; I have, however, her mother's assurance that she was visibly agitated when she rejoined her. As a matter of fact, they returned to the hotel almost immediately, when Cecilia, pleading weariness, retired to her room.

And now this is the part of the story you will find as difficult to believe as I did. Yet I have indisputable evidence that it is true. It was nearly midnight and the large hotel was enjoying the only quiet it knows in the twenty-four hours. I have just said that Cecilia had retired, but in making that assertion I am not telling the exact truth, for though she had bade mother "Goodnight" and had gone to her room, it was not to rest. Regardless of the cold night air she had thrown open the window, and was standing looking out into the moonlit street. Of what she was thinking I do not know, nor can she remember. For my own part, however, I incline to the belief that she was in a semi-hypnotic condition and that for the time being her mind was a blank.

From this point I will let Cecilia tell the story herself.

How long I stood at the window I cannot say; it may have been only five minutes, it might have been an hour. Then, suddenly, an extraordinary thing happened. I knew that it was imprudent, I was aware that it was even wrong, but an overwhelming craving to go out seized me. I felt as if the house were stifling me and that if I did not get out into the cool night air, and within a few minutes, I should die. Stranger still, I felt no desire to battle with the temptation. It was as if a will infinitely stronger than my own was dominating me and that I was powerless to resist. Scarcely conscious of what I was doing I changed my dress, and then, throwing on a cloak, switched off the electric light and stepped out into the corridor. The white-robed Arab servants were lying about on the floor as is their custom; they were all asleep. On the thick carpet of the great staircase my steps made no sound. The hall was in semi-darkness and the watchman must have been absent on his rounds, for there was no one there to spy upon me. Passing through the vestibule I turned the key of the front door. Still success attended me, for the lock shot back with scarcely a sound and I found myself in the street. Even then I had no thought of the folly of this escapade. I was merely conscious of the mysterious power that was dragging me on. Without hesitation I turned to the right and hastened along the pavement, faster I think than I had ever walked in my life. Under the trees it was comparatively dark, but out in the roadway it was well-nigh as bright as day. Once a carriage passed me and I could hear its occupants, who were French, conversing merrily—otherwise I seemed to have the city to myself. Later I heard a muezzin chanting his call to prayer from the minaret of some mosque in the neighbourhood, the cry being taken up and repeated from other mosques. Then at the corner of a street I stopped as if in obedience to a command. I can recall the fact that I was trembling, but for what reason I could not tell. I say this to show that while I was incapable of returning to the hotel, or of exercising my normal will power, I still possessed the faculty of observation.

I had scarcely reached the corner referred to, which, as a matter of fact, I believe I should recognise if I saw it again, when the door of a house opened and a man emerged. It was Professor Constanides, but his appearance at such a place and at such an hour, like everything else that happened that night, did not strike me as being in any way extraordinary.

"You have obeyed me," he said by way of greeting. "That is well. Now let us be going—the hour is late."

As he said it there came the rattle of wheels and a carriage drove swiftly round the corner and pulled up before us. My companion helped me into it and took his place beside me. Even then, unheard-of as my action was, I had no thought of resisting.

"What does it mean?" I asked. "Oh, tell me what it means? Why am I here?"

"You will soon know," was his reply, and his voice took a tone I had never noticed in it before. We had driven some considerable distance, in fact, I believe we had crossed the river, before either of us spoke again.

"Think," said my companion, "and tell me whether you can remember ever having driven with me before?"

"We have driven together many times lately," I replied. "Yesterday to the polo, and the day before to the Pyramids."

"Think again," he said, and as he did so he placed his hand on mine. It was as cold as ice.

However, I only shook my head.

"I cannot remember," I answered, and yet I seemed to be dimly conscious of something that was too intangible to be a recollection. He uttered a little sigh and once more we were silent. The horses must have been good ones for they whirled us along at a fast pace. I did not take much interest in the route we followed, but at last something attracted my attention and I knew that we were on the road to Gizeh. A few moments later the famous Museum, once the palace of the ex-Khedive Ismail, came into view. Almost immediately the carriage pulled up in the shadow of the Lebbek trees and my companion begged me to alight. I did so, whereupon he said something, in what I can only suppose was Arabic, to his coachman, who whipped up his horses and drove swiftly away.

"Come," he said, in the same tone of command as before, and then led the way towards the gates of the old palace. Dominated as my will was by his I could still notice how beautiful the building looked in the moonlight. In the daytime it presents a faded and unsubstantial appearance, but now, with its Oriental tracery, it was almost fairylike. The Professor halted at the gates and unlocked them. How he had admitted us, I cannot say. It suffices that, almost before I was aware of it, we had passed through the garden and were ascending the steps to the main entrance. The doors behind us, we entered the first room. It is only another point in this extraordinary adventure when I declare that even now I was not afraid; and yet to find oneself in such a place and at such an hour at any other time would probably have driven me beside myself with terror.

The moonlight streamed in upon us, revealing the ancient monuments and the other indescribable memorials of those long-dead ages. Once more my conductor uttered his command and we went on through the second room, passed the Sheikh-El-Beled and the Seated Scribe. Room after room we traversed, and to do so it seemed to me that we ascended stairs innumerable. At last we came to one in which Constanides paused. It contained numerous mummy cases and was lighted by a skylight through which the rays of the moon streamed in. We were standing before one which I remembered to have remarked on the occasion of our last visit. I could distinguish the paintings upon it distinctly. Professor Constanides, with the deftness which showed his familiarity with the work, removed the lid and revealed to me the swathed-up figure within. The face was uncovered and was strangely well-preserved. I gazed down on it, and as I did so a sensation that I had never known before passed over me. My body seemed to be shrinking, my blood to be turning to ice.

For the first time I endeavoured to exert myself, to tear myself from the bonds that were holding me. But it was in vain. I was sinking—sinking—sinking—into I knew not what. Then the voice of the man who had brought me to the place sounded in my ears as if he were speaking from a long way off. After that a great light burst upon me, and it was as if I were walking in a dream; yet I knew it was too real, too true to life to be a mere creation of my fancy.

It was night and the heavens were studded with stars. In the distance a great army was encamped and at intervals the calls of the sentries reached me. Somehow I seemed to feel no wonderment at my position. Even my dress caused me no surprise. To my left, as I looked towards the river, was a large tent, before which armed men paced continually. I looked about me as if I expected to see someone, but there was no one.

"It is for the last time," I told myself. "Come what may, it shall be the last time!"

Still I waited, and as I did so I could hear the night wind sighing through the rushes on the river's bank. From the tent near me—for Usirtasen, son of Amenemhait—was then fighting against the Libyans and was commanding his army in person—came the sound of revelry. The air blew cold from the desert and I shivered, for I was but thinly clad. Then I hid myself in the shadow of a great rock that was near at hand. Presently I caught the sound of a footstep, and there came into view a tall man, walking carefully, as though he had no desire that the sentries on guard before the Royal tent should become aware of his presence in the neighbourhood. As I saw him I moved from where I was standing to meet him. He was none other than Sinfihit—younger son of Amenemhait and brother of Usirtasen—who was at that moment conferring with his generals in the tent.

I can see him now as he came towards me, tall, handsome, and defiant in his bearing as a man should be. He walked with the assured step of one who has been a soldier and trained to warlike exercises from his youth up. For a moment I regretted the news I had to tell him—but only for a moment. I could hear the voice of Usirtasen in the tent, and after that I had no thought for anyone else.

"Is it thou, Nofrit?" he asked as soon as he saw me.

"It is I!" I replied. "You are late, Sinfihit. You tarry too long over the wine cups."

"You wrong me, Nofrit," he answered, with all the fierceness for which he was celebrated. "I have drunk no wine this night. Had I not been kept by the Captain of the Guard I should have been here sooner. Thou art not angry with me, Nofrit?"

"Nay, that were presumption on my part, my lord," I answered. "Art thou not the King's son, Sinfihit?"

"And by the Holy Ones I swear that it were better for me if I were not," he replied. "Usirtasen, my brother, takes all and I am but the jackal that gathers up the scraps wheresoever he may find them." He paused for a moment. "However, all goes well with our plot. Let me but have time and I will yet be ruler of this land and of all the Land of Khem beside." He drew himself up to his full height and looked towards the sleeping camp. It was well known that between the brothers there was but little love, and still less trust.

"Peace, peace," I whispered, fearing lest his words might be overheard. "You must not talk so, my lord. Should you by chance be heard you know what the punishment would be!"

He laughed a short and bitter laugh. He was well aware that Usirtasen would show him no mercy. It was not the first time he had been suspected, and he was playing a desperate game. He came a step closer to me and took my hand in his. I would have withdrawn it—but he gave me no opportunity. Never was a man more in earnest than he was then.

"Nofrit," he said, and I could feel his breath upon my cheek, "what is my answer to be? The time for talking is past; now we must act. As thou knowest, I prefer deeds to words, and to-morrow my brother Usirtasen shall learn that I am as powerful as he."

Knowing what I knew I could have laughed him to scorn for his boastful speech. The time, however, was not yet ripe, so I held my peace. He was plotting against his brother, whom I loved, and it was his desire that I should help him. That, however, I would not do. "Listen," he said, drawing even closer to me, and speaking in a voice that showed me plainly how much in earnest he was, "thou knowest how much I love thee. Thou knowest that there is nought I would not do for thee or for thy sake. Be but faithful to me now and there is nothing thou shalt ask in vain of me hereafter. All is prepared, and ere the moon is gone I shall be Pharaoh and reign beside Amenemhait, my father." "Are you so sure that your plans will not miscarry?" I asked, with what was almost a sneer at his recklessness—for recklessness it surely was to think that he could induce an army that had been admittedly successful to swerve in its allegiance to the general who had won its battles for it, and to desert in the face of the enemy. Moreover, I knew that he was wrong in believing that his father cared more for him than for Usirtasen, who had done so much for the kingdom, and who was beloved by high and low alike. But it was not in Sinfihit's nature to look upon the dark side of things. He had complete confidence in himself and in his power to bring his conspiracy against his father and brother to a successful issue. He revealed to me his plans, and, bold though they were, I could see that it was impossible that they could succeed.

And in the event of his failing, what mercy could he hope to receive? I knew Usirtasen too well to think that he would show any. With all the eloquence I could command I implored him to abandon the attempt, or at least to delay it for a time. He seized my wrist and pulled me to him, peering fiercely into my face.

"Art playing me false?" he asked. "If it is so it were better that you should drown yourself in yonder river. Betray me and nothing shall save you—not even Pharaoh himself."

That he meant what he said I felt convinced. The man was desperate; he was staking all he had in the world upon the issue of his venture. I can say with truth that it was not my fault that we had been drawn together, and yet on this night of all others it seemed as if there were nothing left for me but to side with him or to bring about his downfall.

"Nofrit," he said, after a short pause, "is it nothing, thinkest thou, to be the wife of a Pharaoh? Is it not worth striving for, particularly when it can be so easily accomplished?"

I knew, however, that he was deluding himself with false hopes. What he had in his mind could never come to pass. I was like dry grass between two fires. All that was required was one small spark to bring about a conflagration in which I should be consumed.

"Harken to me, Nofrit," he continued. "You have means of learning Usirtasen's plans. Send me word to-morrow as to what is in his mind and the rest will be easy. Your reward shall be greater than you dream of."

Though I had no intention of doing what he asked, I knew that in his present humour it would be little short of madness to thwart him. I therefore temporised with him, and allowed him to suppose that I would do as he wished, and then, bidding him good-night, I sped away towards the hut where I was lodged. I had not been there many minutes when a messenger came to me from Usirtasen, summoning me to his presence. Though I could not understand what it meant I hastened to obey.

On arrival there I found him surrounded by the chief officers of his army. One glance at his face was sufficient to tell me that he was violently angry with someone, and I had the best of reasons for believing that that someone was myself. Alas! it was as I had expected.

Sinfihit's plot had been discovered; he had been followed and watched, and my meeting with him that evening was known. I protested my innocence in vain. The evidence was too strong against me.

"Speak, girl, and tell what thou knowest," said Usirtasen, in a voice I had never heard him use before. "It is the only way by which thou canst save thyself. Look to it that thy story tallies with the tales of others!"

I trembled in every limb as I answered the questions he put to me. It was plain that he no longer trusted me, and that the favour I had once found in his eyes was gone, never to return. "It is well," he said when I had finished my story. "And now we will see thy partner—the man who would have put me—the Pharaoh who is to be—to the sword had I not been warned in time."

He made a sign to one of the officers who stood by, whereupon the latter left the tent, to return a few moments later with Sinfihit.

"Hail, brother!" said Usirtasen, mockingly, as he leaned back in his chair and looked at him through half-shut eyes. "You tarried but a short time over the wine cup this night. I fear it pleased thee but little. Forgive me; on another occasion better shall be found for thee lest thou shouldst deem us lacking in our hospitality."

"There were matters that needed my attention and I could not stay," Sinfihit replied, looking his brother in the face. "Thou wouldst not have me neglect my duties."

"Nay! nay! Maybe they were matters that concerned our personal safety?" Usirtasen continued, still with the same gentleness. "Maybe you heard that there were those in our army who were not well disposed towards us? Give me their names, my brother, that due punishment may be meted out to them."

Before Sinfihit could reply, Usirtasen had sprung to his feet.

"Dog!" he cried, "darest thou prate to me of matters of importance when thou knowest thou hast been plotting against me and my father's throne. I have doubted thee these many months and now all is made clear. By the Gods, the Holy Ones, I swear that thou shalt die for this ere cock-crow.

It was at this moment that Sinfihit became aware of my presence. A little cry escaped him, and his face told me as plainly as any words could speak that he believed that I had betrayed him. He was about to speak, probably to denounce me, when the sound of voices reached us from outside.

Usirtasen bade the guards to ascertain what it meant, and presently a messenger entered the tent.

He was travel-stained and weary. Advancing towards where Usirtasen was seated, he knelt before him.

"Hail, Pharaoh," he said. "I come to three from the Palace of Titoui."

An anxious expression came over Usirtasen's face as he heard this. I also detected beads of perspiration on the brow of Sinfihit. A moment latter it was known to us that Amenemhait was dead, and, therefore, Usirtasen reigned in his stead. The news was so sudden, and the consequences so vast, that it was impossible to realise quite what it meant. I looked across at Sinfihit and his eyes met mine. He seemed to be making up his mind about something. Then with lightning speed he sprang upon me; a dagger gleamed in the air; I felt as if a hot iron had been thrust into my breast, and after that I remember no more.

As I felt myself falling I seemed to wake from my dream—if dream it were—to find myself standing in the Museum by the mummy case, and with Professor Constanides by my side.

"You have seen," he said. "You have looked back across the centuries to that day when, as Nofrit, I believed you had betrayed me, and killed you. After that I escaped from the camp and fled into Kaduma. There I died; but it was decreed that my soul should never know peace till we had met again and you had forgiven me. I have waited all these years, and see—we meet at last."

Strange to say, even then the situation did not strike me as being in any way improbable. Yet now, when I see it set down in black and white, I find myself wondering that I dare to ask anyone in their sober senses to believe it to be true. Was I in truth that same Nofrit who, four thousand years before, had been killed by Sinfihit, son of Amenemhait, because he believed that I had betrayed him? It seemed incredible, and yet, if it were a creation of my imagination, what did the dream mean? I fear it is a riddle of which I shall probably never know the answer. My failure to reply to his question seemed to cause him pain.

"Nofrit," he said, and his voice shook with emotion, "think what your forgiveness means to me. Without it I am lost both here and hereafter."

His voice was low and pleading and his face in the moonlight was like that of a man who knew the uttermost depths of despair.

"Forgive—forgive," he cried again, holding out his hands to me. "If you do not, I must go back to the sufferings which have been my portion since I did the deed which wrought my ruin."

I felt myself trembling like a leaf.

"If it is as you say, though I cannot believe it, I forgive you freely," I answered, in a voice that I scarcely recognised as my own.

For some moments he was silent, then he knelt before me and took my hand, which he raised to his lips. After that, rising, he laid his head upon the breast of the mummy before which we were standing. Looking down at it he addressed it thus:

"Rest, Sinfihit, son of Amenemhait—for that which was foretold for thee is now accomplished, and the punishment which was decreed is at an end. Henceforth thou mayest sleep in peace."

After that he replaced the lid of the coffin, and when this was done he turned to me.

"Let us be going," he said, and we went together through the rooms by the way we had come.

Together we left the building and passed through the gardens out into the road beyond. There we found the carriage waiting for us, and we took our places in it. Once more the horses sped along the silent road, carrying us swiftly back to Cairo. During the drive not a word was spoken by either of us. The only desire I had left was to get back to the hotel and lay my aching head upon my pillow. We crossed the bridge and entered the city. What the time was I had no idea, but I was conscious that the wind blew chill as if in anticipation of the dawn. At the same corner whence we had started, the coachman stopped his horses and I alighted, after which he drove away as if he had received his orders before-hand.

"Will you permit me to walk with you as far as your hotel?" said Constanides, with his customary politeness.

I tried to say something in reply, but my voice failed me. I would much rather have been alone, but as he would not allow this we set off together. At the corner of the street in which the hotel is situated we stopped.

"Here we must part," he said. Then, after a pause, he added, "And for ever. From this moment I shall never see your face again."

"You are leaving Cairo?" was the only thing I could say.

"Yes, I am leaving Cairo," he replied with peculiar emphasis. "My errand here is accomplished. You need have no fear that I shall ever trouble you again."

"I have no fear," I answered, though I am afraid it was only a half truth.

He looked earnestly into my face.

"Nofrit," he said, "for, say what you will, you are the Nofrit I would have made my Queen and have loved beyond all other women, never again will it be permitted you to look into the past as you did to-night. Had things been ordained otherwise we might have done great things together, but the gods willed that it should not be. Let it rest therefore. And now—farewell! To-night I go to the rest for which I have so long been seeking."

Without another word he turned and left me. Then I went on to the hotel. How it came about I cannot say, but the door was open and I passed quickly in. Once more, to my joy, I found the watchman was absent from the hall. Trembling lest anyone might see me, I sped up the stairs and along the corridor, where the servants lay sleeping just as I had left them, and so to my room. Everything was exactly as I had left it, and there was nothing to show that my absence had been suspected. Again I went to the window, and, in a feeling of extraordinary agitation, looked out. Already there were signs of dawn in the sky. I sat down and tried to think over all that had happened to me that evening, endeavouring to convince myself, in the face of indisputable evidence, that it was not real and that I had only dreamt it. Yet it would not do! At last, worn out, I retired to rest. As a rule I sleep soundly; it is scarcely, however, a matter for wonderment that I did not do so on this occasion.

Hour after hour I tumbled and tossed—thinking—thinking—thinking. When I rose and looked into the glass I scarcely recognised myself. Indeed, my mother commented on my fagged appearance when we met at the breakfast table.

"My dear child, you look as if you had been up all night," she said, and little did she guess, as she nibbled her toast, that there was a considerable amount of truth in her remark.

Later she went shopping with a lady staying in the hotel, while I went to my room to lie down.

When we met again at lunch it was easy to see that she had some news of importance to communicate.

"My dear Cecilia," she said, "I have just seen Dr. Forsyth, and he has given me a terrible shock. I don't want to frighten you, my girl, but have you heard that Professor Constanides was found dead in bed this morning? It is a most terrible affair! He must have died during the night!"

I am not going to pretend that I had any reply ready to offer her at that moment.

The Story of Baelbrow

E. and H. Heron

It is a matter for regret that so many of Mr. Flaxman Low's reminiscences should deal with the darker episodes of his experiences. Yet this is almost unavoidable, as the more purely scientific and less strongly marked cases would not, perhaps, contain the same elements of interest for the general public, however valuable and instructive they might be to the expert student. It has also been considered better to choose the completer cases, those that ended in something like satisfactory proof, rather than the many instances where the thread broke off abruptly amongst surmisings, which it was never possible to subject to convincing tests.

North of a low-lying strip of country on the East Anglian coast, the promontory of Bael Ness thrusts out a blunt nose into the sea. On the Ness, backed by pinewoods, stands a square, comfortable stone mansion, known to the countryside as Baelbrow. It has faced the east winds for close upon three hundred years, and during the whole period has been the home of the Swaffam family, who were never in anywise put out of conceit of their ancestral dwelling by the fact that it had always been haunted.

Indeed, the Swaffams were proud of the Baelbrow Ghost, which enjoyed a wide notoriety, and no one dreamt of complaining of its behaviour until Professor Van der Voort of Louvain laid information against it, and sent an urgent appeal for help to Mr. Flaxman Low.

The Professor, who was well acquainted with Mr. Low, detailed the circumstances of his tenancy of Baelbrow, and the unpleasant events that had followed thereupon.

It appeared that Mr. Swaffam, senior, who spent a large portion of his time abroad, had offered to lend his house to the Professor for the summer season. When the Van der Voorts arrived at Baelbrow, they were charmed with the place. The prospect, though not very varied, was at least extensive, and the air exhilarating. Also the Professor's daughter enjoyed frequent visits from her betrothed—Harold Swaffam—and the Professor was delightfully employed in overhauling the Swaffam library. o.

The Van der Voorts had been duly told of the ghost, which lent distinction to the old house, but never in any way interfered with the comfort of the inmates. For some time they found this description to be strictly true, but with the beginning of October came a change. Up to this time and as far back as the Swaffam annals reached, the ghost had been a shadow, a rustle, a passing sigh—nothing definite or troublesome. But early in October strange things began to occur, and the terror culminated when a housemaid was found dead in a corridor three weeks later. Upon this the Professor felt that it was time to send for Flaxman Low.

Mr. Low arrived upon a chilly evening when the house was already beginning to blur in the purple twilight, and the resinous scent of the pines came sweetly on the land breeze. Van der Voort welcomed him in the spacious, fire-lit hall. He was a stout man with a quantity of white hair, round eyes emphasised by spectacles, and a kindly, dreamy face. His life-study was philology, and his two relaxations chess and the smoking of a big bowled meerschaum.

"Now, Professor," said Mr. Low when they had settled themselves in the smoking-room, "how did it all begin?"

"I will tell you," replied Van der Voort, thrusting out his chin, and tapping his broad chest, and speaking as if an unwarrantable liberty had been taken with him. "First of all, it has shown itself to me!" Mr. Flaxman Low smiled and assured him that nothing could be more satisfactory.

"But not at all satisfactory!" exclaimed the Professor. "I was sitting here alone, it might have been midnight—when I hear something come creeping like a little dog with its nails, tick-tick, upon the oak flooring of the hall. I whistle, for I think it is the little 'Rags' of my daughter, and afterwards opened the door, and I saw"—he hesitated and looked hard at Low through his spectacles, "something that was just disappearing into the passage which connects the two wings of the house. It was a figure, not unlike the human figure, but narrow and straight. I fancied I saw a bunch of black hair, and a flutter of something detached, which may have been a handkerchief.

I was overcome by a feeling of repulsion. I heard a few clicking steps, then it stopped, as I thought, at the museum door. Come, I will show you the spot."

The Professor conducted Mr. Low into the hall. The main staircase, dark and massive, yawned above them, and directly behind it ran the passage referred to by the Professor. It was over twenty feet long, and about midway led past a deep arch containing a door reached by two steps.

Van der Voort explained that this door formed the entrance to a large room called the Museum, in which Mr. Swaffam, senior, who was something of a dilettante, stored the various curios he picked up during his excursions abroad. The Professor went on to say that he immediately followed the figure, which he believed had gone into the museum, but he found nothing there except the cases containing Swaffam's treasures.

"I mentioned my experience to no one. I concluded that I had seen the ghost. But two days after, one of the female servants coming through the passage, in the dark, declared that a man leapt out at her from the embrasure of the Museum door, but she released herself and ran screaming into the servants' hall. We at once made a search but found nothing to substantiate her story.

"I took no notice of this, though it coincided pretty well with my own experience. The week after, my daughter Lena came down late one night for a book. As she was about to cross the hall, something leapt upon her from behind. Women are of little use in serious investigations—she fainted! Since then she has been ill and the doctor says 'run down'." Here the Professor spread out his hands. "So she leaves for a change tomorrow. Since then other members of the household have been attacked in much the same manner, with always the same result, they faint and are weak and useless when they recover.

"But, last Wednesday, the affair became a tragedy. By that time the servants had refused to come through the passage except in a crowd of three or four,—most of them preferring to go round by the terrace to reach this part of the house. But one maid, named Eliza Freeman, said she was not afraid of the Baelbrow Ghost, and undertook to put out the lights in the hall one night.

When she had done so, and was returning through the passage past the Museum door, she appears to have been attacked, or at any rate frightened. In the grey of the morning they found her lying beside the steps dead. There was a little blood upon her sleeve but no mark upon her body except a small raised pustule under the ear. The doctor said the girl was extraordinarily anæmic, and that she probably died from fright, her heart being weak. I was surprised at this, for she had always seemed to be a particularly strong and active young woman."

"Can I see Miss Van der Voort to-morrow before she goes?" asked Low, as the Professor signified he had nothing more to tell.

The Professor was rather unwilling that his daughter should be questioned, but he at last gave his permission, and next morning Low had a short talk with the girl before she left the house. He found her a very pretty girl, though listless and startlingly pale, and with a frightened stare in her light brown eyes. Mr. Low asked if she could describe her assailant. "No," she answered. "I could not see him for he was behind me. I only saw a dark, bony hand, with shining nails, and a bandaged arm pass just under my eyes before I fainted."

"Bandaged arm? I have heard nothing of this."

"Tut—tut, mere fancy!" put in the Professor impatiently.

"I saw the bandages on the arm," repeated the girl, turning her head wearily away, "and I smelt the antiseptics it was dressed with."

"You have hurt your neck," remarked Mr. Low, who noticed a small circular patch of pink under her ear.

She flushed and paled, raising her hand to her neck with a nervous jerk, as she said in a low voice: "It has almost killed me. Before he touched me, I knew he was there! I felt it!"

When they left her the Professor apologised for the unreliability of her evidence, and pointed out the discrepancy between her statement and his own.

"She says she sees nothing but an arm, yet I tell you it had no arms! Preposterous! Conceive a wounded man entering this house to frighten the young women! I do not know what to make of it! Is it a man, or is it the Baelbrow Ghost?"

During the afternoon when Mr. Low and the Professor returned from a stroll on the shore, they found a dark-browed young man with a bull neck, and strongly marked features, standing sullenly before the hall fire. The Professor presented him to Mr. Low as Harold Swaffam.

Swaffam seemed to be about thirty, but was already known as a far-seeing and successful member of the Stock Exchange.

"I am pleased to meet you, Mr. Low," he began, with a keen glance, "though you don't look sufficiently high-strung for one of your profession."

Mr. Low merely bowed.

"Come, you don't defend your craft against my insinuations?" went on Swaffam. "And so you have come to rout out our poor old ghost from Baelbrow? You forget that he is an heirloom, a family possession! What's this about his having turned rabid, eh, Professor?" he ended, wheeling round upon Van der Voort in his brusque way.

The Professor told the story over again. It was plain that he stood rather in awe of his prospective son-in-law.

"I heard much the same from Lena, whom I met at the station," said Swaffam. "It is my opinion that the women in this house are suffering from an epidemic of hysteria. You agree with me, Mr. Low?"

"Possibly. Though hysteria could hardly account for Freeman's death."

"I can't say as to that until I have looked further into the particulars. I have not been idle since I arrived. I have examined the Museum. No one has entered it from the outside, and there is no other way of entrance except through the passage. The flooring is laid, I happen to know, on a thick layer of concrete. And there the case for the ghost stands at present." After a few moments of dogged reflection, he swung round on Mr. Low, in a manner that seemed peculiar to him when about to address any person. "What do you say to this plan, Mr. Low? I propose to drive the Professor over to Ferryvale, to stop there for a day or two at the hotel, and I will also dispose of the servants who still remain in the house for, say, forty-eight hours. Meanwhile you and I can try to go further into the secret of the ghost's new pranks?"

Flaxman Low replied that this scheme exactly met his views, but the Professor protested against being sent away. Harold Swaffam, however, was a man who liked to arrange things in his own fashion, and within forty-five minutes he and Van der Voort departed in the dogcart. The evening was lowering, and Baelbrow, like all houses built in exposed situations, was extremely susceptible to the changes of the weather. Therefore, before many hours were over, the place was full of creaking noises as the screaming gale battered at the shuttered windows, and the tree-branches tapped and groaned against the walls.

Harold Swaffam on his way back was caught in the storm and drenched to the skin. It was, therefore, settled that after he had changed his clothes he should have a couple of hours' rest on the smoking-room sofa, while Mr. Low kept watch in the hall.

The early part of the night passed over uneventfully. A light burned faintly in the great wainscotted hall, but the passage was dark. There was nothing to be heard but the wild moan and whistle of the wind coming in from the sea, and the squalls of rain dashing against the windows.

As the hours advanced, Mr. Low lit a lantern that lay at hand, and, carrying it along the passage tried the Museum door. It yielded, and the wind came muttering through to meet him. He looked round at the shutters and behind the big cases which held Mr. Swaffam's treasures, to make sure that the room contained no living occupant but himself.

Suddenly he fancied he heard a scraping noise behind him, and turned round, but discovered nothing to account for it. Finally, he laid the lantern on a bench so that its light should fall through the door into the passage, and returned again to the hall, where he put out the lamp, and then once more took up his station by the closed door of the smoking-room.

A long hour passed, during which the wind continued to roar down the wide hall chimney, and the old boards creaked as if furtive footsteps were gathering from every corner of the house. But Flaxman Low heeded none of these; he was awaiting for a certain sound.

After a while, he heard it—the cautious scraping of wood on wood. He leant forward to watch the Museum door. Click, click, came the curious dog-like tread upon the tiled floor of the Museum, till the thing, whatever it was, paused and listened behind the open door. The wind lulled at the moment, and Low listened also, but no further sound was to be heard, only slowly across the broad ray of light falling through the door grew a stealthy shadow.

Again the wind rose, and blew in heavy gusts about the house, till even the flame in the lantern flickered; but when it steadied once more, Flaxman Low saw that the silent form had passed through the door, and was now on the steps outside. He could just make out a dim shadow in the dark angle of the embrasure.

Presently, from the shapeless shadow came a sound Mr. Low was not prepared to hear. The thing sniffed the air with the strong, audible inspiration of a bear, or some large animal. At the same moment, carried on the draughts of the hall, a faint, unfamiliar odour reached his nostrils.

Lena Van der Voort's words flashed back upon him—this, then, was the creature with the bandaged arm!

Again, as the storm shrieked and shook the windows, a darkness passed across the light. The thing had sprung out from the angle of the door, and Flaxman Low knew that it was making its way towards him through the illusive blackness of the hall. He hesitated for a second; then he opened the smoking-room door.

Harold Swaffam sat up on the sofa, dazed with sleep. "What has happened? Has it come?"

Low told him what he had just seen. Swaffam listened half-smilingly.

"What do you make of it now?" he said.

"I must ask you to defer that question for a little," replied Low.

"Then you mean me to suppose that you have a theory to fit all these incongruous items?"

"I have a theory, which may be modified by further knowledge," said Low. "Meantime, am I right in concluding from the name of this house that it was built on a barrow or burying-place?"

"You are right, though that has nothing to do with the latest freaks of our ghost," returned Swaffam decidedly.

"I also gather that Mr. Swaffam has lately sent home one of the many cases now lying in the Museum?" went on Mr. Low.

"He sent one, certainly, last September."

"And you have opened it," asserted Low.

"Yes; though I flattered myself I had left no trace of my handiwork."

"I have not examined the cases," said Low. "I inferred that you had done so from other facts."

"Now, one thing more," went on Swaffam, still smiling. "Do you imagine there is any danger—I mean to men like ourselves? Hysterical women cannot be taken into serious account."

"Certainly; the gravest danger to any person who moves about this part of the house alone after dark," replied Low.

Harold Swaffam leant back and crossed his legs.

"To go back to the beginning of our conversation, Mr. Low, may I remind you of the various conflicting particulars you will have to reconcile before you can present any decent theory to the world?"

"I am quite aware of that."

"First of all, our original ghost was a mere misty presence, rather guessed at from vague sounds and shadows—now we have a something that is tangible, and that can, as we have proof, kill with fright. Next Van der Voort declares the thing was a narrow, long and distinctly armless object, while Miss Van der Voort has not only seen the arm and hand of a human being, but saw them clearly enough to tell us that the nails were gleaming and the arm bandaged. She also felt its strength. Van der Voort, on the other hand, maintained that it clicked along like a dog—you bear out this description with the additional information that it sniffs like a wild beast. Now what can this thing be? It is capable of being seen, smelt, and felt, yet it hides itself, successfully in a room where there is no cavity or space sufficient to afford covert to a cat! You still tell me that you believe that you can explain?"

"Most certainly," replied Flaxman Low with conviction.

"I have not the slightest intention or desire to be rude, but as a mere matter of common sense, I must express my opinion plainly. I believe the whole thing to be the result of excited imaginations, and I am about to prove it. Do you think there is any further danger to-night?"

"Very great danger to-night," replied Low.

"Very well; as I said, I am going to prove it. I will ask you to allow me to lock you up in one of the distant rooms, where I can get no help from you, and I will pass the remainder of the night walking about the passage and hall in the dark. That should give proof one way or the other."

"You can do so if you wish, but I must at least beg to be allowed to look on. I will leave the house and watch what goes on from the window in the passage, which I saw opposite the Museum door. You cannot, in any fairness, refuse to let me be a witness."

"I cannot, of course," returned Swaffam. "Still, the night is too bad to turn a dog out into, and I warn you that I shall lock you out."

"That will not matter. Lend me a macintosh, and leave the lantern lit in the Museum, where I placed it."

Swaffam agreed to this. Mr. Low gives a graphic account of what followed. He left the house and was duly locked out, and, after groping his way round the house, found himself at length outside the window of the passage, which was almost opposite to the door of the Museum. The door was still ajar and a thin band of light cut out into the gloom. Further down the hall gaped black and void. Low, sheltering himself as well as he could from the rain, waited for Swaffam's appearance. Was the terrible yellow watcher balancing itself upon its lean legs in the dim corner opposite, ready to spring out with its deadly strength upon the passer-by? Presently Low heard a door bang inside the house, and the next moment Swaffam appeared with a candle in his hand, an isolated spread of weak rays against the vast darkness behind. He advanced steadily down the passage, his dark face grim and set, and as he came Mr. Low experienced that tingling sensation, which is so often the forerunner of some strange experience.

Swaffam passed on towards the other end of the passage. There was a quick vibration of the Museum door as a lean shape with a shrunken head leapt out into the passage after him. Then all together came a hoarse shout, the noise of a fall and utter darkness.

In an instant, Mr. Low had broken the glass, opened the window, and swung himself into the passage. There he lit a match and as it flared he saw by its dim light a picture painted for a second upon the obscurity beyond.

Swaffam's big figure lay with outstretched arms, face downwards, and as Low looked a crouching shape extricated itself from the fallen man, raising a narrow vicious head from his shoulder.

The match spluttered feebly and went out, and Low heard a flying step click on the boards, before he could find the candle Swaffam had dropped. Lighting it, he stooped over Swaffam and turned him on his back. The man's strong colour had gone, and the wax-white face looked whiter still against the blackness of hair and brows, and upon his neck under the ear was a little raised pustule, from which a thin line of blood was streaked up to the angle of his cheekbone.

Some instinctive feeling prompted Low to glance up at this moment. Half extended from the Museum doorway were a face and bony neck—a high-nosed, dull-eyed, malignant face, the eye-sockets hollow, and the darkened teeth showing. Low plunged his hand into his pocket, and a shot rang out in the echoing passage-way and hall. The wind sighed through the broken panes, a ribbon of stuff fluttered along the polished flooring, and that was all, as Flaxman Low half dragged, half carried Swaffam into the smoking-room.

It was some time before Swaffam recovered consciousness. He listened to Low's story of how he had found him with a red angry gleam in his sombre eyes.

"The ghost has scored off me," he said, with an odd, sullen laugh, "but now I fancy it's my turn! But before we adjourn to the Museum to examine the place, I will ask you to let me hear your notion of things. You have been right in saying there was real danger. For myself I can only tell you that I felt something spring upon me, and I knew no more. Had this not happened I am afraid I should never have asked you a second time what your idea of the matter might be," he added with a sort of sulky frankness.

"There are two main indications," replied Low. "This strip of yellow bandage, which I have just now picked up from the passage floor, and the mark on your neck."

"What's that you say?" Swaffam rose quickly and examined his neck in a small glass beside the mantelshelf.

"Connect those two, and I think I can leave you to work it out for yourself," said Low.

"Pray let us have your theory in full," requested Swaffam shortly.

"Very well," answered Low good-humouredly—he thought Swaffam's annoyance natural in the circumstances— "The long, narrow figure which seemed to the Professor to be armless is developed on the next occasion. For Miss Van der Voort sees a bandaged arm and a dark hand with gleaming—which means, of course, gilded—nails. The clicking sound of the footsteps coincides with these particulars, for we know that sandals made of strips of leather are not uncommon in company with gilt nails and bandages. Old and dry leather would naturally click upon your polished floor."

"Bravo, Mr. Low! So you mean to say that this house is haunted by a mummy!"

"That is my idea, and all I have seen confirms me in my opinion."

"To do you justice, you held this theory before to-night—before, in fact, you had seen anything for yourself. You gathered that my father had sent home a mummy, and you went on to conclude that I had opened the case?"

"Yes. I imagine you took off most of, or rather all, the outer bandages, thus leaving the limbs free, wrapped only in the inner bandages which were swathed round each separate limb. I fancy this mummy was preserved on the Theban method with aromatic spices, which left the skin olive-coloured, dry and flexible, like tanned leather, the features remaining distinct, and the hair, teeth, and eyebrows perfect."

"So far, good," said Swaffam. "But now, how about the intermittent vitality? The postule on the neck of those whom it attacks? And where is our old Baelbrow ghost to come in?"

Swaffam tried to speak in a rallying tone, but his excitement and lowering temper were visible enough, in spite of the attempts he made to suppress them.

"To begin at the beginning," said Flaxman Low, "everybody who, in a rational and honest manner, investigates the phenomena of spiritism will, sooner or later, meet in them some perplexing element, which is not to be explained by any of the ordinary theories. For reasons into which I need not now enter, this present case appears to me to be one of these. I am led to believe that the ghost which has for so many years given dim and vague manifestations of its existence in this house is a vampire."

Swaffam threw back his head with an incredulous gesture.

"We no longer live in the middle ages, Mr. Low! And besides, how could a vampire come here?" he said scoffingly.

"It is held by some authorities on these subjects that under certain conditions a vampire may be self-created. You tell me that this house is built upon an ancient barrow, in fact, on a spot where we might naturally expect to find such an elemental psychic germ. In those dead human systems were contained all the seeds for good and evil.

"The power which causes these psychic seeds or germs to grow is thought, and from being long dwelt on and indulged, a thought might finally gain a mysterious vitality, which could go on increasing more and more by attracting to itself suitable and appropriate elements from its environment. For a long period this germ remained a helpless intelligence, awaiting the opportunity to assume some material form, by means of which to carry out its desires. The invisible is the real; the material only subserves its manifestation.

"The impalpable reality already existed, when you provided for it a physical medium for action by unwrapping the mummy's form. Now, we can only judge of the nature of the germ by its manifestation through matter. Here we have every indication of a vampire intelligence touching into life and energy the dead human frame. Hence the mark on the neck of its victims, and their bloodless and anæmic condition. For a vampire, as you know, sucks blood."

Swaffam rose, and took up the lamp.

"Now, for proof," he said bluntly. "Wait a second, Mr. Low. You say you fired at this appearance?" And he took up the pistol which Low had laid down on the table.

"Yes, I aimed at a small portion of its foot which I saw on the step."

Without more words, and with the pistol still in his hand, Swaffam led the way to the Museum. The wind howled round the house, and the darkness, which precedes the dawn, lay upon the world, when the two men looked upon one of the strangest sights it has ever been given to men to shudder at.

Half in and half out of an oblong wooden box in a corner of the great room, lay a lean shape in its rotten yellow bandages, the scraggy neck surmounted by a mop of frizzled hair. The toe strap of a sandal and a portion of the right foot had been shot away.

Swaffam, with a working face, gazed down at it, then seizing it by its tearing bandages, he flung it into the box, where it fell into a life-like posture, its wide, moist-lipped mouth gaping up at them.

For a moment Swaffam stood over the thing; then with a curse he raised the revolver and shot into the grinning face again and again with a deliberate vindictiveness. Finally he rammed the thing down into the box, and, clubbing the weapon, smashed the head into fragments with a vicious energy that coloured the whole horrible scene with a suggestion of murder done.

Then, turning to Low, he said: "Help me to fasten the cover on it."

"Are you going to bury it?"

"No, we must rid the earth of it," he answered savagely. "I'll put it into the old canoe and burn it."

The rain had ceased when in the daybreak they carried the old canoe down to the shore. In it they placed the mummy case with its ghastly occupant, and piled faggots about it. The sail was raised and the pile lighted, and Low and Swaffam watched it creep out on the ebb-tide, at first a twinkling spark, then a flare and waving fire, until far out to sea the history of that dead thing ended 3000 years after the priests of Armen had laid it to rest in its appointed pyramid.

The Mysterious Mummy

Sax Rohmer

It was about five o'clock on a hot August afternoon, that a tall, thin man, wearing a weedy beard, and made conspicuous by an ill-fitting frock-coat and an almost napless silk hat, walked into the entrance hall of the Great Portland Square Museum. He carried no stick, and, looking about him, as though unfamiliar with the building, he ultimately mounted the principal staircase, walking with a pronounced stoop, and at intervals coughing with a hollow sound.

His gaunt figure attracted the attention of several people, among them the attendant in the Egyptian room. Hardened though he was to the eccentric in humanity, the man who hung so eagerly over the mummies of departed kings and coughed so frequently, nevertheless secured his instant attention. Visitors of the regulation type were rapidly thinning out, so that the gaunt man, during the whole of the time he remained in the room, was kept under close surveillance by the vigilant official. Seeing him go in the direction of the stairs, the attendant supposed the strange visitor to be about to leave the Museum. But that he did not immediately do so was shown by subsequent testimony.

The day's business being concluded, the staff of police who patrol nightly the Great Square Museum duly filed into the building. A man is placed in each room, it being his duty to examine thoroughly every nook and cranny; having done which, all doors of communication are closed, the officer on guard in one room being unable to leave his post or to enter another. Every hour the inspector, a sergeant, and a fireman make a round of the entire building: from which it will be seen that a person having designs on any of the numerous treasures of the place would require more than average ingenuity to bring his plans to a successful issue.

In recording this very singular case, the only incident of the night to demand attention is that of the mummy in the Etruscan room.

Persons familiar with the Great Portland Square Museum will know that certain of the tombs in the Etruscan room are used as receptacles for Egyptian mummies that have, for various reasons, never been put upon exhibition. Anyone who has peered under the partially raised lid of a huge sarcophagus and found within the rigid form of a mummy, will appreciate the feelings of the man on night duty amid surroundings so lugubrious. The electric light, it should be mentioned, is not extinguished until the various apartments have been examined, and its extinction immediately precedes the locking of the door.

The constable in the Etruscan room glanced into the various sarcophagi and cast the rays of his bull's-eye lantern into the shadows of the great stone tombs. Satisfied that no one lurked there, he mounted the steps leading up to the Roman gallery, turning out the lights in the room below from the switch at the top. The light was still burning on the ground floor, and the sergeant had not yet arrived with the keys. It was whilst the man stood awaiting his coming that a singular thing occurred.

From somewhere within the darkened chamber beneath, there came the sound of a hollow cough!

By no means deficient in courage, the constable went down the steps in three bounds, his lantern throwing discs of light on stately statues and gloomy tombs. The sound was not repeated:

and having nothing to guide him to its source, he commenced a second methodical search of the sarcophagi, as offering the most likely hiding places. When all save one had been examined, the constable began to believe that the coughing had existed only in his imagination. It was upon casting the rays of his bull's-eye into the last sarcophagus that he experienced a sudden sensation of fear. It was empty; yet he distinctly remembered, from his previous examination, that a mummy had lain there!

At the moment of making this weird discovery, he realised that he would have done better, before commencing his search for the man with the cough, first to turn on the light; for it must be remembered that he had extinguished the electric lamps. Determined to do so before pursuing his investigations further, he ran up the steps—to find the Roman gallery in darkness. The bright disc of a lantern was approaching from the upper end, and the man ran forward.

"Who turned off the lights here?" came the voice of the sergeant.

"That's what I want to know! Somebody did it while I was downstairs!" said the constable, and gave a hurried account of the mysterious coughing and the missing mummy.

"How long has there been a mummy in this tomb?" asked the sergeant.

"There was one there a month back, but they took it upstairs. They may have brought it down again last week though, or it may have been a fresh one. You see, the other lot were on duty up to last night."

This was quite true, as the sergeant was aware. Three bodies of picked men share the night duties at the Great Portland Square Museum, and those on duty upon this particular occasion had not been in the place during the previous two weeks.

"Very strange!" muttered the sergeant; and a moment later his whistle was sounding.

From all over the building men came running, for none of the doors had yet been locked.

"There seems to be someone concealed in the Museum: search all the rooms again!" was the brief order.

The constables disappeared, and the sergeant, accompanied by the inspector, went down to examine the Etruscan room. Nothing was found there; nor were any of the other searchers more successful. There was no trace anywhere of a man in hiding. Beyond leaving open the door between the Roman gallery and the steps of the Etruscan room, no more could be done in the matter. The gallery communicates with the entrance hall, where the inspector, together with the sergeant and fireman, spends the night, and the idea of the former was to keep in touch with the scene of these singular happenings. His action was perfectly natural; but these precautions were subsequently proved to be absolutely useless.

The night passed without any disturbing event, and the mystery of the vanishing mummy and the ghostly cough seemed likely to remain a mystery. The night-police filed out in the early morning, and the inspector, with the sergeant, returned, as soon as possible, to the Museum, to make further inquiries concerning the missing occupant of the sarcophagus.

"A mummy in the end tomb!" exclaimed the curator of Etruscan antiquities; "my dear sir, there has been no mummy there for nearly a month!"

"But my man states that he saw one there last night!" declared the inspector.

The curator looked puzzled. Turning to an attendant, he said: "Who was in charge of the Etruscan room immediately before six last night?"

"I was, sir!"

"Were there any visitors?"

"No one came in between five-forty and six."

"And before that?"

"I was away at tea, sir!"

"Who was in charge then?"

"Mr. Robins."

"Call Robins."

The commissionaire in question arrived.

"How long were you in the Etruscan room last night?"

"About half-an-hour, sir."

"Are you sure that no one concealed himself?"

The man looked startled. "Well, sir," he said hesitatingly, "I'm sorry I didn't report it before; but when Mr. Barton called me, at about twenty-five minutes to six, there was someone there, a gent in a seedy frock-coat and a high hat, and I don't remember seeing him come out."

"Did you search the room?"

"Yes, sir; but there was no one to be seen!"

"You should have reported the matter at once. I must see Barton."

Barton, the head attendant, remembered speaking to Robins at the top of the steps leading to the Etruscan room. He saw no one come out, but it was just possible for a person to have done so and yet be seen by neither himself nor Robins.

"Let three of you thoroughly overhaul the room for any sign of a man having hidden there," directed the curator briskly.

He turned to the sergeant and inspector with a smile, "I rather fancy it will prove to be a mare's nest!" he said. "We have had these mysteries before."

The words had but just left his lips when a Museum official, a well-known antiquarian expert, ran up in a perfect frenzy of excitement. "Good heavens, Peters!" he gasped. "The Rienzi Vase has gone!"

"What!" came an incredulous chorus.

"The circular top of the case has been completely cut out and ingeniously replaced, and a plausible imitation of the vase substituted!"

They waited for no more, but hurried upstairs to the Vase room, which, in the Great Portland Square Museum, is really only a part of the Egyptian room. The Rienzi Vase, though no larger than an ordinary breakfast-cup, all the world knows to be of fabulous value. It seemed inconceivable that anyone could have stolen it. Yet there, in the midst of a knot of excited officials, stood the empty case, whilst the imitation antique was being passed from hand to hand.

Never before nor since has such a scene been witnessed in the Museum. The staff, to a man, had lost their wits. What is to be done? was the general inquiry. In less than half an hour the doors would have to be opened to the public, and the absence of the famous vase would inevitably be noticed. It was at this juncture, and whilst everyone was speaking at once, that one of the party, standing close to a wall-cabinet, suddenly held up a warning finger. "Hush!" he said; "listen!"

A sudden silence fell upon the room so that people running about in other apartments could be plainly heard. And presently, from somewhere behind the glass doors surrounding the place, came a low moan, electrifying the already excited listeners. The keys were promptly forthcoming and then was made the second astounding discovery of the eventful morning.

A man, gagged and bound, was imprisoned behind a great mummy case!

Eager hands set to work to release him, and restoratives were applied, as he seemed to be in a very weak condition. He was but partially dressed, and breathed heavily through his nose, like a man in a drunken slumber. All waited breathlessly for his return to consciousness; for certainly he, if anyone, should be in a position to furnish some clue to the deep mystery. On regaining his senses, he had disappointingly little to tell. He was Constable Smith, who had been on night-duty in the Egyptian room. Sometime during the first hour, and not long after the alarm in the basement, he had been mysteriously pinioned as he paraded the apartment. He caught no glimpse of his opponent, who held him from behind in such a manner that he was totally unable to defend himself. Some sweet-smelling drug had been applied to his nostrils, and he remembered no more until regaining consciousness in the mummy case! That was the whole of his testimony. In setting out the particulars of this remarkable affair, a third and final discovery must be noted. The three men who had been directed to examine the Etruscan room brought to light a bundle of old garments, containing an ancient opera-hat, a faded frock-coat, a pair of shiny trousers, and a pair of elastic-sided boots. They were wedged high up at the back of a tall statue, where they had evidently escaped the eyes of all previous searchers. That constituted the entire data on which investigations had to be based. The Egyptian room was closed indefinitely, "for repairs." No further useful evidence could be obtained from anyone. Several witnesses furnished consistent descriptions of the shabby stranger with the hollow cough; but it may here be mentioned that no one of them ever set eyes upon him again. The inspector, the sergeant, and the fireman solemnly swore to having visited the Egyptian room at the end of each hour throughout the night, and to having found the constable on duty as usual! Smith swore, with equal solemnity, that he had been drugged during the first hour and subsequently confined in the mummy case.

The matter was carefully kept out of the papers, although the Museum, throughout many following days, positively bristled with detectives. As the second week drew to a close and the Egyptian room still remained locked, well-informed persons began to whisper that a scandal could no longer be avoided. There can be no doubt that, in many quarters, Constable Smith's share in the proceedings was regarded with grave suspicion. It was at this critical juncture, when it seemed inevitable that the loss of the world-famous Rienzi Vase must be made known to an unsympathetic public, that certain high authorities gave out that the vase had been removed, and that none of the night staff were in any way implicated in its disappearance!

On this announcement being made, several strange theories were mooted. Some stated that the vase had never left the Museum! Others averred that it had been pawned to a foreign government!

Whatever the real explanation, and the secret was jealously guarded by the highly-placed officials who alone knew the truth, suffice it that the Egyptian room was again thrown open and the Rienzi Vase shown to be reposing in its usual position.

Now that it again stands in its place for all to see, there can be no objection to my relating how I once held the famous Rienzi Vase in my possession for twelve days. If there be any objection...

I am sorry. You must understand that I am no common thief—no footpad: I am a person of keenly observant character, and my business is to detect vital weaknesses in great institutions and to charge a moderately high fee for my services. Thus I discovered that a certain famous tiara in a French museum was inadequately protected, and accordingly removed it, replacing it by a substitute. The authorities refused me my fee, and all the world knows that my clever forgery was detected by the experts. That brought them to their senses; it is the genuine tiara that reposes in their cabinet now!

In the same way I removed a world-renowned, historical mummy from its resting place in Cairo, and two days later they grew suspicious of my imitation—it was the handiwork of a clever Birmingham artist—and the department was closed. The bulky character of the mummy nearly brought about my downfall, and it was only by abandoning it that I succeeded in leaving Cairo. I am not proud of that case; I was clumsy. But of the case of the Rienzi Vase I have every reason to be highly proud. That you may judge of the neatness and dispatch with which I acted, I will relate how the whole business was conducted.

You must know, then, that the first flaw I discovered in the arrangements at the Great Portland Square Museum was this: the wall-cases were badly guarded. I learnt this interesting fact one afternoon as I strolled about the Egyptian room. A certain gentleman—I will not name him—was showing a party of ladies round the apartment. He had unlocked a wall-case, and was standing with a handsome bead-necklet in his hand, explaining where and when it was found. He was only a few yards away, but with his back toward the case. Enough! The key, with others attached, was in the glass door. You will admit that this was exceedingly careless; but the presence of four charming American ladies ... one can excuse him!

I regret to have to confess that I was somewhat awkward—the keys rattled. The whole party looked in my direction. But the immaculate man-about-town, with his cultivated manner and his very considerable knowledge of Egyptology—how should they suspect? I apologised; I had brushed against them in passing; I made myself agreeable, and the uncomfortable incident was forgotten, by them—not by me. I had a beautiful wax impression to keep my memory fresh!

The scheme formed then. I knew that a body of picked police promenaded the Museum at night, and that each of the rooms was usually in charge of the same man. I learnt, later, that there were three bodies of men, so that the same police were in the Museum but one week in every three. I made the acquaintance of seven constables and frequented eight different public-houses before I met the man of whom I was in search.

The first policeman I found, who paraded the Egyptian room at night, was short and thick-set, and I gave him up as a bad job. I learnt from him, however, who was to occupy the post during the coming week, and presently I unearthed the private bar which this latter officer, his name was Smith, used. Eureka! He was tall and thin. Incidentally, he was also surly. But the winning ways of the jovial master-plumber, who was so free with his money, ultimately thawed him.

Every night throughout the rest of the week I spent in this constable's company, studying his somewhat colourless personality. Then, one afternoon, I entered the Museum. My weedy beard, my gaunt expression, and my hollow cough—they were all in the part! I went up to the Egyptian room to assure myself that a certain mummy case had not been removed, and having found it to occupy its usual place, I descended to the Etruscan basement.

For half-an-hour I occupied myself there, but the commissionaire never budged from his seat. I knew that this particular man was only in temporary charge whilst another was at tea, for I was well posted, and wondered if his companion were ever coming back. Luckily, an incident occurred to serve my purpose. The chief attendant appeared at the head of the steps. "Robins!" he called.

Robins ran briskly upstairs at his command, and then—in fifteen seconds my transformation was complete. Gone were the weedy grey beard and moustache—gone the seedy, black garments and the elastic-sided boots—gone the old opera-hat—and, behold, I was Constable Smith, attired in mummy wrappings!

An acrobatic spring, and the bundle of aged garments was wedged behind a tall statue, where nothing but a most minute search could reveal it. Down again, not a second to spare! Into the empty sarcophagus at the further end of the room; and, lastly, a hideous rubber mask slipped over the ruddy features of Constable Smith and attached behind the ears, my arms stiffened and my hands concealed in the wrappings, and I was a long-dead mummy—

with a neat leather case hidden beneath my arched back! Brisk work, I assure you; but one grows accustomed to it in time. The commissionaire entered the room very shortly afterwards. He had not seen me go out, but, as I expected, neither was he absolutely sure that I had not done so. He peered about suspiciously, but I did not mind. The real ordeal came a couple of hours later, when a police officer flashed his lantern into all the tombs.

For a moment my heart seemed to cease beating as the light shone on my rubber countenance.

But he was satisfied, this stupid policeman, and I heard his footsteps retreating to the door. I allowed him time to get to the top, and extinguished the light in the Etruscan room, and then... I was out of my tomb and hidden in the little niche immediately beside the foot of the stairs. I coughed loudly. Heavens! He came back down the steps with such velocity that he was carried halfway along the room. He began to flash his lantern into the tombs again; but, before he had examined the first of them, I was upstairs in the Roman gallery!

Without the electric light it was quite dark in the Etruscan room, which is in the basement; but, being a bright night, I knew I could find what I required in the Roman gallery without the aid of artificial light; besides, I had not to act in the open—someone might arrive too soon. So, thoroughly well posted as to the situation of the switches, I extinguished the lamps, and dodged in among the Roman stonework to the foot of a great pillar, towering almost to the lofty roof and surmounted by an ornate capital.

I had planned all this beforehand, you see; but I must confess it was an awful scramble to the top. I had only just curled up on the summit, the handle of my invaluable leather-case held fast in my teeth, when a sergeant came running down the gallery, almost into the arms of the constable who was running up the steps from the Etruscan room.

A moment's hurried conversation, and then the lights turned on and the sound of a whistle. It was foolish, of course; but I had expected it. From all over the building the police arrived, and, fatigued as I was with my climb, yet another acrobatic feat was before me.

The top of my pillar was no great distance from the stone balustrade of the first-floor landing, on which the Egyptian room opens, and a narrow ledge, perhaps of eleven inches, runs all round the wall of the Roman gallery some four feet below the ceiling. I cautiously stepped from the pillar to the ledge—I was invisible from the other end of the place—and, pressing my body close against the wall, reached the balustrade. Before Constable Smith—who had left his post and descended to the lower gallery on hearing the sergeant's whistle—re-entered the Egyptian room, my bright, new key had found the lock of a certain cabinet, and I was secure behind a mummy case—whilst a little steel pin prevented the spring of the lock from shutting me in.

Poor Constable Smith! I was sorry to have to act so: but, ten minutes after the closing of the doors of communication, I came on him from behind, having silently crept from the case as he passed me, and followed him down the darkened room, the thin linen wrappings that covered my feet making no sound upon the wooden floor. I had a pad ready in my hand, saturated with the contents of a small phial that had reposed in my mummy garments.

I thrust my knee in his spine and seized his hands by a trick which you may learn for a peseta any day in the purlieus of Tangier. A muscular man, he tried hard to cope with his unseen opponent; but the pad never left his mouth and nostrils, and the few muffled cries that escaped him were luckily unheard. He soon became unconscious, and I had to work hard lest the inspector should make his round before I was ready for him. The mummy case had to be lowered on to the floor, and the heavy body tightly bound and lifted into it, then stood up again and securely locked behind the glass doors. It was hot work, and I had but just accomplished the task and climbed into the constable's uniform, when the inspector's key sounded in the door. Ah! it is an exciting profession! The rest was easy. Wrapped up in my yellow mummy linen were the various appliances I required, and in the leather box was the imitation Rienzi Vase. The circular glass top of the case gave some trouble. So hard and thick was it that I had to desist five times and conceal my tools, owing to the hourly visits of the inspector. Poor Constable Smith began to groan toward six o'clock, and a second dose of medicine was necessary to keep him quiet for another hour or so.

I filed out with the other police in the morning, the Rienzi Vase inside my helmet. As to the sequel, it is brief. Of course the detectives tried their hands at the affair; but, pooh! I am too old a bird to leave "clues"! It is only amateurs that do that!

My fee, and the conditions to be observed in paying it, I conveyed to the authorities privately.

They thought they had a "clue" then, and delayed another week. They actually detained my unhappy agent, a most guileless and upright person, who knew positively nothing. Oh! it was too funny! But, realising that only by the vase being returned to its place could a scandal be avoided—they met me in the matter.

The Mummy of Thompson-Pratt

C. J. Cutcliffe Hyne

Gargrave was a fellow of Clare with rooms in College, who lectured twice a week on Constructive Egyptology, as a rule to empty benches. He was one of the most profound Egyptologists of the day, and had a clever knack of keeping all interesting items to himself, and discoursing the dry bran of theory only. At the beginning of each October term he had quite a crowd to hear him. The undergraduate who thought he ought to do something up at Cambridge on which to report progress to parent or guardian, would run his eye down the list, and pitch upon Constructive Egyptology as a subject likely to be of the light fiction order, and one which would probably offer him pleasant entertainment. But one hearing of Gargrave soon knocked this notion on the head, and that undergraduate in future wasted no more time drawing caricatures on lecture-room foolscap with spluttering lecture-room quills, whilst Gargrave prosed about the true significance of an accidental scratch on a scarabeus, but spent his mornings in bed, or on the river, or merely playing poker, as Nature had originally intended. And the lecture-room benches remained vacant till the next batch of green freshmen arrived in the succeeding October.

This result was pointed out clearly to Gargrave by candid friends. But this made no difference in the discourses. He held to the solid Cambridge theory that Varsity lectures were not intended to amuse, or teach anything that was useful; but merely to educate; which was a very different matter. "D'ye think I'm a music hall?" Gargrave would say. "Or is it a damned board-school you take me for?" The rest of the Clare fellows wished Gargrave would take orders, and then they could give him a college living and get rid of him. But Gargrave refused to do this thing, on the plea of religious scruples; and rumour got about in Cambridge that his creed was that of the ancient gods of Egypt.

Of the same college, and the bye-term senior to Gargrave, was Thompson-Pratt, Demonstrator in Chemistry at the Cavendish laboratories. He was not a Fellow of Clare, or even likely to be made one. Why he had ever got a first class in the National Science tripos was an abstruse mystery. He was not a man of brilliant intellect, nor did he, in his undergraduate days, ever resort to excessive reading. When he graduated at the end of his third year, he tried schoolmastering for a twelve-month, disliked it, and stumbled into this demonstratorship in chemistry which was then vacant. Envious people said he got it by sheer favouritism. He himself suggested that it was a just reward for his powers of blarney.

Thompson-Pratt always had matches and strong tobacco ready in his pocket for any one who needed them, and in the waiting spaces during a lingering experiment he could re-spin a yarn from back numbers of the *Pink 'Un* as deftly as one could wish to hear it. He was a distinctly popular man in a small way, and got asked out more than was good for his health.

Gargrave dined daily at the high table in hall, drank two glasses of port and ate four walnuts in the Combination Room afterwards, and then returned to his own rooms on the Don's staircase and worked till 2 A.M. Thompson-Pratt kept in Green Street, dined at the Hoop, and spent his evenings at threepenny-rise poker with four other Bachelors who entertained one another in turn and sat up till daylight. He knew Gargrave and disliked him candidly, and Gargrave despised Thompson-Pratt. So here are the men, and these are the relations between them.

Gargrave brought home the mummy himself by long sea from Alexandria in a P. & O. boat, and as I happened to be on board, and was a man of his own year and college, he looked upon me as his especial prey and bored me accordingly. I told him at the outset that except as fuel I was not interested in mummies in any degree whatever. But that did not choke him off in the least; and he poured conversational mummy-dust into my ears all down the Mediterranean, and through the Straits, and across the Bay, and down Channel till we fetched up in Southampton. I gave him the slip there in the Custom-House, and hoped he'd get run over by a cab in the street.

Two years later I went up to Cambridge to take my M.A. degree. I was paying my fees in the butteries, when in came Gargrave and passed the time of day. “Look here,” he said, “I wish you’d come round to my rooms after you’ve finished your business in the Senate House. I’ve got an experiment I want you to be in at.”

“What sort of experiment?” I asked. “Not mummies?”

“It has to do with a mummy. The one you saw me bring home from Egypt.”

“No, thanks, old man,” I said. “I hate the whole breed of them. Besides, I’ve another engagement.”

He pawed my coat sleeve. “I know you hate them. That’s just the very reason I want you. You’ll be an unprejudiced witness. Now do stay. You needn’t put up at the Bull. I’ve got a spare bed, and I’ll tell my gyp to make it up for you. I believe I’ve got hold of the finest thing that was ever hit upon since Egyptology started, and I want you to be there to confirm my notes.”

“But I should be no good at taking down notes. I’m merely a novelist. I haven’t climbed as far as being a reporter yet. Shorthand is clean beyond me.”

“I’ve got a phonograph to take it all down,” he said. “Writing would be no use even though you knew the language, which you don’t. The accent we use now is probably quite wrong. You wouldn’t be able to catch hold of one word in ten.”

“I wish you wouldn’t talk hieroglyphics.”

“I can’t explain it more to you here,” he said. “You must come and see for yourself, and I can promise you the entertainment will be exciting enough and suit even your lively tastes. If you stay away, you’ll regret it all the rest of your life.”

“Why?”

He was getting exasperated. “You’ll see why, you fool, when my book comes out in a year’s time.”

It was really cheering to see Gargrave human enough to lose his temper. “All right,” I said, “I’ll come after I’ve been through the mill in the Senate House and can smoke in Cambridge streets at night without danger of being proctorised and fined the gentle six-and-eight. So-long,” I said, and turned into the butteries to talk over past undergraduate high-jinks with my old gyp.

Now if anything better had turned up, it is more than possible that I should have forgotten my engagement with Gargrave and gone elsewhere. I had had a very excellent three years in Cambridge some time before, as an irresponsible undergraduate, and was by no means averse to having a short retaste of the old lively scenes. But I could find no one that I knew who seemed at all interesting; the current undergraduates, looked at from the light of after years, seemed mere schoolboys; and in fact the larger part of my acquaintance seemed to consist of gyps, bedmakers, or tradesmen's assistants; and so *faute de mieuz*, after I had been raised to the sublime degree of Magister Artium, I restored my borrowed hood, cap, gown, and bands to the tailor's, and strolled across to Gargrave's staircase.

I went in without knocking, *more Cantab*. He was fitting a new wax cylinder to a phonograph, and as he leaned over the machine and I saw the curves of his head, I thought of what a thousand pities it was that a man with such a magnificent brain should fritter it on such a useless life-work. The mummy case stood open against one of the walls, the mummy in it stripped of its swathings. The air was full of the sickly flavour of spices. I pulled out a cigar and lit it.

"Don't smoke," said Gargrave. "I must have the air here quite clear."

"Then open the window," I said. "The place stinks."

"You'll be used to the atmosphere directly. There's the mummy. What do you think of him?"

"Toughish *biltong*. Newer meat for me. He's well tattooed about the chest and arms, though."

"Those are not tattoo marks. Look closer. They are a pattern in the grain of the epidermis."

"So they are. Mr. Menen-Ra—isn't that his name?—is a curious beast."

"Curious! He's unique. Or at least he and his descendants are."

"Oh, those markings would not pass on to his son."

"So you say. But it appears they did."

"Have you got another mummy here, then?"

"I've got more than that. I've got one of his living descendants, he's due in this room almost directly."

"Humbug."

"You shall judge for yourself. You know the very man. He's Thompson-Pratt, of the bye-term above us."

"What, the demonstrator in the labs?"

"That same man. He's the lineal descendant of this mummy, as I've been at infinite pains to find out."

"And has he got the strawberry mark, or whatever you call it?"

"He has, line for line, pustule for pustule."

"Did he see your mummy and come up and claim it as a cousin?"

"He did not. I discovered his markings for myself long before I saw the mummy. It was the term after you had gone down. He'd been on this staircase here to see the Dean, who was out. He slipped in coming down, and took a header, and got all the sense knocked out of him. I heard the noise. I was the only man in. So I went and picked him up, and brought him in here. He lay so still I thought he was dead, so I ripped open his shirt to see if I could feel his heart beating; and it was then that incidentally I came across the markings. I got him back to his senses again soon afterwards, and whilst he was lying on my sofa getting his nerves straight again, I told him what I had seen and asked him how they came there.

"He was furiously angry and said I'd taken a great liberty.

"'My good man,' I said, 'I didn't look for the things. I merely stumbled across them by accident.'

"'They are the curse of my life,' said he. 'I love swimming, and yet I daren't bathe in public. People hoot at me if I do. Look,' he said, and pulled back his shirt, and showed me his chest and the tops of his arms. 'I'm marked like the spotted man at the fair. I'm a blooming spectacle. My father's the same way, and so's the grand gov'nor, and so was his father before him. I suppose it's a sort of family curse, or some such rot as that, only we're too ashamed of the whole thing to have any yarn about it.' And then he pinned me not to tell about him, and then he went. I didn't worry my head more about the matter. Biology's outside my line, and Thompson-Pratt was not a man I had any special interest in at that period.

"Well, then, of course I went on with my work, and in time went to Egypt and got this mummy of Menen-Ra. I brought it home in its swathings, and didn't open it out till I got here. I'd procured it, as you know, for a certain purpose connected with one of my theories. But when I'd had the first glance at those markings on its skin, I let my original ideas go to the winds for the time being. So far as I could remember, they were the exact repetition of those carried by Thompson-Pratt.

"Here was a strange thing! I sat and thought of it hour after hour, and day after day. I tell you theories fairly bubbled out of me. At last I made up my mind what was to be done. But before I went further, I had got to know if the markings were exactly the same as Thompson-Pratt's. He made a big difficulty about it, and for a man who pretends to be scientific, I must say he was absurdly prejudiced. But he gave in at last, and let me take a photograph. I tell you it was simply marvellous: line for line, pustule for pustule, his markings were the same as the mummy's.

"Well, that was strong evidence, you'll say, but I wanted to go deeper. I've put an enormous amount of work into it; I've had scores of genealogy experts working for me; and I've had amazing luck. I've worked out the chain of descent in Egypt, Italy, France, England, Scotland, and England again without a break; and I've learned for an absolute certainty that Thompson-Pratt is the direct descendant of the Egyptian Menen-Ra, whose mummy you see against the wall yonder.

"And now," he went on, "I'll explain to you what I intend to do." But he did not explain to me then. The door opened and Thompson-Pratt came into the room. He nodded curtly enough to Gargrave, but he greeted me kindly. "Hullo, old man. How's the world using you? Heard you were up taking out your M.A. Staying up long?"

"Going down to-morrow. I've just come in here because Gargrave wanted to show me some tricks with his mummy."

"Damnation," said Thompson-Pratt to the owner of the rooms, "you haven't been talking about—er—secrets, have you?"

"No secrets will be given away unless you do it yourself," said Gargrave, oracularly. "I've just asked him in to be an independent witness."

"Oh, I see," said Thompson-Pratt, getting into a chair. "But look here, you know. I don't half like this experiment of yours."

"It's in the cause of science."

"Science be sugared." He stared thoughtfully into the fire and then turned round and faced Gargrave squarely. "Look here, sir, if you are going to make use of me, I'm going to share some of the profits. You say that wrinkled, smelly person in the coffin yonder is my ancestor, and you are going to make me to talk his thoughts. Well, you may do it, or you mayn't. But if it does come off, it's just on the cards the old boy may let slip something in the natural science line which is strange to us to-day. I've a notion those old Egyptians were a lot ahead of us in some branches of chemistry, and if I could get hold of the way of making some new dye, for instance, to use with alizerene—"

"You shall have a copy of every word that's said," Gargrave promised.

"From the phonograph? Yes, I see. But it'll be in what-d'you-call-em language—hieroglyphics, isn't it? Ancient Egyptian, I mean."

"You shall overlook my translation as I make it. Man, I mean to do fairly by you."

"Oh, all right," said Thompson-Pratt. "Don't get shirty. Only, a man must look after his own interests, y'know, that's all; and besides, it's a hundred to one the whole thing's a fizzle."

Gargrave set his teeth. "Have you any more to say?" he inquired.

"No," said Thompson-Pratt, with a bored yawn. "Wire in."

Now from where I sat on the table, I was watching the proceedings pretty carefully; and it struck me that Gargrave merely got a hypnotic influence over Thompson-Pratt in the usual way. He has told me since that he did something more, and perhaps this may be so; but anyway the patient seemed to go to sleep and to wake up again, and be entirely under the control of Gar-grave's will. He made him lie down on the hearthrug in front of the fire, and then he took the mummy out of its case and laid that down on the hearthrug also, side by side with its living descendant. Then he told me to go out of the room.

"Whatever for?" I asked. "I thought you invited me here to see an experiment?"

"So I did. And you shall see it when the time comes. But I have one or two more preparations to make first, which I don't choose to be overlooked. You must go into my inner room."

"I have a rare big mind to go out of the place altogether."

"You can do it if you like, of course, but you are a fool if you do."

Well, perhaps it was undignified, but I shrugged my shoulders, and swallowed my pride, and marched off into the inner room. I will own I was getting curious as to what was coming next.

Gargrave came after me, and had the impertinence to lock the door on my heels. So there I was anyway, and as he seemed to have a dislike for smoking, I lit a pipe and filled the room with heavy reek.

I will give him credit for one thing, though. He did not keep me waiting long. He opened the door in a minute or so and said: "Sorry, old man, but I must keep my processes secret at any cost. Come in."

I went in. Thompson-Pratt and the man who had predeceased him some 3000 years were lying side by side on the hearthrug, to all appearance exactly as I had left them.

Evening was come on, the lamps had not been lit, and only the dancing, uncanny firelight illuminated the faces; and as I gazed a little closer, a curious thrill went through me. It was Thompson-Pratt's which seemed to be the dead face now. Behind the shrivelled mask of the mummy there was surely some flicker of life. Gargrave was bending down, arranging the mouthpiece of the phonograph over the mummy's lips, and as he moved aside I could have sworn I saw the long-dead limbs twitch. I took out a handkerchief and wiped my forehead. Gargrave saw me do it.

"Now don't be an idiot," he said. "There's nothing to be scared of. Just keep cool, and take accurate mental notes of all you see and hear." He tried to talk calmly, but I saw he was quivering with excitement for all that. He turned to the mummy and said something in a tongue I could not understand, enunciating each syllable most distinctly. I distinguished the word "Menen-Ra," but could make out nothing else.

Neither the mummy nor Thompson-Pratt gave any sign of having heard.

He repeated the sentence again, varying the pronunciation of the words, and this time got a reply.

"You must speak English if you wish me to understand," came the answer in a stifled, dusty voice directly from the mummy's lips.

Gargrave started, and I think he swore. "Why?" he asked savagely.

"Because I have forgotten the other—the old tongue."

"If I am being played with," said Gargrave, "there is one man here who will carry out of this room my marks on him for life."

There was no answer. He went on: "Do you know your name?"

"Menen-Ra."

"Where buried?"

"Thebes."

"You were not."

"I was buried at Thebes; but I should be taken afterwards to our family vault on the estate by Koorkoor, according to our custom."

"It was in the desert by the oasis of Koorkoor I found you. In what manner of grave?"

"Rock-hewn, with my titles carved above me."

"Alone?"

"No, my four uncles, killed in war, would be with me."

"Were they all sound men?"

"No, my uncle Nepo, the last buried and so the next to me, had his right arm lopped off at the elbow: an old wound."

Gargrave broke off his questioning and hit the table excitedly. "That settles it," he cried. "No living soul knows what the grave was like except myself, and no one could have guessed it. And it's all absolutely exact. It's a miracle, but I've done it. The soul of Thompson-Pratt has gone back to its old abiding-place, and now I shall be told the history of 3000 years ago exactly as it happened, and I can give that history to the modern world. When he spoke English I thought there was fraud; but there isn't; it's just part of the natural lapse." He rubbed his hands. "Lord! how simple it is, and I'm the only man that's got the key." He turned again to the mummy. "Menen-Ra, I command you that you lift up your voice now in history, and tell us of the Government of Egypt, and of Pharaoh, and of Pharaoh's inner life, and the daily life you lived yourself, and the daily life of the people."

And the mummy in its dusty tones began to speak. There was no doubt about the genuineness of it all, that I can vouch for. The phraseology was certainly that of Thompson-Pratt, reader of the *Pink 'Un*, and Demonstrator in Chemistry at the Cavendish Labs. But the sentiments were those of ancient Egypt, spoken as no other men now living (except Gargrave and myself)) ever heard them, but startlingly fresh and real. Not even the most imaginative student, redolent in the lore of that long-dead land, could have invented them. They were marvellous in their vivid truth. They were nothing short of a revelation.

But Gargrave cursed as he listened. He had looked for a dissertation on history, and he was getting *chroniques scandaleuses*; he had expected talk about Kings' policies, and he was hearing the tales of flirtations with their housemaids. He wanted descriptions of Council Chambers, and he got the dimensions of wine-shops. He had fallen into the error of thinking that all the men of bygone Egypt were as thoughtful and ponderous as the hoary few whose scribings have remained; and when he found that the ancient land contained devil-may-care pleasure-eaters like those that live in this land of ours to-day, he could have beaten himself in the fury of his disappointment.

For myself, as I listened whilst Menen-Ra prattled on, I laughed till the tears came, and my only regret—a professional one—was that I could not use up that unmatchable subject-matter hereafter. I was listening to the talk of a man-about-town, who lived in Thebes 3000 years ago, and learning in detail exactly how he wasted his days and how he enjoyed his nights. He told us of his bets, his bouts, his light loves, and his serious entanglements. Every third sentence referred to a long-dead Chloe, evidently the Thäis of her day in that far-forgotten Thebes. Even allowing for Menen-Ra's obvious partiality, Chloe must have been a lady of wonderful powers, albeit she was a mere dancer by recognised profession. It was a gorgeous piece of description. But as it was given to us it would not publish; no, not even inside a yellow cover. And though I did note down a few items to make into future copy, I think I shall give them as my own. They are quite new, and no one will accuse me of lifting them; and, besides, it is merely foolishness to offer unasked-for explanations which no one will believe.

But I cannot say I heard as much as I wished. It was evident that Menen-Ra, after his silence of 3000 years, was equal to going on till midnight. But his was a mouth which could only speak on its own topic. Again and again Gargrave tried to lead this wanderer from a long-forgotten past on to the more weighty matters of state, and time after time he got back to talk about cockfights, and dicing bouts, and ape-racing on the dry Nile banks; or else he would speak to us of Chloe and his other loves with a freedom which is quite obsolete to-day. He brimmed with these reminiscences. But he had no others of a graver sort. This Menen-Ra had lived for nothing but his own personal pleasure, and beyond the limits of that he knew no more than we moderns did about the larger affairs of his country.

Gargrave tried him on every topic. He asked about the army. Menen-Ra started off loud in the praises of his favourite gladiator, and gave us the latest betting on his approaching fight. Gargrave asked for some song of the priests of Osiris, and this faded roysterer promptly trolled forth a drinking chant that nearly split his dusky throat.

And at last, seeing the futility of getting what he wanted, Gargrave savagely put an end to the inquisition. He clapped a large sponge over the still white face of Thompson-Pratt, and took a green powder from the mantelpiece and threw it on the sponge. There was a *paff* of streaky flame, and Thompson-Pratt sprang up choking and spluttering.

"I say, good Lord, Gargrave, what devil's game have you been up to now? What have you been putting me to bed on the hearthrug with that old image for? Here! I say, have you got a whisky-and-soda? Get me some whisky, for heaven's sake. I'm nearly parched to death."

I mixed a drink, and handed it to him. He gulped half of it thirstily. Then he bethought him of a toast. He nodded towards the mummy on the floor. "Here's to you, old cock," said he, and emptied his tumbler to the dregs. "I wonder what the equivalent of whisky was in your benighted day? I bet you had your share of it, if you are ancestor of mine."

"You're a Goth," I said.

"I know," said Thompson-Pratt, "and I had a far better time of it than—say—a Constructive Egyptologist has. Come along to the Hoop and have some dinner. We'll leave Gargrave to go on thumbing at my unpleasant forefather."

Mustapha

S. Baring-Gould

Among the many hangers-on at the Hotel de l'Europe at Luxor—donkey-boys, porters, guides, antiquity dealers—was one, a young man named Mustapha, who proved a general favourite.

I spent three winters at Luxor, partly for my health, partly for pleasure, mainly to make artistic studies, as I am by profession a painter. So I came to know Mustapha fairly well in three stages, during those three winters.

When first I made his acquaintance he was in the transition condition from boyhood to manhood. He had an intelligent face, with bright eyes, a skin soft as brown silk, with a velvety hue on it. His features were regular, and if his face was a little too round to quite satisfy an English artistic eye, yet this was a peculiarity to which one soon became accustomed. He was unflaggingly good-natured and obliging. A mongrel, no doubt, he was; Arab and native Egyptian blood were mingled in his veins. But the result was happy; he combined the patience and gentleness of the child of Mizraim with the energy and pluck of the son of the desert.

Mustapha had been a donkey-boy, but had risen a stage higher, and looked, as the object of his supreme ambition, to become some day a dragoman, and blaze like one of these gilded beetles in lace and chains, rings and weapons. To become a dragoman—one of the most obsequious of men till engaged, one of the veriest tyrants when engaged—to what higher could an Egyptian boy aspire?

To become a dragoman means to go in broadcloth and with gold chains when his fellows are half naked; to lounge and twist the moustache when his kinsfolk are toiling under the water- buckets; to be able to extort backsheesh from all the tradesmen to whom he can introduce a master; to do nothing himself and make others work for him; to be able to look to purchase two, three, even four wives when his father contented himself with one; to soar out of the region of native virtues into that of foreign vices; to be superior to all instilled prejudices against spirits and wine—that is the ideal set before young Egypt through contact with the English and the American tourist.

We all liked Mustapha. No one had a bad word to say of him. Some pious individuals rejoiced to see that he had broken with the Koran, as if this were a first step towards taking up with the Bible. A free-thinking professor was glad to find that Mustapha had emancipated himself from some of those shackles which religion places on august, divine humanity, and that by getting drunk he gave pledge that he had risen into a sphere of pure emancipation, which eventuates in ideal perfection.

As I made my studies I engaged Mustapha to carry my easel and canvas, or camp-stool. I was glad to have him as a study, to make him stand by a wall or sit on a pillar that was prostrate, as artistic exigencies required. He was always ready to accompany me. There was an understanding between us that when a drove of tourists came to Luxor he might leave me for the day to pick up what he could then from the natural prey; but I found him not always keen to be off duty to me. Though he could get more from the occasional visitor than from me, he was above the ravenous appetite for backsheesh which consumed his fellows.

He who has much to do with the native Egyptian will have discovered that there are in him a fund of kindliness and a treasure of good qualities. He is delighted to be treated with humanity, pleased to be noticed, and ready to repay attention with touching gratitude. He is by no means as rapacious for backsheesh as the passing traveller supposes; he is shrewd to distinguish between man and man; likes this one, and will do anything for him unrewarded, and will do naught for another for any bribe.

The Egyptian is now in a transitional state. If it be quite true that the touch of England is restoring life to his crippled limbs, and the voice of England bidding him rise up and walk, there are occasions on which association with Englishmen is a disadvantage to him. Such an instance is that of poor, good Mustapha.

It was not my place to caution Mustapha against the pernicious influences to which he was subjected, and, to speak plainly, I did not know what line to adopt, on what ground to take my stand, if I did. He was breaking with the old life, and taking up with what was new, retaining of the old only what was bad in it, and acquiring of the new none of its good parts. Civilisation—European civilisation—is excellent, but cannot be swallowed at a gulp, nor does it wholly suit the oriental digestion.

That which impelled Mustapha still further in his course was the attitude assumed towards him by his own relatives and the natives of his own village. They were strict Moslems, and they regarded him as one on the highway to becoming a renegade. They treated him with mistrust, showed him aversion, and loaded him with reproaches. Mustapha had a high spirit, and he resented rebuke. Let his fellows grumble and objurgate, said he; they would cringe to him when he became a dragoman, with his pockets stuffed with piastres.

There was in our hotel, the second winter, a young fellow of the name of Jameson, a man with plenty of money, superficial good nature, little intellect, very conceited and egotistic, and this fellow was Mustapha's evil genius. It was Jameson's delight to encourage Mustapha in drinking and gambling. Time hung heavy on his hands. He cared nothing for hieroglyphics, scenery bored him, antiquities, art, had no charm for him. Natural history presented to him no attraction, and the only amusement level with his mental faculties was that of hoaxing natives, or breaking down their religious prejudices.

Matters were in this condition as regarded Mustapha, when an incident occurred during my second winter at Luxor that completely altered the tenor of Mustapha's life.

One night a fire broke out in the nearest village. It originated in a mud hovel belonging to a fellah; his wife had spilled some oil on the hearth, and the flames leaping up had caught the low thatch, which immediately burst into a blaze. A wind was blowing from the direction of the Arabian desert, and it carried the flames and ignited the thatch before it on other roofs; the conflagration spread, and the whole village was menaced with destruction. The greatest excitement and alarm prevailed. The inhabitants lost their heads. Men ran about rescuing from their hovels their only treasures—old sardine tins and empty marmalade pots; women wailed, children sobbed; no one made any attempt to stay the fire; and, above all, were heard the screams of the woman whose incaution had caused the mischief, and who was being beaten unmercifully by her husband.

The few English in the hotel came on the scene, and with their instinctive energy and system set to work to organise a corps and subdue the flames. The women and girls who were rescued from the menaced hovels, or plucked out of those already on fire, were in many cases unveiled, and so it came to pass that Mustapha, who, under English direction, was ablest and most vigorous in his efforts to stop the conflagration, met his fate in the shape of the daughter of Ibraim the Earner.

By the light of the flames he saw her, and at once resolved to make that fair girl his wife.

No reasonable obstacle intervened, so thought Mustapha. He had amassed a sufficient sum to entitle him to buy a wife and set up a household of his own. A house consists of four mud walls and a low thatch, and housekeeping in an Egyptian house is as elementary and economical as the domestic architecture. The maintenance of a wife and family is not costly after the first outlay, which consists in indemnifying the father for the expense to which he has been put in rearing a daughter.

The ceremony of courting is also elementary, and the addresses of the suitor are not paid to the bride, but to her father, and not in person by the candidate, but by an intermediary.

Mustapha negotiated with a friend, a fellow hanger-on at the hotel, to open proceedings with the farrier. He was to represent to the worthy man that the suitor entertained the most ardent admiration for the virtues of Ibraim personally, that he was inspired with but one ambition, which was alliance with so distinguished a family as his. He was to assure the father of the damsel that Mustapha undertook to proclaim through Upper and Lower Egypt, in the ears of Egyptians, Arabs, and Europeans, that Ibraim was the most remarkable man that ever existed for solidity of judgment, excellence of parts, uprightness of dealing, nobility of sentiment, strictness in observance of the precepts of the Koran, and that finally Mustapha was anxious to indemnify this same paragon of genius and virtue for his condescension in having cared to breed and clothe and feed for several years a certain girl, his daughter, if Mustapha might have that daughter as his wife. Not that he cared for the daughter in herself, but as a means whereby he might have the honour of entering into alliance with one so distinguished and so esteemed of Allah as Ibraim the Farrier.

To the infinite surprise of the intermediary, and to the no less surprise and mortification of the suitor, Mustapha was refused. He was a bad Moslem. Ibraim would have no alliance with one who had turned his back on the Prophet and drunk bottled beer.

Till this moment Mustapha had not realised how great was the alienation between his fellows and himself—what a barrier he had set up between himself and the men of his own blood. The refusal of his suit struck the young man to the quick. He had known and played with the farrier's daughter in childhood, till she had come of age to veil her face; now that he had seen her in her ripe charms, his heart was deeply stirred and engaged. He entered into himself, and going to the mosque he there made a solemn vow that if he ever touched wine, ale, or spirits again he would cut his throat, and he sent word to Ibraim that he had done so, and begged that he would not dispose of his daughter and finally reject him till he had seen how that he who had turned in thought and manner of life from the Prophet would return with firm resolution to the right way.

II

From this time Mustapha changed his conduct. He was obliging and attentive as before, ready to exert himself to do for me what I wanted, ready also to extort money from the ordinary tourist for doing nothing, to go with me and carry my tools when I went forth painting, and to joke and laugh with Jameson; but, unless he were unavoidably detained, he said his prayers five times daily in the mosque, and no inducement whatever would make him touch anything save sherbet, milk, or water.

Mustapha had no easy time of it. The strict Mohammedans mistrusted this sudden conversion, and believed that he was playing a part. Ibraim gave him no encouragement. His relatives maintained their reserve and stiffness towards him.

His companions, moreover, who were in the transitional stage, and those who had completely shaken off all faith in Allah and trust in the Prophet and respect for the Koran, were incensed at his desertion. He was ridiculed, insulted; he was waylaid and beaten. The young fellows mimicked him, the elder scoffed at him.

Jameson took his change to heart, and laid himself out to bring him out of his pot of scruples.

"Mustapha ain't any sport at all now," said he. "I'm hanged if he has another para from me." He offered him bribes in gold, he united with the others in ridicule, he turned his back on him, and refused to employ him. Nothing availed. Mustapha was respectful, courteous, obliging as before, but he had returned, he said, to the faith and rule of life in which he had been brought up, and he would never again leave it.

"I have sworn," said he, "that if I do I will cut my throat." I had been, perhaps, negligent in cautioning the young fellow the first winter that I knew him against the harm likely to be done him by taking up with European habits contrary to his law and the feelings and prejudices of his people. Now, however, I had no hesitation in expressing to him the satisfaction I felt at the courageous and determined manner in which he had broken with acquired habits that could do him no good. For one thing, we were now better acquaintances, and I felt that as one who had known him for more than a few months in the winter, I had a good right to speak. And, again, it is always easier or pleasanter to praise than to reprimand.

One day when sketching I cut my pencil with a pruning-knife I happened to have in my pocket; my proper knife of many blades had been left behind by misadventure.

Mustapha noticed the knife and admired it, and asked if it had cost a great sum.

"Not at all," I answered. "I did not even buy it. It was given me. I ordered some flower seeds from a seeds-man, and when he sent me the consignment he included this knife in the case as a present. It is not worth more than a shilling in England."

He turned it about, with looks of admiration.

"It is just the sort that would suit me," he said. "I know your other knife with many blades. It is very fine, but it is too small. I do not want it to cut pencils. It has other things in it, a hook for taking stones from a horse's hoof, a pair of tweezers for removing hairs. I do not want such, but a knife such as this, with such a curve, is just the thing."

"Then you shall have it," said I. "You are welcome. It was for rough work only that I brought the knife to Egypt with me."

I finished a painting that winter that gave me real satisfaction. It was of the great court of the temple of Luxor by evening light, with the last red glare of the sun over the distant desert hills, and the eastern sky above of a purple depth. What colours I used! the intensest on my palette, and yet fell short of the effect.

The picture was in the Academy, was well hung, abominably represented in one of the illustrated guides to the galleries, as a blotch, by some sort of photographic process on gelatine; my picture sold, which concerned me most of all, and not only did it sell at a respectable figure, but it also brought me two or three orders for Egyptian pictures. So many English and Americans go up the Nile, and carry away with them pleasant reminiscences of the Land of the Pharaohs, that when in England they are fain to buy pictures which shall remind them of scenes in that land.

I returned to my hotel at Luxor in November, to spend there a third winter. The fellaheen about there saluted me as a friend with an affectionate delight, which I am quite certain was not assumed, as they got nothing out of me save kindly salutations. I had the Egyptian fever on me, which, when once acquired, is not to be shaken off—an enthusiasm for everything Egyptian, the antiquities, the history of the Pharaohs, the very desert, the brown Nile, the desolate hill ranges, the ever blue sky, the marvellous colorations at rise and set of sun, and last, but not least, the prosperity of the poor peasants.

I am quite certain that the very warmest welcome accorded to me was from Mustapha, and almost the first words he said to me on my meeting him again were:

"I have been very good. I say my prayers. I drink no wine, and Ibraim will give me his daughter in the second Iomada—what you call January."

"Not before, Mustapha?"

"No, sir; he says I must be tried for one whole year, and he is right."

"Then soon after Christmas you will be happy!"

"I have got a house and made it ready. Yes. After Christmas there will be one very happy man—one very, very happy man in Egypt, and that will be your humble servant, Mustapha."

III

We were a pleasant party at Luxor, this third winter, not numerous, but for the most part of congenial tastes. For the most part we were keen on hieroglyphics, we admired Queen Hatasou and we hated Rameses II. We could distinguish the artistic work of one dynasty from that of another. We were learned on cartouches, and flourished our knowledge before the tourists dropping in.

One of those staying in the hotel was an Oxford don, very good company, interested in everything, and able to talk well on everything—I mean everything more or less remotely connected with Egypt. Another was a young fellow who had been an attaché at Berlin, but was out of health—nothing organic the matter with his lungs, but they were weak. He was keen on the political situation, and very anti-Gallican, as every man who has been in Egypt naturally is, who is not a Frenchman.

There was also staying in the hotel an American lady, fresh and delightful, whose mind and conversation twinkled like frost crystals in the sun, a woman full of good-humour, of the most generous sympathies, and so droll that she kept us ever amused.

And, alas! Jameson was back again, not entering into any of our pursuits, not understanding our little jokes, not at all content to be there. He grumbled at the food— and, indeed, that might have been better; at the monotony of the life at Luxor, at his London doctor for putting the veto on Cairo because of its drainage, or rather the absence of all drainage. I really think we did our utmost to draw Jameson into our circle, to amuse him, to interest him in something; but one by one we gave him up, and the last to do this was the little American lady.

From the outset he had attacked Mustapha, and endeavoured to persuade him to shake off his "squeamish nonsense," as Jameson called his resolve. "I'll tell you what it is, old fellow," he said, "life isn't worth living without good liquor, and as for that blessed Prophet of yours, he showed he was a fool when he put a bar on drinks."

But as Mustapha was not pliable he gave him up. "He's become just as great a bore as that old Rameses," said he. "I'm sick of the whole concern, and I don't think anything of fresh dates, that you fellows make such a fuss about. As for that stupid old Nile—there ain't a fish worth eating comes out of it. And those old Egyptians were arrant humbugs. I haven't seen a lotus since I came here, and they made such a fuss about them too."

The little American lady was not weary of asking questions relative to English home life, and especially to country-house living and amusements.

"Oh, my dear!" said she, "I would give my ears to spend a Christmas in the fine old fashion in a good ancient manor-house in the country."

"There is nothing remarkable in that," said an English lady.

"Not to you, maybe; but there would be to us. What we read of and make pictures of in our fancies, that is what you live. Your facts are our fairy tales. Look at your hunting."

"That, if you like, is fun," threw in Jameson. "But I don't myself think anything save Luxor can be a bigger bore than country-house life at Christmas time—when all the boys are back from school."

"With us," said the little American, "our sportsmen dress in pink like yours—the whole thing—and canter after a bag of anise seed that is trailed before them."

"Why do they not import foxes?"

"Because a fox would not keep to the road. Our farmers object pretty freely to trespass; so the hunting must of necessity be done on the highway, and the game is but a bag of anise seed. I would like to see an English meet and a run."

This subject was thrashed out after having been prolonged unduly for the sake of Jameson.

"Oh, dear me!" said the Yankee lady. "If but that chef could be persuaded to give us plum-puddings for Christmas, I would try to think I was in England."

"Plum-pudding is exploded," said Jameson. "Only children ask for it now. A good trifle or a tipsy-cake is much more to my taste; but this hanged cook here can give us nothing but his blooming custard pudding and burnt sugar."

"I do not think it would be wise to let him attempt a plum-pudding," said the English lady. "But if we can persuade him to permit me I will mix and make the pudding, and then he cannot go far wrong in the boiling and dishing up."

"That is the only thing wanting to make me perfectly happy," said the American. "I'll confront monsieur. I am sure I can talk him into a good humour, and we shall have our plum-pudding."

No one has yet been found, I do believe, who could resist that little woman. She carried everything before her. The cook placed himself and all his culinary apparatus at her feet. We took part in the stoning of the raisins, and the washing of the currants, even the chopping of the suet; we stirred the pudding, threw in sixpence apiece, and a ring, and then it was tied up in a cloth, and set aside to be boiled. Christmas Day came, and the English chaplain preached us a practical sermon on "Goodwill towards men." That was his text, and his sermon was but a swelling out of the words just as rice is swelled to thrice its size by boiling.

We dined. There was an attempt at roast beef—it was more like baked leather. The event of the dinner was to be the bringing in and eating of the plum-pudding.

Surely all would be perfect. We could answer for the materials and the mixing. The English lady could guarantee the boiling. She had seen the plum-pudding on the boil,'' and had given strict injunctions as to the length of time during which it was to boil.

But, alas! the pudding was not right when brought on the table. It was not enveloped in lambent blue flame—it was not crackling in the burning brandy. It was sent in dry, and the brandy arrived separate in a white sauceboat, hot indeed, and sugared, but not on fire.

There ensued outcries of disappointment. Attempts were made to redress the mistake by setting fire to the brandy in a spoon, but the spoon was cold. The flame would not catch, and finally, with a sigh, we had to take our plum-pudding as served.

"I say, chaplain!" exclaimed Jameson, "practice is better than precept, is it not?"

"To be sure it is."

"You gave us a deuced good sermon. It was short, as it ought to be; but I'll go better on it, I'll practise where you preached, and have larks, too!"

Then Jameson started from table with a plate of plum-pudding in one hand and the sauce-boat in the other. "By Jove!" he said, "I'll teach these fellows to open their eyes. I'll show them that we know how to feed. We can't turn out scarabs and cartouches in England, that are no good to anyone, but we can produce the finest roast beef in the world, and do a thing or two in puddings."

And he left the room.

We paid no heed to anything Jameson said or did. We were rather relieved that he was out of the room, and did not concern ourselves about the "larks" he promised himself, and which we were quite certain would be as insipid as were the quails of the Israelites.

In ten minutes he was back, laughing and red in the face. "I've had splitting fun," he said. "You should have been there."

"Where, Jameson?"

"Why, outside. There were a lot of old moolahs and other hoky-pokies sitting and contemplating the setting sun and all that sort of thing, and I gave Mustapha the pudding. I told him I wished him to try our great national English dish, on which her Majesty the Queen dines daily. Well, he ate and enjoyed it, by George. Then I said, 'Old fellow, it's uncommonly dry, so you must take the sauce to it.' He asked if it was only sauce—flour and water. 'It's sauce, by Jove,' said I, 'a little sugar to it; no bar on the sugar, Musty.' So I put the boat to his lips and gave him a pull. By George, you should have seen his face! It was just thundering fun. 'I've done you at last, old Musty,' I said. 'It is best cognac.' He gave me such a look! He'd have eaten me, I believe—and he walked away. It was just splitting fun. I wish you had been there to see it."

I went out after dinner, to take my usual stroll along the river-bank, and to watch the evening lights die away on the columns and obelisk. On my return I saw at once that something had happened which had produced commotion among the servants of the hotel. I had reached the salon before I inquired what was the matter.

The boy who was taking the coffee round said: "Mustapha is dead. He cut his throat at the door of the mosque. He could not help himself. He had broken his vow."

I looked at Jameson without a word. Indeed, I could not speak; I was choking. The little American lady was trembling, the English lady crying. The gentlemen stood silent in the windows, not speaking a word.

Jameson's colour changed. He was honestly distressed, uneasy, and tried to cover his confusion with bravado and a jest.

"After all," he said, "it is only a n— the less."

"N—!" said the American lady. "He was no n—, but an Egyptian."

"Oh! I don't pretend to distinguish between your blacks and whity-browns any more than I do between your cartouches," returned Jameson.

"He was no black," said the American lady, standing up. "But I do mean to say that I consider you an utterly unredeemed black—"

"My dear, don't," said the Englishwoman, drawing the other down. "It's no good. The thing is done. He meant no harm."

IV

I could not sleep. My blood was in a boil. I felt that I could not speak to Jameson again. He would have to leave Luxor. That was tacitly understood among us. Coventry was the place to which he would be consigned.

I tried to finish in a little sketch I had made in my notebook when I was in my room, but my hand shook, and I was constrained to lay my pencil aside. Then I took up an Egyptian grammar, but could not fix my mind on study. The hotel was very still. Everyone had gone to bed at an early hour that night, disinclined for conversation. No one was moving. There was a lamp in the passage; it was partly turned down. Jameson's room was next to mine. I heard him stir as he undressed, and talk to himself. Then he was quiet. I wound up my watch, and emptying my pocket, put my purse under the pillow. I was not in the least heavy with sleep. If I did go to bed I should not be able to close my eyes. But then—if I sat up I could do nothing.

I was about leisurely to undress, when I heard a sharp cry, or exclamation of mingled pain and alarm, from the adjoining room. In another moment there was a rap at my door. I opened, and Jameson came in. He was in his nightshirt, and looking agitated and frightened.

"Look here, old fellow," said he in a shaking voice, "there is Musty in my room. He has been hiding there, and just as I dropped asleep he ran that—knife of yours into my throat."

"My knife?"

"Yes—that pruning-knife you gave him, you know. Look here—I must have the place sewn up. Do go for a doctor, there's a good chap."

"Where is the place?"

"Here on my right gill."

Jameson turned his head to the left, and I raised the lamp. There was no wound of any sort there.

I told him so.

"Oh, yes! That's fine—I tell you I felt his knife go in."

"Nonsense, you were dreaming."

"Dreaming! Not I. I saw Musty as distinctly as I now see you."

"This is a delusion, Jameson," I replied. "The poor fellow is dead."

"Oh, that's very fine," said Jameson. "It is not the first of April, and I don't believe the yarns that you've been spinning. You tried to make believe he was dead, but I know he is not. He has got into my room, and he made a dig at my throat with your pruning-knife."

"I'll go into your room with you."

"Do so. But he's gone by this time. Trust him to cut and run." I followed Jameson, and looked about. There was no trace of anyone beside himself having been in the room. Moreover, there was no place but the nut-wood wardrobe in the bedroom in which anyone could have secreted himself I opened this and showed that it was empty.

After a while I pacified Jameson, and induced him to go to bed again, and then I left his room. I did not now attempt to court sleep. I wrote letters with a hand not the steadiest, and did my accounts.

As the hour approached midnight I was again startled by a cry from the adjoining room, and in another moment Jameson was at my door.

"That blooming fellow Musty is in my room still," said he. "He has been at my throat again."

"Nonsense," I said. "You are labouring under hallucinations. You locked your door."

"Oh, by Jove, yes—of course I did; but, hang it, in this hole, neither doors nor windows fit, and the locks are no good, and the bolts nowhere. He got in again somehow, and if I had not started up the moment I felt the knife, he'd have done for me. He would, by George. I wish I had a revolver."

I went into Jameson's room. Again he insisted on my looking at his throat.

"It's very good of you to say there is no wound," said he. "But you won't gull me with words. I felt his knife in my windpipe, and if I had not jumped out of bed—"

"You locked your door. No one could enter. Look in the glass, there is not even a scratch. This is pure imagination."

"I'll tell you what, old fellow, I won't sleep in that room again. Change with me, there's a charitable buffer. If you don't believe in Musty, Musty won't hurt you, maybe—anyhow you can try if he's solid or a phantom. Blow me if the knife felt like a phantom."

"I do not quite see my way to changing rooms," I replied; "but this I will do for you. If you like to go to bed again in your own apartment, I will sit up with you till morning."

"All right," answered Jameson. "And if Musty comes in again, let out at him and do not spare him. Swear that."

I accompanied Jameson once more to his bedroom. Little as I liked the man, I could not deny him my presence and assistance at this time. It was obvious that his nerves were shaken by what had occurred, and he felt his relation to Mustapha much more than he cared to show. The thought that he had been the cause of the poor fellow's death preyed on his mind, never strong, and now it was upset with imaginary terrors.

I gave up letter writing, and brought my Baedeker's *Upper Egypt* into Jameson's room, one of the best of all guide-books, and one crammed with information. I seated myself near the light, and with my back to the bed, on which the young man had once more flung himself.

"I say," said Jameson, raising his head, "is it too late for a brandy-and-soda?"

"Everyone is in bed."

"What lazy dogs they are. One never can get anything one wants here."

"Well, try to go to sleep."

He tossed from side to side for some time, but after a while, either he was quiet, or I was engrossed in my Baedeker, and I heard nothing till a clock struck twelve. At the last stroke I heard a snort and then a gasp and a cry from the bed. I started up, and looked round. Jameson was slipping out with his feet onto the floor.

"Confound you!" said he angrily, "you are a fine watch, you are, to let Mustapha steal in on tiptoe whilst you are cartouching and all that sort of rubbish. He was at me again, and if I had not been sharp he'd have cut my throat. I won't go to bed any more!"

"Well, sit up. But I assure you no one has been here."

"That's fine. How can you tell? You had your back to me, and these devils of fellows steal about like cats. You can't hear them till they are at you."

It was of no use arguing with Jameson, so I let him have his way.

"I can feel all the three places in my throat where he ran the knife in," said he. "And—don't you notice?—I speak with difficulty."

So we sat up together the rest of the night. He became more reasonable as dawn came on, and inclined to admit that he had been a prey to fancies. The day passed very much as did others—Jameson was dull and sulky. After *déjeuner* he sat on at table when the ladies had risen and retired, and the gentlemen had formed in knots at the window, discussing what was to be done in the afternoon. Suddenly Jameson, whose head had begun to nod, started up with an oath and threw down his chair.

"You fellows!" he said, "you are all in league against me. You let that Mustapha come in without a word, and try to stick his knife into me."

"He has not been here."

"It's a plant. You are combined to bully me and drive me away. You don't like me. You have engaged Mustapha to murder me. This is the fourth time he has tried to cut my throat, and in the *sale à manger*, too, with you all standing round. You ought to be ashamed to call yourselves Englishmen. I'll go to Cairo. I'll complain."

It really seemed that the feeble brain of Jameson was affected. The Oxford don undertook to sit up in the room the following night.

The young man was fagged and sleep-weary, but no sooner did his eyes close, and clouds form about his head, than he was brought to wakefulness again by the same fancy or dream. The Oxford don had more trouble with him on the second night than I had on the first, for his lapses into sleep were more frequent, and each such lapse was succeeded by a start and a panic.

The next day he was worse, and we felt that he could no longer be left alone. The third night the attaché sat up to watch him.

Jameson had now sunk into a sullen mood. He would not speak, except to himself, and then only to grumble.

During the night, without being aware of it, the young attaché, who had taken a couple of magazines with him to read, fell asleep. When he went off he did not know. He woke just before dawn, and in a spasm of terror and self-reproach saw that Jameson's chair was empty.

Jameson was not on his bed. He could not be found in the hotel. At dawn he was found—dead, at the door of the mosque, with his throat cut.

The Nemesis of Fire

Algernon Blackwood

I

By some means which I never could fathom, John Silence always contrived to keep the compartment to himself, and as the train had a clear run of two hours before the first stop, there was ample time to go over the preliminary facts of the case. He had telephoned to me that very morning, and even through the disguise of the miles of wire the thrill of incalculable adventure had sounded in his voice.

"As if it were an ordinary country visit," he called, in reply to my question; "and don't forgot to bring your gun."

"With blank cartridges, I suppose?" for I knew his rigid principles with regard to the taking of life, and guessed that the guns were merely for some obvious purpose of disguise

Then he thanked me for coming, mentioned the train, snapped down the receiver, and left me, vibrating with the excitement of anticipation, to do my packing. For the honour of accompanying Dr. John Silence on one of his big cases was what many would have considered an empty honour—and risky. Certainly the adventure held all manner of possibilities, and I arrived at Waterloo with the feelings of a man who is about to embark on some dangerous and peculiar mission in which the dangers he expects to run will not be the ordinary dangers to life and limb, but of some secret character difficult to name and still more difficult to cope with.

"The Manor House has a high sound," he told me, as we sat with our feet up and talked, "but I believe it is little more than an overgrown farmhouse in the desolate heather country beyond D—, and its owner, Colonel Wragge, a retired soldier with a taste for books, lives there practically alone, I understand, with an elderly invalid sister. So you need not look forward to a lively visit, unless the case provides some excitement of its own."

"Which is likely?"

By way of reply he handed me a letter marked "Private." It was dated a week ago, and signed "Yours faithfully, Horace Wragge."

"He heard of me, you see, through Captain Anderson," the doctor explained modestly, as though his fame were not almost world-wide; "you remember that Indian obsession case—"

I read the letter. Why it should have been marked private was difficult to understand. It was very brief, direct, and to the point. It referred by way of introduction to Captain Anderson, and then stated quite simply that the writer needed help of a peculiar kind and asked for a personal interview—a morning interview, since it was impossible for him to be absent from the house at night. The letter was dignified even to the point of abruptness, and it is difficult to explain how it managed to convey to me the impression of a strong man, shaken and perplexed. Perhaps the restraint of the wording, and the mystery of the affair had something to do with it; and the reference to the Anderson case, the horror of which lay still vivid in my memory, may have touched the sense of something rather ominous and alarming. But, whatever the cause, there was no doubt that an impression of serious peril rose somehow out of that white paper with the few lines of firm writing, and the spirit of a deep uneasiness ran between the words and reached the mind without any visible form of expression.

"And when you saw him—?" I asked, returning the letter as the train rushed clattering noisily through Clapham Junction.

"I have not seen him," was the reply. "The man's mind was charged to the brim when he wrote that; full of vivid mental pictures. Notice the restraint of it. For the main character of his case psychometry could be depended upon, and the scrap of paper his hand has touched is sufficient to give to another mind—a sensitive and sympathetic mind—clear mental pictures of what is going on. I think I have a very sound general idea of his problem."

"So there may be excitement, after all?"

John Silence waited a moment before he replied.

"Something very serious is amiss there," he said gravely, at length. "Some one—not himself, I gather,—has been meddling with a rather dangerous kind of gunpowder. So—yes, there may be excitement, as you put it."

"And my duties?" I asked, with a decidedly growing interest. "Remember, I am your 'assistant.'"

"Behave like an intelligent confidential secretary. Observe everything, without seeming to. Say nothing—nothing that means anything. Be present at all interviews. I may ask a good deal of you, for if my impressions are correct this is—"

He broke off suddenly.

"But I won't tell you my impressions yet," he resumed after a moment's thought. "Just watch and listen as the case proceeds. Form your own impressions and cultivate your intuitions. We come as ordinary visitors, of course," he added, a twinkle showing for an instant in his eye; "hence, the guns."

Though disappointed not to hear more, I recognised the wisdom of his words and knew how valueless my impressions would be once the powerful suggestion of having heard his own lay behind them. I likewise reflected that intuition joined to a sense of humour was of more use to a man than double the quantity of mere "brains," as such.

Before putting the letter away, however, he handed it back, telling me to place it against my forehead for a few moments and then describe any pictures that came spontaneously into my mind.

"Don't deliberately look for anything. Just imagine you see the inside of the eyelid, and wait for pictures that rise against its dark screen."

I followed his instructions, making my mind as nearly blank as possible. But no visions came. I saw nothing but the lines of light that pass to and fro like the changes of a kaleidoscope across the blackness. A momentary sensation of warmth came and went curiously.

"You see—what?" he asked presently.

"Nothing," I was obliged to admit disappointedly; "nothing but the usual flashes of light one always sees. Only, perhaps, they are more vivid than usual."

He said nothing by way of comment or reply.

"And they group themselves now and then," I continued, with painful candour, for I longed to see the pictures he had spoken of, "group themselves into globes and round balls of fire, and the lines that flash about sometimes look like triangles and crosses—almost like geometrical figures. Nothing more."

I opened my eyes again, and gave him back the letter.

"It makes my head hot," I said, feeling somehow unworthy for not seeing anything of interest. But the look in his eyes arrested my attention at once.

"That sensation of heat is important," he said significantly.

"It was certainly real, and rather uncomfortable," I replied, hoping he would expand and explain. "There was a distinct feeling of warmth—internal warmth somewhere—oppressive in a sense."

"That is interesting," he remarked, putting the letter back in his pocket, and settling himself in the corner with newspapers and books. He vouchsafed nothing more, and I knew the uselessness of trying to make him talk. Following his example I settled likewise with magazines into my corner. But when I closed my eyes again to look for the flashing lights and the sensation of heat, I found nothing but the usual phantasmagoria of the day's events—faces, scenes, memories,—and in due course I fell asleep and then saw nothing at all of any kind.

When we left the train, after six hours' travelling, at a little wayside station standing without trees in a world of sand and heather, the late October shadows had already dropped their sombre veil upon the landscape, and the sun dipped almost out of sight behind the moorland hills. In a high dogcart, behind a fast horse, we were soon rattling across the undulating stretches of an open and bleak country, the keen air stinging our cheeks and the scents of pine and bracken strong about us. Bare hills were faintly visible against the horizon, and the coachman pointed to a bank of distant shadows on our left where he told us the sea lay. Occasional stone farmhouses, standing back from the road among straggling fir trees, and large black barns that seemed to shift past us with a movement of their own in the gloom, were the only signs of humanity and civilisation that we saw, until at the end of a bracing five miles the lights of the lodge gates flared before us and we plunged into a thick grove of pine trees that concealed the Manor House up to the moment of actual arrival.

Colonel Wragge himself met us in the hall. He was the typical army officer who had seen service, real service, and found himself in the process. He was tall and well built, broad in the shoulders, but lean as a greyhound, with grave eyes, rather stern, and a moustache turning grey. I judged him to be about sixty years of age, but his movements showed a suppleness of strength and agility that contradicted the years. The face was full of character and resolution, the face of a man to be depended upon, and the straight grey eyes, it seemed to me, wore a veil of perplexed anxiety that he made no attempt to disguise. The whole appearance of the man at once clothed the adventure with gravity and importance. A matter that gave such a man cause for serious alarm, I felt, must be something real and of genuine moment.

His speech and manner, as he welcomed us, were like his letter, simple and sincere. He had a nature as direct and undeviating as a bullet. Thus, he showed plainly his surprise that Dr. Silence had not come alone.

"My confidential secretary, Mr. Hubbard," the doctor said, introducing me, and the steady gaze and powerful shake of the hand I then received were well calculated, I remember thinking, to drive home the impression that here was a man who was not to be trifled with, and whose perplexity must spring from some very real and tangible cause. And, quite obviously, he was relieved that we had come. His welcome was unmistakably genuine.

He led us at once into a room, half library, half smoking-room, that opened out of the low-ceilinged hall. The Manor House gave the impression of a rambling and glorified farmhouse, solid, ancient, comfortable, and wholly unpretentious. And so it was. Only the heat of the place struck me as unnatural. This room with the blazing fire may have seemed uncomfortably warm after the long drive through the night air; yet it seemed to me that the hall itself, and the whole atmosphere of the house, breathed a warmth that hardly belonged to well-filled grates or the pipes of hot air and water. It was not the heat of the greenhouse; it was an oppressive heat that somehow got into the head and mind. It stirred a curious sense of uneasiness in me, and I caught myself thinking of the sensation of warmth that had emanated from the letter in the train.

I heard him thanking Dr. Silence for having come; there was no preamble, and the exchange of civilities was of the briefest description. Evidently here was a man who, like my companion, loved action rather than talk. His manner was straightforward and direct. I saw him in a flash: puzzled, worried, harassed into a state of alarm by something he could not comprehend; forced to deal with things he would have preferred to despise, yet facing it all with dogged seriousness and making no attempt to conceal that he felt secretly ashamed of his incompetence.

"So I cannot offer you much entertainment beyond that of my own company, and the queer business that has been going on here, and is still going on," he said, with a slight inclination of the head towards me by way of including me in his confidence.

"I think, Colonel Wragge," replied John Silence impressively, "that we shall none of us find the time hangs heavy. I gather we shall have our hands full."

The two men looked at one another for the space of some seconds, and there was an indefinable quality in their silence which for the first time made me admit a swift question into my mind; and I wondered a little at my rashness in coming with so little reflection into a big case of this incalculable doctor. But no answer suggested itself, and to withdraw was, of course, inconceivable. The gates had closed behind me now, and the spirit of the adventure was already besieging my mind with its advance guard of a thousand little hopes and fears.

Explaining that he would wait till after dinner to discuss anything serious, as no reference was ever made before his sister, he led the way upstairs and showed us personally to our rooms; and it was just as I was finishing dressing that a knock came at my door and Dr. Silence entered.

He was always what is called a serious man, so that even in moments of comedy you felt he never lost sight of the profound gravity of life, but as he came across the room to me I caught the expression of his face and understood in a flash that he was now in his most grave and earnest mood. He looked almost troubled. I stopped fumbling with my black tie and stared.

"It is serious," he said, speaking in a low voice, "more so even than I imagined. Colonel Wragge's control over his thoughts concealed a great deal in my psychometrising of the letter. I looked in to warn you to keep yourself well in hand—generally speaking."

"Haunted house?" I asked, conscious of a distinct shiver down my back.

But he smiled gravely at the question.

"Haunted House of Life more likely," he replied, and a look came into his eyes which I had only seen there when a human soul was in the toils and he was thick in the fight of rescue. He was stirred in the deeps.

"Colonel Wragge—or the sister?" I asked hurriedly, for the gong was sounding.

"Neither directly," he said from the door. "Something far older, something very, very remote indeed. This thing has to do with the ages, unless I am mistaken greatly, the ages on which the mists of memory have long lain undisturbed."

He came across the floor very quickly with a finger on his lips, looking at me with a peculiar searchingness of gaze.

"Are you aware yet of anything—odd here?" he asked in a whisper. "Anything you cannot quite define, for instance. Tell me, Hubbard, for I want to know all your impressions. They may help me."

I shook my head, avoiding his gaze, for there was something in the eyes that scared me a little. But he was so in earnest that I set my mind keenly searching.

"Nothing yet," I replied truthfully, wishing I could confess to a real emotion; "nothing but the strange heat of the place."

He gave a little jump forward in my direction.

"The heat again, that's it!" he exclaimed, as though glad of my corroboration. "And how would you describe it, perhaps?" he asked quickly, with a hand on the door knob.

"It doesn't seem like ordinary physical heat," I said, casting about in my thoughts for a definition.

"More a mental heat," he interrupted, "a glowing of thought and desire, a sort of feverish warmth of the spirit. Isn't that it?"

I admitted that he had exactly described my sensations.

"Good!" he said, as he opened the door, and with an indescribable gesture that combined a warning to be ready with a sign of praise for my correct intuition, he was gone.

I hurried after him, and found the two men waiting for me in front of the fire.

"I ought to warn you," our host was saying as I came in, "that my sister, whom you will meet at dinner, is not aware of the real object of your visit. She is under the impression that we are interested in the same line of study—folklore—and that your researches have led to my seeking acquaintance. She comes to dinner in her chair, you know. It will be a great pleasure to her to meet you both. We have few visitors."

So that on entering the dining-room we were prepared to find Miss Wragge already at her place, seated in a sort of bath-chair. She was a vivacious and charming old lady, with smiling expression and bright eyes, and she chatted all through dinner with unfailing spontaneity. She had that face, unlined and fresh, that some people carry through life from the cradle to the grave; her smooth plump cheeks were all pink and white, and her hair, still dark, was divided into two glossy and sleek halves on either side of a careful parting. She wore gold-rimmed glasses, and at her throat was a large scarab of green jasper that made a very handsome brooch.

Her brother and Dr. Silence talked little, so that most of the conversation was carried on between herself and me, and she told me a great deal about the history of the old house, most of which I fear I listened to with but half an ear.

"And when Cromwell stayed here," she babbled on, "he occupied the very rooms upstairs that used to be mine. But my brother thinks it safer for me to sleep on the ground floor now in case of fire."

And this sentence has stayed in my memory only because of the sudden way her brother interrupted her and instantly led the conversation on to another topic. The passing reference to fire seemed to have disturbed him, and thenceforward he directed the talk himself.

It was difficult to believe that this lively and animated old lady, sitting beside me and taking so eager an interest in the affairs of life, was practically, we understood, without the use of her lower limbs, and that her whole existence for years had been passed between the sofa, the bed, and the bath-chair in which she chatted so naturally at the dinner table. She made no allusion to her affliction until the dessert was reached, and then, touching a bell, she made us a witty little speech about leaving us "like time, on noiseless feet," and was wheeled out of the room by the butler and carried off to her apartments at the other end of the house.

And the rest of us were not long in following suit, for Dr. Silence and myself were quite as eager to learn the nature of our errand as our host was to impart it to us. He led us down a long flagged passage to a room at the very end of the house, a room provided with double doors, and windows, I saw, heavily shuttered. Books lined the walls on every side, and a large desk in the bow window was piled up with volumes, some open, some shut, some showing scraps of paper stuck between the leaves, and all smothered in a general cataract of untidy foolscap and loose-half sheets.

"My study and workroom," explained Colonel Wragge, with a delightful touch of innocent pride, as though he were a very serious scholar. He placed arm-chairs for us round the fire. "Here," he added significantly, "we shall be safe from interruption and can talk securely."

During dinner the manner of the doctor had been all that was natural and spontaneous, though it was impossible for me, knowing him as I did, not to be aware that he was subconsciously very keenly alert and already receiving upon the ultra-sensitive surface of his mind various and vivid impressions; and there was now something in the gravity of his face, as well as in the significant tone of Colonel Wragge's speech, and something, too, in the fact that we three were shut away in this private chamber about to listen to things probably strange, and certainly mysterious—something in all this that touched my imagination sharply and sent an undeniable thrill along my nerves. Taking the chair indicated by my host, I lit my cigar and waited for the opening of the attack, fully conscious that we were now too far gone in the adventure to admit of withdrawal, and wondering a little anxiously where it was going to lead.

What I expected precisely, it is hard to say. Nothing definite, perhaps. Only the sudden change was dramatic. A few hours before the prosaic atmosphere of Piccadilly was about me, and now I was sitting in a secret chamber of this remote old building waiting to hear an account of things that held possibly the genuine heart of terror. I thought of the dreary moors and hills outside, and the dark pine copses soughing in the wind of night; I remembered my companion's singular words up in my bedroom before dinner; and then I turned and noted carefully the stern countenance of the Colonel as he faced us and lit his big black cigar before speaking.

The threshold of an adventure, I reflected as I waited for the first words, is always the most thrilling moment—until the climax comes.

But Colonel Wragge hesitated—mentally—a long time before he began. He talked briefly of our journey, the weather, the country, and other comparatively trivial topics, while he sought about in his mind for an appropriate entry into the subject that was uppermost in the thoughts of all of us. The fact was he found it a difficult matter to speak of at all, and it was Dr. Silence who finally showed him the way over the hedge.

"Mr. Hubbard will take a few notes when you are ready—you won't object," he suggested; "I can give my undivided attention in this way."

"By all means," turning to reach some of the loose sheets on the writing table, and glancing at me. He still hesitated a little, I thought. "The fact is," he said apologetically, "I wondered if it was quite fair to trouble you so soon. The daylight might suit you better to hear what I have to tell. Your sleep, I mean, might be less disturbed, perhaps."

"I appreciate your thoughtfulness," John Silence replied with his gentle smile, taking command as it were from that moment, "but really we are both quite immune. There is nothing, I think, that could prevent either of us sleeping, except—an outbreak of fire, or some such very physical disturbance."

Colonel Wragge raised his eyes and looked fixedly at him. This reference to an outbreak of fire I felt sure was made with a purpose. It certainly had the desired effect of removing from our host's manner the last signs of hesitancy.

"Forgive me," he said. "Of course, I know nothing of your methods in matters of this kind—so, perhaps, you would like me to begin at once and give you an outline of the situation?"

Dr. Silence bowed his agreement. "I can then take my precautions accordingly," he added calmly.

The soldier looked up for a moment as though he did not quite gather the meaning of these words; but he made no further comment and turned at once to tackle a subject on which he evidently talked with diffidence and unwillingness.

"It's all so utterly out of my line of things," he began, puffing out clouds of cigar smoke between his words, "and there's so little to tell with any real evidence behind it, that it's almost impossible to make a consecutive story for you. It's the total cumulative effect that is so—so disquieting." He chose his words with care, as though determined not to travel one hair's breadth beyond the truth.

"I came into this place twenty years ago when my elder brother died," he continued, "but could not afford to live here then. My sister, whom you met at dinner, kept house for him till the end, and during all these years, while I was seeing service abroad, she had an eye to the place—for we never got a satisfactory tenant—and saw that it was not allowed to go to ruin. I myself took possession, however, only a year ago.

"My brother," he went on, after a perceptible pause, "spent much of his time away, too. He was a great traveller, and filled the house with stuff he brought home from all over the world. The laundry—a small detached building beyond the servants' quarters—he turned into a regular little museum. The curios and things I have cleared away—they collected dust and were always getting broken—but the laundry-house you shall see tomorrow."

Colonel Wragge spoke with such deliberation and with so many pauses that this beginning took him a long time. But at this point he came to a full stop altogether. Evidently there was something he wished to say that cost him considerable effort. At length he looked up steadily into my companion's face.

"May I ask you—that is, if you won't think it strange," he said, and a sort of hush came over his voice and manner, "whether you have noticed anything at all unusual—anything queer, since you came into the house?"

Dr. Silence answered without a moment's hesitation.

"I have," he said. "There is a curious sensation of heat in the place."

"Ah!" exclaimed the other, with a slight start. "You *have* noticed it. This unaccountable heat—"

"But its cause, I gather, is not in the house itself—but outside," I was astonished to hear the doctor add.

Colonel Wragge rose from his chair and turned to unhook a framed map that hung upon the wall. I got the impression that the movement was made with the deliberate purpose of concealing his face.

"Your diagnosis, I believe, is amazingly accurate," he said after a moment, turning round with the map in his hands. "Though, of course, I can have no idea how you should guess—"

John Silence shrugged his shoulders expressively. "Merely my impression," he said. "If you pay attention to impressions, and do not allow them to be confused by deductions of the intellect, you will often find them surprisingly, uncannily, accurate."

Colonel Wragge resumed his seat and laid the map upon his knees. His face was very thoughtful as he plunged abruptly again into his story.

"On coming into possession," he said, looking us alternately in the face, "I found a crop of stories of the most extraordinary and impossible kind I had ever heard—stories which at first I treated with amused indifference, but later was forced to regard seriously, if only to keep my servants. These stories I thought I traced to the fact of my brother's death—and, in a way, I think so still."

He leant forward and handed the map to Dr. Silence.

"It's an old plan of the estate," he explained, "but accurate enough for our purpose, and I wish you would note the position of the plantations marked upon it, especially those near the house. That one," indicating the spot with his finger, "is called the Twelve Acre Plantation. It was just there, on the side nearest the house, that my brother and the head keeper met their deaths."

He spoke as a man forced to recognise facts that he deplored, and would have preferred to leave untouched—things he personally would rather have treated with ridicule if possible. It made his words peculiarly dignified and impressive, and I listened with an increasing uneasiness as to the sort of help the doctor would look to me for later. It seemed as though I were a spectator of some drama of mystery in which any moment I might be summoned to play a part.

"It was twenty years ago," continued the Colonel, "but there was much talk about it at the time, unfortunately, and you may, perhaps, have heard of the affair. Stride, the keeper, was a passionate, hot-tempered man but I regret to say, so was my brother, and quarrels between them seem to have been frequent."

"I do not recall the affair," said the doctor. "May I ask what was the cause of death?" Something in his voice made me prick up my ears for the reply.

"The keeper, it was said, from suffocation. And at the inquest the doctors averred that both men had been dead the same length of time when found."

"And your brother?" asked John Silence, noticing the omission, and listening intently.

"Equally mysterious," said our host, speaking in a low voice with effort. "But there was one distressing feature I think I ought to mention. For those who saw the face—I did not see it myself—and though Stride carried a gun its chambers were undischarged—" He stammered and hesitated with confusion. Again that sense of terror moved between his words. He stuck.

"Yes," said the chief listener sympathetically.

"My brother's face, they said, looked as though it had been scorched. It had been swept, as it were, by something that burned—blasted. It was, I am told, quite dreadful. The bodies were found lying side by side, faces downwards, both pointing away from the wood, as though they had been in the act of running, and not more than a dozen yards from its edge."

Dr. Silence made no comment. He appeared to be studying the map attentively.

"I did not see the face myself," repeated the other, his manner somehow expressing the sense of awe he contrived to keep out of his voice, "but my sister unfortunately did, and her present state I believe to be entirely due to the shock it gave to her nerves. She never can be brought to refer to it, naturally, and I am even inclined to think that the memory has mercifully been permitted to vanish from her mind. But she spoke of it at the time as a face swept by flame—blasted."

John Silence looked up from his contemplation of the map, but with the air of one who wished to listen, not to speak, and presently Colonel Wragge went on with his account. He stood on the mat, his broad shoulders hiding most of the mantelpiece.

"They all centred about this particular plantation, these stories. That was to be expected, for the people here are as superstitious as Irish peasantry, and though I made one or two examples among them to stop the foolish talk, it had no effect, and new versions came to my ears every week. You may imagine how little good dismissals did, when I tell you that the servants dismissed themselves. It was not the house servants, but the men who worked on the estate outside. The keepers gave notice one after another, none of them with any reason I could accept; the foresters refused to enter the wood, and the beaters to beat in it. Word flew all over the countryside that Twelve Acre Plantation was a place to be avoided, day or night.

"There came a point," the Colonel went on, now well in his swing, "when I felt compelled to make investigations on my own account. I could not kill the thing by ignoring it; so I collected and analysed the stories at first hand. For this Twelve Acre Wood, you will see by the map, comes rather near home. Its lower end, if you will look, almost touches the end of the back lawn, as I will show you tomorrow, and its dense growth of pines forms the chief protection the house enjoys from the east winds that blow up from the sea. And in olden days, before my brother interfered with it and frightened all the game away, it was one of the best pheasant coverts on the whole estate."

"And what form, if I may ask, did this interference take?" asked Dr. Silence.

"In detail, I cannot tell you, for I do not know—except that I understand it was the subject of his frequent differences with the head keeper; but during the last two years of his life, when he gave up travelling and settled down here, he took a special interest in this wood, and for some unaccountable reason began to build a low stone wall around it. This wall was never finished, but you shall see the ruins tomorrow in the daylight."

"And the result of your investigations—these stories, I mean?" the doctor broke in, anxious to keep him to the main issues.

"Yes, I'm coming to that," he said slowly, "but the wood first, for this wood out of which they grew like mushrooms has nothing in any way peculiar about it. It is very thickly grown, and rises to a clearer part in the centre, a sort of mound where there is a circle of large boulders—old Druid stones, I'm told. At another place there's a small pond. There's nothing distinctive about it that I could mention—just an ordinary pine-wood, a very ordinary pine-wood—only the trees are a bit twisted in the trunks, some of 'em, and very dense. Nothing more.

"And the stories? Well, none of them had anything to do with my poor brother, or the keeper, as you might have expected; and they were all odd—such odd things, I mean, to invent or imagine. I never could make out how these people got such notions into their heads."

He paused a moment to relight his cigar.

"There's no regular path through it," he resumed, puffing vigorously, "but the fields round it are constantly used, and one of the gardeners whose cottage lies over that way declared he often saw moving lights in it at night, and luminous shapes like globes of fire over the tops of the trees, skimming and floating, and making a soft hissing sound—most of 'em said that, in fact—and another man saw shapes flitting in and out among the trees, things that were neither men nor animals, and all faintly luminous. No one ever pretended to see human forms—always queer, huge things they could not properly describe. Sometimes the whole wood was lit up, and one fellow—he's still here and you shall see him—has a most circumstantial yarn about having seen great stars lying on the ground round the edge of the wood at regular intervals—"

"What kind of stars?" put in John Silence sharply, in a sudden way that made me start.

"Oh, I don't know quite; ordinary stars, I think he said, only very large, and apparently blazing as though the ground was alight. He was too terrified to go close and examine, and he has never seen them since."

He stooped and stirred the fire into a welcome blaze—welcome for its blaze of light rather than for its heat. In the room there was already a strange pervading sensation of warmth that was oppressive in its effect and far from comforting.

"Of course," he went on, straightening up again on the mat, "this was all commonplace enough—this seeing lights and figures at night. Most of these fellows drink, and imagination and terror between them may account for almost anything. But others saw things in broad daylight. One of the woodmen, a sober, respectable man, took the shortcut home to his midday meal, and swore he was followed the whole length of the wood by something that never showed itself, but dodged from tree to tree, always keeping out of sight, yet solid enough to make the branches sway and the twigs snap on the ground. And it made a noise, he declared—but really" —the speaker stopped and gave a short laugh— "it's too absurd—"

"*Please!*" insisted the doctor; "for it is these small details that give me the best clues always."

"—it made a crackling noise, he said, like a bonfire. Those were his very words: like the crackling of a bonfire," finished the soldier, with a repetition of his short laugh.

"Most interesting," Dr. Silence observed gravely. "Please omit nothing."

"Yes," he went on, "and it was soon after that the fires began—the fires in the wood. They started mysteriously burning in the patches of coarse white grass that cover the more open parts of the plantation. No one ever actually saw them start, but many, myself among the number, have seen them burning and smouldering. They are always small and circular in shape, and for all the world like a picnic fire. The head keeper has a dozen explanations, from sparks flying out of the house chimneys to the sunlight focusing through a dewdrop, but none of them, I must admit, convince me as being in the least likely or probable. They are most singular, I consider, most singular, these mysterious fires, and I am glad to say that they come only at rather long intervals and never seem to spread.

"But the keeper had other queer stories as well, and about things that are verifiable. He declared that no life ever willingly entered the plantation; more, that no life existed in it at all. No birds nested in the trees, or flew into their shade. He set countless traps, but never caught so much as a rabbit or a weasel. Animals avoided it, and more than once he had picked up dead creatures round the edges that bore no obvious signs of how they had met their death.

"Moreover, he told me one extraordinary tale about his retriever chasing some invisible creature across the field one day when he was out with his gun. The dog suddenly pointed at something in the field at his feet, and then gave chase, yelping like a mad thing. It followed its imaginary quarry to the borders of the wood, and then went in—a thing he had never known it to do before. The moment it crossed the edge—it is darkish in there even in daylight—it began fighting in the most frenzied and terrific fashion. It made him afraid to interfere, he said. And at last, when the dog came out, hanging its tail down and panting, he found something like white hair stuck to its jaws, and brought it to show me. I tell you these details because—"

"They are important, believe me," the doctor stopped him. "And you have it still, this hair?" he asked.

"It disappeared in the oddest way," the Colonel explained. "It was curious looking stuff, something like asbestos, and I sent it to be analysed by the local chemist. But either the man got wind of its origin, or else he didn't like the look of it for some reason, because he returned it to me and said it was neither animal, vegetable, nor mineral, so far as he could make out, and he didn't wish to have anything to do with it. I put it away in paper, but a week later, on opening the package—it was gone! Oh, the stories are simply endless. I could tell you hundreds all on the same lines."

"And personal experiences of your own, Colonel Wragge?" asked John Silence earnestly, his manner showing the greatest possible interest and sympathy.

The soldier gave an almost imperceptible start. He looked distinctly uncomfortable.

"Nothing, I think," he said slowly, "nothing—er—I should like to rely on. I mean nothing I have the right to speak of, perhaps—yet."

His mouth closed with a snap. Dr. Silence, after waiting a little to see if he would add to his reply, did not seek to press him on the point.

"Well," he resumed presently, and as though he would speak contemptuously, yet dared not, "this sort of thing has gone on at intervals ever since. It spreads like wildfire, of course, mysterious chatter of this kind, and people began trespassing all over the estate, coming to see the wood, and making themselves a general nuisance. Notices of man-traps and spring-guns only seemed to increase their persistence; and—think of it," he snorted, "some local Research Society actually wrote and asked permission for one of their members to spend a night in the wood! Bolder fools, who didn't write for leave, came and took away bits of bark from the trees and gave them to clairvoyants, who invented in their turn a further batch of tales. There was simply no end to it all."

"Most distressing and annoying, I can well believe," interposed the doctor.

"Then suddenly, the phenomena ceased as mysteriously as they had begun, and the interest flagged. The tales stopped. People got interested in something else. It all seemed to die out. This was last July. I can tell you exactly, for I've kept a diary more or less of what happened."

"Ah!"

"But now, quite recently, within the past three weeks, it has all revived again with a rush—with a kind of furious attack, so to speak. It has really become unbearable. You may imagine what it means, and the general state of affairs, when I say that the possibility of leaving has occurred to me."

"Incendiarism?" suggested Dr. Silence, half under his breath, but not so low that Colonel Wragge did not hear him.

"By Jove, sir, you take the very words out of my mouth!" exclaimed the astonished man, glancing from the doctor to me and from me to the doctor, and rattling the money in his pocket as though some explanation of my friend's divining powers were to be found that way.

"It's only that you are thinking very vividly," the doctor said quietly, "and your thoughts form pictures in my mind before you utter them. It's merely a little elementary thought-reading."

His intention, I saw, was not to perplex the good man, but to impress him with his powers so as to ensure obedience later.

"Good Lord! I had no idea—" He did not finish the sentence, and dived again abruptly into his narrative.

"I did not see anything myself, I must admit, but the stories of independent eye-witnesses were to the effect that lines of light, like streams of thin fire, moved through the wood and sometimes were seen to shoot out precisely as flames might shoot out—in the direction of this house. There," he explained, in a louder voice that made me jump, pointing with a thick finger to the map, "where the westerly fringe of the plantation comes up to the end of the lower lawn at the back of the house—where it links on to those dark patches, which are laurel shrubberies, running right up to the back premises—that's where these lights were seen. They passed from the wood to the shrubberies, and in this way reached the house itself. Like silent rockets, one man described them, rapid as lightning and exceedingly bright."

"And this evidence you spoke of?"

"They actually reached the sides of the house. They've left a mark of scorching on the walls—the walls of the laundry building at the other end. You shall see 'em tomorrow." He pointed to the map to indicate the spot, and then straightened himself and glared about the room as though he had said something no one could believe and expected contradiction.

"Scorched—just as the faces were," the doctor murmured, looking significantly at me.

"Scorched—yes," repeated the Colonel, failing to catch the rest of the sentence in his excitement.

There was a prolonged silence in the room, in which I heard the gurgling of the oil in the lamp and the click of the coals and the heavy breathing of our host. The most unwelcome sensations were creeping about my spine, and I wondered whether my companion would scorn me utterly if I asked to sleep on the sofa in his room. It was eleven o'clock, I saw by the clock on the mantelpiece. We had crossed the dividing line and were now well in the movement of the adventure. The fight between my interest and my dread became acute. But, even if turning back had been possible, I think the interest would have easily gained the day.

"I have enemies, of course," I heard the Colonel's rough voice break into the pause presently, "and have discharged a number of servants—"

"It's not that," put in John Silence briefly.

"You think not? In a sense I am glad, and yet—there are some things that can be met and dealt with—"

He left the sentence unfinished, and looked down at the floor with an expression of grim severity that betrayed a momentary glimpse of character. This fighting man loathed and abhorred the thought of an enemy he could not see and come to grips with. Presently he moved over and sat down in the chair between us. Something like a sigh escaped him. Dr. Silence said nothing.

"My sister, of course, is kept in ignorance, as far as possible, of all this," he said disconnectedly, and as if talking to himself. "But even if she knew she would find matter-of-fact explanations. I only wish I could. I'm sure they exist."

There came then an interval in the conversation that was very significant. It did not seem a real pause, or the silence real silence, for both men continued to think so rapidly and strongly that one almost imagined their thoughts clothed themselves in words in the air of the room. I was more than a little keyed up with the strange excitement of all I had heard, but what stimulated my nerves more than anything else was the obvious fact that the doctor was clearly upon the trail of discovery. In his mind at that moment, I believe, he had already solved the nature of this perplexing psychical problem. His face was like a mask, and he employed the absolute minimum of gesture and words. All his energies were directed inwards, and by those incalculable methods and processes he had mastered with such infinite patience and study, I felt sure he was already in touch with the forces behind these singular phenomena and laying his deep plans for bringing them into the open, and then effectively dealing with them.

Colonel Wragge meanwhile grew more and more fidgety. From time to time he turned towards my companion, as though about to speak, yet always changing his mind at the last moment. Once he went over and opened the door suddenly, apparently to see if any one were listening at the keyhole, for he disappeared a moment between the two doors, and I then heard him open the outer one. He stood there for some seconds and made a noise as though he were sniffing the air like a dog. Then he closed both doors cautiously and came back to the fireplace. A strange excitement seemed growing upon him. Evidently he was trying to make up his mind to say something that he found it difficult to say. And John Silence, as I rightly judged, was waiting patiently for him to choose his own opportunity and his own way of saying it. At last he turned and faced us, squaring his great shoulders, and stiffening perceptibly.

Dr. Silence looked up sympathetically.

"Your own experiences help me most," he observed quietly.

"The fact is," the Colonel said, speaking very low, "this past week there have been outbreaks of fire in the house itself. Three separate outbreaks—and all—in my sister's room."

"Yes," the doctor said, as if this was just what he had expected to hear.

"Utterly unaccountable—all of them," added the other, and then sat down. I began to understand something of the reason of his excitement. He was realising at last that the "natural" explanation he had held to all along was becoming impossible, and he hated it. It made him angry.

"Fortunately," he went on, "she was out each time and does not know. But I have made her sleep now in a room on the ground floor."

"A wise precaution," the doctor said simply. He asked one or two questions. The fires had started in the curtains—once by the window and once by the bed. The third time smoke had been discovered by the maid coming from the cupboard, and it was found that Miss Wragge's clothes hanging on the hooks were smouldering. The doctor listened attentively, but made no comment.

"And now can you tell me," he said presently, "what your own feeling about it is—your general impression?"

"It sounds foolish to say so," replied the soldier, after a moment's hesitation, "but I feel exactly as I have often felt on active service in my Indian campaigns: just as if the house and all in it were in a state of siege; as though a concealed enemy were encamped about us—in ambush somewhere." He uttered a soft nervous laugh. "As if the next sign of smoke would precipitate a panic—a dreadful panic."

The picture came before me of the night shadowing the house, and the twisted pine trees he had described crowding about it, concealing some powerful enemy; and, glancing at the resolute face and figure of the old soldier, forced at length to his confession, I understood something of all he had been through before he sought the assistance of John Silence.

"And tomorrow, unless I am mistaken, is full moon," said the doctor suddenly, watching the other's face for the effect of his apparently careless words.

Colonel Wragge gave an uncontrollable start, and his face for the first time showed unmistakable pallor.

"What in the world—?" he began, his lip quivering.

"Only that I am beginning to see light in this extraordinary affair," returned the other calmly, "and, if my theory is correct, each month when the moon is at the full should witness an increase in the activity of the phenomena."

"I don't see the connection," Colonel Wragge answered almost savagely, "but I am bound to say my diary bears you out." He wore the most puzzled expression I have ever seen upon an honest face, but he abhorred this additional corroboration of an explanation that perplexed him.

"I confess," he repeated, "I cannot see the connection."

"Why should you?" said the doctor, with his first laugh that evening. He got up and hung the map upon the wall again. "But I do—because these things are my special study—and let me add that I have yet to come across a problem that is not natural, and has not a natural explanation. It's merely a question of how much one knows—and admits."

Colonel Wragge eyed him with a new and curious respect in his face. But his feelings were soothed. Moreover, the doctor's laugh and change of manner came as a relief to all, and broke the spell of grave suspense that had held us so long. We all rose and stretched our limbs, and took little walks about the room.

"I am glad, Dr. Silence, if you will allow me to say so, that you are here," he said simply, "very glad indeed. And now I fear I have kept you both up very late," with a glance to include me, "for you must be tired, and ready for your beds. I have told you all there is to tell," he added, "and tomorrow you must feel perfectly free to take any steps you think necessary."

The end was abrupt, yet natural, for there was nothing more to say, and neither of these men talked for mere talking's sake.

Out in the cold and chilly hall he lit our candles and took us upstairs. The house was at rest and still, every one asleep. We moved softly. Through the windows on the stairs we saw the moonlight falling across the lawn, throwing deep shadows. The nearer pine trees were just visible in the distance, a wall of impenetrable blackness.

Our host came for a moment to our rooms to see that we had everything. He pointed to a coil of strong rope lying beside the window, fastened to the wall by means of an iron ring. Evidently it had been recently put in.

"I don't think we shall need it," Dr. Silence said, with a smile.

"I trust not," replied our host gravely. "I sleep quite close to you across the landing," he whispered, pointing to his door, "and if you—if you want anything in the night you will know where to find me."

He wished us pleasant dreams and disappeared down the passage into his room, shading the candle with his big muscular hand from the draughts.

John Silence stopped me a moment before I went.

"You know what it is?" I asked, with an excitement that even overcame my weariness.

"Yes," he said, "I'm almost sure. And you?"

"Not the smallest notion."

He looked disappointed, but not half as disappointed as I felt.

"Egypt," he whispered, "Egypt!"

II

Nothing happened to disturb me in the night—nothing, that is, except a nightmare in which Colonel Wragge chased me amid thin streaks of fire, and his sister always prevented my escape by suddenly rising up out of the ground in her chair—dead. The deep baying of dogs woke me once, just before the dawn, it must have been, for I saw the window frame against the sky; there was a flash of lightning, too, I thought, as I turned over in bed. And it was warm, for October oppressively warm.

It was after eleven o'clock when our host suggested going out with the guns, these, we understood, being a somewhat thin disguise for our true purpose. Personally, I was glad to be in the open air, for the atmosphere of the house was heavy with presentiment. The sense of impending disaster hung over all. Fear stalked the passages, and lurked in the corners of every room. It was a house haunted, but really haunted; not by some vague shadow of the dead, but by a definite though incalculable influence that was actively alive, and dangerous. At the least smell of smoke the entire household quivered. An odour of burning, I was convinced, would paralyse all the inmates. For the servants, though professedly ignorant by the master's unspoken orders, yet shared the common dread; and the hideous uncertainty, joined with this display of so spiteful and calculated a spirit of malignity, provided a kind of black doom that draped not only the walls, but also the minds of the people living within them.

Only the bright and cheerful vision of old Miss Wragge being pushed about the house in her noiseless chair, chatting and nodding briskly to every one she met, prevented us from giving way entirely to the depression which governed the majority. The sight of her was like a gleam of sunshine through the depths of some ill-omened wood, and just as we went out I saw her being wheeled along by her attendant into the sunshine of the back lawn, and caught her cheery smile as she turned her head and wished us good sport.

The morning was October at its best. Sunshine glistened on the dew-drenched grass and on leaves turned golden-red. The dainty messengers of coming hoar-frost were already in the air, a search for permanent winter quarters. From the wide moors that everywhere swept up against the sky, like a purple sea splashed by the occasional grey of rocky clefts, there stole down the cool and perfumed wind of the west. And the keen taste of the sea ran through all like a master-flavour, borne over the spaces perhaps by the seagulls that cried and circled high in the air.

But our host took little interest in this sparkling beauty, and had no thought of showing off the scenery of his property. His mind was otherwise intent, and, for that matter, so were our own.

"Those bleak moors and hills stretch unbroken for hours," he said, with a sweep of the hand; "and over there, some four miles," pointing in another direction, "lies S— Bay, a long, swampy inlet of the sea, haunted by myriads of seabirds. On the other side of the house are the plantations and pine-woods. I thought we would get the dogs and go first to the Twelve Acre Wood I told you about last night. It's quite near."

We found the dogs in the stable, and I recalled the deep baying of the night when a fine bloodhound and two great Danes leaped out to greet us. Singular companions for guns, I thought to myself, as we struck out across the fields and the great creatures bounded and ran beside us, nose to ground.

The conversation was scanty. John Silence's grave face did not encourage talk. He wore the expression I knew well—that look of earnest solicitude which meant that his whole being was deeply absorbed and preoccupied. Frightened, I had never seen him, but anxious often—it always moved me to witness it—and he was anxious now.

"On the way back you shall see the laundry building," Colonel Wragge observed shortly, for he, too, found little to say. "We shall attract less attention then."

Yet not all the crisp beauty of the morning seemed able to dispel the feelings of uneasy dread that gathered increasingly about our minds as we went.

In a very few minutes a clump of pine trees concealed the house from view, and we found ourselves on the outskirts of a densely grown plantation of conifers. Colonel Wragge stopped abruptly, and, producing a map from his pocket, explained once more very briefly its position with regard to the house. He showed how it ran up almost to the walls of the laundry building—though at the moment beyond our actual view—and pointed to the windows of his sister's bedroom where the fires had been. The room, now empty, looked straight on to the wood. Then, glancing nervously about him, and calling the dogs to heel, he proposed that we should enter the plantation and make as thorough examination of it as we thought worth while. The dogs, he added, might perhaps be persuaded to accompany us a little way—and he pointed to where they cowered at his feet—but he doubted it. "Neither voice nor whip will get them very far, I'm afraid," he said. "I know by experience."

"If you have no objection," replied Dr. Silence, with decision, and speaking almost for the first time, "we will make our examination alone—Mr. Hubbard and myself. It will be best so."

His tone was absolutely final, and the Colonel acquiesced so politely that even a less intuitive man than myself must have seen that he was genuinely relieved.

"You doubtless have good reasons," he said.

"Merely that I wish to obtain my impressions uncoloured. This delicate clue I am working on might be so easily blurred by the thought-currents of another mind with strongly preconceived ideas."

"Perfectly. I understand," rejoined the soldier, though with an expression of countenance that plainly contradicted his words. "Then I will wait here with the dogs; and we'll have a look at the laundry on our way home."

I turned once to look back as we clambered over the low stone wall built by the late owner, and saw his straight, soldierly figure standing in the sunlit field watching us with a curiously intent look on his face. There was something to me incongruous, yet distinctly pathetic, in the man's efforts to meet all far-fetched explanations of the mystery with contempt, and at the same time in his stolid, unswerving investigation of it all. He nodded at me and made a gesture of farewell with his hand. That picture of him, standing in the sunshine with his big dogs, steadily watching us, remains with me to this day.

Dr. Silence led the way in among the twisted trunks, planted closely together in serried ranks, and I followed sharp at his heels. The moment we were out of sight he turned and put down his gun against the roots of a big tree, and I did likewise.

"We shall hardly want these cumbersome weapons of murder," he observed, with a passing smile.

"You are sure of your clue, then?" I asked at once, bursting with curiosity, yet fearing to betray it lest he should think me unworthy. His own methods were so absolutely simple and untheatrical.

"I am sure of my clue," he answered gravely. "And I think we have come just in time. You shall know in due course. For the present—be content to follow and observe. And think, steadily. The support of your mind will help me."

His voice had that quiet mastery in it which leads men to face death with a sort of happiness and pride. I would have followed him anywhere at that moment. At the same time his words conveyed a sense of dread seriousness. I caught the thrill of his confidence; but also, in this broad light of day, I felt the measure of alarm that lay behind.

"You still have no strong impressions?" he asked. "Nothing happened in the night, for instance? No vivid dreamings?"

He looked closely for my answer, I was aware.

"I slept almost an unbroken sleep. I was tremendously tired, you know, and, but for the oppressive heat—"

"Good! You still notice the heat, then," he said to himself, rather than expecting an answer. "And the lightning?" he added, "that lightning out of a clear sky—that flashing—did you notice *that?*"

I answered truly that I thought I had seen a flash during a moment of wakefulness, and he then drew my attention to certain facts before moving on.

"You remember the sensation of warmth when you put the letter to your forehead in the train; the heat generally in the house last evening, and, as you now mention, in the night. You heard, too, the Colonel's stories about the appearances of fire in this wood and in the house itself, and the way his brother and the gamekeeper came to their deaths twenty years ago."

I nodded, wondering what in the world it all meant.

"And you get no clue from these facts?" he asked, a trifle surprised.

I searched every corner of my mind and imagination for some inkling of his meaning, but was obliged to admit that I understood nothing so far.

"Never mind, you will later. And now," he added, "we will go over the wood and see what we can find."

His words explained to me something of his method. We were to keep our minds alert and report to each other the least fancy that crossed the picture-gallery of our thoughts. Then, just as we started, he turned again to me with a final warning.

"And, for your safety," he said earnestly, "imagine *now*—and for that matter, imagine always until we leave this place—imagine with the utmost keenness, that you are surrounded by a shell that protects you. Picture yourself inside a protective envelope, and build it up with the most intense imagination you can evoke. Pour the whole force of your thought and will into it. Believe vividly all through this adventure that such a shell, constructed of your thought, will and imagination, surrounds you completely, and that nothing can pierce it to attack."

He spoke with dramatic conviction, gazing hard at me as though to enforce his meaning, and then moved forward and began to pick his way over the rough, tussocky ground into the wood. And meanwhile, knowing the efficacy of his prescription, I adopted it to the best of my ability.

The trees at once closed about us like the night. Their branches met overhead in a continuous tangle, their stems crept closer and closer, the brambly undergrowth thickened and multiplied. We tore our trousers, scratched our hands, and our eyes filled with fine dust that made it most difficult to avoid the clinging, prickly network of branches and creepers. Coarse white grass that caught our feet like string grew here and there in patches. It crowned the lumps of peaty growth that stuck up like human heads, fantastically dressed, thrusting up at us out of the ground with crests of dead hair. We stumbled and floundered among them. It was hard going, and I could well conceive it impossible to find a way at all in the night-time. We jumped, when possible, from tussock to tussock, and it seemed as though we were springing among heads on a battlefield, and that this dead white grass concealed eyes that turned to stare as we passed.

Here and there the sunlight shot in with vivid spots of white light, dazzling the sight, but only making the surrounding gloom deeper by contrast. And on two occasions we passed dark circular places in the grass where fires had eaten their mark and left a ring of ashes. Dr. Silence pointed to them, but without comment and without pausing, and the sight of them woke in me a singular realisation of the dread that lay so far only just out of sight in this adventure.

It was exhausting work, and heavy going. We kept close together. The warmth, too, was extraordinary. Yet it did not seem the warmth of the body due to violent exertion, but rather an inner heat of the mind that laid glowing hands of fire upon the heart and set the brain in a kind of steady blaze. When my companion found himself too far in advance, he waited for me to come up. The place had evidently been untouched by hand of man, keeper, forester or sportsman, for many a year; and my thoughts, as we advanced painfully, were not unlike the state of the wood itself—dark, confused, full of a haunting wonder and the shadow of fear.

By this time all signs of the open field behind us were hid. No single gleam penetrated. We might have been groping in the heart of some primeval forest. Then, suddenly, the brambles and tussocks and stringlike grass came to an end; the trees opened out; and the ground began to slope upwards towards a large central mound. We had reached the middle of the plantation, and before us stood the broken Druid stones our host had mentioned. We walked easily up the little hill, between the sparser stems, and, resting upon one of the ivy-covered boulders, looked round upon a comparatively open space, as large, perhaps, as a small London Square.

Thinking of the ceremonies and sacrifices this rough circle of prehistoric monoliths might have witnessed, I looked up into my companion's face with an unspoken question. But he read my thought and shook his head.

"Our mystery has nothing to do with these dead symbols," he said, "but with something perhaps even more ancient, and of another country altogether."

"Egypt?" I said half under my breath, hopelessly puzzled, but recalling his words in my bedroom.

He nodded. Mentally I still floundered, but he seemed intensely preoccupied and it was no time for asking questions; so while his words circled unintelligibly in my mind I looked round at the scene before me, glad of the opportunity to recover breath and some measure of composure. But hardly had I time to notice the twisted and contorted shapes of many of the pine trees close at hand when Dr. Silence leaned over and touched me on the shoulder. He pointed down the slope. And the look I saw in his eyes keyed up every nerve in my body to its utmost pitch.

A thin, almost imperceptible column of blue smoke was rising among the trees some twenty yards away at the foot of the mound. It curled up and up, and disappeared from sight among the tangled branches overhead. It was scarcely thicker than the smoke from a small brand of burning wood.

"Protect yourself! Imagine your shell strongly," whispered the doctor sharply, "and follow me closely."

He rose at once and moved swiftly down the slope towards the smoke, and I followed, afraid to remain alone. I heard the soft crunching of our steps on the pine needles. Over his shoulder I watched the thin blue spiral, without once taking my eyes off it. I hardly know how to describe the peculiar sense of vague horror inspired in me by the sight of that streak of smoke pencilling its way upwards among the dark trees. And the sensation of increasing heat as we approached was phenomenal. It was like walking towards a glowing yet invisible fire.

As we drew nearer his pace slackened. Then he stopped and pointed, and I saw a small circle of burnt grass upon the ground. The tussocks were blackened and smouldering, and from the centre rose this line of smoke, pale, blue, steady. Then I noticed a movement of the atmosphere beside us, as if the warm air were rising and the cooler air rushing in to take its place: a little centre of wind in the stillness. Overhead the boughs stirred and trembled where the smoke disappeared. Otherwise, not a tree sighed, not a sound made itself heard. The wood was still as a graveyard. A horrible idea came to me that the course of nature was about to change without warning, had changed a little already, that the sky would drop, or the surface of the earth crash inwards like a broken bubble. Something, certainly, reached up to the citadel of my reason, causing its throne to shake.

John Silence moved forward again. I could not see his face, but his attitude was plainly one of resolution, of muscles and mind ready for vigorous action. We were within ten feet of the blackened circle when the smoke of a sudden ceased to rise, and vanished. The tail of the column disappeared in the air above, and at the same instant it seemed to me that the sensation of heat passed from my face, and the motion of the wind was gone. The calm spirit of the fresh October day resumed command.

Side by side we advanced and examined the place. The grass was smouldering, the ground still hot. The circle of burned earth was a foot to a foot and a half in diameter. It looked like an ordinary picnic fireplace. I bent down cautiously to look, but in a second I sprang back with an involuntary cry of alarm, for, as the doctor stamped on the ashes to prevent them spreading, a sound of hissing rose from the spot as though he had kicked a living creature. This hissing was faintly audible in the air. It moved past us, away towards the thicker portion of the wood in the direction of our field, and in a second Dr. Silence had left the fire and started in pursuit.

And then began the most extraordinary hunt of invisibility I can ever conceive.

He went fast even at the beginning, and, of course, it was perfectly obvious that he was following something. To judge by the poise of his head he kept his eyes steadily at a certain level—just above the height of a man—and the consequence was he stumbled a good deal over the roughness of the ground. The hissing sound had stopped. There was no sound of any kind, and what he saw to follow was utterly beyond me. I only know, that in mortal dread of being left behind, and with a biting curiosity to see whatever there was to be seen, I followed as quickly as I could, and even then barely succeeded in keeping up with him.

And, as we went, the whole mad jumble of the Colonel's stories ran through my brain, touching a sense of frightened laughter that was only held in check by the sight of this earnest, hurrying figure before me. For John Silence at work inspired me with a kind of awe. He looked so diminutive among these giant twisted trees, while yet I knew that his purpose and his knowledge were so great, and even in hurry he was dignified. The fancy that we were playing some queer, exaggerated game together met the fact that we were two men dancing upon the brink of some possible tragedy, and the mingling of the two emotions in my mind was both grotesque and terrifying.

He never turned in his mad chase, but pushed rapidly on, while I panted after him like a figure in some unreasoning nightmare. And, as I ran, it came upon me that he had been aware all the time, in his quiet, internal way, of many things that he had kept for his own secret consideration; he had been watching, waiting, planning from the very moment we entered the shade of the wood. By some inner, concentrated process of mind, dynamic if not actually magical, he had been in direct contact with the source of the whole adventure, the very essence of the real mystery. And now the forces were moving to a climax. Something was about to happen, something important, something possibly dreadful. Every nerve, every sense, every significant gesture of the plunging figure before me proclaimed the fact just as surely as the skies, the winds, and the face of the earth tell the birds the time to migrate and warn the animals that danger lurks and they must move.

In a few moments we reached the foot of the mound and entered the tangled undergrowth that lay between us and the sunlight of the field. Here the difficulties of fast travelling increased a hundredfold. There were brambles to dodge, low boughs to dive under, and countless tree trunks closing up to make a direct path impossible. Yet Dr. Silence never seemed to falter or hesitate. He went, diving, jumping, dodging, ducking, but ever in the same main direction, following a clean trail. Twice I tripped and fell, and both times, when I picked myself up again, I saw him ahead of me, still forcing a way like a dog after its quarry. And sometimes, like a dog, he stopped and pointed—human pointing it was, psychic pointing, and each time he stopped to point I heard that faint high hissing in the air beyond us. The instinct of an infallible dowser possessed him, and he made no mistakes.

At length, abruptly, I caught up with him, and found that we stood at the edge of the shallow pond Colonel Wragge had mentioned in his account the night before. It was long and narrow, filled with dark brown water, in which the trees were dimly reflected. Not a ripple stirred its surface.

"Watch!" he cried out, as I came up. "It's going to cross. It's bound to betray itself. The water is its natural enemy, and we shall see the direction."

And, even as he spoke, a thin line like the track of a water-spider, shot swiftly across the shiny surface; there was a ghost of steam in the air above; and immediately I became aware of an odour of burning.

Dr. Silence turned and shot a glance at me that made me think of lightning. I began to shake all over.

"Quick!" he cried with excitement, "to the trail again! We must run around. It's going to the house!"

The alarm in his voice quite terrified me. Without a false step I dashed round the slippery banks and dived again at his heels into the sea of bushes and tree trunks. We were now in the thick of the very dense belt that ran around the outer edge of the plantation, and the field was near; yet so dark was the tangle that it was some time before the first shafts of white sunlight became visible. The doctor now ran in zigzags. He was following something that dodged and doubled quite wonderfully, yet had begun, I fancied, to move more slowly than before.

"Quick!" he cried. "In the light we shall lose it!"

I still saw nothing, heard nothing, caught no suggestion of a trail; yet this man, guided by some interior divining that seemed infallible, made no false turns, though how he failed to crash headlong into the trees has remained a mystery to me ever since. And then, with a sudden rush, we found ourselves on the skirts of the wood with the open field lying in bright sunshine before our eyes.

"Too late!" I heard him cry, a note of anguish in his voice. "It's out—and, by God, it's making for the house!"

I saw the Colonel standing in the field with his dogs where we had left him. He was bending double, peering into the wood where he heard us running, and he straightened up like a bent whip released. John Silence dashed passed, calling him to follow.

"We shall lose the trail in the light," I heard him cry as he ran. "But quick! We may yet get there in time!"

That wild rush across the open field, with the dogs at our heels, leaping and barking, and the elderly Colonel behind us running as though for his life, shall I ever forget it? Though I had only vague ideas of the meaning of it all, I put my best foot forward, and, being the youngest of the three, I reached the house an easy first. I drew up, panting, and turned to wait for the others. But, as I turned, something moving a little distance away caught my eye, and in that moment I swear I experienced the most overwhelming and singular shock of surprise and terror I have ever known, or can conceive as possible.

For the front door was open, and the waist of the house being narrow, I could see through the hall into the dining-room beyond, and so out on to the back lawn, and there I saw no less a sight than the figure of Miss Wragge—running. Even at that distance it was plain that she had seen me, and was coming fast towards me, running with the frantic gait of a terror-stricken woman. She had recovered the use of her legs.

Her face was a livid grey, as of death itself, but the general expression was one of laughter, for her mouth was gaping, and her eyes, always bright, shone with the light of a wild merriment that seemed the merriment of a child, yet was singularly ghastly. And that very second, as she fled past me into her brother's arms behind, I smelt again most unmistakably the odour of burning, and to this day the smell of smoke and fire can come very near to turning me sick with the memory of what I had seen.

Fast on her heels, too, came the terrified attendant, more mistress of herself, and able to speak—which the old lady could not do—but with a face almost, if not quite, as fearful.

"We were down by the bushes in the sun,"—she gasped and screamed in reply to Colonel Wragge's distracted questionings,—"I was wheeling the chair as usual when she shrieked and leaped—I don't know exactly—I was too frightened to see—Oh, my God! she jumped clean out of the chair—*and ran!* There was a blast of hot air from the wood, and she hid her face and jumped. She didn't make a sound—she didn't cry out, or make a sound. She just ran."

But the nightmare horror of it all reached the breaking point a few minutes later, and while I was still standing in the hall temporarily bereft of speech and movement; for while the doctor, the Colonel and the attendant were half-way up the staircase, helping the fainting woman to the privacy of her room, and all in a confused group of dark figures, there sounded a voice behind me, and I turned to see the butler, his face dripping with perspiration, his eyes starting out of his head.

"The laundry's on fire!" he cried; "the laundry building's a-caught!"

I remember his odd expression "a-caught," and wanting to laugh, but finding my face rigid and inflexible.

"The devil's about again, s'help me Gawd!" he cried, in a voice thin with terror, running about in circles.

And then the group on the stairs scattered as at the sound of a shot, and the Colonel and Dr. Silence came down three steps at a time, leaving the afflicted Miss Wragge to the care of her single attendant.

We were out across the front lawn in a moment and round the corner of the house, the Colonel leading, Silence and I at his heels, and the portly butler puffing some distance in the rear, getting more and more mixed in his addresses to God and the devil; and the moment we passed the stables and came into view of the laundry building, we saw a wicked-looking volume of smoke pouring out of the narrow windows, and the frightened women-servants and grooms running hither and thither, calling aloud as they ran.

The arrival of the master restored order instantly, and this retired soldier, poor thinker perhaps, but capable man of action, had the matter in hand from the start. He issued orders like a martinet, and, almost before I could realise it, there were streaming buckets on the scene and a line of men and women formed between the building and the stable pump.

"Inside," I heard John Silence cry, and the Colonel followed him through the door, while I was just quick enough at their heels to hear him add, "the smoke's the worst part of it. There's no fire yet, I think."

And, true enough, there was no fire. The interior was thick with smoke, but it speedily cleared and not a single bucket was used upon the floor or walls. The air was stifling, the heat fearful.

"There's precious little to burn in here; it's all stone," the Colonel exclaimed, coughing. But the doctor was pointing to the wooden covers of the great cauldron in which the clothes were washed, and we saw that these were smouldering and charred. And when we sprinkled half a bucket of water on them the surrounding bricks hissed and fizzed and sent up clouds of steam. Through the open door and windows this passed out with the rest of the smoke, and we three stood there on the brick floor staring at the spot and wondering, each in our own fashion, how in the name of natural law the place could have caught fire or smoked at all. And each was silent—myself from sheer incapacity and befuddlement, the Colonel from the quiet pluck that faces all things yet speaks little, and John Silence from the intense mental grappling with this latest manifestation of a profound problem that called for concentration of thought rather than for any words.

There was really nothing to say. The facts were indisputable.

Colonel Wragge was the first to utter.

"My sister," he said briefly, and moved off. In the yard I heard him sending the frightened servants about their business in an excellently matter-of-fact voice, scolding some one roundly for making such a big fire and letting the flues get over-heated, and paying no heed to the stammering reply that no fire had been lit there for several days. Then he dispatched a groom on horseback for the local doctor.

Then Dr. Silence turned and looked at me. The absolute control he possessed, not only over the outward expression of emotion by gesture, change of colour, light in the eyes, and so forth, but also, as I well knew, over its very birth in his heart, the masklike face of the dead he could assume at will, made it extremely difficult to know at any given moment what was at work in his inner consciousness. But now, when he turned and looked at me, there was no sphinx-expression there, but rather the keen triumphant face of a man who had solved a dangerous and complicated problem, and saw his way to a clean victory.

"*Now* do you guess?" he asked quietly, as though it were the simplest matter in the world, and ignorance were impossible.

I could only stare stupidly and remain silent. He glanced down at the charred cauldron-lids, and traced a figure in the air with his finger. But I was too excited, or too mortified, or still too dazed, perhaps, to see what it was he outlined, or what it was he meant to convey. I could only go on staring and shaking my puzzled head.

"A fire-elemental," he cried, "a fire-elemental of the most powerful and malignant kind—"

"A what?" thundered the voice of Colonel Wragge behind us, having returned suddenly and overheard.

"It's a fire-elemental," repeated Dr. Silence more calmly, but with a note of triumph in his voice he could not keep out, "and a fire-elemental enraged."

The light began to dawn in my mind at last. But the Colonel—who had never heard the term before, and was besides feeling considerably worked up for a plain man with all this mystery he knew not how to grapple with—the Colonel stood, with the most dumfoundered look ever seen on a human countenance, and continued to roar, and stammer, and stare.

"And why," he began, savage with the desire to find something visible he could fight— "why, in the name of all the blazes—?" and then stopped as John Silence moved up and took his arm.

"There, my dear Colonel Wragge," he said gently, "you touch the heart of the whole thing. You ask 'Why.' That is precisely our problem." He held the soldier's eyes firmly with his own. "And that, too, I think, we shall soon know. Come and let us talk over a plan of action—that room with the double doors, perhaps."

The word "action" calmed him a little, and he led the way, without further speech, back into the house, and down the long stone passage to the room where we had heard his stories on the night of our arrival. I understood from the doctor's glance that my presence would not make the interview easier for our host, and I went upstairs to my own room—shaking.

But in the solitude of my room the vivid memories of the last hour revived so mercilessly that I began to feel I should never in my whole life lose the dreadful picture of Miss Wragge running—that dreadful human climax after all the non-human mystery in the wood—and I was not sorry when a servant knocked at my door and said that Colonel Wragge would be glad if I would join them in the little smoking-room.

"I think it is better you should be present," was all Colonel Wragge said as I entered the room. I took the chair with my back to the window. There was still an hour before lunch, though I imagine that the usual divisions of the day hardly found a place in the thoughts of any one of us.

The atmosphere of the room was what I might call electric. The Colonel was positively bristling; he stood with his back to the fire, fingering an unlit black cigar, his face flushed, his being obviously roused and ready for action. He hated this mystery. It was poisonous to his nature, and he longed to meet something face to face—something he could gauge and fight. Dr. Silence, I noticed at once, was sitting before the map of the estate which was spread upon a table. I knew by his expression the state of his mind. He was in the thick of it all, knew it, delighted in it, and was working at high pressure. He recognised my presence with a lifted eyelid, and the flash of the eye, contrasted with his stillness and composure, told me volumes.

"I was about to explain to our host briefly what seems to me afoot in all this business," he said without looking up, "when he asked that you should join us so that we can all work together." And, while signifying my assent, I caught myself wondering what quality it was in the calm speech of this undemonstrative man that was so full of power, so charged with the strange, virile personality behind it and that seemed to inspire us with his own confidence as by a process of radiation.

"Mr. Hubbard," he went on gravely, turning to the soldier, "knows something of my methods, and in more than one—er—interesting situation has proved of assistance. What we want now"—and here he suddenly got up and took his place on the mat beside the Colonel, and looked hard at him— "is men who have self-control, who are sure of themselves, whose minds at the critical moment will emit positive forces, instead of the wavering and uncertain currents due to negative feelings—due, for instance, to fear."

He looked at us each in turn. Colonel Wragge moved his feet farther apart, and squared his shoulders; and I felt guilty but said nothing, conscious that my latent store of courage was being deliberately hauled to the front. He was winding me up like a clock.

"So that, in what is yet to come," continued our leader, "each of us will contribute his share of power, and ensure success for my plan."

"I'm not afraid of anything I can *see*," said the Colonel bluntly.

"I'm ready," I heard myself say, as it were automatically, "for anything," and then added, feeling the declaration was lamely insufficient, "and everything."

Dr. Silence left the mat and began walking to and fro about the room, both hands plunged deep into the pockets of his shooting-jacket. Tremendous vitality streamed from him. I never took my eyes off the small, moving figure; small yes,—and yet somehow making me think of a giant plotting the destruction of worlds. And his manner was gentle, as always, soothing almost, and his words uttered quietly without emphasis or emotion. Most of what he said was addressed, though not too obviously, to the Colonel.

"The violence of this sudden attack," he said softly, pacing to and fro beneath the bookcase at the end of the room, "is due, of course, partly to the fact that tonight the moon is at the full"—here he glanced at me for a moment— "and partly to the fact that we have all been so deliberately concentrating upon the matter. Our thinking, our investigation, has stirred it into unusual activity. I mean that the intelligent force behind these manifestations has realised that some one is busied about its destruction. And it is now on the defensive: more, it is aggressive."

"But 'it'—what is 'it'?" began the soldier, fuming. "What, in the name of all that's dreadful, *is* a fire-elemental?"

"I cannot give you at this moment," replied Dr. Silence, turning to him, but undisturbed by the interruption, "a lecture on the nature and history of magic, but can only say that an Elemental is the active force behind the elements,—whether earth, air, water, *or fire*,—it is impersonal in its essential nature, but can be focused, personified, ensouled, so to say, by those who know how—by magicians, if you will—for certain purposes of their own, much in the same way that steam and electricity can be harnessed by the practical man of this century.

"Alone, these blind elemental energies can accomplish little, but governed and directed by the trained will of a powerful manipulator they may become potent activities for good or evil. They are the basis of all magic, and it is the motive behind them that constitutes the magic 'black' or 'white'; they can be the vehicles of curses or of blessings, for a curse is nothing more than the thought of a violent will perpetuated. And in such cases—cases like this—the conscious, directing will of the mind that is using the elemental stands always behind the phenomena—"

"You think that my brother—!" broke in the Colonel, aghast.

"Has nothing whatever to do with it—directly. The fire-elemental that has here been tormenting you and your household was sent upon its mission long before you, or your family, or your ancestors, or even the nation you belong to—unless I am much mistaken—was even in existence. We will come to that a little later; after the experiment I propose to make we shall be more positive. At present I can only say we have to deal now, not only with the phenomenon of Attacking Fire merely, but with the vindictive and enraged intelligence that is directing it from behind the scenes—vindictive and enraged,"—he repeated the words.

"That explains—" began Colonel Wragge, seeking furiously for words he could not find quickly enough.

"Much," said John Silence, with a gesture to restrain him.

He stopped a moment in the middle of his walk, and a deep silence came down over the little room. Through the windows the sunlight seemed less bright, the long line of dark hills less friendly, making me think of a vast wave towering to heaven and about to break and overwhelm us. Something formidable had crept into the world about us. For, undoubtedly, there was a disquieting thought, holding terror as well as awe, in the picture his words conjured up: the conception of a human will reaching its deathless hand, spiteful and destructive, down through the ages, to strike the living and afflict the innocent.

"But what is its object?" burst out the soldier, unable to restrain himself longer in the silence. "Why does it come from that plantation? And why should it attack us, or any one in particular?" Questions began to pour from him in a stream.

"All in good time," the doctor answered quietly, having let him run on for several minutes. "But I must first discover positively what, or who, it is that directs this particular fire-elemental. And, to do that, we must first"—he spoke with slow deliberation— "seek to capture—to confine by visibility—to limit its sphere in a concrete form."

"Good heavens almighty!" exclaimed the soldier, mixing his words in his unfeigned surprise.

"Quite so," pursued the other calmly; "for in so doing I think we can release it from the purpose that binds it, restore it to its normal condition of latent fire, and also"—he lowered his voice perceptibly— "also discover the face and form of the Being that ensouls it."

"The man behind the gun!" cried the Colonel, beginning to understand something, and leaning forward so as not to miss a single syllable.

"I mean that in the last resort, before it returns to the womb of potential fire, it will probably assume the face and figure of its Director, of the man of magical knowledge who originally bound it with his incantations and sent it forth upon its mission of centuries."

The soldier sat down and gasped openly in his face, breathing hard; but it was a very subdued voice that framed the question.

"And how do you propose to make it visible? How capture and confine it? What d'ye mean, Dr. John Silence?"

"By furnishing it with the materials for a form. By the process of materialisation simply. Once limited by dimensions, it will become slow, heavy, visible. We can then dissipate it. Invisible fire, you see, is dangerous and incalculable; locked up in a form we can perhaps manage it. We must betray it—to its death."

"And this material?" we asked in the same breath, although I think I had already guessed.

"Not pleasant, but effective," came the quiet reply; "the exhalations of freshly spilled blood."

"Not human blood!" cried Colonel Wragge, starting up from his chair with a voice like an explosion. I thought his eyes would start from their sockets.

The face of Dr. Silence relaxed in spite of himself, and his spontaneous little laugh brought a welcome though momentary relief.

"The days of human sacrifice, I hope, will never come again," he explained. "Animal blood will answer the purpose, and we can make the experiment as pleasant as possible. Only, the blood must be freshly spilled and strong with the vital emanations that attract this peculiar class of elemental creature. Perhaps—perhaps if some pig on the estate is ready for the market—"

He turned to hide a smile; but the passing touch of comedy found no echo in the mind of our host, who did not understand how to change quickly from one emotion to another. Clearly he was debating many things laboriously in his honest brain. But, in the end, the earnestness and scientific disinterestedness of the doctor, whose influence over him was already very great, won the day, and he presently looked up more calmly, and observed shortly that he thought perhaps the matter could be arranged.

"There are other and pleasanter methods," Dr. Silence went on to explain, "but they require time and preparation, and things have gone much too far, in my opinion, to admit of delay. And the process need cause you no distress: we sit round the bowl and await results. Nothing more. The emanations of blood—which, as Levi says, is the first incarnation of the universal fluid—furnish the materials out of which the creatures of discarnate life, spirits if you prefer, can fashion themselves a temporary appearance. The process is old, and lies at the root of all blood sacrifice. It was known to the priests of Baal, and it is known to the modern ecstasy dancers who cut themselves to produce objective phantoms who dance with them. And the least gifted clairvoyant could tell you that the forms to be seen in the vicinity of slaughter-houses, or hovering above the deserted battlefields, are—well, simply beyond all description. I do not mean," he added, noticing the uneasy fidgeting of his host, "that anything in our laundry-experiment need appear to terrify us, for this case seems a comparatively simple one, and it is only the vindictive character of the intelligence directing this fire-elemental that causes anxiety and makes for personal danger."

"It is curious," said the Colonel, with a sudden rush of words, drawing a deep breath, and as though speaking of things distasteful to him, "that during my years among the Hill Tribes of Northern India I came across—personally came across—instances of the sacrifices of blood to certain deities being stopped suddenly, and all manner of disasters happening until they were resumed. Fires broke out in the huts, and even on the clothes, of the natives—and—and I admit I have read, in the course of my studies,"—he made a gesture toward his books and heavily laden table,— "of the Yezidis of Syria evoking phantoms by means of cutting their bodies with knives during their whirling dances—enormous globes of fire which turned into monstrous and terrible forms—and I remember an account somewhere, too, how the emaciated forms and pallid countenances of the spectres, that appeared to the Emperor Julian, claimed to be the true Immortals, and told him to renew the sacrifices of blood 'for the fumes of which, since the establishment of Christianity, they had been pining'—that these were in reality the phantoms evoked by the rites of blood."

Both Dr. Silence and myself listened in amazement, for this sudden speech was so unexpected, and betrayed so much more knowledge than we had either of us suspected in the old soldier.

"Then perhaps you have read, too," said the doctor, "how the Cosmic Deities of savage races, elemental in their nature, have been kept alive through many ages by these blood rites?"

"No," he answered; "that is new to me."

"In any case," Dr. Silence added, "I am glad you are not wholly unfamiliar with the subject, for you will now bring more sympathy, and therefore more help, to our experiment. For, of course, in this case, we only want the blood to tempt the creature from its lair and enclose it in a form—"

"I quite understand. And I only hesitated just now," he went on, his words coming much more slowly, as though he felt he had already said too much, "because I wished to be quite sure it was no mere curiosity, but an actual sense of necessity that dictated this horrible experiment."

"It is your safety, and that of your household, and of your sister, that is at stake," replied the doctor. "Once I have *seen*, I hope to discover whence this elemental comes, and what its real purpose is."

Colonel Wragge signified his assent with a bow.

"And the moon will help us," the other said, "for it will be full in the early hours of the morning, and this kind of elemental-being is always most active at the period of full moon. Hence, you see, the clue furnished by your diary."

So it was finally settled. Colonel Wragge would provide the materials for the experiment, and we were to meet at midnight. How he would contrive at that hour—but that was his business. I only know we both realised that he would keep his word, and whether a pig died at midnight, or at noon, was after all perhaps only a question of the sleep and personal comfort of the executioner.

"Tonight, then, in the laundry," said Dr. Silence finally, to clinch the plan; "we three alone—and at midnight, when the household is asleep and we shall be free from disturbance."

He exchanged significant glances with our host, who, at that moment, was called away by the announcement that the family doctor had arrived, and was ready to see him in his sister's room.

For the remainder of the afternoon John Silence disappeared. I had my suspicions that he made a secret visit to the plantation and also to the laundry building; but, in any case, we saw nothing of him, and he kept strictly to himself. He was preparing for the night, I felt sure, but the nature of his preparations I could only guess. There was movement in his room, I heard, and an odour like incense hung about the door, and knowing that he regarded rites as the vehicles of energies, my guesses were probably not far wrong.

Colonel Wragge, too, remained absent the greater part of the afternoon, and, deeply afflicted, had scarcely left his sister's bedside, but in response to my inquiry when we met for a moment at tea-time, he told me that although she had moments of attempted speech, her talk was quite incoherent and hysterical, and she was still quite unable to explain the nature of what she had seen. The doctor, he said, feared she had recovered the use of her limbs, only to lose that of her memory, and perhaps even of her mind.

"Then the recovery of her legs, I trust, may be permanent, at any rate," I ventured, finding it difficult to know what sympathy to offer. And he replied with a curious short laugh, "Oh yes; about that there can be no doubt whatever."

And it was due merely to the chance of my overhearing a fragment of conversation—unwillingly, of course—that a little further light was thrown upon the state in which the old lady actually lay. For, as I came out of my room, it happened that Colonel Wragge and the doctor were going downstairs together, and their words floated up to my ears before I could make my presence known by so much as a cough.

"Then you must find a way," the doctor was saying with decision; "for I cannot insist too strongly upon that—and at all costs she must be kept quiet. These attempts to go out must be prevented—if necessary, by force. This desire to visit some wood or other she keeps talking about is, of course, hysterical in nature. It cannot be permitted for a moment."

"It shall not be permitted," I heard the soldier reply, as they reached the hall below.

"It has impressed her mind for some reason—" the doctor went on, by way evidently of soothing explanation, and then the distance made it impossible for me to hear more.

At dinner Dr. Silence was still absent, on the public plea of a headache, and though food was sent to his room, I am inclined to believe he did not touch it, but spent the entire time fasting.

We retired early, desiring that the household should do likewise, and I must confess that at ten o'clock when I bid my host a temporary good-night, and sought my room to make what mental preparation I could, I realised in no very pleasant fashion that it was a singular and formidable assignation, this midnight meeting in the laundry building, and that there were moments in every adventure of life when a wise man, and one who knew his own limitations, owed it to his dignity to withdraw discreetly. And, but for the character of our leader, I probably should have then and there offered the best excuse I could think of, and have allowed myself quietly to fall asleep and wait for an exciting story in the morning of what had happened. But with a man like John Silence, such a lapse was out of the question, and I sat before my fire counting the minutes and doing everything I could think of to fortify my resolution and fasten my will at the point where I could be reasonably sure that my self-control would hold against all attacks of men, devils, or elementals.

III

At a quarter before midnight, clad in a heavy ulster, and with slippered feet, I crept cautiously from my room and stole down the passage to the top of the stairs. Outside the doctor's door I waited a moment to listen. All was still; the house in utter darkness; no gleam of light beneath any door; only, down the length of the corridor, from the direction of the sick-room, came faint sounds of laughter and incoherent talk that were not things to reassure a mind already half a-tremble, and I made haste to reach the hall and let myself out through the front door into the night.

The air was keen and frosty, perfumed with night smells, and exquisitely fresh; all the million candles of the sky were alight, and a faint breeze rose and fell with far-away sighings in the tops of the pine trees. My blood leaped for a moment in the spaciousness of the night, for the splendid stars brought courage; but the next instant, as I turned the corner of the house, moving stealthily down the gravel drive, my spirits sank again ominously. For, yonder, over the funereal plumes of the Twelve Acre Plantation, I saw the broken, yellow disc of the half-moon just rising in the east, staring down like some vast Being come to watch upon the progress of our doom. Seen through the distorting vapours of the earth's atmosphere, her face looked weirdly unfamiliar, her usual expression of benignant vacancy somehow a-twist. I slipped along by the shadows of the wall, keeping my eyes upon the ground.

The laundry-house, as already described, stood detached from the other offices, with laurel shrubberies crowding thickly behind it, and the kitchen-garden so close on the other side that the strong smells of soil and growing things came across almost heavily. The shadows of the haunted plantation, hugely lengthened by the rising moon behind them, reached to the very walls and covered the stone tiles of the roof with a dark pall. So keenly were my senses alert at this moment that I believe I could fill a chapter with the endless small details of the impression I received—shadows, odour, shapes, sounds—in the space of the few seconds I stood and waited before the closed wooden door.

Then I became aware of some one moving towards me through the moonlight, and the figure of John Silence, without overcoat and bareheaded, came quickly and without noise to join me. His eyes, I saw at once, were wonderfully bright, and so marked was the shining pallor of his face that I could hardly tell when he passed from the moonlight into the shade.

He passed without a word, beckoning me to follow, and then pushed the door open, and went in.

The chill air of the place met us like that of an underground vault; and the brick floor and whitewashed walls, streaked with damp and smoke, threw back the cold in our faces. Directly opposite gaped the black throat of the huge open fireplace, the ashes of wood fires still piled and scattered about the hearth, and on either side of the projecting chimney-column were the deep recesses holding the big twin cauldrons for boiling clothes. Upon the lids of these cauldrons stood the two little oil lamps, shaded red, which gave all the light there was, and immediately in front of the fireplace there was a small circular table with three chairs set about it. Overhead, the narrow slit windows, high up the walls, pointed to a dim network of wooden rafters half lost among the shadows, and then came the dark vault of the roof. Cheerless and unalluring, for all the red light, it certainly was, reminding me of some unused conventicle, bare of pews or pulpit, ugly and severe, and I was forcibly struck by the contrast between the normal uses to which the place was ordinarily put, and the strange and medieval purpose which had brought us under its roof tonight.

Possibly an involuntary shudder ran over me, for my companion turned with a confident look to reassure me, and he was so completely master of himself that I at once absorbed from his abundance, and felt the chinks of my failing courage beginning to close up. To meet his eye in the presence of danger was like finding a mental railing that guided and supported thought along the giddy edges of alarm.

"I am quite ready," I whispered, turning to listen for approaching footsteps.

He nodded, still keeping his eyes on mine. Our whispers sounded hollow as they echoed overhead among the rafters.

"I'm glad you are here," he said. "Not all would have the courage. Keep your thoughts controlled, and imagine the protective shell round you—round your inner being."

"I'm all right," I repeated, cursing my chattering teeth.

He took my hand and shook it, and the contact seemed to shake into me something of his supreme confidence. The eyes and hands of a strong man can touch the soul. I think he guessed my thought, for a passing smile flashed about the corners of his mouth.

"You will feel more comfortable," he said, in a low tone, "when the chain is complete. The Colonel we can count on, of course. Remember, though," he added warningly, "he may perhaps become controlled—possessed—when the thing comes, because he won't know how to resist. And to explain the business to such a man—!" He shrugged his shoulders expressively. "But it will only be temporary, and I will see that no harm comes to him."

He glanced round at the arrangements with approval.

"Red light," he said, indicating the shaded lamps, "has the lowest rate of vibration. Materialisations are dissipated by strong light—won't form, or hold together—in rapid vibrations."

I was not sure that I approved altogether of this dim light, for in complete darkness there is something protective—the knowledge that one cannot be seen, probably—which a half-light destroys, but I remembered the warning to keep my thoughts steady, and forbore to give them expression.

There was a step outside, and the figure of Colonel Wragge stood in the doorway. Though entering on tiptoe, he made considerable noise and clatter, for his free movements were impeded by the burden he carried, and we saw a large yellowish bowl held out at arms' length from his body, the mouth covered with a white cloth. His face, I noted, was rigidly composed. He, too, was master of himself. And, as I thought of this old soldier moving through the long series of alarms, worn with watching and wearied with assault, unenlightened yet undismayed, even down to the dreadful shock of his sister's terror, and still showing the dogged pluck that persists in the face of defeat, I understood what Dr. Silence meant when he described him as a man "to be counted on."

I think there was nothing beyond this rigidity of his stern features, and a certain greyness of the complexion, to betray the turmoil of the emotions that were doubtless going on within; and the quality of these two men, each in his own way, so keyed me up that, by the time the door was shut and we had exchanged silent greetings, all the latent courage I possessed was well to the fore, and I felt as sure of myself as I knew I ever could feel.

Colonel Wragge set the bowl carefully in the centre of the table.

"Midnight," he said shortly, glancing at his watch, and we all three moved to our chairs.

There, in the middle of that cold and silent place, we sat, with the vile bowl before us, and a thin, hardly perceptible steam rising through the damp air from the surface of the white cloth and disappearing upwards the moment it passed beyond the zone of red light and entered the deep shadows thrown forward by the projecting wall of chimney.

The doctor had indicated our respective places, and I found myself seated with my back to the door and opposite the black hearth. The Colonel was on my left, and Dr. Silence on my right, both half facing me, the latter more in shadow than the former. We thus divided the little table into even sections, and sitting back in our chairs we awaited events in silence.

For something like an hour I do not think there was even the faintest sound within those four walls and under the canopy of that vaulted roof. Our slippers made no scratching on the gritty floor, and our breathing was suppressed almost to nothing; even the rustle of our clothes as we shifted from time to time upon our seats was inaudible. Silence smothered us absolutely—the silence of night, of listening, the silence of a haunted expectancy. The very gurgling of the lamps was too soft to be heard, and if light itself had sound, I do not think we should have noticed the silvery tread of the moonlight as it entered the high narrow windows and threw upon the floor the slender traces of its pallid footsteps.

Colonel Wragge and the doctor, and myself too for that matter, sat thus like figures of stone, without speech and without gesture. My eyes passed in ceaseless journeys from the bowl to their faces, and from their faces to the bowl. They might have been masks, however, for all the signs of life they gave; and the light steaming from the horrid contents beneath the white cloth had long ceased to be visible.

Then presently, as the moon rose higher, the wind rose with it. It sighed, like the lightest of passing wings, over the roof; it crept most softly round the walls; it made the brick floor like ice beneath our feet. With it I saw mentally the desolate moorland flowing like a sea about the old house, the treeless expanse of lonely hills, the nearer copses, sombre and mysterious in the night. The plantation, too, in particular I saw, and imagined I heard the mournful whisperings that must now be a-stirring among its tree-tops as the breeze played down between the twisted stems. In the depth of the room behind us the shafts of moonlight met and crossed in a growing network.

It was after an hour of this wearing and unbroken attention, and I should judge about one o'clock in the morning, when the baying of the dogs in the stableyard first began, and I saw John Silence move suddenly in his chair and sit up in an attitude of attention. Every force in my being instantly leaped into the keenest vigilance. Colonel Wragge moved too, though slowly, and without raising his eyes from the table before him.

The doctor stretched his arm out and took the white cloth from the bowl.

It was perhaps imagination that persuaded me the red glare of the lamps grew fainter and the air over the table before us thickened. I had been expecting something for so long that the movement of my companions, and the lifting of the cloth, may easily have caused the momentary delusion that something hovered in the air before my face, touching the skin of my cheeks with a silken run. But it was certainly not a delusion that the Colonel looked up at the same moment and glanced over his shoulder, as though his eyes followed the movements of something to and fro about the room, and that he then buttoned his overcoat more tightly about him and his eyes sought my own face first, and then the doctor's. And it was no delusion that his face seemed somehow to have turned dark, become spread as it were with a shadowy blackness. I saw his lips tighten and his expression grow hard and stern, and it came to me then with a rush that, of course, this man had told us but a part of the experiences he had been through in the house, and that there was much more he had never been able to bring himself to reveal at all. I felt sure of it. The way he turned and stared about him betrayed a familiarity with other things than those he had described to us. It was not merely a sight of fire he looked for; it was a sight of something alive, intelligent, something able to evade his searching; it was *a person*. It was the watch for the ancient Being who sought to obsess him.

And the way in which Dr. Silence answered his look—though it was only by a glance of subtlest sympathy—confirmed my impression.

"We may be ready now," I heard him say in a whisper, and I understood that his words were intended as a steadying warning, and braced myself mentally to the utmost of my power.

Yet long before Colonel Wragge had turned to stare about the room, and long before the doctor had confirmed my impression that things were at last beginning to stir, I had become aware in most singular fashion that the place held more than our three selves. With the rising of the wind this increase to our numbers had first taken place. The baying of the hounds almost seemed to have signalled it. I cannot say how it may be possible to realise that an empty place has suddenly become—not empty, when the new arrival is nothing that appeals to any one of the senses; for this recognition of an "invisible," as of the change in the balance of personal forces in a human group, is indefinable and beyond proof. Yet it is unmistakable. And I knew perfectly well at what given moment the atmosphere within these four walls became charged with the presence of other living beings besides ourselves. And, on reflection, I am convinced that both my companions knew it too.

"Watch the light," said the doctor under his breath, and then I knew too that it was no fancy of my own that had turned the air darker, and the way he turned to examine the face of our host sent an electric thrill of wonder and expectancy shivering along every nerve in my body.

Yet it was no kind of terror that I experienced, but rather a sort of mental dizziness, and a sensation as of being suspended in some remote and dreadful altitude where things might happen, indeed were about to happen, that had never before happened within the ken of man. Horror may have formed an ingredient, but it was not chiefly horror, and in no sense ghostly horror.

Uncommon thoughts kept beating on my brain like tiny hammers, soft yet persistent, seeking admission; their unbidden tide began to wash along the far fringes of my mind, the currents of unwonted sensations to rise over the remote frontiers of my consciousness. I was aware of thoughts, and the fantasies of thoughts, that I never knew before existed. Portions of my being stirred that had never stirred before, and things ancient and inexplicable rose to the surface and beckoned me to follow. I felt as though I were about to fly off, at some immense tangent, into an outer space hitherto unknown even in dreams. And so singular was the result produced upon me that I was uncommonly glad to anchor my mind, as well as my eyes, upon the masterful personality of the doctor at my side, for there, I realised, I could draw always upon the forces of sanity and safety.

With a vigorous effort of will I returned to the scene before me, and tried to focus my attention, with steadier thoughts, upon the table, and upon the silent figures seated round it. And then I saw that certain changes had come about in the place where we sat.

The patches of moonlight on the floor, I noted, had become curiously shaded; the faces of my companions opposite were not so clearly visible as before; and the forehead and cheeks of Colonel Wragge were glistening with perspiration. I realised further, that an extraordinary change had come about in the temperature of the atmosphere. The increased warmth had a painful effect, not alone on Colonel Wragge, but upon all of us. It was oppressive and unnatural. We gasped figuratively as well as actually.

"You are the first to feel it," said Dr. Silence in low tones, looking across at him. "You are in more intimate touch, of course—"

The Colonel was trembling, and appeared to be in considerable distress. His knees shook, so that the shuffling of his slippered feet became audible. He inclined his head to show that he had heard, but made no other reply. I think, even then, he was sore put to it to keep himself in hand. I knew what he was struggling against. As Dr. Silence had warned me, he was about to be obsessed, and was savagely, though vainly, resisting.

But, meanwhile, a curious and whirling sense of exhilaration began to come over me. The increasing heat was delightful, bringing a sensation of intense activity, of thoughts pouring through the mind at high speed, of vivid pictures in the brain, of fierce desires and lightning energies alive in every part of the body. I was conscious of no physical distress, such as the Colonel felt, but only of a vague feeling that it might all grow suddenly too intense—that I might be consumed—that my personality as well as my body, might become resolved into the flame of pure spirit. I began to live at a speed too intense to last. It was as if a thousand ecstasies besieged me—

"Steady!" whispered the voice of John Silence in my ear, and I looked up with a start to see that the Colonel had risen from his chair. The doctor rose too. I followed suit, and for the first time saw down into the bowl. To my amazement and horror I saw that the contents were troubled. The blood was astir with movement.

The rest of the experiment was witnessed by us standing. It came, too, with a curious suddenness. There was no more dreaming, for me at any rate.

I shall never forget the figure of Colonel Wragge standing there beside me, upright and unshaken, squarely planted on his feet, looking about him, puzzled beyond belief, yet full of a fighting anger. Framed by the white walls, the red glow of the lamps upon his streaming cheeks, his eyes glowing against the deathly pallor of his skin, breathing hard and making convulsive efforts of hands and body to keep himself under control, his whole being roused to the point of savage fighting, yet with nothing visible to get at anywhere—he stood there, immovable against odds. And the strange contrast of the pale skin and the burning face I had never seen before, or wish to see again.

But what has left an even sharper impression on my memory was the blackness that then began crawling over his face, obliterating the features, concealing their human outline, and hiding him inch by inch from view. This was my first realisation that the process of materialisation was at work. His visage became shrouded. I moved from one side to the other to keep him in view, and it was only then I understood that, properly speaking, the blackness was not upon the countenance of Colonel Wragge, but that something had inserted itself between me and him, thus screening his face with the effect of a dark veil. Something that apparently rose through the floor was passing slowly into the air above the table and above the bowl. The blood in the bowl, moreover, was considerably less than before.

And, with this change in the air before us, there came at the same time a further change, I thought, in the face of the soldier. One-half was turned towards the red lamps, while the other caught the pale illumination of the moonlight falling aslant from the high windows, so that it was difficult to estimate this change with accuracy of detail. But it seemed to me that, while the features—eyes, nose, mouth—remained the same, the life informing them had undergone some profound transformation. The signature of a new power had crept into the face and left its traces there—an expression dark, and in some unexplained way, terrible.

Then suddenly he opened his mouth and spoke, and the sound of this changed voice, deep and musical though it was, made me cold and set my heart beating with uncomfortable rapidity. The Being, as he had dreaded, was already in control of his brain, using his mouth.

"I see a blackness like the blackness of Egypt before my face," said the tones of this unknown voice that seemed half his own and half another's. "And out of this darkness they come, they come."

I gave a dreadful start. The doctor turned to look at me for an instant, and then turned to centre his attention upon the figure of our host, and I understood in some intuitive fashion that he was there to watch over the strangest contest man ever saw—to watch over and, if necessary, to protect.

"He is being controlled—possessed," he whispered to me through the shadows. His face wore a wonderful expression, half triumph, half admiration.

Even as Colonel Wragge spoke, it seemed to me that this visible darkness began to increase, pouring up thickly out of the ground by the hearth, rising up in sheets and veils, shrouding our eyes and faces. It stole up from below—an awful blackness that seemed to drink in all the radiations of light in the building, leaving nothing but the ghost of a radiance in their place. Then, out of this rising sea of shadows, issued a pale and spectral light that gradually spread itself about us, and from the heart of this light I saw the shapes of fire crowd and gather. And these were not human shapes, or the shapes of anything I recognised as alive in the world, but outlines of fire that traced globes, triangles, crosses, and the luminous bodies of various geometrical figures. They grew bright, faded, and then grew bright again with an effect almost of pulsation. They passed swiftly to and fro through the air, rising and falling, and particularly in the immediate neighbourhood of the Colonel, often gathering about his head and shoulders, and even appearing to settle upon him like giant insects of flame. They were accompanied, moreover, by a faint sound of hissing—the same sound we had heard that afternoon in the plantation.

"The fire-elementals that precede their master," the doctor said in an undertone. "Be ready."

And while this weird display of the shapes of fire alternately flashed and faded, and the hissing echoed faintly among the dim rafters overhead, we heard the awful voice issue at intervals from the lips of the afflicted soldier. It was a voice of power, splendid in some way I cannot describe, and with a certain sense of majesty in its cadences, and, as I listened to it with quickly beating heart, I could fancy it was some ancient voice of Time itself, echoing down immense corridors of stone, from the depths of vast temples, from the very heart of mountain tombs.

"I have seen my divine Father, Osiris," thundered the great tones. "I have scattered the gloom of the night. I have burst through the earth, and am one with the starry Deities!"

Something grand came into the soldier's face. He was staring fixedly before him, as though seeing nothing.

"Watch," whispered Dr. Silence in my ear, and his whisper seemed to come from very far away.

Again the mouth opened and the awesome voice issued forth.

"Thoth," it boomed, "has loosened the bandages of Set which fettered my mouth. I have taken my place in the great winds of heaven."

I heard the little wind of night, with its mournful voice of ages, sighing round the walls and over the roof.

"Listen!" came from the doctor at my side, and the thunder of the voice continued—

"I have hidden myself with you, O ye stars that never diminish. I remember my name—in—the—House—of—Fire!"

The voice ceased and the sound died away. Something about the face and figure of Colonel Wragge relaxed, I thought. The terrible look passed from his face. The Being that obsessed him was gone.

"The great Ritual," said Dr. Silence aside to me, very low, "the Book of the Dead. Now it's leaving him. Soon the blood will fashion it a body."

Colonel Wragge, who had stood absolutely motionless all this time, suddenly swayed, so that I thought he was going to fall,—and, but for the quick support of the doctor's arm, he probably would have fallen, for he staggered as in the beginning of collapse.

"I am drunk with the wine of Osiris," he cried,—and it was half with his own voice this time— "but Horus, the Eternal Watcher, is about my path—for—safety." The voice dwindled and failed, dying away into something almost like a cry of distress.

"Now, watch closely," said Dr. Silence, speaking loud, "for after the cry will come the Fire!"

I began to tremble involuntarily; an awful change had come without warning into the air; my legs grew weak as paper beneath my weight and I had to support myself by leaning on the table. Colonel Wragge, I saw, was also leaning forward with a kind of droop. The shapes of fire had vanished all, but his face was lit by the red lamps and the pale, shifting moonlight rose behind him like mist.

We were both gazing at the bowl, now almost empty; the Colonel stooped so low I feared every minute he would lose his balance and drop into it; and the shadow, that had so long been in process of forming, now at length began to assume material outline in the air before us.

Then John Silence moved forward quickly. He took his place between us and the shadow. Erect, formidable, absolute master of the situation, I saw him stand there, his face calm and almost smiling, and fire in his eyes. His protective influence was astounding and incalculable. Even the abhorrent dread I felt at the sight of the creature growing into life and substance before us, lessened in some way so that I was able to keep my eyes fixed on the air above the bowl without too vivid a terror.

But as it took shape, rising out of nothing as it were, and growing momentarily more defined in outline, a period of utter and wonderful silence settled down upon the building and all it contained. A hush of ages, like the sudden centre of peace at the heart of the travelling cyclone, descended through the night, and out of this hush, as out of the emanations of the steaming blood, issued the form of the ancient being who had first sent the elemental of fire upon its mission. It grew and darkened and solidified before our eyes. It rose from just beyond the table so that the lower portions remained invisible, but I saw the outline limn itself upon the air, as though slowly revealed by the rising of a curtain. It apparently had not then quite concentrated to the normal proportions, but was spread out on all sides into space, huge, though rapidly condensing, for I saw the colossal shoulders, the neck, the lower portion of the dark jaws, the terrible mouth, and then the teeth and lips—and, as the veil seemed to lift further upon the tremendous face—I saw the nose and cheek bones. In another moment I should have looked straight into the eyes—

But what Dr. Silence did at that moment was so unexpected, and took me so by surprise, that I have never yet properly understood its nature, and he has never yet seen fit to explain in detail to me. He uttered some sound that had a note of command in it—and, in so doing, stepped forward and intervened between me and the face. The figure, just nearing completeness, he therefore hid from my sight—and I have always thought purposely hid from my sight.

"The fire!" he cried out. "The fire! Beware!"

There was a sudden roar as of flame from the very mouth of the pit, and for the space of a single second all grew light as day. A blinding flash passed across my face, and there was heat for an instant that seemed to shrivel skin, and flesh, and bone. Then came steps, and I heard Colonel Wragge utter a great cry, wilder than any human cry I have ever known. The heat sucked all the breath out of my lungs with a rush, and the blaze of light, as it vanished, swept my vision with it into enveloping darkness.

When I recovered the use of my senses a few moments later I saw that Colonel Wragge with a face of death, its whiteness strangely stained, had moved closer to me. Dr. Silence stood beside him, an expression of triumph and success in his eyes. The next minute the soldier tried to clutch me with his hand. Then he reeled, staggered, and, unable to save himself, fell with a great crash upon the brick floor.

After the sheet of flame, a wind raged round the building as though it would lift the roof off, but then passed as suddenly as it came. And in the intense calm that followed I saw that the form had vanished, and the doctor was stooping over Colonel Wragge upon the floor, trying to lift him to a sitting position.

"Light," he said quietly, "more light. Take the shades off."

Colonel Wragge sat up and the glare of the unshaded lamps fell upon his face. It was grey and drawn, still running heat, and there was a look in the eyes and about the corners of the mouth that seemed in this short space of time to have added years to its age. At the same time, the expression of effort and anxiety had left it. It showed relief.

"Gone!" he said, looking up at the doctor in a dazed fashion, and struggling to his feet. "Thank God! it's gone at last." He stared round the laundry as though to find out where he was. "Did it control me—take possession of me? Did I talk nonsense?" he asked bluntly. "After the heat came, I remember nothing—"

"You'll feel yourself again in a few minutes," the doctor said. To my infinite horror I saw that he was surreptitiously wiping sundry dark stains from the face. "Our experiment has been a success and—"

He gave me a swift glance to hide the bowl, standing between me and our host while I hurriedly stuffed it down under the lid of the nearest cauldron.

"—and none of us the worse for it," he finished.

"And fires?" he asked, still dazed, "there'll be no more fires?"

"It is dissipated—partly, at any rate," replied Dr. Silence cautiously.

"And the man behind the gun," he went on, only half realising what he was saying, I think; "have you discovered *that?*"

"A form materialised," said the doctor briefly. "I know for certain now what the directing intelligence was behind it all."

Colonel Wragge pulled himself together and got upon his feet. The words conveyed no clear meaning to him yet. But his memory was returning gradually, and he was trying to piece together the fragments into a connected whole. He shivered a little, for the place had grown suddenly chilly. The air was empty again, lifeless.

"You feel all right again now," Dr. Silence said, in the tone of a man stating a fact rather than asking a question.

"Thanks to you—both, yes." He drew a deep breath, and mopped his face, and even attempted a smile. He made me think of a man coming from the battlefield with the stains of fighting still upon him, but scornful of his wounds. Then he turned gravely towards the doctor with a question in his eyes. Memory had returned and he was himself again.

"Precisely what I expected," the doctor said calmly; "a fire-elemental sent upon its mission in the days of Thebes, centuries before Christ, and tonight, for the first time all these thousands of years, released from the spell that originally bound it."

We stared at him in amazement, Colonel Wragge opening his lips for words that refused to shape themselves.

"And, if we dig," he continued significantly, pointing to the floor where the blackness had poured up, "we shall find some underground connection—a tunnel most likely—leading to the Twelve Acre Wood. It was made by—your predecessor."

"A tunnel made by my brother!" gasped the soldier. "Then my sister should know—she lived here with him—" He stopped suddenly.

John Silence inclined his head slowly. "I think so," he said quietly. "Your brother, no doubt, was as much tormented as you have been," he continued after a pause in which Colonel Wragge seemed deeply preoccupied with his thoughts, "and tried to find peace by burying it in the wood, and surrounding the wood then, like a large magic circle, with the enchantments of the old formulae. So the stars the man saw blazing—"

"But burying what?" asked the soldier faintly, stepping backwards towards the support of the wall.

Dr. Silence regarded us both intently for a moment before he replied. I think he weighed in his mind whether to tell us now, or when the investigation was absolutely complete.

"The mummy," he said softly, after a moment; "the mummy that your brother took from its resting place of centuries, and brought home—here."

Colonel Wragge dropped down upon the nearest chair, hanging breathlessly on every word. He was far too amazed for speech.

"The mummy of some important person—a priest most likely—protected from disturbance and desecration by the ceremonial magic of the time. For they understood how to attach to the mummy, to lock up with it in the tomb, an elemental force that would direct itself even after ages upon any one who dared to molest it. In this case it was an elemental of fire."

Dr. Silence crossed the floor and turned out the lamps one by one. He had nothing more to say for the moment. Following his example, I folded the table together and took up the chairs, and our host, still dazed and silent, mechanically obeyed him and moved to the door.

We removed all traces of the experiment, taking the empty bowl back to the house concealed beneath an ulster.

The air was cool and fragrant as we walked to the house, the stars beginning to fade overhead and a fresh wind of early morning blowing up out of the east where the sky was already hinting of the coming day. It was after five o'clock.

Stealthily we entered the front hall and locked the door, and as we went on tiptoe upstairs to our rooms, the Colonel, peering at us over his candle as he nodded good-night, whispered that if we were ready the digging should be begun that very day.

Then I saw him steal along to his sister's room and disappear.

IV

But not even the mysterious references to the mummy, or the prospect of a revelation by digging, were able to hinder the reaction that followed the intense excitement of the past twelve hours, and I slept the sleep of the dead, dreamless and undisturbed. A touch on the shoulder woke me, and I saw Dr. Silence standing beside the bed, dressed to go out.

"Come," he said, "it's tea-time. You've slept the best part of a dozen hours."

I sprang up and made a hurried toilet, while my companion sat and talked. He looked fresh and rested, and his manner was even quieter than usual.

"Colonel Wragge has provided spades and pickaxes. We're going out to unearth this mummy at once," he said; "and there's no reason we should not get away by the morning train."

"I'm ready to go tonight, if you are," I said honestly.

But Dr. Silence shook his head.

"I must see this through to the end," he said gravely, and in a tone that made me think he still anticipated serious things, perhaps. He went on talking while I dressed.

"This case is really typical of all stories of mummy-haunting, and none of them are cases to trifle with," he explained, "for the mummies of important people—kings, priests, magicians—were laid away with profoundly significant ceremonial, and were very effectively protected, as you have seen, against desecration, and especially against destruction.

"The general belief," he went on, anticipating my questions, "held, of course, that the perpetuity of the mummy guaranteed that of its Ka,—the owner's spirit,—but it is not improbable that the magical embalming was also used to retard reincarnation, the preservation of the body preventing the return of the spirit to the toil and discipline of earth-life; and, in any case, they knew how to attach powerful guardian-forces to keep off trespassers. And any one who dared to remove the mummy, or especially to unwind it—well," he added, with meaning, "you have seen—and you will see."

I caught his face in the mirror while I struggled with my collar. It was deeply serious. There could be no question that he spoke of what he believed and knew.

"The traveller-brother who brought it here must have been haunted too," he continued, "for he tried to banish it by burial in the wood, making a magic circle to enclose it. Something of genuine ceremonial he must have known, for the stars the man saw were of course the remains of the still flaming pentagrams he traced at intervals in the circle. Only he did not know enough, or possibly was ignorant that the mummy's guardian was a fire-force. Fire cannot be enclosed by fire, though, as you saw, it can be released by it."

"Then that awful figure in the laundry?" I asked, thrilled to find him so communicative.

"Undoubtedly the actual Ka of the mummy operating always behind its agent, the elemental, and most likely thousands of years old."

"And Miss Wragge—?" I ventured once more.

"Ah, Miss Wragge," he repeated with increased gravity, "Miss Wragge—"

A knock at the door brought a servant with word that tea was ready, and the Colonel had sent to ask if we were coming down. The thread was broken. Dr. Silence moved to the door and signed to me to follow. But his manner told me that in any case no real answer would have been forthcoming to my question.

"And the place to dig in," I asked, unable to restrain my curiosity, "will you find it by some process of divination or—?"

He paused at the door and looked back at me, and with that he left me to finish my dressing.

It was growing dark when the three of us silently made our way to the Twelve Acre Plantation; the sky was overcast, and a black wind came out of the east. Gloom hung about the old house and the air seemed full of sighings. We found the tools ready laid at the edge of the wood, and each shouldering his piece, we followed our leader at once in among the trees. He went straight forward for some twenty yards and then stopped. At his feet lay the blackened circle of one of the burned places. It was just discernible against the surrounding white grass.

"There are three of these," he said, "and they all lie in a line with one another. Any one of them will tap the tunnel that connects the laundry—the former Museum—with the chamber where the mummy now lies buried."

He at once cleared away the burnt grass and began to dig; we all began to dig. While I used the pick, the others shovelled vigorously. No one spoke. Colonel Wragge worked the hardest of the three. The soil was light and sandy, and there were only a few snake-like roots and occasional loose stones to delay us. The pick made short work of these. And meanwhile the darkness settled about us and the biting wind swept roaring through the trees overhead.

Then, quite suddenly, without a cry, Colonel Wragge disappeared up to his neck.

"The tunnel!" cried the doctor, helping to drag him out, red, breathless, and covered with sand and perspiration. "Now, let me lead the way." And he slipped down nimbly into the hole, so that a moment later we heard his voice, muffled by sand and distance, rising up to us.

"Hubbard, you come next, and then Colonel Wragge—if he wishes," we heard.

"I'll follow you, of course," he said, looking at me as I scrambled in.

The hole was bigger now, and I got down on all-fours in a channel not much bigger than a large sewer-pipe and found myself in total darkness. A minute later a heavy thud, followed by a cataract of loose sand, announced the arrival of the Colonel.

"Catch hold of my heel," called Dr. Silence, "and Colonel Wragge can take yours."

In this slow, laborious fashion we wormed our way along a tunnel that had been roughly dug out of the shifting sand, and was shored up clumsily by means of wooden pillars and posts. Any moment, it seemed to me, we might be buried alive. We could not see an inch before our eyes, but had to grope our way feeling the pillars and the walls. It was difficult to breathe, and the Colonel behind me made but slow progress, for the cramped position of our bodies was very severe.

We had travelled in this way for ten minutes, and gone perhaps as much as ten yards, when I lost my grasp of the doctor's heel.

"Ah!" I heard his voice, sounding above me somewhere. He was standing up in a clear space, and the next moment I was standing beside him. Colonel Wragge came heavily after, and he too rose up and stood. Then Dr. Silence produced his candles and we heard preparations for striking matches.

Yet even before there was light, an indefinable sensation of awe came over us all. In this hole in the sand, some three feet under ground, we stood side by side, cramped and huddled, struck suddenly with an over whelming apprehension of something ancient, something formidable, something incalculably wonderful, that touched in each one of us a sense of the sublime and the terrible even before we could see an inch before our faces. I know not how to express in language this singular emotion that caught us here in utter darkness, touching no sense directly, it seemed, yet with the recognition that before us in the blackness of this underground night there lay something that was mighty with the mightiness of long past ages.

I felt Colonel Wragge press in closely to my side, and I understood the pressure and welcomed it. No human touch, to me at least, has ever been more eloquent.

Then the match flared, a thousand shadows fled on black wings, and I saw John Silence fumbling with the candle, his face lit up grotesquely by the flickering light below it.

I had dreaded this light, yet when it came there was apparently nothing to explain the profound sensations of dread that preceded it. We stood in a small vaulted chamber in the sand, the sides and roof shored with bars of wood, and the ground laid roughly with what seemed to be tiles. It was six feet high, so that we could all stand comfortably, and may have been ten feet long by eight feet wide. Upon the wooden pillars at the side I saw that Egyptian hieroglyphics had been rudely traced by burning.

Dr. Silence lit three candles and handed one to each of us. He placed a fourth in the sand against the wall on his right, and another to mark the entrance to the tunnel. We stood and stared about us, instinctively holding our breath.

"Empty, by God!" exclaimed Colonel Wragge. His voice trembled with excitement. And then, as his eyes rested on the ground, he added, "And footsteps—look—footsteps in the sand!"

Dr. Silence said nothing. He stooped down and began to make a search of the chamber, and as he moved, my eyes followed his crouching figure and noted the queer distorted shadows that poured over the walls and ceiling after him. Here and there thin trickles of loose sand ran fizzing down the sides. The atmosphere, heavily charged with faint yet pungent odours, lay utterly still, and the flames of the candles might have been painted on the air for all the movement they betrayed.

And, as I watched, it was almost necessary to persuade myself forcibly that I was only standing upright with difficulty in this little sand-hole of a modern garden in the south of England, for it seemed to me that I stood, as in vision, at the entrance of some vast rock-hewn Temple far, far down the river of Time. The illusion was powerful, and persisted. Granite columns, that rose to heaven, piled themselves about me, majestically uprearing, and a roof like the sky itself spread above a line of colossal figures that moved in shadowy procession along endless and stupendous aisles. This huge and splendid fantasy, borne I knew not whence, possessed me so vividly that I was actually obliged to concentrate my attention upon the small stooping figure of the doctor, as he groped about the walls, in order to keep the eye of imagination on the scene before me.

But the limited space rendered a long search out of the question, and his footsteps, instead of shuffling through loose sand, presently struck something of a different quality that gave forth a hollow and resounding echo. He stooped to examine more closely.

He was standing exactly in the centre of the little chamber when this happened, and he at once began scraping away the sand with his feet. In less than a minute a smooth surface became visible—the surface of a wooden covering. The next thing I saw was that he had raised it and was peering down into a space below. Instantly, a strong odour of nitre and bitumen, mingled with the strange perfume of unknown and powdered aromatics, rose up from the uncovered space and filled the vault, stinging the throat and making the eyes water and smart.

"The mummy!" whispered Dr. Silence, looking up into our faces over his candle; and as he said the word I felt the soldier lurch against me, and heard his breathing in my very ear.

"The mummy!" he repeated under his breath, as we pressed forward to look.

It is difficult to say exactly why the sight should have stirred in me so prodigious an emotion of wonder and veneration, for I have had not a little to do with mummies, have unwound scores of them, and even experimented magically with not a few. But there was something in the sight of that grey and silent figure, lying in its modern box of lead and wood at the bottom of this sandy grave, swathed in the bandages of centuries and wrapped in the perfumed linen that the priests of Egypt had prayed over with their mighty enchantments thousands of years before—something in the sight of it lying there and breathing its own spice-laden atmosphere even in the darkness of its exile in this remote land, something that pierced to the very core of my being and touched that root of awe which slumbers in every man near the birth of tears and the passion of true worship.

I remember turning quickly from the Colonel, lest he should see my emotion, yet fail to understand its cause, turn and clutch John Silence by the arm, and then fall trembling to see that he, too, had lowered his head and was hiding his face in his hands.

A kind of whirling storm came over me, rising out of I know not what utter deeps of memory, and in a whiteness of vision I heard the magical old chauntings from the Book of the Dead, and saw the Gods pass by in dim procession, the mighty, immemorial Beings who were yet themselves only the personified attributes of the true Gods, the God with the Eyes of Fire, the God with the Face of Smoke. I saw again Anubis, the dog-faced deity, and the children of Horus, eternal watcher of the ages, as they swathed Osiris, the first mummy of the world, in the scented and mystic bands, and I tasted again something of the ecstasy of the justified soul as it embarked in the golden Boat of Ra, and journeyed onwards to rest in the fields of the blessed.

And then, as Dr. Silence, with infinite reverence, stooped and touched the still face, so dreadfully staring with its painted eyes, there rose again to our nostrils wave upon wave of this perfume of thousands of years, and time fled backwards like a thing of naught, showing me in haunted panorama the most wonderful dream of the whole world.

A gentle hissing became audible in the air, and the doctor moved quickly backwards. It came close to our faces and then seemed to play about the walls and ceiling.

"The last of the Fire—still waiting for its full accomplishment," he muttered; but I heard both words and hissing as things far away, for I was still busy with the journey of the soul through the Seven Halls of Death, listening for echoes of the grandest ritual ever known to men.

The earthen plates covered with hieroglyphics still lay beside the mummy, and round it, carefully arranged at the points of the compass, stood the four jars with the heads of the hawk, the jackal, the cynocephalus, and man, the jars in which were placed the hair, the nail parings, the heart, and other special portions of the body. Even the amulets, the mirror, the blue clay statues of the Ka, and the lamp with seven wicks were there. Only the sacred scarabaeus was missing.

"Not only has it been torn from its ancient resting-place," I heard Dr. Silence saying in a solemn voice as he looked at Colonel Wragge with fixed gaze, "but it has been partially unwound,"—he pointed to the wrappings of the breast,— "and—the scarabaeus has been removed from the throat."

The hissing, that was like the hissing of an invisible flame, had ceased; only from time to time we heard it as though it passed backwards and forwards in the tunnel; and we stood looking into each other's faces without speaking.

Presently Colonel Wragge made a great effort and braced himself. I heard the sound catch in his throat before the words actually became audible.

"My sister," he said, very low. And then there followed a long pause, broken at length by John Silence.

"It must be replaced," he said significantly.

"I knew nothing," the soldier said, forcing himself to speak the words he hated saying. "Absolutely nothing."

"It must be returned," repeated the other, "if it is not now too late. For I fear—I fear—"

Colonel Wragge made a movement of assent with his head.

"It shall be," he said.

The place was still as the grave.

I do not know what it was then that made us all three turn round with so sudden a start, for there was no sound audible to my ears, at least.

The doctor was on the point of replacing the lid over the mummy, when he straightened up as if he had been shot.

"There's something coming," said Colonel Wragge under his breath, and the doctor's eyes, peering down the small opening of the tunnel, showed me the true direction.

A distant shuffling noise became distinctly audible coming from a point about half-way down the tunnel we had so laboriously penetrated.

"It's the sand falling in," I said, though I knew it was foolish.

"No," said the Colonel calmly, in a voice that seemed to have the ring of iron, "I've heard it for some time past. It is something alive—and it is coming nearer."

He stared about him with a look of resolution that made his face almost noble. The horror in his heart was overmastering, yet he stood there prepared for anything that might come.

"There's no other way out," John Silence said.

He leaned the lid against the sand, and waited. I knew by the masklike expression of his face, the pallor, and the steadiness of the eyes, that he anticipated something that might be very terrible—appalling.

The Colonel and myself stood on either side of the opening. I still held my candle and was ashamed of the way it shook, dripping the grease all over me; but the soldier had set his into the sand just behind his feet.

Thoughts of being buried alive, of being smothered like rats in a trap, of being caught and done to death by some invisible and merciless force we could not grapple with, rushed into my mind. Then I thought of fire—of suffocation—of being roasted alive. The perspiration began to pour from my face.

"Steady!" came the voice of Dr. Silence to me through the vault.

For five minutes, that seemed fifty, we stood waiting, looking from each other's faces to the mummy, and from the mummy to the hole, and all the time the shuffling sound, soft and stealthy, came gradually nearer. The tension, for me at least, was very near the breaking point when at last the cause of the disturbance reached the edge. It was hidden for a moment just behind the broken rim of soil. A jet of sand, shaken by the close vibration, trickled down on to the ground; I have never in my life seen anything fall with such laborious leisure. The next second, uttering a cry of curious quality, it came into view.

And it was far more distressingly horrible than anything I had anticipated.

For the sight of some Egyptian monster, some god of the tombs, or even of some demon of fire, I think I was already half prepared; but when, instead, I saw the white visage of Miss Wragge framed in that round opening of sand, followed by her body crawling on all fours, her eyes bulging and reflecting the yellow glare of the candles, my first instinct was to turn and run like a frantic animal seeking a way of escape.

But Dr. Silence, who seemed no whit surprised, caught my arm and steadied me, and we both saw the Colonel then drop upon his knees and come thus to a level with his sister. For more than a whole minute, as though struck in stone, the two faces gazed silently at each other: hers, for all the dreadful emotion in it, more like a gargoyle than anything human; and his, white and blank with an expression that was beyond either astonishment or alarm. She looked up; he looked down. It was a picture in a nightmare, and the candle, stuck in the sand close to the hole, threw upon it the glare of impromptu footlights.

Then John Silence moved forward and spoke in a voice that was very low, yet perfectly calm and natural.

"I am glad you have come," he said. "You are the one person whose presence at this moment is most required. And I hope that you may yet be in time to appease the anger of the Fire, and to bring peace again to your household, and," he added lower still so that no one heard it but myself, "*safety to yourself.*"

And while her brother stumbled backwards, crushing a candle into the sand in his awkwardness, the old lady crawled farther into the vaulted chamber and slowly rose upon her feet.

At the sight of the wrapped figure of the mummy I was fully prepared to see her scream and faint, but on the contrary, to my complete amazement, she merely bowed her head and dropped quietly upon her knees. Then, after a pause of more than a minute, she raised her eyes to the roof and her lips began to mutter as in prayer. Her right hand, meanwhile, which had been fumbling for some time at her throat suddenly came away, and before the gaze of all of us she held it out, palm upwards, over the grey and ancient figure outstretched below. And in it we beheld glistening the green jasper of the stolen scarabaeus.

Her brother, leaning heavily against the wall behind, uttered a sound that was half cry, half exclamation, but John Silence, standing directly in front of her, merely fixed his eyes on her and pointed downwards to the staring face below.

"Replace it," he said sternly, "where it belongs."

Miss Wragge was kneeling at the feet of the mummy when this happened. We three men all had our eyes riveted on what followed. Only the reader who by some remote chance may have witnessed a line of mummies, freshly laid from their tombs upon the sand, slowly stir and bend as the heat of the Egyptian sun warms their ancient bodies into the semblance of life, can form any conception of the ultimate horror we experienced when the silent figure before us moved in its grave of lead and sand. Slowly, before our eyes, it writhed, and, with a faint rustling of the immemorial cerements, rose up, and, through sightless and bandaged eyes, stared across the yellow candlelight at the woman who had violated it.

I tried to move—her brother tried to move—but the sand seemed to hold our feet. I tried to cry—her brother tried to cry—but the sand seemed to fill our lungs and throat. We could only stare—and, even so, the sand seemed to rise like a desert storm and cloud our vision ...

And when I managed at length to open my eyes again, the mummy was lying once more upon its back, motionless, the shrunken and painted face upturned towards the ceiling, and the old lady had tumbled forward and was lying in the semblance of death with her head and arms upon its crumbling body.

But upon the wrappings of the throat I saw the green jasper of the sacred scarabaeus shining again like a living eye.

Colonel Wragge and the doctor recovered themselves long before I did, and I found myself helping them clumsily and unintelligently to raise the frail body of the old lady, while John Silence carefully replaced the covering over the grave and scraped back the sand with his foot, while he issued brief directions.

I heard his voice as in a dream; but the journey back along that cramped tunnel, weighted by a dead woman, blinded with sand, suffocated with heat, was in no sense a dream. It took us the best part of half an hour to reach the open air. And, even then, we had to wait a considerable time for the appearance of Dr. Silence. We carried her undiscovered into the house and up to her own room.

"The mummy will cause no further disturbance," I heard Dr. Silence say to our host later that evening as we prepared to drive for the night train, "provided always," he added significantly, "that you, and yours, cause it no disturbance."

It was in a dream, too, that we left.

"You did not see her face, I know," he said to me as we wrapped our rugs about us in the empty compartment. And when I shook my head, quite unable to explain the instinct that had come to me not to look, he turned toward me, his face pale, and genuinely sad.

"Scorched and blasted," he whispered.

Sand

Algernon Blackwood

I

As Felix Henriot came through the streets that January night the fog was stifling, but when he reached his little flat upon the top floor there came a sound of wind. Wind was stirring about the world. It blew against his windows, but at first so faintly that he hardly noticed it. Then, with an abrupt rise and fall like a wailing voice that sought to claim attention, it called him. He peered through the window into the blurred darkness, listening.

There is no cry in the world like that of the homeless wind. A vague excitement, scarcely to be analysed, ran through his blood. The curtain of fog waved momentarily aside. Henriot fancied a star peeped down at him.

"It will change things a bit—at last," he sighed, settling back into his chair. "It will bring movement!"

Already something in himself had changed. A restlessness, as of that wandering wind, woke in his heart—the desire to be off and away. Other things could rouse this wildness too: falling water, the singing of a bird, an odour of wood-fire, a glimpse of winding road. But the cry of wind, always searching, questioning, travelling the world's great routes, remained ever the master-touch. High longing took his mood in hand. Mid seven millions he felt suddenly—lonely.

"I will arise and go now, for always night and day I hear lake water lapping with low sounds by the shore; While I stand on the roadway, or on the pavements gray, I hear it in the deep heart's core."

He murmured the words over softly to himself. The emotion that produced Innisfree passed strongly through him. He too would be over the hills and far away. He craved movement, change, adventure—somewhere far from shops and crowds and motor-'busses. For a week the fog had stifled London. This wind brought life.

Where should he go? Desire was long; his purse was short.

He glanced at his books, letters, newspapers. They had no interest now. Instead he listened. The panorama of other journeys rolled in colour through the little room, flying on one another's heels. Henriot enjoyed this remembered essence of his travels more than the travels themselves. The crying wind brought so many voices, all of them seductive:

There was a soft crashing of waves upon the Black Sea shores, where the huge Caucasus beckoned in the sky beyond; a rustling in the umbrella pines and cactus at Marseilles, whence magic steamers start about the world like flying dreams. He heard the plash of fountains upon Mount Ida's slopes, and the whisper of the tamarisk on Marathon. It was dawn once more upon the Ionian Sea, and he smelt the perfume of the Cyclades. Blue-veiled islands melted in the sunshine, and across the dewy lawns of Tempe, moistened by the spray of many waterfalls, he saw—Great Heavens above!—the dancing of white forms ... or was it only mist the sunshine painted against Pelion?... "Methought, among the lawns together, we wandered underneath the young grey dawn. And multitudes of dense white fleecy clouds shepherded by the slow, unwilling wind...."

And then, into his stuffy room, slipped the singing perfume of a wall-flower on a ruined tower, and with it the sweetness of hot ivy. He heard the "yellow bees in the ivy bloom." Wind whipped over the open hills—this very wind that laboured drearily through the London fog.

And—he was caught. The darkness melted from the city. The fog whisked off into an azure sky. The roar of traffic turned into booming of the sea. There was a whistling among cordage, and the floor swayed to and fro. He saw a sailor touch his cap and pocket the two-franc piece. The syren hooted—ominous sound that had started him on many a journey of adventure—and the roar of London became mere insignificant clatter of a child's toy carriages.

He loved that syren's call; there was something deep and pitiless in it. It drew the wanderers forth from cities everywhere:

"Leave your known world behind you, and come with me for better or for worse! The anchor is up; it is too late to change. Only—beware! You shall know curious things—and alone!"

Henriot stirred uneasily in his chair. He turned with sudden energy to the shelf of guide-books, maps and time-tables—possessions he most valued in the whole room. He was a happy-go-lucky, adventure-loving soul, careless of common standards, athirst ever for the new and strange.

"That's the best of having a cheap flat," he laughed, "and no ties in the world. I can turn the key and disappear. No one cares or knows—no one but the thieving caretaker. And he's long ago found out that there's nothing here worth taking!"

There followed then no lengthy indecision. Preparation was even shorter still. He was always ready for a move, and his sojourn in cities was but breathing-space while he gathered pennies for further wanderings. An enormous kit-bag—sack-shaped, very worn and dirty—emerged speedily from the bottom of a cupboard in the wall. It was of limitless capacity. The key and padlock rattled in its depths. Cigarette ashes covered everything while he stuffed it full of ancient, indescribable garments. And his voice, singing of those "yellow bees in the ivy bloom," mingled with the crying of the rising wind about his windows. His restlessness had disappeared by magic.

This time, however, there could be no haunted Pelion, nor shady groves of Tempe, for he lived in sophisticated times when money markets regulated movement sternly. Travelling was only for the rich; mere wanderers must pig it. He remembered instead an opportune invitation to the Desert. "Objective" invitation, his genial hosts had called it, knowing his hatred of convention. And Helouan danced into letters of brilliance upon the inner map of his mind. For Egypt had ever held his spirit in thrall, though as yet he had tried in vain to touch the great buried soul of her. The excavators, the Egyptologists, the archaeologists most of all, plastered her grey ancient face with labels like hotel advertisements on travellers' portmanteaux. They told where she had come from last, but nothing of what she dreamed and thought and loved. The heart of Egypt lay beneath the sand, and the trifling robbery of little details that poked forth from tombs and temples brought no true revelation of her stupendous spiritual splendour. Henriot, in his youth, had searched and dived among what material he could find, believing once—or half believing—that the ceremonial of that ancient system veiled a weight of symbol that was reflected from genuine supersensual knowledge. The rituals, now taken literally, and so pityingly explained away, had once been genuine pathways of approach. But never yet, and least of all in his previous visits to Egypt itself, had he discovered one single person, worthy of speech, who caught at his idea. "Curious," they said, then turned away—to go on digging in the sand. Sand smothered her world to-day. Excavators discovered skeletons. Museums everywhere stored them—grinning, literal relics that told nothing.

But now, while he packed and sang, these hopes of enthusiastic younger days stirred again—because the emotion that gave them birth was real and true in him. Through the morning mists upon the Nile an old pyramid bowed hugely at him across London roofs: "Come," he heard its awful whisper beneath the ceiling, "I have things to show you, and to tell." He saw the flock of them sailing the Desert like weird grey solemn ships that make no earthly port. And he imagined them as one: multiple expressions of some single unearthly portent they adumbrated in mighty form—dead symbols of some spiritual conception long vanished from the world.

"I mustn't dream like this," he laughed, "or I shall get absent-minded and pack fire-tongs instead of boots. It looks like a jumble sale already!" And he stood on a heap of things to wedge them down still tighter.

But the pictures would not cease. He saw the kites circling high in the blue air. A couple of white vultures flapped lazily away over shining miles. Felucca sails, like giant wings emerging from the ground, curved towards him from the Nile. The palm-trees dropped long shadows over Memphis. He felt the delicious, drenching heat, and the Khamasin, that over-wind from Nubia, brushed his very cheeks. In the little gardens the mish-mish was in bloom.... He smelt the Desert ... grey sepulchre of cancelled cycles.... The stillness of her interminable reaches dropped down upon old London....

The magic of the sand stole round him in its silent-footed tempest.

And while he struggled with that strange, capacious sack, the piles of clothing ran into shapes of gleaming Bedouin faces; London garments settled down with the mournful sound of camels' feet, half dropping wind, half water flowing underground—sound that old Time has brought over into modern life and left a moment for our wonder and perhaps our tears.

He rose at length with the excitement of some deep enchantment in his eyes. The thought of Egypt plunged ever so deeply into him, carrying him into depths where he found it difficult to breathe, so strangely far away it seemed, yet indefinably familiar. He lost his way. A touch of fear came with it.

"A sack like that is the wonder of the world," he laughed again, kicking the unwieldy, sausage-shaped monster into a corner of the room, and sitting down to write the thrilling labels: "Felix Henriot, Alexandria via Marseilles." But his pen blotted the letters; there was sand in it. He rewrote the words. Then he remembered a dozen things he had left out. Impatiently, yet with confusion somewhere, he stuffed them in. They ran away into shifting heaps; they disappeared; they emerged suddenly again. It was like packing hot, dry, flowing sand. From the pockets of a coat—he had worn it last summer down Dorset way—out trickled sand. There was sand in his mind and thoughts.

And his dreams that night were full of winds, the old sad winds of Egypt, and of moving, sifting sand. Arabs and Afreets danced amazingly together across dunes he could never reach. For he could not follow fast enough. Something infinitely older than these ever caught his feet and held him back. A million tiny fingers stung and pricked him. Something flung a veil before his eyes. Once it touched him—his face and hands and neck. "Stay here with us," he heard a host of muffled voices crying, but their sound was smothered, buried, rising through the ground. A myriad throats were choked. Till, at last, with a violent effort he turned and seized it. And then the thing he grasped at slipped between his fingers and ran easily away. It had a grey and yellow face, and it moved through all its parts. It flowed as water flows, and yet was solid. It was centuries old.

He cried out to it. "Who are you? What is your name? I surely know you ... but I have forgotten ...?"

And it stopped, turning from far away its great uncovered countenance of nameless colouring. He caught a voice. It rolled and boomed and whispered like the wind. And then he woke, with a curious shaking in his heart, and a little touch of chilly perspiration on the skin.

But the voice seemed in the room still—close beside him:

"I am the Sand," he heard, before it died away.

And next he realised that the glitter of Paris lay behind him, and a steamer was taking him with much unnecessary motion across a sparkling sea towards Alexandria. Gladly he saw the Riviera fade below the horizon, with its hard bright sunshine, treacherous winds, and its smear of rich, conventional English. All restlessness now had left him. True vagabond still at forty, he only felt the unrest and discomfort of life when caught in the network of routine and rigid streets, no chance of breaking loose. He was off again at last, money scarce enough indeed, but the joy of wandering expressing itself in happy emotions of release. Every warning of calculation was stifled. He thought of the American woman who walked out of her Long Island house one summer's day to look at a passing sail—and was gone eight years before she walked in again. Eight years of roving travel! He had always felt respect and admiration for that woman.

For Felix Henriot, with his admixture of foreign blood, was philosopher as well as vagabond, a strong poetic and religious strain sometimes breaking out through fissures in his complex nature. He had seen much life; had read many books. The passionate desire of youth to solve the world's big riddles had given place to a resignation filled to the brim with wonder. Anything might be true. Nothing surprised him. The most outlandish beliefs, for all he knew, might fringe truth somewhere. He had escaped that cheap cynicism with which disappointed men soothe their vanity when they realise that an intelligible explanation of the universe lies beyond their powers. He no longer expected final answers.

For him, even the smallest journeys held the spice of some adventure; all minutes were loaded with enticing potentialities. And they shaped for themselves somehow a dramatic form. "It's like a story," his friends said when he told his travels. It always was a story.

But the adventure that lay waiting for him where the silent streets of little Helouan kiss the great Desert's lips, was of a different kind to any Henriot had yet encountered. Looking back, he has often asked himself, "How in the world can I accept it?"

And, perhaps, he never yet has accepted it. It was sand that brought it. For the Desert, the stupendous thing that mothers little Helouan, produced it.

II

He slipped through Cairo with the same relief that he left the Riviera, resenting its social vulgarity so close to the imperial aristocracy of the Desert; he settled down into the peace of soft and silent little Helouan. The hotel in which he had a room on the top floor had been formerly a Khedivial Palace. It had the air of a palace still. He felt himself in a country-house, with lofty ceilings, cool and airy corridors, spacious halls. Soft-footed Arabs attended to his wants; white walls let in light and air without a sign of heat; there was a feeling of a large, spread tent pitched on the very sand; and the wind that stirred the oleanders in the shady gardens also crept in to rustle the palm leaves of his favourite corner seat. Through the large windows where once the Khedive held high court, the sunshine blazed upon vistaed leagues of Desert.

And from his bedroom windows he watched the sun dip into gold and crimson behind the swelling Libyan sands. This side of the pyramids he saw the Nile meander among palm groves and tilled fields. Across his balcony railings the Egyptian stars trooped down beside his very bed, shaping old constellations for his dreams; while, to the south, he looked out upon the vast untamable Body of the sands that carpeted the world for thousands of miles towards Upper Egypt, Nubia, and the dread Sahara itself. He wondered again why people thought it necessary to go so far afield to know the Desert. Here, within half an hour of Cairo, it lay breathing solemnly at his very doors.

For little Helouan, caught thus between the shoulders of the Libyan and Arabian Deserts, is utterly sand-haunted. The Desert lies all round it like a sea. Henriot felt he never could escape from it, as he moved about the island whose coasts are washed with sand. Down each broad and shining street the two end houses framed a vista of its dim immensity—glimpses of shimmering blue, or flame-touched purple. There were stretches of deep sea-green as well, far off upon its bosom. The streets were open channels of approach, and the eye ran down them as along the tube of a telescope laid to catch incredible distance out of space. Through them the Desert reached in with long, thin feelers towards the village. Its Being flooded into Helouan, and over it. Past walls and houses, churches and hotels, the sea of Desert pressed in silently with its myriad soft feet of sand. It poured in everywhere, through crack and slit and crannie. These were reminders of possession and ownership. And every passing wind that lifted eddies of dust at the street corners were messages from the quiet, powerful Thing that permitted Helouan to lie and dream so peacefully in the sunshine. Mere artificial oasis, its existence was temporary, held on lease, just for ninety-nine centuries or so.

This sea idea became insistent. For, in certain lights, and especially in the brief, bewildering dusk, the Desert rose—swaying towards the small white houses. The waves of it ran for fifty miles without a break. It was too deep for foam or surface agitation, yet it knew the swell of tides. And underneath flowed resolute currents, linking distance to the centre. These many deserts were really one. A storm, just retreated, had tossed Helouan upon the shore and left it there to dry; but any morning he would wake to find it had been carried off again into the depths. Some fragment, at least, would disappear. The grim Mokattam Hills were rollers that ever threatened to topple down and submerge the sandy bar that men called Helouan.

Being soundless, and devoid of perfume, the Desert's message reached him through two senses only—sight and touch; chiefly, of course, the former. Its invasion was concentrated through the eyes. And vision, thus uncorrected, went what pace it pleased. The Desert played with him. Sand stole into his being—through the eyes.

And so obsessing was this majesty of its close presence, that Henriot sometimes wondered how people dared their little social activities within its very sight and hearing; how they played golf and tennis upon reclaimed edges of its face, picnicked so blithely hard upon its frontiers, and danced at night while this stern, unfathomable Thing lay breathing just beyond the trumpery walls that kept it out. The challenge of their shallow admiration seemed presumptuous, almost provocative. Their pursuit of pleasure suggested insolent indifference. They ran fool-hardy hazards, he felt; for there was no worship in their vulgar hearts. With a mental shudder, sometimes he watched the cheap tourist horde go laughing, chattering past within view of its ancient, half-closed eyes. It was like defying deity.

For, to his stirred imagination the sublimity of the Desert dwarfed humanity. These people had been wiser to choose another place for the flaunting of their tawdry insignificance. Any minute this Wilderness, "huddled in grey annihilation," might awake and notice them ...!

In his own hotel were several "smart," so-called "Society" people who emphasised the protest in him to the point of definite contempt. Overdressed, the latest worldly novel under their arms, they strutted the narrow pavements of their tiny world, immensely pleased with themselves. Their vacuous minds expressed themselves in the slang of their exclusive circle—value being the element excluded. The pettiness of their outlook hardly distressed him—he was too familiar with it at home—but their essential vulgarity, their innate ugliness, seemed more than usually offensive in the grandeur of its present setting. Into the mighty sands they took the latest London scandal, gabbling it over even among the Tombs and Temples. And "it was to laugh," the pains they spent wondering whom they might condescend to know, never dreaming that they themselves were not worth knowing. Against the background of the noble Desert their titles seemed the cap and bells of clowns.

And Henriot, knowing some of them personally, could not always escape their insipid company. Yet he was the gainer. They little guessed how their commonness heightened contrast, set mercilessly thus beside the strange, eternal beauty of the sand.

Occasionally the protest in his soul betrayed itself in words, which of course they did not understand. "He is so clever, isn't he?" And then, having relieved his feelings, he would comfort himself characteristically:

"The Desert has not noticed them. The Sand is not aware of their existence. How should the sea take note of rubbish that lies above its tide-line?"

For Henriot drew near to its great shifting altars in an attitude of worship. The wilderness made him kneel in heart. Its shining reaches led to the oldest Temple in the world, and every journey that he made was like a sacrament. For him the Desert was a consecrated place. It was sacred.

And his tactful hosts, knowing his peculiarities, left their house open to him when he cared to come—they lived upon the northern edge of the oasis—and he was as free as though he were absolutely alone. He blessed them; he rejoiced that he had come. Little Helouan accepted him. The Desert knew that he was there.

From his corner of the big dining-room he could see the other guests, but his roving eye always returned to the figure of a solitary man who sat at an adjoining table, and whose personality stirred his interest. While affecting to look elsewhere, he studied him as closely as might be. There was something about the stranger that touched his curiosity—a certain air of expectation that he wore. But it was more than that: it was anticipation, apprehension in it somewhere. The man was nervous, uneasy. His restless way of suddenly looking about him proved it. Henriot tried every one else in the room as well; but, though his thought settled on others too, he always came back to the figure of this solitary being opposite, who ate his dinner as if afraid of being seen, and glanced up sometimes as if fearful of being watched. Henriot's curiosity, before he knew it, became suspicion. There was mystery here. The table, he noticed, was laid for two.

"Is he an actor, a priest of some strange religion, an enquiry agent, or just—a crank?" was the thought that first occurred to him. And the question suggested itself without amusement. The impression of subterfuge and caution he conveyed left his observer unsatisfied.

The face was clean shaven, dark, and strong; thick hair, straight yet bushy, was slightly unkempt; it was streaked with grey; and an unexpected mobility when he smiled ran over the features that he seemed to hold rigid by deliberate effort. The man was cut to no quite common measure. Henriot jumped to an intuitive conclusion: "He's not here for pleasure or merely sight-seeing. Something serious has brought him out to Egypt." For the face combined too ill-assorted qualities: an obstinate tenacity that might even mean brutality, and was certainly repulsive, yet, with it, an undecipherable dreaminess betrayed by lines of the mouth, but above all in the very light blue eyes, so rarely raised. Those eyes, he felt, had looked upon unusual things; "dreaminess" was not an adequate description; "searching" conveyed it better. The true source of the queer impression remained elusive. And hence, perhaps, the incongruous marriage in the face—mobility laid upon a matter-of-fact foundation underneath. The face showed conflict.

And Henriot, watching him, felt decidedly intrigued. "I'd like to know that man, and all about him." His name, he learned later, was Richard Vance; from Birmingham; a business man. But it was not the Birmingham he wished to know; it was the—other: cause of the elusive, dreamy searching. Though facing one another at so short a distance, their eyes, however, did not meet. And this, Henriot well knew, was a sure sign that he himself was also under observation. Richard Vance, from Birmingham, was equally taking careful note of Felix Henriot, from London.

Thus, he could wait his time. They would come together later. An opportunity would certainly present itself. The first links in a curious chain had already caught; soon the chain would tighten, pull as though by chance, and bring their lives into one and the same circle. Wondering in particular for what kind of a companion the second cover was laid, Henriot felt certain that their eventual coming together was inevitable. He possessed this kind of divination from first impressions, and not uncommonly it proved correct.

Following instinct, therefore, he took no steps towards acquaintance, and for several days, owing to the fact that he dined frequently with his hosts, he saw nothing more of Richard Vance, the business man from Birmingham. Then, one night, coming home late from his friend's house, he had passed along the great corridor, and was actually a step or so into his bedroom, when a drawling voice sounded close behind him. It was an unpleasant sound. It was very near him too—

"I beg your pardon, but have you, by any chance, such a thing as a compass you could lend me?"

The voice was so close that he started. Vance stood within touching distance of his body. He had stolen up like a ghostly Arab, must have followed him, too, some little distance, for further down the passage the light of an open door—he had passed it on his way—showed where he came from.

"Eh? I beg your pardon? A—compass, did you say?" He felt disconcerted for a moment. How short the man was, now that he saw him standing. Broad and powerful too. Henriot looked down upon his thick head of hair. The personality and voice repelled him. Possibly his face, caught unawares, betrayed this.

"Forgive my startling you," said the other apologetically, while the softer expression danced in for a moment and disorganised the rigid set of the face. "The soft carpet, you know. I'm afraid you didn't hear my tread. I wondered"—he smiled again slightly at the nature of the request— "if—by any chance—you had a pocket compass you could lend me?"

"Ah, a compass, yes! Please don't apologise. I believe I have one—if you'll wait a moment. Come in, won't you? I'll have a look."

The other thanked him but waited in the passage. Henriot, it so happened, had a compass, and produced it after a moment's search.

"I am greatly indebted to you—if I may return it in the morning. You will forgive my disturbing you at such an hour. My own is broken, and I wanted—er—to find the true north."

Henriot stammered some reply, and the man was gone. It was all over in a minute. He locked his door and sat down in his chair to think. The little incident had upset him, though for the life of him he could not imagine why. It ought by rights to have been almost ludicrous, yet instead it was the exact reverse—half threatening. Why should not a man want a compass? But, again, why should he? And at midnight? The voice, the eyes, the near presence—what did they bring that set his nerves thus asking unusual questions? This strange impression that something grave was happening, something unearthly—how was it born exactly? The man's proximity came like a shock. It had made him start. He brought—thus the idea came unbidden to his mind—something with him that galvanised him quite absurdly, as fear does, or delight, or great wonder. There was a music in his voice too—a certain—well, he could only call it lilt, that reminded him of plainsong, intoning, chanting. Drawling was not the word at all.

He tried to dismiss it as imagination, but it would not be dismissed. The disturbance in himself was caused by something not imaginary, but real. And then, for the first time, he discovered that the man had brought a faint, elusive suggestion of perfume with him, an aromatic odour, that made him think of priests and churches. The ghost of it still lingered in the air. Ah, here then was the origin of the notion that his voice had chanted: it was surely the suggestion of incense. But incense, intoning, a compass to find the true north—at midnight in a Desert hotel!

A touch of uneasiness ran through the curiosity and excitement that he felt.

And he undressed for bed. "Confound my old imagination," he thought, "what tricks it plays me! It'll keep me awake!"

But the questions, once started in his mind, continued. He must find explanation of one kind or another before he could lie down and sleep, and he found it at length in—the stars. The man was an astronomer of sorts; possibly an astrologer into the bargain! Why not? The stars were wonderful above Helouan. Was there not an observatory on the Mokattam Hills, too, where tourists could use the telescopes on privileged days? He had it at last. He even stole out on to his balcony to see if the stranger perhaps was looking through some wonderful apparatus at the heavens. Their rooms were on the same side. But the shuttered windows revealed no stooping figure with eyes glued to a telescope. The stars blinked in their many thousands down upon the silent desert. The night held neither sound nor movement. There was a cool breeze blowing across the Nile from the Lybian Sands. It nipped; and he stepped back quickly into the room again. Drawing the mosquito curtains carefully about the bed, he put the light out and turned over to sleep.

And sleep came quickly, contrary to his expectations, though it was a light and surface sleep. That last glimpse of the darkened Desert lying beneath the Egyptian stars had touched him with some hand of awful power that ousted the first, lesser excitement. It calmed and soothed him in one sense, yet in another, a sense he could not understand, it caught him in a net of deep, deep feelings whose mesh, while infinitely delicate, was utterly stupendous. His nerves this deeper emotion left alone: it reached instead to something infinite in him that mere nerves could neither deal with nor interpret. The soul awoke and whispered in him while his body slept.

And the little, foolish dreams that ran to and fro across this veil of surface sleep brought oddly tangled pictures of things quite tiny and at the same time of others that were mighty beyond words. With these two counters Nightmare played. They interwove. There was the figure of this dark-faced man with the compass, measuring the sky to find the true north, and there were hints of giant Presences that hovered just outside some curious outline that he traced upon the ground, copied in some nightmare fashion from the heavens. The excitement caused by his visitor's singular request mingled with the profounder sensations his final look at the stars and Desert stirred. The two were somehow inter-related.

Some hours later, before this surface sleep passed into genuine slumber, Henriot woke—with an appalling feeling that the Desert had come creeping into his room and now stared down upon him where he lay in bed. The wind was crying audibly about the walls outside. A faint, sharp tapping came against the window panes.

He sprang instantly out of bed, not yet awake enough to feel actual alarm, yet with the nightmare touch still close enough to cause a sort of feverish, loose bewilderment. He switched the lights on. A moment later he knew the meaning of that curious tapping, for the rising wind was flinging tiny specks of sand against the glass. The idea that they had summoned him belonged, of course, to dream.

He opened the window, and stepped out on to the balcony. The stone was very cold under his bare feet. There was a wash of wind all over him. He saw the sheet of glimmering, pale desert near and far; and something stung his skin below the eyes.

"The sand," he whispered, "again the sand; always the sand. Waking or sleeping, the sand is everywhere—nothing but sand, sand, Sand...."

He rubbed his eyes. It was like talking in his sleep, talking to Someone who had questioned him just before he woke. But was he really properly awake? It seemed next day that he had dreamed it. Something enormous, with rustling skirts of sand, had just retreated far into the Desert. Sand went with it—flowing, trailing, smothering the world. The wind died down.

And Henriot went back to sleep, caught instantly away into unconsciousness; covered, blinded, swept over by this spreading thing of reddish brown with the great, grey face, whose Being was colossal yet quite tiny, and whose fingers, wings and eyes were countless as the stars.

But all night long it watched and waited, rising to peer above the little balcony, and sometimes entering the room and piling up beside his very pillow. He dreamed of Sand.

III

For some days Henriot saw little of the man who came from Birmingham and pushed curiosity to a climax by asking for a compass in the middle of the night. For one thing, he was a good deal with his friends upon the other side of Helouan, and for another, he slept several nights in the Desert.

He loved the gigantic peace the Desert gave him. The world was forgotten there; and not the world merely, but all memory of it. Everything faded out. The soul turned inwards upon itself.

An Arab boy and donkey took out sleeping-bag, food and water to the Wadi Hof, a desolate gorge about an hour eastwards. It winds between cliffs whose summits rise some thousand feet above the sea. It opens suddenly, cut deep into the swaying world of level plateaux and undulating hills. It moves about too; he never found it in the same place twice—like an arm of the Desert that shifted with the changing lights. Here he watched dawns and sunsets, slept through the mid-day heat, and enjoyed the unearthly colouring that swept Day and Night across the huge horizons. In solitude the Desert soaked down into him. At night the jackals cried in the darkness round his cautiously-fed camp fire—small, because wood had to be carried—and in the day-time kites circled overhead to inspect him, and an occasional white vulture flapped across the blue. The weird desolation of this rocky valley, he thought, was like the scenery of the moon. He took no watch with him, and the arrival of the donkey boy an hour after sunrise came almost from another planet, bringing things of time and common life out of some distant gulf where they had lain forgotten among lost ages.

The short hour of twilight brought, too, a bewitchment into the silence that was a little less than comfortable. Full light or darkness he could manage, but this time of half things made him want to shut his eyes and hide. Its effect stepped over imagination. The mind got lost. He could not understand it. For the cliffs and boulders of discoloured limestone shone then with an inward glow that signalled to the Desert with veiled lanterns. The misshappen hills, carved by wind and rain into ominous outlines, stirred and nodded. In the morning light they retired into themselves, asleep. But at dusk the tide retreated. They rose from the sea, emerging naked, threatening. They ran together and joined shoulders, the entire army of them. And the glow of their sandy bodies, self-luminous, continued even beneath the stars. Only the moonlight drowned it. For the moonrise over the Mokattam Hills brought a white, grand loveliness that drenched the entire Desert. It drew a marvellous sweetness from the sand. It shone across a world as yet unfinished, whereon no life might show itself for ages yet to come. He was alone then upon an empty star, before the creation of things that breathed and moved.

What impressed him, however, more than everything else was the enormous vitality that rose out of all this apparent death. There was no hint of the melancholy that belongs commonly to flatness; the sadness of wide, monotonous landscape was not here. The endless repetition of sweeping vale and plateau brought infinity within measurable comprehension. He grasped a definite meaning in the phrase "world without end": the Desert had no end and no beginning. It gave him a sense of eternal peace, the silent peace that star-fields know. Instead of subduing the soul with bewilderment, it inspired with courage, confidence, hope. Through this sand which was the wreck of countless geological ages, rushed life that was terrific and uplifting, too huge to include melancholy, too deep to betray itself in movement. Here was the stillness of eternity. Behind the spread grey masque of apparent death lay stores of accumulated life, ready to break forth at any point. In the Desert he felt himself absolutely royal.

And this contrast of Life, veiling itself in Death, was a contradiction that somehow intoxicated. The Desert exhilaration never left him. He was never alone. A companionship of millions went with him, and he felt the Desert close, as stars are close to one another, or grains of sand.

It was the Khamasin, the hot wind bringing sand, that drove him in—with the feeling that these few days and nights had been immeasurable, and that he had been away a thousand years. He came back with the magic of the Desert in his blood, hotel-life tasteless and insipid by comparison. To human impressions thus he was fresh and vividly sensitive. His being, cleaned and sensitized by pure grandeur, "felt" people—for a time at any rate—with an uncommon sharpness of receptive judgment. He returned to a life somehow mean and meagre, resuming insignificance with his dinner jacket. Out with the sand he had been regal; now, like a slave, he strutted self-conscious and reduced.

But this imperial standard of the Desert stayed a little time beside him, its purity focusing judgment like a lens. The specks of smaller emotions left it clear at first, and as his eye wandered vaguely over the people assembled in the dining-room, it was arrested with a vivid shock upon two figures at the little table facing him.

He had forgotten Vance, the Birmingham man who sought the North at midnight with a pocket compass. He now saw him again, with an intuitive discernment entirely fresh. Before memory brought up her clouding associations, some brilliance flashed a light upon him. "That man," Henriot thought, "might have come with me. He would have understood and loved it!" But the thought was really this—a moment's reflection spread it, rather: "He belongs somewhere to the Desert; the Desert brought him out here." And, again, hidden swiftly behind it like a movement running below water— "What does he want with it? What is the deeper motive he conceals? For there is a deeper motive; and it is concealed."

But it was the woman seated next him who absorbed his attention really, even while this thought flashed and went its way. The empty chair was occupied at last. Unlike his first encounter with the man, she looked straight at him. Their eyes met fully. For several seconds there was steady mutual inspection, while her penetrating stare, intent without being rude, passed searchingly all over his face. It was disconcerting. Crumbling his bread, he looked equally hard at her, unable to turn away, determined not to be the first to shift his gaze. And when at length she lowered her eyes he felt that many things had happened, as in a long period of intimate conversation. Her mind had judged him through and through. Questions and answer flashed. They were no longer strangers. For the rest of dinner, though he was careful to avoid direct inspection, he was aware that she felt his presence and was secretly speaking with him. She asked questions beneath her breath. The answers rose with the quickened pulses in his blood. Moreover, she explained Richard Vance. It was this woman's power that shone reflected in the man. She was the one who knew the big, unusual things. Vance merely echoed the rush of her vital personality.

This was the first impression that he got—from the most striking, curious face he had ever seen in a woman. It remained very near him all through the meal: she had moved to his table, it seemed she sat beside him. Their minds certainly knew contact from that moment.

It is never difficult to credit strangers with the qualities and knowledge that oneself craves for, and no doubt Henriot's active fancy went busily to work. But, none the less, this thing remained and grew: that this woman was aware of the hidden things of Egypt he had always longed to know. There was knowledge and guidance she could impart. Her soul was searching among ancient things. Her face brought the Desert back into his thoughts. And with it came—the sand.

Here was the flash. The sight of her restored the peace and splendour he had left behind him in his Desert camps. The rest, of course, was what his imagination constructed upon this slender basis. Only,—not all of it was imagination.

Now, Henriot knew little enough of women, and had no pose of "understanding" them. His experience was of the slightest; the love and veneration felt for his own mother had set the entire sex upon the heights. His affairs with women, if so they may be called, had been transient—all but those of early youth, which having never known the devastating test of fulfilment, still remained ideal and superb. There was unconscious humour in his attitude—from a distance; for he regarded women with wonder and respect, as puzzles that sweetened but complicated life, might even endanger it. He certainly was not a marrying man! But now, as he felt the presence of this woman so deliberately possess him, there came over him two clear, strong messages, each vivid with certainty. One was that banal suggestion of familiarity claimed by lovers and the like—he had often heard of it— "I have known that woman before; I have met her ages ago somewhere; she is strangely familiar to me"; and the other, growing out of it almost: "Have nothing to do with her; she will bring you trouble and confusion; avoid her, and be warned";—in fact, a distinct presentiment.

Yet, although Henriot dismissed both impressions as having no shred of evidence to justify them, the original clear judgment, as he studied her extraordinary countenance, persisted through all denials The familiarity, and the presentiment, remained. There also remained this other—an enormous imaginative leap!—that she could teach him "Egypt."

He watched her carefully, in a sense fascinated. He could only describe the face as black, so dark it was with the darkness of great age. Elderly was the obvious, natural word; but elderly described the features only. The expression of the face wore centuries. Nor was it merely the coal-black eyes that betrayed an ancient, age-travelled soul behind them. The entire presentment mysteriously conveyed it. This woman's heart knew long-forgotten things—the thought kept beating up against him. There were cheek-bones, oddly high, that made him think involuntarily of the well-advertised Pharaoh, Rameses; a square, deep jaw; and an aquiline nose that gave the final touch of power. For the power undeniably was there, and while the general effect had grimness in it, there was neither harshness nor any forbidding touch about it. There was an implacable sternness in the set of lips and jaw, and, most curious of all, the eyelids over the steady eyes of black were level as a ruler. This level framing made the woman's stare remarkable beyond description. Henriot thought of an idol carved in stone, stone hard and black, with eyes that stared across the sand into a world of things non-human, very far away, forgotten of men. The face was finely ugly. This strange dark beauty flashed flame about it.

And, as the way ever was with him, Henriot next fell to constructing the possible lives of herself and her companion, though without much success. Imagination soon stopped dead. She was not old enough to be Vance's mother, and assuredly she was not his wife. His interest was more than merely piqued—it was puzzled uncommonly. What was the contrast that made the man seem beside her—vile? Whence came, too, the impression that she exercised some strong authority, though never directly exercised, that held him at her mercy? How did he guess that the man resented it, yet did not dare oppose, and that, apparently acquiescing good-humouredly, his will was deliberately held in abeyance, and that he waited sulkily, biding his time? There was furtiveness in every gesture and expression. A hidden motive lurked in him; unworthiness somewhere; he was determined yet ashamed. He watched her ceaselessly and with such uncanny closeness.

Henriot imagined he divined all this. He leaped to the guess that his expenses were being paid. A good deal more was being paid besides. She was a rich relation, from whom he had expectations; he was serving his seven years, ashamed of his servitude, ever calculating escape—but, perhaps, no ordinary escape. A faint shudder ran over him. He drew in the reins of imagination.

Of course, the probabilities were that he was hopelessly astray—one usually is on such occasions—but this time, it so happened, he was singularly right. Before one thing only his ready invention stopped every time. This vileness, this notion of unworthiness in Vance, could not be negative merely. A man with that face was no inactive weakling. The motive he was at such pains to conceal, betraying its existence by that very fact, moved, surely, towards aggressive action. Disguised, it never slept. Vance was sharply on the alert. He had a plan deep out of sight. And Henriot remembered how the man's soft approach along the carpeted corridor had made him start. He recalled the quasi shock it gave him. He thought again of the feeling of discomfort he had experienced.

Next, his eager fancy sought to plumb the business these two had together in Egypt—in the Desert. For the Desert, he felt convinced, had brought them out. But here, though he constructed numerous explanations, another barrier stopped him. Because he knew. This woman was in touch with that aspect of ancient Egypt he himself had ever sought in vain; and not merely with stones the sand had buried so deep, but with the meanings they once represented, buried so utterly by the sands of later thought.

And here, being ignorant, he found no clue that could lead to any satisfactory result, for he possessed no knowledge that might guide him. He floundered—until Fate helped him. And the instant Fate helped him, the warning and presentiment he had dismissed as fanciful, became real again. He hesitated. Caution acted. He would think twice before taking steps to form acquaintance. "Better not," thought whispered. "Better leave them alone, this queer couple.

They're after things that won't do you any good." This idea of mischief, almost of danger, in their purposes was oddly insistent; for what could possibly convey it? But, while he hesitated, Fate, who sent the warning, pushed him at the same time into the circle of their lives: at first tentatively—he might still have escaped; but soon urgently—curiosity led him inexorably towards the end.

IV

It was so simple a manoeuvre by which Fate began the innocent game. The woman left a couple of books behind her on the table one night, and Henriot, after a moment's hesitation, took them out after her. He knew the titles—*The House of the Master*, and *The House of the Hidden Places*, both singular interpretations of the Pyramids that once had held his own mind spellbound. Their ideas had been since disproved, if he remembered rightly, yet the titles were a clue—a clue to that imaginative part of his mind that was so busy constructing theories and had found its stride. Loose sheets of paper, covered with notes in a minute handwriting, lay between the pages; but these, of course, he did not read, noticing only that they were written round designs of various kinds—intricate designs.

He discovered Vance in a corner of the smoking-lounge. The woman had disappeared.

Vance thanked him politely. "My aunt is so forgetful sometimes," he said, and took them with a covert eagerness that did not escape the other's observation. He folded up the sheets and put them carefully in his pocket. On one there was an ink-sketched map, crammed with detail, that might well have referred to some portion of the Desert. The points of the compass stood out boldly at the bottom. There were involved geometrical designs again. Henriot saw them. They exchanged, then, the commonplaces of conversation, but these led to nothing further. Vance was nervous and betrayed impatience. He presently excused himself and left the lounge. Ten minutes later he passed through the outer hall, the woman beside him, and the pair of them, wrapped up in cloak and ulster, went out into the night. At the door, Vance turned and threw a quick, investigating glance in his direction. There seemed a hint of questioning in that glance; it might almost have been a tentative invitation. But, also, he wanted to see if their exit had been particularly noticed—and by whom.

This, briefly told, was the first manoeuvre by which Fate introduced them. There was nothing in it. The details were so insignificant, so slight the conversation, so meagre the pieces thus added to Henriot's imaginative structure. Yet they somehow built it up and made it solid; the outline in his mind began to stand four-square. That writing, those designs, the manner of the man, their going out together, the final curious look—each and all betrayed points of a hidden thing. Subconsciously he was excavating their buried purposes. The sand was shifting. The concentration of his mind incessantly upon them removed it grain by grain and speck by speck. Tips of the smothered thing emerged. Presently a subsidence would follow with a rush and light would blaze upon its skeleton. He felt it stirring underneath his feet—this flowing movement of light, dry, heaped-up sand. It was always—sand.

Then other incidents of a similar kind came about, clearing the way to a natural acquaintanceship. Henriot watched the process with amusement, yet with another feeling too that was only a little less than anxiety. A keen observer, no detail escaped him; he saw the forces of their lives draw closer. It made him think of the devices of young people who desire to know one another, yet cannot get a proper introduction. Fate condescended to such little tricks. They wanted a third person, he began to feel. A third was necessary to some plan they had on hand, and—they waited to see if he could fill the place. This woman, with whom he had yet exchanged no single word, seemed so familiar to him, well known for years. They weighed and watched him, wondering if he would do.

None of the devices were too obviously used, but at length Henriot picked up so many forgotten articles, and heard so many significant phrases, casually let fall, that he began to feel like the villain in a machine-made play, where the hero for ever drops clues his enemy is intended to discover.

Introduction followed inevitably. "My aunt can tell you; she knows Arabic perfectly." He had been discussing the meaning of some local name or other with a neighbour after dinner, and Vance had joined them. The neighbour moved away; these two were left standing alone, and he accepted a cigarette from the other's case. There was a rustle of skirts behind them. "Here she comes," said Vance; "you will let me introduce you." He did not ask for Henriot's name; he had already taken the trouble to find it out—another little betrayal, and another clue.

It was in a secluded corner of the great hall, and Henriot turned to see the woman's stately figure coming towards them across the thick carpet that deadened her footsteps. She came sailing up, her black eyes fixed upon his face. Very erect, head upright, shoulders almost squared, she moved wonderfully well; there was dignity and power in her walk. She was dressed in black, and her face was like the night. He found it impossible to say what lent her this air of impressiveness and solemnity that was almost majestic. But there was this touch of darkness and of power in the way she came that made him think of some sphinx-like figure of stone, some idol motionless in all its parts but moving as a whole, and gliding across—sand. Beneath those level lids her eyes stared hard at him. And a faint sensation of distress stirred in him deep, deep down. Where had he seen those eyes before?

He bowed, as she joined them, and Vance led the way to the armchairs in a corner of the lounge. The meeting, as the talk that followed, he felt, were all part of a preconceived plan. It had happened before. The woman, that is, was familiar to him—to some part of his being that had dropped stitches of old, old memory.

Lady Statham! At first the name had disappointed him. So many folk wear titles, as syllables in certain tongues wear accents—without them being mute, unnoticed, unpronounced. Nonentities, born to names, so often claim attention for their insignificance in this way. But this woman, had she been Jemima Jones, would have made the name distinguished and select. She was a big and sombre personality. Why was it, he wondered afterwards, that for a moment something in him shrank, and that his mind, metaphorically speaking, flung up an arm in self-protection? The instinct flashed and passed. But it seemed to him born of an automatic feeling that he must protect—not himself, but the woman from the man. There was confusion in it all; links were missing. He studied her intently. She was a woman who had none of the external feminine signals in either dress or manner, no graces, no little womanly hesitations and alarms, no daintiness, yet neither anything distinctly masculine. Her charm was strong, possessing; only he kept forgetting that he was talking to a—woman; and the thing she inspired in him included, with respect and wonder, somewhere also this curious hint of dread. This instinct to protect her fled as soon as it was born, for the interest of the conversation in which she so quickly plunged him obliterated all minor emotions whatsoever. Here, for the first time, he drew close to Egypt, the Egypt he had sought so long. It was not to be explained. He felt it.

Beginning with commonplaces, such as "You like Egypt? You find here what you expected?" she led him into better regions with "One finds here what one brings." He knew the delightful experience of talking fluently on subjects he was at home in, and to some one who understood. The feeling at first that to this woman he could not say mere anythings, slipped into its opposite—that he could say everything. Strangers ten minutes ago, they were at once in deep and intimate talk together. He found his ideas readily followed, agreed with up to a point—the point which permits discussion to start from a basis of general accord towards speculation. In the excitement of ideas he neglected the uncomfortable note that had stirred his caution, forgot the warning too. Her mind, moreover, seemed known to him; he was often aware of what she was going to say before he actually heard it; the current of her thoughts struck a familiar gait, and more than once he experienced vividly again the odd sensation that it all had happened before. The very sentences and phrases with which she pointed the turns of her unusual ideas were never wholly unexpected.

For her ideas were decidedly unusual, in the sense that she accepted without question speculations not commonly deemed worth consideration at all, indeed not ordinarily even known. Henriot knew them, because he had read in many fields. It was the strength of her belief that fascinated him. She offered no apologies. She knew. And while he talked, she listening with folded arms and her black eyes fixed upon his own, Richard Vance watched with vigilant eyes and listened too, ceaselessly alert. Vance joined in little enough, however, gave no opinions, his attitude one of general acquiescence. Twice, when pauses of slackening interest made it possible, Henriot fancied he surprised another quality in this negative attitude. Interpreting it each time differently, he yet dismissed both interpretations with a smile. His imagination leaped so absurdly to violent conclusions. They were not tenable: Vance was neither her keeper, nor was he in some fashion a detective. Yet in his manner was sometimes this suggestion of the detective order. He watched with such deep attention, and he concealed it so clumsily with an affectation of careless indifference.

There is nothing more dangerous than that impulsive intimacy strangers sometimes adopt when an atmosphere of mutual sympathy takes them by surprise, for it is akin to the false frankness friends affect when telling "candidly" one another's faults. The mood is invariably regretted later. Henriot, however, yielded to it now with something like abandon. The pleasure of talking with this woman was so unexpected, and so keen.

For Lady Statham believed apparently in some Egypt of her dreams. Her interest was neither historical, archaeological, nor political. It was religious—yet hardly of this earth at all. The conversation turned upon the knowledge of the ancient Egyptians from an unearthly point of view, and even while he talked he was vaguely aware that it was her mind talking through his own. She drew out his ideas and made him say them. But this he was properly aware of only afterwards—that she had cleverly, mercilessly pumped him of all he had ever known or read upon the subject. Moreover, what Vance watched so intently was himself, and the reactions in himself this remarkable woman produced. That also he realised later.

His first impression that these two belonged to what may be called the "crank" order was justified by the conversation. But, at least, it was interesting crankiness, and the belief behind it made it even fascinating. Long before the end he surprised in her a more vital form of his own attitude that anything may be true, since knowledge has never yet found final answers to any of the biggest questions.

He understood, from sentences dropped early in the talk, that she was among those few "superstitious" folk who think that the old Egyptians came closer to reading the eternal riddles of the world than any others, and that their knowledge was a remnant of that ancient Wisdom Religion which existed in the superb, dark civilization of the sunken Atlantis, lost continent that once joined Africa to Mexico. Eighty thousand years ago the dim sands of Poseidonis, great island adjoining the main continent which itself had vanished a vast period before, sank down beneath the waves, and the entire known world to-day was descended from its survivors.

Hence the significant fact that all religions and "mythological" systems begin with a story of a flood—some cataclysmic upheaval that destroyed the world. Egypt itself was colonised by a group of Atlantean priests who brought their curious, deep knowledge with them. They had foreseen the cataclysm.

Lady Statham talked well, bringing into her great dream this strong, insistent quality of belief and fact. She knew, from Plato to

Donelly, all that the minds of men have ever speculated upon the gorgeous legend. The evidence for such a sunken continent—Henriot had skimmed it too in years gone by—she made bewilderingly complete. He had heard Baconians demolish Shakespeare with an array of evidence equally overwhelming. It catches the imagination though not the mind. Yet out of her facts, as she presented them, grew a strange likelihood. The force of this woman's personality, and her calm and quiet way of believing all she talked about, took her listener to some extent—further than ever before, certainly—into the great dream after her. And the dream, to say the least, was a picturesque one, laden with wonderful possibilities. For as she talked the spirit of old Egypt moved up, staring down upon him out of eyes lidded so curiously level. Hitherto all had prated to him of the Arabs, their ancient faith and customs, and the splendour of the Bedouins, those Princes of the Desert. But what he sought, barely confessed in words even to himself, was something older far than this. And this strange, dark woman brought it close. Deeps in his soul, long slumbering, awoke. He heard forgotten questions.

Only in this brief way could he attempt to sum up the storm she roused in him.

She carried him far beyond mere outline, however, though afterwards he recalled the details with difficulty. So much more was suggested than actually expressed. She contrived to make the general modern scepticism an evidence of cheap mentality. It was so easy; the depth it affects to conceal, mere emptiness. "We have tried all things, and found all wanting"—the mind, as measuring instrument, merely confessed inadequate. Various shrewd judgments of this kind increased his respect, although her acceptance went so far beyond his own. And, while the label of credulity refused to stick to her, her sense of imaginative wonder enabled her to escape that dreadful compromise, a man's mind in a woman's temperament. She fascinated him.

The spiritual worship of the ancient Egyptians, she held, was a symbolical explanation of things generally alluded to as the secrets of life and death; their knowledge was a remnant of the wisdom of Atlantis. Material relics, equally misunderstood, still stood to-day at Karnac, Stonehenge, and in the mysterious writings on buried Mexican temples and cities, so significantly akin to the hieroglyphics upon the Egyptian tombs.

"The one misinterpreted as literally as the other," she suggested, "yet both fragments of an advanced knowledge that found its grave in the sea. The Wisdom of that old spiritual system has vanished from the world, only a degraded literalism left of its undecipherable language. The jewel has been lost, and the casket is filled with sand, sand, sand."

How keenly her black eyes searched his own as she said it, and how oddly she made the little word resound. The syllable drew out almost into chanting. Echoes answered from the depths within him, carrying it on and on across some desert of forgotten belief. Veils of sand flew everywhere about his mind. Curtains lifted. Whole hills of sand went shifting into level surfaces whence gardens of dim outline emerged to meet the sunlight.

"But the sand may be removed." It was her nephew, speaking almost for the first time, and the interruption had an odd effect, introducing a sharply practical element. For the tone expressed, so far as he dared express it, disapproval. It was a baited observation, an invitation to opinion.

"We are not sand-diggers, Mr. Henriot," put in Lady Statham, before he decided to respond. "Our object is quite another one; and I believe—I have a feeling," she added almost questioningly, "that you might be interested enough to help us perhaps."

He only wondered the direct attack had not come sooner. Its bluntness hardly surprised him. He felt himself leap forward to accept it. A sudden subsidence had freed his feet.

Then the warning operated suddenly—for an instant. Henriot was interested; more, he was half seduced; but, as yet, he did not mean to be included in their purposes, whatever these might be. That shrinking dread came back a moment, and was gone again before he could question it. His eyes looked full at Lady Statham. "What is it that you know?" they asked her. "Tell me the things we once knew together, you and I. These words are merely trifling. And why does another man now stand in my place? For the sands heaped upon my memory are shifting, and it is you who are moving them away."

His soul whispered it; his voice said quite another thing, although the words he used seemed oddly chosen:

"There is much in the ideas of ancient Egypt that has attracted me ever since I can remember, though I have never caught up with anything definite enough to follow. There was majesty somewhere in their conceptions—a large, calm majesty of spiritual dominion, one might call it perhaps. I am interested."

Her face remained expressionless as she listened, but there was grave conviction in the eyes that held him like a spell. He saw through them into dim, faint pictures whose background was always sand. He forgot that he was speaking with a woman, a woman who half an hour ago had been a stranger to him. He followed these faded mental pictures, though he never caught them up.... It was like his dream in London.

Lady Statham was talking—he had not noticed the means by which she effected the abrupt transition—of familiar beliefs of old Egypt; of the Ka, or Double, by whose existence the survival of the soul was possible, even its return into manifested, physical life; of the astrology, or influence of the heavenly bodies upon all sublunar activities; of terrific forms of other life, known to the ancient worship of Atlantis, great Potencies that might be invoked by ritual and ceremonial, and of their lesser influence as recognised in certain lower forms, hence treated with veneration as the "Sacred Animal" branch of this dim religion. And she spoke lightly of the modern learning which so glibly imagined it was the animals themselves that were looked upon as "gods"—the bull, the bird, the crocodile, the cat. "It's there they all go so absurdly wrong," she said, "taking the symbol for the power symbolised. Yet natural enough. The mind to-day wears blinkers, studies only the details seen directly before it. Had none of us experienced love, we should think the first lover mad. Few to-day know the Powers they knew, hence deny them. If the world were deaf it would stand with mockery before a hearing group swayed by an orchestra, pitying both listeners and performers. It would deem our admiration of a great swinging bell mere foolish worship of form and movement. Similarly, with high Powers that once expressed themselves in common forms—where best they could—being themselves bodiless. The learned men classify the forms with painstaking detail. But deity has gone out of life. The Powers symbolised are no longer experienced."

"These Powers, you suggest, then—their Kas, as it were—may still—"

But she waved aside the interruption. "They are satisfied, as the common people were, with a degraded literalism," she went on. "Nut was the Heavens, who spread herself across the earth in the form of a woman; Shu, the vastness of space; the ibis typified

Thoth, and Hathor was the Patron of the Western Hills; Khonsu, the moon, was personified, as was the deity of the Nile. But the high priest of Ra, the sun, you notice, remained ever the Great One of Visions."

The High Priest, the Great One of Visions!—How wonderfully again she made the sentence sing. She put splendour into it. The pictures shifted suddenly closer in his mind. He saw the grandeur of Memphis and Heliopolis rise against the stars and shake the sand of ages from their stern old temples.

"You think it possible, then, to get into touch with these High Powers you speak of, Powers once manifested in common forms?"

Henriot asked the question with a degree of conviction and solemnity that surprised himself. The scenery changed about him as he listened. The spacious halls of this former khedivial Palace melted into Desert spaces. He smelt the open wilderness, the sand that haunted Helouan. The soft-footed Arab servants moved across the hall in their white sheets like eddies of dust the wind stirred from the Libyan dunes. And over these two strangers close beside him stole a queer, indefinite alteration. Moods and emotions, nameless as unknown stars, rose through his soul, trailing dark mists of memory from unfathomable distances.

Lady Statham answered him indirectly. He found himself wishing that those steady eyes would sometimes close.

"Love is known only by feeling it," she said, her voice deepening a little. "Behind the form you feel the person loved. The process is an evocation, pure and simple. An arduous ceremonial, involving worship and devotional preparation, is the means. It is a difficult ritual—the only one acknowledged by the world as still effectual. Ritual is the passage way of the soul into the Infinite."

He might have said the words himself. The thought lay in him while she uttered it. Evocation everywhere in life was as true as assimilation. Nevertheless, he stared his companion full in the eyes with a touch of almost rude amazement. But no further questions prompted themselves; or, rather, he declined to ask them. He recalled, somehow uneasily, that in ceremonial the points of the compass have significance, standing for forces and activities that sleep there until invoked, and a passing light fell upon that curious midnight request in the corridor upstairs. These two were on the track of undesirable experiments, he thought.... They wished to include him too.

"You go at night sometimes into the Desert?" he heard himself saying. It was impulsive and miscalculated. His feeling that it would be wise to change the conversation resulted in giving it fresh impetus instead.

"We saw you there—in the Wadi Hof," put in Vance, suddenly breaking his long silence; "you too sleep out, then? It means, you know, the Valley of Fear."

"We wondered—" It was Lady Statham's voice, and she leaned forward eagerly as she said it, then abruptly left the sentence incomplete. Henriot started; a sense of momentary acute discomfort again ran over him. The same second she continued, though obviously changing the phrase— "we wondered how you spent your day there, during the heat. But you paint, don't you? You draw, I mean?"

The commonplace question, he realised in every fibre of his being, meant something they deemed significant. Was it his talent for drawing that they sought to use him for? Even as he answered with a simple affirmative, he had a flash of intuition that might be fanciful, yet that might be true: that this extraordinary pair were intent upon some ceremony of evocation that should summon into actual physical expression some Power—some type of life—known long ago to ancient worship, and that they even sought to fix its bodily outline with the pencil—his pencil.

A gateway of incredible adventure opened at his feet. He balanced on the edge of knowing unutterable things. Here was a clue that might lead him towards the hidden Egypt he had ever craved to know. An awful hand was beckoning. The sands were shifting. He saw the million eyes of the Desert watching him from beneath the level lids of centuries. Speck by speck, and grain by grain, the sand that smothered memory lifted the countless wrappings that embalmed it.

And he was willing, yet afraid. Why in the world did he hesitate and shrink? Why was it that the presence of this silent, watching personality in the chair beside him kept caution still alive, with warning close behind? The pictures in his mind were gorgeously coloured. It was Richard Vance who somehow streaked them through with black. A thing of darkness, born of this man's unassertive presence, flitted ever across the scenery, marring its grandeur with something evil, petty, dreadful. He held a horrible thought alive. His mind was thinking venal purposes.

In Henriot himself imagination had grown curiously heated, fed by what had been suggested rather than actually said. Ideas of immensity crowded his brain, yet never assumed definite shape. They were familiar, even as this strange woman was familiar. Once, long ago, he had known them well; had even practised them beneath these bright Egyptian stars. Whence came this prodigious glad excitement in his heart, this sense of mighty Powers coaxed down to influence the very details of daily life? Behind them, for all their vagueness, lay an archetypal splendour, fraught with forgotten meanings. He had always been aware of it in this mysterious land, but it had ever hitherto eluded him. It hovered everywhere. He had felt it brooding behind the towering Colossi at Thebes, in the skeletons of wasted temples, in the uncouth comeliness of the Sphinx, and in the crude terror of the Pyramids even. Over the whole of Egypt hung its invisible wings. These were but isolated fragments of the Body that might express it. And the Desert remained its cleanest, truest symbol. Sand knew it closest. Sand might even give it bodily form and outline.

But, while it escaped description in his mind, as equally it eluded visualisation in his soul, he felt that it combined with its vastness something infinitely small as well. Of such wee particles is the giant Desert born....

Henriot started nervously in his chair, convicted once more of unconscionable staring; and at the same moment a group of hotel people, returning from a dance, passed through the hall and nodded him good-night. The scent of the women reached him; and with it the sound of their voices discussing personalities just left behind. A London atmosphere came with them. He caught trivial phrases, uttered in a drawling tone, and followed by the shrill laughter of a girl. They passed upstairs, discussing their little things, like marionettes upon a tiny stage.

But their passage brought him back to things of modern life, and to some standard of familiar measurement. The pictures that his soul had gazed at so deep within, he realised, were a pictorial transfer caught incompletely from this woman's vivid mind. He had seen the Desert as the grey, enormous Tomb where hovered still the Ka of ancient Egypt. Sand screened her visage with the veil of centuries. But She was there, and She was living. Egypt herself had pitched a temporary camp in him, and then moved on.

There was a momentary break, a sense of abruptness and dislocation. And then he became aware that Lady Statham had been speaking for some time before he caught her actual words, and that a certain change had come into her voice as also into her manner.

V

She was leaning closer to him, her face suddenly glowing and alive. Through the stone figure coursed the fires of a passion that deepened the coal-black eyes and communicated a hint of light—of exaltation—to her whole person. It was incredibly moving. To this deep passion was due the power he had felt. It was her entire life; she lived for it, she would die for it. Her calmness of manner enhanced its effect. Hence the strength of those first impressions that had stormed him. The woman had belief; however wild and strange, it was sacred to her. The secret of her influence was—conviction.

His attitude shifted several points then. The wonder in him passed over into awe. The things she knew were real. They were not merely imaginative speculations.

"I knew I was not wrong in thinking you in sympathy with this line of thought," she was saying in lower voice, steady with earnestness, and as though she had read his mind. "You, too, know, though perhaps you hardly realise that you know. It lies so deep in you that you only get vague feelings of it—intimations of memory. Isn't that the case?"

Henriot gave assent with his eyes; it was the truth.

"What we know instinctively," she continued, "is simply what we are trying to remember. Knowledge is memory." She paused a moment watching his face closely. "At least, you are free from that cheap scepticism which labels these old beliefs as superstition." It was not even a question.

"I—worship real belief—of any kind," he stammered, for her words and the close proximity of her atmosphere caused a strange upheaval in his heart that he could not account for. He faltered in his speech. "It is the most vital quality in life—rarer than deity." He was using her own phrases even. "It is creative. It constructs the world anew—"

"And may reconstruct the old."

She said it, lifting her face above him a little, so that her eyes looked down into his own. It grew big and somehow masculine. It was the face of a priest, spiritual power in it. Where, oh where in the echoing Past had he known this woman's soul? He saw her in another setting, a forest of columns dim about her, towering above giant aisles. Again he felt the Desert had come close. Into this tent-like hall of the hotel came the sifting of tiny sand. It heaped softly about the very furniture against his feet, blocking the exits of door and window. It shrouded the little present. The wind that brought it stirred a veil that had hung for ages motionless....

She had been saying many things that he had missed while his mind went searching. "There were types of life the Atlantean system knew it might revive—life unmanifested to-day in any bodily form," was the sentence he caught with his return to the actual present.

"A type of life?" he whispered, looking about him, as though to see who it was had joined them; "you mean a—soul? Some kind of soul, alien to humanity, or to—to any forms of living thing in the world to-day?" What she had been saying reached him somehow, it seemed, though he had not heard the words themselves. Still hesitating, he was yet so eager to hear. Already he felt she meant to include him in her purposes, and that in the end he must go willingly. So strong was her persuasion on his mind.

And he felt as if he knew vaguely what was coming. Before she answered his curious question—prompting it indeed—rose in his mind that strange idea of the Group-Soul: the theory that big souls cannot express themselves in a single individual, but need an entire group for their full manifestation.

He listened intently. The reflection that this sudden intimacy was unnatural, he rejected, for many conversations were really gathered into one. Long watching and preparation on both sides had cleared the way for the ripening of acquaintance into confidence—how long he dimly wondered? But if this conception of the Group-Soul was not new, the suggestion Lady Statham developed out of it was both new and startling—and yet always so curiously familiar. Its value for him lay, not in far-fetched evidence that supported it, but in the deep belief which made it a vital asset in an honest inner life.

"An individual," she said quietly, "one soul expressed completely in a single person, I mean, is exceedingly rare. Not often is a physical instrument found perfect enough to provide it with adequate expression. In the lower ranges of humanity—certainly in animal and insect life—one soul is shared by many. Behind a tribe of savages stands one Savage. A flock of birds is a single Bird, scattered through the consciousness of all. They wheel in mid-air, they migrate, they obey the deep intelligence called instinct—all as one. The life of any one lion is the life of all—the lion group-soul that manifests itself in the entire genus. An ant-heap is a single Ant; through the bees spreads the consciousness of a single Bee."

Henriot knew what she was working up to. In his eagerness to hasten disclosure he interrupted—

"And there may be types of life that have no corresponding bodily expression at all, then?" he asked as though the question were forced out of him. "They exist as Powers—unmanifested on the earth to-day?"

"Powers," she answered, watching him closely with unswerving stare, "that need a group to provide their body—their physical expression—if they came back."

"Came back!" he repeated below his breath.

But she heard him. "They once had expression. Egypt, Atlantis knew them—spiritual Powers that never visit the world to-day."

"Bodies," he whispered softly, "actual bodies?"

"Their sphere of action, you see, would be their body. And it might be physical outline. So potent a descent of spiritual life would select materials for its body where it could find them. Our conventional notion of a body—what is it? A single outline moving altogether in one direction. For little human souls, or fragments, this is sufficient. But for vaster types of soul an entire host would be required."

"A church?" he ventured. "Some Body of belief, you surely mean?"

She bowed her head a moment in assent. She was determined he should seize her meaning fully.

"A wave of spiritual awakening—a descent of spiritual life upon a nation," she answered slowly, "forms itself a church, and the body of true believers are its sphere of action. They are literally its bodily expression. Each individual believer is a corpuscle in that Body. The Power has provided itself with a vehicle of manifestation. Otherwise we could not know it. And the more real the belief of each individual, the more perfect the expression of the spiritual life behind them all. A Group-soul walks the earth. Moreover, a nation naturally devout could attract a type of soul unknown to a nation that denies all faith. Faith brings back the gods.... But to-day belief is dead, and Deity has left the world."

She talked on and on, developing this main idea that in days of older faiths there were deific types of life upon the earth, evoked by worship and beneficial to humanity. They had long ago withdrawn because the worship which brought them down had died the death. The world had grown pettier. These vast centres of Spiritual Power found no "Body" in which they now could express themselves or manifest.... Her thoughts and phrases poured over him like sand. It was always sand he felt—burying the Present and uncovering the Past....

He tried to steady his mind upon familiar objects, but wherever he looked Sand stared him in the face. Outside these trivial walls the Desert lay listening. It lay waiting too. Vance himself had dropped out of recognition. He belonged to the world of things to-day. But this woman and himself stood thousands of years away, beneath the columns of a Temple in the sands. And the sands were moving. His feet went shifting with them ... running down vistas of ageless memory that woke terror by their sheer immensity of distance....

Like a muffled voice that called to him through many veils and wrappings, he heard her describe the stupendous Powers that evocation might coax down again among the world of men.

"To what useful end?" he asked at length, amazed at his own temerity, and because he knew instinctively the answer in advance. It rose through these layers of coiling memory in his soul.

"The extension of spiritual knowledge and the widening of life," she answered. "The link with the 'unearthly kingdom' wherein this ancient system went forever searching, would be re-established. Complete rehabilitation might follow. Portions—little portions of these Powers—expressed themselves naturally once in certain animal types, instinctive life that did not deny or reject them. The worship of sacred animals was the relic of a once gigantic system of evocation—not of monsters," and she smiled sadly, "but of Powers that were willing and ready to descend when worship summoned them."

Again, beneath his breath, Henriot heard himself murmur—his own voice startled him as he whispered it: "Actual bodily shape and outline?"

"Material for bodies is everywhere," she answered, equally low; "dust to which we all return; sand, if you prefer it, fine, fine sand. Life moulds it easily enough, when that life is potent."

A certain confusion spread slowly through his mind as he heard her. He lit a cigarette and smoked some minutes in silence. Lady Statham and her nephew waited for him to speak. At length, after some inner battling and hesitation, he put the question that he knew they waited for. It was impossible to resist any longer.

"It would be interesting to know the method," he said, "and to revive, perhaps, by experiment—"

Before he could complete his thought, she took him up:

"There are some who claim to know it," she said gravely—her eyes a moment masterful. "A clue, thus followed, might lead to the entire reconstruction I spoke of."

"And the method?" he repeated faintly.

"Evoke the Power by ceremonial evocation—the ritual is obtainable—and note the form it assumes. Then establish it. This shape or outline once secured, could then be made permanent—a mould for its return at will—its natural physical expression here on earth."

"Idol!" he exclaimed.

"Image," she replied at once. "Life, before we can know it, must have a body. Our souls, in order to manifest here, need a material vehicle."

"And—to obtain this form or outline?" he began; "to fix it, rather?"

"Would be required the clever pencil of a fearless looker-on—some one not engaged in the actual evocation. This form, accurately made permanent in solid matter, say in stone, would provide a channel always open. Experiment, properly speaking, might then begin. The cisterns of Power behind would be accessible."

"An amazing proposition!" Henriot exclaimed. What surprised him was that he felt no desire to laugh, and little even to doubt.

"Yet known to every religion that ever deserved the name," put in Vance like a voice from a distance. Blackness came somehow with his interruption—a touch of darkness. He spoke eagerly.

To all the talk that followed, and there was much of it, Henriot listened with but half an ear. This one idea stormed through him with an uproar that killed attention. Judgment was held utterly in abeyance. He carried away from it some vague suggestion that this woman had hinted at previous lives she half remembered, and that every year she came to Egypt, haunting the sands and temples in the effort to recover lost clues. And he recalled afterwards that she said, "This all came to me as a child, just as though it was something half remembered." There was the further suggestion that he himself was not unknown to her; that they, too, had met before. But this, compared to the grave certainty of the rest, was merest fantasy that did not hold his attention. He answered, hardly knowing what he said. His preoccupation with other thoughts deep down was so intense, that he was probably barely polite, uttering empty phrases, with his mind elsewhere. His one desire was to escape and be alone, and it was with genuine relief that he presently excused himself and went upstairs to bed. The halls, he noticed, were empty; an Arab servant waited to put the lights out. He walked up, for the lift had long ceased running.

And the magic of old Egypt stalked beside him. The studies that had fascinated his mind in earlier youth returned with the power that had subdued his mind in boyhood. The cult of Osiris woke in his blood again; Horus and Nephthys stirred in their long-forgotten centres. There revived in him, too long buried, the awful glamour of those liturgal rites and vast body of observances, those spells and formulae of incantation of the oldest known recension that years ago had captured his imagination and belief—the Book of the Dead. Trumpet voices called to his heart again across the desert of some dim past. There were forms of life—impulses from the Creative Power which is the Universe—other than the soul of man. They could be known. A spiritual exaltation, roused by the words and presence of this singular woman, shouted to him as he went.

Then, as he closed his bedroom door, carefully locking it, there stood beside him—Vance. The forgotten figure of Vance came up close—the watching eyes, the simulated interest, the feigned belief, the detective mental attitude, these broke through the grandiose panorama, bringing darkness. Vance, strong personality that hid behind assumed nonentity for some purpose of his own, intruded with sudden violence, demanding an explanation of his presence.

And, with an equal suddenness, explanation offered itself then and there. It came unsought, its horror of certainty utterly unjustified; and it came in this unexpected fashion:

Behind the interest and acquiescence of the man ran—fear: but behind the vivid fear ran another thing that Henriot now perceived was vile. For the first time in his life, Henriot knew it at close quarters, actual, ready to operate. Though familiar enough in daily life to be of common occurrence, Henriot had never realised it as he did now, so close and terrible. In the same way he had never realised that he would die—vanish from the busy world of men and women, forgotten as though he had never existed, an eddy of wind-blown dust. And in the man named Richard Vance this thing was close upon blossom. Henriot could not name it to himself. Even in thought it appalled him.

He undressed hurriedly, almost with the child's idea of finding safety between the sheets. His mind undressed itself as well. The business of the day laid itself automatically aside; the will sank down; desire grew inactive. Henriot was exhausted. But, in that stage towards slumber when thinking stops, and only fugitive pictures pass across the mind in shadowy dance, his brain ceased shouting its mechanical explanations, and his soul unveiled a peering eye. Great limbs of memory, smothered by the activities of the Present, stirred their stiffened lengths through the sands of long ago—sands this woman had begun to excavate from some far-off pre-existence they had surely known together. Vagueness and certainty ran hand in hand. Details were unrecoverable, but the emotions in which they were embedded moved.

He turned restlessly in his bed, striving to seize the amazing clues and follow them. But deliberate effort hid them instantly again; they retired instantly into the subconsciousness. With the brain of this body he now occupied they had nothing to do. The brain stored memories of each life only. This ancient script was graven in his soul. Subconsciousness alone could interpret and reveal. And it was his subconscious memory that Lady Statham had been so busily excavating.

Dimly it stirred and moved about the depths within him, never clearly seen, indefinite, felt as a yearning after unrecoverable knowledge. Against the darker background of Vance's fear and sinister purpose—both of this present life, and recent—he saw the grandeur of this woman's impossible dream, and knew, beyond argument or reason, that it was true. Judgment and will asleep, he left the impossibility aside, and took the grandeur. The Belief of Lady Statham was not credulity and superstition; it was Memory. Still to this day, over the sands of Egypt, hovered immense spiritual potencies, so vast that they could only know physical expression in a group—in many. Their sphere of bodily manifestation must be a host, each individual unit in that host a corpuscle in the whole.

The wind, rising from the Lybian wastes across the Nile, swept up against the exposed side of the hotel, and made his windows rattle—the old, sad winds of Egypt. Henriot got out of bed to fasten the outside shutters. He stood a moment and watched the moon floating down behind the Sakkara Pyramids. The Pleiades and Orion's Belt hung brilliantly; the Great Bear was close to the horizon. In the sky above the Desert swung ten thousand stars. No sounds rose from the streets of Helouan. The tide of sand was coming slowly in.

And a flock of enormous thoughts swooped past him from fields of this unbelievable, lost memory. The Desert, pale in the moon, was coextensive with the night, too huge for comfort or understanding, yet charged to the brim with infinite peace. Behind its majesty of silence lay whispers of a vanished language that once could call with power upon mighty spiritual Agencies. Its skirts were folded now, but, slowly across the leagues of sand, they began to stir and rearrange themselves. He grew suddenly aware of this enveloping shroud of sand—as the raw material of bodily expression: Form.

The sand was in his imagination and his mind. Shaking loosely the folds of its gigantic skirts, it rose; it moved a little towards him. He saw the eternal countenance of the Desert watching him—immobile and unchanging behind these shifting veils the winds laid so carefully over it. Egypt, the ancient Egypt, turned in her vast sarcophagus of Desert, wakening from her sleep of ages at the Belief of approaching worshippers.

Only in this insignificant manner could he express a letter of the terrific language that crowded to seek expression through his soul.... He closed the shutters and carefully fastened them. He turned to go back to bed, curiously trembling. Then, as he did so, the whole singular delusion caught him with a shock that held him motionless. Up rose the stupendous apparition of the entire Desert and stood behind him on that balcony. Swift as thought, in silence, the Desert stood on end against his very face. It towered across the sky, hiding Orion and the moon; it dipped below the horizons. The whole grey sheet of it rose up before his eyes and stood. Through its unfolding skirts ran ten thousand eddies of swirling sand as the creases of its grave-clothes smoothed themselves out in moonlight. And a bleak, scarred countenance, huge as a planet, gazed down into his own....

Through his dreamless sleep that night two things lay active and awake ... in the subconscious part that knows no slumber. They were incongruous. One was evil, small and human; the other unearthly and sublime. For the memory of the fear that haunted Vance, and the sinister cause of it, pricked at him all night long. But behind, beyond this common, intelligible emotion, lay the crowding wonder that caught his soul with glory:

The Sand was stirring, the Desert was awake. Ready to mate with them in material form, brooded close the Ka of that colossal Entity that once expressed itself through the myriad life of ancient Egypt.

VI

Next day, and for several days following, Henriot kept out of the path of Lady Statham and her nephew. The acquaintanceship had grown too rapidly to be quite comfortable. It was easy to pretend that he took people at their face value, but it was a pose; one liked to know something of antecedents. It was otherwise difficult to "place" them. And Henriot, for the life of him, could not "place" these two. His Subconsciousness brought explanation when it came—but the Subconsciousness is only temporarily active. When it retired he floundered without a rudder, in confusion.

With the flood of morning sunshine the value of much she had said evaporated. Her presence alone had supplied the key to the cipher. But while the indigestible portions he rejected, there remained a good deal he had already assimilated. The discomfort remained; and with it the grave, unholy reality of it all. It was something more than theory. Results would follow—if he joined them. He would witness curious things.

The force with which it drew him brought hesitation. It operated in him like a shock that numbs at first by its abrupt arrival, and needs time to realise in the right proportions to the rest of life. These right proportions, however, did not come readily, and his emotions ranged between sceptical laughter and complete acceptance. The one detail he felt certain of was this dreadful thing he had divined in Vance. Trying hard to disbelieve it, he found he could not. It was true. Though without a shred of real evidence to support it, the horror of it remained. He knew it in his very bones.

And this, perhaps, was what drove him to seek the comforting companionship of folk he understood and felt at home with. He told his host and hostess about the strangers, though omitting the actual conversation because they would merely smile in blank miscomprehension. But the moment he described the strong black eyes beneath the level eyelids, his hostess turned with a start, her interest deeply roused: "Why, it's that awful Statham woman," she exclaimed, "that must be Lady Statham, and the man she calls her nephew."

"Sounds like it, certainly," her husband added. "Felix, you'd better clear out. They'll bewitch you too."

And Henriot bridled, yet wondering why he did so. He drew into his shell a little, giving the merest sketch of what had happened. But he listened closely while these two practical old friends supplied him with information in the gossiping way that human nature loves. No doubt there was much embroidery, and more perversion, exaggeration too, but the account evidently rested upon some basis of solid foundation for all that. Smoke and fire go together always.

"He is her nephew right enough," Mansfield corrected his wife, before proceeding to his own man's form of elaboration; "no question about that, I believe. He's her favourite nephew, and she's as rich as a pig. He follows her out here every year, waiting for her empty shoes. But they are an unsavoury couple. I've met 'em in various parts, all over Egypt, but they always come back to Helouan in the end. And the stories about them are simply legion. You remember—" he turned hesitatingly to his wife— "some people, I heard," he changed his sentence, "were made quite ill by her."

"I'm sure Felix ought to know, yes," his wife boldly took him up, "my niece, Fanny, had the most extraordinary experience." She turned to Henriot. "Her room was next to Lady Statham in some hotel or other at Assouan or Edfu, and one night she woke and heard a kind of mysterious chanting or intoning next her. Hotel doors are so dreadfully thin. There was a funny smell too, like incense of something sickly, and a man's voice kept chiming in. It went on for hours, while she lay terrified in bed—"

"Frightened, you say?" asked Henriot.

"Out of her skin, yes; she said it was so uncanny—made her feel icy. She wanted to ring the bell, but was afraid to leave her bed. The room was full of—of things, yet she could see nothing. She felt them, you see. And after a bit the sound of this sing-song voice so got on her nerves, it half dazed her—a kind of enchantment—she felt choked and suffocated. And then—" It was her turn to hesitate.

"Tell it all," her husband said, quite gravely too.

"Well—something came in. At least, she describes it oddly, rather; she said it made the door bulge inwards from the next room, but not the door alone; the walls bulged or swayed as if a huge thing pressed against them from the other side. And at the same moment her windows—she had two big balconies, and the venetian shutters were fastened—both her windows darkened—though it was two in the morning and pitch dark outside. She said it was all one thing—trying to get in; just as water, you see, would rush in through every hole and opening it could find, and all at once. And in spite of her terror—that's the odd part of it—she says she felt a kind of splendour in her—a sort of elation."

"She saw nothing?"

"She says she doesn't remember. Her senses left her, I believe—though she won't admit it."

"Fainted for a minute, probably," said Mansfield.

"So there it is," his wife concluded, after a silence. "And that's true. It happened to my niece, didn't it, John?"

Stories and legendary accounts of strange things that the presence of these two brought poured out then. They were obviously somewhat mixed, one account borrowing picturesque details from another, and all in disproportion, as when people tell stories in a language they are little familiar with. But, listening with avidity, yet also with uneasiness, somehow, Henriot put two and two together. Truth stood behind them somewhere. These two held traffic with the powers that ancient Egypt knew.

"Tell Felix, dear, about the time you met the nephew—horrid creature—in the Valley of the Kings," he heard his wife say presently. And Mansfield told it plainly enough, evidently glad to get it done, though.

"It was some years ago now, and I didn't know who he was then, or anything about him. I don't know much more now—except that he's a dangerous sort of charlatan-devil, I think. But I came across him one night up there by Thebes in the Valley of the Kings—you know, where they buried all their Johnnies with so much magnificence and processions and masses, and all the rest. It's the most astounding, the most haunted place you ever saw, gloomy, silent, full of gorgeous lights and shadows that seem alive—terribly impressive; it makes you creep and shudder. You feel old Egypt watching you."

"Get on, dear," said his wife.

"Well, I was coming home late on a blasted lazy donkey, dog-tired into the bargain, when my donkey boy suddenly ran for his life and left me alone. It was after sunset. The sand was red and shining, and the big cliffs sort of fiery. And my donkey stuck its four feet in the ground and wouldn't budge. Then, about fifty yards away, I saw a fellow—European apparently—doing something—Heaven knows what, for I can't describe it—among the boulders that lie all over the ground there. Ceremony, I suppose you'd call it. I was so interested that at first I watched. Then I saw he wasn't alone. There were a lot of moving things round him, towering big things, that came and went like shadows. That twilight is fearfully bewildering; perspective changes, and distance gets all confused. It's fearfully hard to see properly. I only remember that I got off my donkey and went up closer, and when I was within a dozen yards of him—well, it sounds such rot, you know, but I swear the things suddenly rushed off and left him there alone. They went with a roaring noise like wind; shadowy but tremendously big, they were, and they vanished up against the fiery precipices as though they slipped bang into the stone itself. The only thing I can think of to describe 'em is—well, those sand-storms the Khamasin raises—the hot winds, you know."

"They probably were sand," his wife suggested, burning to tell another story of her own.

"Possibly, only there wasn't a breath of wind, and it was hot as blazes—and—I had such extraordinary sensations—never felt anything like it before—wild and exhilarated—drunk, I tell you, drunk."

"You saw them?" asked Henriot. "You made out their shape at all, or outline?"

"Sphinx," he replied at once, "for all the world like sphinxes. You know the kind of face and head these limestone strata in the Desert take—great visages with square Egyptian head-dresses where the driven sand has eaten away the softer stuff beneath? You see it everywhere—enormous idols they seem, with faces and eyes and lips awfully like the sphinx—well, that's the nearest I can get to it." He puffed his pipe hard. But there was no sign of levity in him. He told the actual truth as far as in him lay, yet half ashamed of what he told. And a good deal he left out, too.

"She's got a face of the same sort, that Statham horror," his wife said with a shiver. "Reduce the size, and paint in awful black eyes, and you've got her exactly—a living idol." And all three laughed, yet a laughter without merriment in it.

"And you spoke to the man?"

"I did," the Englishman answered, "though I confess I'm a bit ashamed of the way I spoke. Fact is, I was excited, thunderingly excited, and felt a kind of anger. I wanted to kick the beggar for practising such bally rubbish, and in such a place too. Yet all the time—well, well, I believe it was sheer funk now," he laughed; "for I felt uncommonly queer out there in the dusk, alone with—with that kind of business; and I was angry with myself for feeling it. Anyhow, I went up—I'd lost my donkey boy as well, remember—and slated him like a dog. I can't remember what I said exactly—only that he stood and stared at me in silence. That made it worse—seemed twice as real then. The beggar said no single word the whole time. He signed to me with one hand to clear out. And then, suddenly out of nothing—she—that woman—appeared and stood beside him. I never saw her come. She must have been behind some boulder or other, for she simply rose out of the ground. She stood there and stared at me too—bang in the face. She was turned towards the sunset—what was left of it in the west—and her black eyes shone like—ugh! I can't describe it—it was shocking."

"She spoke?"

"She said five words—and her voice—it'll make you laugh—it was metallic like a gong: 'You are in danger here.' That's all she said. I simply turned and cleared out as fast as ever I could. But I had to go on foot. My donkey had followed its boy long before. I tell you—smile as you may—my blood was all curdled for an hour afterwards."

Then he explained that he felt some kind of explanation or apology was due, since the couple lodged in his own hotel, and how he approached the man in the smoking-room after dinner. A conversation resulted—the man was quite intelligent after all—of which only one sentence had remained in his mind.

"Perhaps you can explain it, Felix. I wrote it down, as well as I could remember. The rest confused me beyond words or memory; though I must confess it did not seem—well, not utter rot exactly. It was about astrology and rituals and the worship of the old Egyptians, and I don't know what else besides. Only, he made it intelligible and almost sensible, if only I could have got the hang of the thing enough to remember it. You know," he added, as though believing in spite of himself, "there is a lot of that wonderful old Egyptian religious business still hanging about in the atmosphere of this place, say what you like."

"But this sentence?" Henriot asked. And the other went off to get a note-book where he had written it down.

"He was jawing, you see," he continued when he came back, Henriot and his wife having kept silence meanwhile, "about direction being of importance in religious ceremonies, West and North symbolising certain powers, or something of the kind, why people turn to the East and all that sort of thing, and speaking of the whole Universe as if it had living forces tucked away in it that expressed themselves somehow when roused up. That's how I remember it anyhow. And then he said this thing—in answer to some fool question probably that I put." And he read out of the note-book:

"'You were in danger because you came through the Gateway of the West, and the Powers from the Gateway of the East were at that moment rising, and therefore in direct opposition to you.'"

Then came the following, apparently a simile offered by way of explanation. Mansfield read it in a shamefaced tone, evidently prepared for laughter:

"'Whether I strike you on the back or in the face determines what kind of answering force I rouse in you. Direction is significant.' And he said it was the period called the Night of Power—time when the Desert encroaches and spirits are close."

And tossing the book aside, he lit his pipe again and waited a moment to hear what might be said. "Can you explain such gibberish?" he asked at length, as neither of his listeners spoke. But Henriot said he couldn't. And the wife then took up her own tale of stories that had grown about this singular couple.

These were less detailed, and therefore less impressive, but all contributed something towards the atmosphere of reality that framed the entire picture. They belonged to the type one hears at every dinner party in Egypt—stories of the vengeance mummies seem to take on those who robbed them, desecrating their peace of centuries; of a woman wearing a necklace of scarabs taken from a princess's tomb, who felt hands about her throat to strangle her; of little Ka figures, Pasht goddesses, amulets and the rest, that brought curious disaster to those who kept them. They are many and various, astonishingly circumstantial often, and vouched for by persons the reverse of credulous. The modern superstition that haunts the desert gullies with Afreets has nothing in common with them. They rest upon a basis of indubitable experience; and they remain—inexplicable. And about the personalities of Lady Statham and her nephew they crowded like flies attracted by a dish of fruit. The Arabs, too, were afraid of her. She had difficulty in getting guides and dragomen.

"My dear chap," concluded Mansfield, "take my advice and have nothing to do with 'em. There is a lot of queer business knocking about in this old country, and people like that know ways of reviving it somehow. It's upset you already; you looked scared, I thought, the moment you came in." They laughed, but the Englishman was in earnest. "I tell you what," he added, "we'll go off for a bit of shooting together. The fields along the Delta are packed with birds now: they're home early this year on their way to the North. What d'ye say, eh?"

But Henriot did not care about the quail shooting. He felt more inclined to be alone and think things out by himself. He had come to his friends for comfort, and instead they had made him uneasy and excited. His interest had suddenly doubled. Though half afraid, he longed to know what these two were up to—to follow the adventure to the bitter end. He disregarded the warning of his host as well as the premonition in his own heart. The sand had caught his feet.

There were moments when he laughed in utter disbelief, but these were optimistic moods that did not last. He always returned to the feeling that truth lurked somewhere in the whole strange business, and that if he joined forces with them, as they seemed to wish, he would witness—well, he hardly knew what—but it enticed him as danger does the reckless man, or death the suicide. The sand had caught his mind.

He decided to offer himself to all they wanted—his pencil too. He would see—a shiver ran through him at the thought—what they saw, and know some eddy of that vanished tide of power and splendour the ancient Egyptian priesthood knew, and that perhaps was even common experience in the far-off days of dim Atlantis. The sand had caught his imagination too. He was utterly sand-haunted.

VII

And so he took pains, though without making definite suggestion, to place himself in the way of this woman and her nephew—

only to find that his hints were disregarded. They left him alone, if they did not actually avoid him. Moreover, he rarely came across them now. Only at night, or in the queer dusk hours, he caught glimpses of them moving hurriedly off from the hotel, and always desertwards. And their disregard, well calculated, enflamed his desire to the point when he almost decided to propose himself. Quite suddenly, then, the idea flashed through him—how do they come, these odd revelations, when the mind lies receptive like a plate sensitised by anticipation?—that they were waiting for a certain date, and, with the notion, came Mansfield's remark about "the Night of Power," believed in by the old Egyptian Calendar as a time when the supersensuous world moves close against the minds of men with all its troop of possibilities. And the thought, once lodged in its corner of imagination, grew strong. He looked it up. Ten days from now, he found, Leyel-el-Sud would be upon him, with a moon, too, at the full. And this strange hint of guidance he accepted. In his present mood, as he admitted, smiling to himself, he could accept anything. It was part of it, it belonged to the adventure. But, even while he persuaded himself that it was play, the solemn reality, of what lay ahead increased amazingly, sketched darkly in his very soul.

These intervening days he spent as best he could—impatiently, a prey to quite opposite emotions. In the blazing sunshine he thought of it and laughed; but at night he lay often sleepless, calculating chances of escape. He never did escape, however. The Desert that watched little Helouan with great, unwinking eyes watched also every turn and twist he made. Like this oasis, he basked in the sun of older time, and dreamed beneath forgotten moons. The sand at last had crept into his inmost heart. It sifted over him.

Seeking a reaction from normal, everyday things, he made tourist trips; yet, while recognising the comedy in his attitude, he never could lose sight of the grandeur that banked it up so hauntingly. These two contrary emotions grafted themselves on all he did and saw. He crossed the Nile at Bedrashein, and went again to the Tomb-World of Sakkara; but through all the chatter of veiled and helmeted tourists, the bandar-log of our modern Jungle, ran this dark under-stream of awe their monkey methods could not turn aside. One world lay upon another, but this modern layer was a shallow crust that, like the phenomenon of the "desert-film," a mere angle of falling light could instantly obliterate. Beneath the sand, deep down, he passed along the Street of Tombs, as he had often passed before, moved then merely by historical curiosity and admiration, but now by emotions for which he found no name. He saw the enormous sarcophagi of granite in their gloomy chambers where the sacred bulls once lay, swathed and embalmed like human beings, and, in the flickering candle light, the mood of ancient rites surged round him, menacing his doubts and laughter. The least human whisper in these subterraneans, dug out first four thousand years ago, revived ominous Powers that stalked beside him, forbidding and premonitive. He gazed at the spots where Mariette, unearthing them forty years ago, found fresh as of yesterday the marks of fingers and naked feet—of those who set the sixty-five ton slabs in position. And when he came up again into the sunshine he met the eternal questions of the pyramids, overtopping all his mental horizons. Sand blocked all the avenues of younger emotion, leaving the channels of something in him incalculably older, open and clean swept.

He slipped homewards, uncomfortable and followed, glad to be with a crowd—because he was otherwise alone with more than he could dare to think about. Keeping just ahead of his companions, he crossed the desert edge where the ghost of Memphis walks under rustling palm trees that screen no stone left upon another of all its mile-long populous splendours. For here was a vista his imagination could realise; here he could know the comfort of solid ground his feet could touch. Gigantic Ramases, lying on his back beneath their shade and staring at the sky, similarly helped to steady his swaying thoughts. Imagination could deal with these.

And daily thus he watched the busy world go to and fro to its scale of tips and bargaining, and gladly mingled with it, trying to laugh and study guidebooks, and listen to half-fledged explanations, but always seeing the comedy of his poor attempts. Not all those little donkeys, bells tinkling, beads shining, trotting beneath their comical burdens to the tune of shouting and belabouring, could stem this tide of deeper things the woman had let loose in the subconscious part of him. Everywhere he saw the mysterious camels go slouching through the sand, gurgling the water in their skinny, extended throats. Centuries passed between the enormous knee-stroke of their stride. And, every night, the sunsets restored the forbidding, graver mood, with their crimson, golden splendour, their strange green shafts of light, then—sudden twilight that brought the Past upon him with an awful leap. Upon the stage then stepped the figures of this pair of human beings, chanting their ancient plainsong of incantation in the moonlit desert, and working their rites of unholy evocation as the priests had worked them centuries before in the sands that now buried Sakkara fathoms deep.

Then one morning he woke with a question in his mind, as though it had been asked of him in sleep and he had waked just before the answer came. "Why do I spend my time sight-seeing, instead of going alone into the Desert as before? What has made me change?"

This latest mood now asked for explanation. And the answer, coming up automatically, startled him. It was so clear and sure—had been lying in the background all along. One word contained it:

Vance.

The sinister intentions of this man, forgotten in the rush of other emotions, asserted themselves again convincingly. The human horror, so easily comprehensible, had been smothered for the time by the hint of unearthly revelations. But it had operated all the time. Now it took the lead. He dreaded to be alone in the Desert with this dark picture in his mind of what Vance meant to bring there to completion. This abomination of a selfish human will returned to fix its terror in him. To be alone in the Desert meant to be alone with the imaginative picture of what Vance—he knew it with such strange certainty—hoped to bring about there.

There was absolutely no evidence to justify the grim suspicion. It seemed indeed far-fetched enough, this connection between the sand and the purpose of an evil-minded, violent man. But Henriot saw it true. He could argue it away in a few minutes—easily. Yet the instant thought ceased, it returned, led up by intuition. It possessed him, filled his mind with horrible possibilities. He feared the Desert as he might have feared the scene of some atrocious crime. And, for the time, this dread of a merely human thing corrected the big seduction of the other—the suggested "super-natural."

Side by side with it, his desire to join himself to the purposes of the woman increased steadily. They kept out of his way apparently; the offer seemed withdrawn; he grew restless, unable to settle to anything for long, and once he asked the porter casually if they were leaving the hotel. Lady Statham had been invisible for days, and Vance was somehow never within speaking distance. He heard with relief that they had not gone—but with dread as well.

Keen excitement worked in him underground. He slept badly. Like a schoolboy, he waited for the summons to an important examination that involved portentous issues, and contradictory emotions disturbed his peace of mind abominably.

VIII

But it was not until the end of the week, when Vance approached him with purpose in his eyes and manner, that Henriot knew his fears unfounded, and caught himself trembling with sudden anticipation—because the invitation, so desired yet so dreaded, was actually at hand. Firmly determined to keep caution uppermost, yet he went unresistingly to a secluded corner by the palms where they could talk in privacy. For prudence is of the mind, but desire is of the soul, and while his brain of to-day whispered wariness, voices in his heart of long ago shouted commands that he knew he must obey with joy.

It was evening and the stars were out. Helouan, with her fairy twinkling lights, lay silent against the Desert edge. The sand was at the flood. The period of the Encroaching of the Desert was at hand, and the deeps were all astir with movement. But in the windless air was a great peace. A calm of infinite stillness breathed everywhere. The flow of Time, before it rushed away backwards, stopped somewhere between the dust of stars and Desert. The mystery of sand touched every street with its unutterable softness.

And Vance began without the smallest circumlocution. His voice was low, in keeping with the scene, but the words dropped with a sharp distinctness into the other's heart like grains of sand that pricked the skin before they smothered him. Caution they smothered instantly; resistance too.

"I have a message for you from my aunt," he said, as though he brought an invitation to a picnic. Henriot sat in shadow, but his companion's face was in a patch of light that followed them from the windows of the central hall. There was a shining in the light blue eyes that betrayed the excitement his quiet manner concealed. "We are going—the day after to-morrow—to spend the night in the Desert; she wondered if, perhaps, you would care to join us?"

"For your experiment?" asked Henriot bluntly.

Vance smiled with his lips, holding his eyes steady, though unable to suppress the gleam that flashed in them and was gone so swiftly. There was a hint of shrugging his shoulders.

"It is the Night of Power—in the old Egyptian Calendar, you know," he answered with assumed lightness almost, "the final moment of Leyel-el-Sud, the period of Black Nights when the Desert was held to encroach with—with various possibilities of a supernatural order. She wishes to revive a certain practice of the old Egyptians. There may be curious results. At any rate, the occasion is a picturesque one—better than this cheap imitation of London life." And he indicated the lights, the signs of people in the hall dressed for gaieties and dances, the hotel orchestra that played after dinner.

Henriot at the moment answered nothing, so great was the rush of conflicting emotions that came he knew not whence. Vance went calmly on. He spoke with a simple frankness that was meant to be disarming. Henriot never took his eyes off him. The two men stared steadily at one another.

"She wants to know if you will come and help too—in a certain way only: not in the experiment itself precisely, but by watching merely and—" He hesitated an instant, half lowering his eyes.

"Drawing the picture," Henriot helped him deliberately.

"Drawing what you see, yes," Vance replied, the voice turned graver in spite of himself. "She wants—she hopes to catch the outlines of anything that happens—"

"Comes."

"Exactly. Determine the shape of anything that comes. You may remember your conversation of the other night with her. She is very certain of success."

This was direct enough at any rate. It was as formal as an invitation to a dinner, and as guileless. The thing he thought he wanted lay within his reach. He had merely to say yes. He did say yes; but first he looked about him instinctively, as for guidance. He looked at the stars twinkling high above the distant Libyan Plateau; at the long arms of the Desert, gleaming weirdly white in the moonlight, and reaching towards him down every opening between the houses; at the heavy mass of the Mokattam Hills, guarding the Arabian Wilderness with strange, peaked barriers, their sand-carved ridges dark and still above the Wadi Hof.

These questionings attracted no response. The Desert watched him, but it did not answer. There was only the shrill whistling cry of the lizards, and the sing-song of a white-robed Arab gliding down the sandy street. And through these sounds he heard his own voice answer: "I will come—yes. But how can I help? Tell me what you propose—your plan?"

And the face of Vance, seen plainly in the electric glare, betrayed his satisfaction. The opposing things in the fellow's mind of darkness fought visibly in his eyes and skin. The sordid motive, planning a dreadful act, leaped to his face, and with it a flash of this other yearning that sought unearthly knowledge, perhaps believed it too. No wonder there was conflict written on his features.

Then all expression vanished again; he leaned forward, lowering his voice.

"You remember our conversation about there being types of life too vast to manifest in a single body, and my aunt's belief that these were known to certain of the older religious systems of the world?"

"Perfectly."

"Her experiment, then, is to bring one of these great Powers back—we possess the sympathetic ritual that can rouse some among them to activity—and win it down into the sphere of our minds, our minds heightened, you see, by ceremonial to that stage of clairvoyant vision which can perceive them."

"And then?" They might have been discussing the building of a house, so naturally followed answer upon question. But the whole body of meaning in the old Egyptian symbolism rushed over him with a force that shook his heart. Memory came so marvellously with it.

"If the Power floods down into our minds with sufficient strength for actual form, to note the outline of such form, and from your drawing model it later in permanent substance. Then we should have means of evoking it at will, for we should have its natural Body—the form it built itself, its signature, image, pattern. A starting-point, you see, for more—leading, she hopes, to a complete reconstruction."

"It might take actual shape—assume a bodily form visible to the eye?" repeated Henriot, amazed as before that doubt and laughter did not break through his mind.

"We are on the earth," was the reply, spoken unnecessarily low since no living thing was within earshot, "we are in physical conditions, are we not? Even a human soul we do not recognise unless we see it in a body—parents provide the outline, the signature, the sigil of the returning soul. This," and he tapped himself upon the breast, "is the physical signature of that type of life we call a soul.

Unless there is life of a certain strength behind it, no body forms. And, without a body, we are helpless to control or manage it—deal with it in any way. We could not know it, though being possibly aware of it."

"To be aware, you mean, is not sufficient?" For he noticed the italics Vance made use of.

"Too vague, of no value for future use," was the reply. "But once obtain the form, and we have the natural symbol of that particular Power. And a symbol is more than image, it is a direct and concentrated expression of the life it typifies—possibly terrific."

"It may be a body, then, this symbol you speak of."

"Accurate vehicle of manifestation; but 'body' seems the simplest word."

Vance answered very slowly and deliberately, as though weighing how much he would tell. His language was admirably evasive. Few perhaps would have detected the profound significance the curious words he next used unquestionably concealed. Henriot's mind rejected them, but his heart accepted. For the ancient soul in him was listening and aware.

"Life, using matter to express itself in bodily shape, first traces a geometrical pattern. From the lowest form in crystals, upwards to more complicated patterns in the higher organisations—there is always first this geometrical pattern as skeleton. For geometry lies at the root of all possible phenomena; and is the mind's interpretation of a living movement towards shape that shall express it." He brought his eyes closer to the other, lowering his voice again. "Hence," he said softly, "the signs in all the old magical systems—skeleton forms into which the Powers evoked descended; outlines those Powers automatically built up when using matter to express themselves. Such signs are material symbols of their bodiless existence. They attract the life they represent and interpret. Obtain the correct, true symbol, and the Power corresponding to it can approach—once roused and made aware. It has, you see, a ready-made mould into which it can come down."

"Once roused and made aware?" repeated Henriot questioningly, while this man went stammering the letters of a language that he himself had used too long ago to recapture fully.

"Because they have left the world. They sleep, unmanifested. Their forms are no longer known to men. No forms exist on earth to-day that could contain them. But they may be awakened," he added darkly. "They are bound to answer to the summons, if such summons be accurately made."

"Evocation?" whispered Henriot, more distressed than he cared to admit.

Vance nodded. Leaning still closer, to his companion's face, he thrust his lips forward, speaking eagerly, earnestly, yet somehow at the same time, horribly: "And we want—my aunt would ask—your draughtsman's skill, or at any rate your memory afterwards, to establish the outline of anything that comes."

He waited for the answer, still keeping his face uncomfortably close.

Henriot drew back a little. But his mind was fully made up now. He had known from the beginning that he would consent, for the desire in him was stronger than all the caution in the world. The Past inexorably drew him into the circle of these other lives, and the little human dread Vance woke in him seemed just then insignificant by comparison. It was merely of To-day.

"You two," he said, trying to bring judgment into it, "engaged in evocation, will be in a state of clairvoyant vision. Granted. But shall I, as an outsider, observing with unexcited mind, see anything, know anything, be aware of anything at all, let alone the drawing of it?"

"Unless," the reply came instantly with decision, "the descent of Power is strong enough to take actual material shape, the experiment is a failure. Anybody can induce subjective vision. Such fantasies have no value though. They are born of an overwrought imagination." And then he added quickly, as though to clinch the matter before caution and hesitation could take effect: "You must watch from the heights above. We shall be in the valley—the Wadi Hof is the place. You must not be too close—"

"Why not too close?" asked Henriot, springing forward like a flash before he could prevent the sudden impulse.

With a quickness equal to his own, Vance answered. There was no faintest sign that he was surprised. His self-control was perfect. Only the glare passed darkly through his eyes and went back again into the sombre soul that bore it.

"For your own safety," he answered low. "The Power, the type of life, she would waken is stupendous. And if roused enough to be attracted by the patterned symbol into which she would decoy it down, it will take actual, physical expression. But how? Where is the Body of Worshippers through whom it can manifest? There is none. It will, therefore, press inanimate matter into the service. The terrific impulse to form itself a means of expression will force all loose matter at hand towards it—sand, stones, all it can compel to yield—everything must rush into the sphere of action in which it operates. Alone, we at the centre, and you, upon the outer fringe, will be safe. Only—you must not come too close."

But Henriot was no longer listening. His soul had turned to ice. For here, in this unguarded moment, the cloven hoof had plainly shown itself. In that suggestion of a particular kind of danger Vance had lifted a corner of the curtain behind which crouched his horrible intention. Vance desired a witness of the extraordinary experiment, but he desired this witness, not merely for the purpose of sketching possible shapes that might present themselves to excited vision. He desired a witness for another reason too. Why had Vance put that idea into his mind, this idea of so peculiar danger? It might well have lost him the very assistance he seemed so anxious to obtain.

Henriot could not fathom it quite. Only one thing was clear to him. He, Henriot, was not the only one in danger.

They talked for long after that—far into the night. The lights went out, and the armed patrol, pacing to and fro outside the iron railings that kept the desert back, eyed them curiously. But the only other thing he gathered of importance was the ledge upon the cliff-top where he was to stand and watch; that he was expected to reach there before sunset and wait till the moon concealed all glimmer in the western sky, and—that the woman, who had been engaged for days in secret preparation of soul and body for the awful rite, would not be visible again until he saw her in the depths of the black valley far below, busy with this man upon audacious, ancient purposes.

IX

An hour before sunset Henriot put his rugs and food upon a donkey, and gave the boy directions where to meet him—a considerable distance from the appointed spot. He went himself on foot. He slipped in the heat along the sandy street, where strings of camels still go slouching, shuffling with their loads from the quarries that built the pyramids, and he felt that little friendly Helouan tried to keep him back. But desire now was far too strong for caution.

The desert tide was rising. It easily swept him down the long white street towards the enormous deeps beyond. He felt the pull of a thousand miles before him; and twice a thousand years drove at his back.

Everything still basked in the sunshine. He passed Al Hayat, the stately hotel that dominates the village like a palace built against the sky; and in its pillared colonnades and terraces he saw the throngs of people having late afternoon tea and listening to the music of a regimental band. Men in flannels were playing tennis, parties were climbing off donkeys after long excursions; there was laughter, talking, a babel of many voices. The gaiety called to him; the everyday spirit whispered to stay and join the crowd of lively human beings. Soon there would be merry dinner-parties, dancing, voices of pretty women, sweet white dresses, singing, and the rest. Soft eyes would question and turn dark. He picked out several girls he knew among the palms. But it was all many, oh so many leagues away; centuries lay between him and this modern world. An indescriable loneliness was in his heart. He went searching through the sands of forgotten ages, and wandering among the ruins of a vanished time. He hurried. Already the deeper water caught his breath.

He climbed the steep rise towards the plateau where the Observatory stands, and saw two of the officials whom he knew taking a siesta after their long day's work. He felt that his mind, too, had dived and searched among the heavenly bodies that live in silent, changeless peace remote from the world of men. They recognised him, these two whose eyes also knew tremendous distance close. They beckoned, waving the straws through which they sipped their drinks from tall glasses. Their voices floated down to him as from the star-fields. He saw the sun gleam upon the glasses, and heard the clink of the ice against the sides. The stillness was amazing. He waved an answer, and passed quickly on. He could not stop this sliding current of the years.

The tide moved faster, the draw of piled-up cycles urging it. He emerged upon the plateau, and met the cooler Desert air. His feet went crunching on the "desert-film" that spread its curious dark shiny carpet as far as the eye could reach; it lay everywhere, unswept and smooth as when the feet of vanished civilizations trod its burning surface, then dipped behind the curtains Time pins against the stars. And here the body of the tide set all one way.

There was a greater strength of current, draught and suction. He felt the powerful undertow. Deeper masses drew his feet sideways, and he felt the rushing of the central body of the sand. The sands were moving, from their foundation upwards. He went unresistingly with them.

Turning a moment, he looked back at shining little Helouan in the blaze of evening light. The voices reached him very faintly, merged now in a general murmur. Beyond lay the strip of Delta vivid green, the palms, the roofs of Bedrashein, the blue laughter of the Nile with its flocks of curved felucca sails. Further still, rising above the yellow Libyan horizon, gloomed the vast triangles of a dozen Pyramids, cutting their wedge-shaped clefts out of a sky fast crimsoning through a sea of gold. Seen thus, their dignity imposed upon the entire landscape. They towered darkly, symbolic signatures of the ancient Powers that now watched him taking these little steps across their damaged territory.

He gazed a minute, then went on. He saw the big pale face of the moon in the east. Above the ever-silent Thing these giant symbols once interpreted, she rose, grand, effortless, half-terrible as themselves. And, with her, she lifted up this tide of the Desert that drew his feet across the sand to Wadi Hof. A moment later he dipped below the ridge that buried Helouan and Nile and Pyramids from sight. He entered the ancient waters. Time then, in an instant, flowed back behind his footsteps, obliterating every trace. And with it his mind went too. He stepped across the gulf of centuries, moving into the Past. The Desert lay before him—an open tomb wherein his soul should read presently of things long vanished.

The strange half-lights of sunset began to play their witchery then upon the landscape. A purple glow came down upon the Mokattam Hills. Perspective danced its tricks of false, incredible deception. The soaring kites that were a mile away seemed suddenly close, passing in a moment from the size of gnats to birds with a fabulous stretch of wing. Ridges and cliffs rushed close without a hint of warning, and level places sank into declivities and basins that made him trip and stumble. That indescriable quality of the Desert, which makes timid souls avoid the hour of dusk, emerged; it spread everywhere, undisguised. And the bewilderment it brings is no vain, imagined thing, for it distorts vision utterly, and the effect upon the mind when familiar sight goes floundering is the simplest way in the world of dragging the anchor that grips reality. At the hour of sunset this bewilderment comes upon a man with a disconcerting swiftness. It rose now with all this weird rapidity. Henriot found himself enveloped at a moment's notice.

But, knowing well its effect, he tried to judge it and pass on. The other matters, the object of his journey chief of all, he refused to dwell upon with any imagination. Wisely, his mind, while never losing sight of it, declined to admit the exaggeration that over-elaborate thinking brings. "I'm going to witness an incredible experiment in which two enthusiastic religious dreamers believe firmly," he repeated to himself. "I have agreed to draw—anything I see. There may be truth in it, or they may be merely self-suggested vision due to an artificial exaltation of their minds. I'm interested—perhaps against my better judgment. Yet I'll see the adventure out—because I must."

This was the attitude he told himself to take. Whether it was the real one, or merely adopted to warm a cooling courage, he could not tell. The emotions were so complex and warring. His mind, automatically, kept repeating this comforting formula. Deeper than that he could not see to judge. For a man who knew the full content of his thought at such a time would solve some of the oldest psychological problems in the world. Sand had already buried judgment, and with it all attempt to explain the adventure by the standards acceptable to his brain of to-day. He steered subconsciously through a world of dim, huge, half-remembered wonders.

The sun, with that abrupt Egyptian suddenness, was below the horizon now. The pyramid field had swallowed it. Ra, in his golden boat, sailed distant seas beyond the Libyan wilderness. Henriot walked on and on, aware of utter loneliness. He was walking fields of dream, too remote from modern life to recall companionship he once had surely known. How dim it was, how deep and distant, how lost in this sea of an incalculable Past! He walked into the places that are soundless. The soundlessness of ocean, miles below the surface, was about him. He was with One only—this unfathomable, silent thing where nothing breathes or stirs—nothing but sunshine, shadow and the wind-borne sand. Slowly, in front, the moon climbed up the eastern sky, hanging above the silence—silence that ran unbroken across the horizons to where Suez gleamed upon the waters of a sister sea in motion. That moon was glinting now upon the Arabian Mountains by its desolate shores. Southwards stretched the wastes of Upper Egypt a thousand miles to meet the Nubian wilderness. But over all these separate Deserts stirred the soft whisper of the moving sand—deep murmuring message that Life was on the way to unwind Death. The Ka of Egypt, swathed in centuries of sand, hovered beneath the moon towards her ancient tenement.

For the transformation of the Desert now began in earnest. It grew apace. Before he had gone the first two miles of his hour's journey, the twilight caught the rocky hills and twisted them into those monstrous revelations of physiognomies they barely take the trouble to conceal even in the daytime. And, while he well understood the eroding agencies that have produced them, there yet rose in his mind a deeper interpretation lurking just behind their literal meanings. Here, through the motionless surfaces, that nameless thing the Desert ill conceals urged outwards into embryonic form and shape, akin, he almost felt, to those immense deific symbols of Other Life the Egyptians knew and worshipped. Hence, from the Desert, had first come, he felt, the unearthly life they typified in their monstrous figures of granite, evoked in their stately temples, and communed with in the ritual of their Mystery ceremonials.

This "watching" aspect of the Libyan Desert is really natural enough; but it is just the natural, Henriot knew, that brings the deepest revelations. The surface limestones, resisting the erosion, block themselves ominously against the sky, while the softer sand beneath sets them on altared pedestals that define their isolation splendidly. Blunt and unconquerable, these masses now watched him pass between them. The Desert surface formed them, gave them birth. They rose, they saw, they sank down again—waves upon a sea that carried forgotten life up from the depths below. Of forbidding, even menacing type, they somewhere mated with genuine grandeur. Unformed, according to any standard of human or of animal faces, they achieved an air of giant physiognomy which made them terrible. The unwinking stare of eyes—lidless eyes that yet ever succeed in hiding—looked out under well-marked, level eyebrows, suggesting a vision that included the motives and purposes of his very heart. They looked up grandly, understood why he was there, and then—slowly withdrew their mysterious, penetrating gaze.

The strata built them so marvellously up; the heavy, threatening brows; thick lips, curved by the ages into a semblance of cold smiles; jowls drooping into sandy heaps that climbed against the cheeks; protruding jaws, and the suggestion of shoulders just about to lift the entire bodies out of the sandy beds—this host of countenances conveyed a solemnity of expression that seemed everlasting, implacable as Death. Of human signature they bore no trace, nor was comparison possible between their kind and any animal life. They peopled the Desert here. And their smiles, concealed yet just discernible, went broadening with the darkness into a Desert laughter. The silence bore it underground. But Henriot was aware of it. The troop of faces slipped into that single, enormous countenance which is the visage of the Sand. And he saw it everywhere, yet nowhere.

Thus with the darkness grew his imaginative interpretation of the Desert. Yet there was construction in it, a construction, moreover, that was not entirely his own. Powers, he felt, were rising, stirring, wakening from sleep. Behind the natural faces that he saw, these other things peered gravely at him as he passed. They used, as it were, materials that lay ready to their hand. Imagination furnished these hints of outline, yet the Powers themselves were real. There was this amazing movement of the sand. By no other manner could his mind have conceived of such a thing, nor dreamed of this simple, yet dreadful method of approach.

Approach! that was the word that first stood out and startled him. There was approach; something was drawing nearer. The Desert rose and walked beside him. For not alone these ribs of gleaming limestone contributed towards the elemental visages, but the entire hills, of which they were an outcrop, ran to assist in the formation, and were a necessary part of them. He was watched and stared at from behind, in front, on either side, and even from below. The sand that swept him on, kept even pace with him. It turned luminous too, with a patchwork of glimmering effect that was indescribably weird; lanterns glowed within its substance, and by their light he stumbled on, glad of the Arab boy he would presently meet at the appointed place.

The last torch of the sunset had flickered out, melting into the wilderness, when, suddenly opening at his feet, gaped the deep, wide gully known as Wadi Hof. Its curve swept past him.

This first impression came upon him with a certain violence: that the desolate valley rushed. He saw but a section of its curve and sweep, but through its entire length of several miles the Wadi fled away. The moon whitened it like snow, piling black shadows very close against the cliffs. In the flood of moonlight it went rushing past. It was emptying itself.

For a moment the stream of movement seemed to pause and look up into his face, then instantly went on again upon its swift career. It was like the procession of a river to the sea. The valley emptied itself to make way for what was coming. The approach, moreover, had already begun.

Conscious that he was trembling, he stood and gazed into the depths, seeking to steady his mind by the repetition of the little formula he had used before. He said it half aloud. But, while he did so, his heart whispered quite other things. Thoughts the woman and the man had sown rose up in a flock and fell upon him like a storm of sand. Their impetus drove off all support of ordinary ideas. They shook him where he stood, staring down into this river of strange invisible movement that was hundreds of feet in depth and a quarter of a mile across.

He sought to realise himself as he actually was to-day—mere visitor to Helouan, tempted into this wild adventure with two strangers. But in vain. That seemed a dream, unreal, a transient detail picked out from the enormous Past that now engulfed him, heart and mind and soul. This was the reality.

The shapes and faces that the hills of sand built round him were the play of excited fancy only. By sheer force he pinned his thought against this fact: but further he could not get. There were Powers at work; they were being stirred, wakened somewhere into activity. Evocation had already begun. That sense of their approach as he had walked along from Helouan was not imaginary. A descent of some type of life, vanished from the world too long for recollection, was on the way,—so vast that it would manifest itself in a group of forms, a troop, a host, an army. These two were near him somewhere at this very moment, already long at work, their minds driving beyond this little world. The valley was emptying itself—for the descent of life their ritual invited.

And the movement in the sand was likewise true. He recalled the sentences the woman had used. "My body," he reflected, "like the bodies life makes use of everywhere, is mere upright heap of earth and dust and—sand. Here in the Desert is the raw material, the greatest store of it in the world."

And on the heels of it came sharply that other thing: that this descending Life would press into its service all loose matter within its reach—to form that sphere of action which would be in a literal sense its Body.

In the first few seconds, as he stood there, he realised all this, and realised it with an overwhelming conviction it was futile to deny. The fast-emptying valley would later brim with an unaccustomed and terrific life. Yet Death hid there too—a little, ugly, insignificant death. With the name of Vance it flashed upon his mind and vanished, too tiny to be thought about in this torrent of grander messages that shook the depths within his soul. He bowed his head a moment, hardly knowing what he did. He could have waited thus a thousand years it seemed. He was conscious of a wild desire to run away, to hide, to efface himself utterly, his terror, his curiosity, his little wonder, and not be seen of anything. But it was all vain and foolish. The Desert saw him. The Gigantic knew that he was there. No escape was possible any longer. Caught by the sand, he stood amid eternal things. The river of movement swept him too.

These hills, now motionless as statues, would presently glide forward into the cavalcade, sway like vessels, and go past with the procession. At present only the contents, not the frame, of the Wadi moved. An immense soft brush of moonlight swept it empty for what was on the way.... But presently the entire Desert would stand up and also go.

Then, making a sideways movement, his feet kicked against something soft and yielding that lay heaped upon the Desert floor, and Henriot discovered the rugs the Arab boy had carefully set down before he made full speed for the friendly lights of Helouan. The sound of his departing footsteps had long since died away. He was alone.

The detail restored to him his consciousness of the immediate present, and, stooping, he gathered up the rugs and overcoat and began to make preparations for the night. But the appointed spot, whence he was to watch, lay upon the summit of the opposite cliffs. He must cross the Wadi bed and climb. Slowly and with labour he made his way down a steep cleft into the depth of the Wadi Hof, sliding and stumbling often, till at length he stood upon the floor of shining moonlight. It was very smooth; windless utterly; still as space; each particle of sand lay in its ancient place asleep. The movement, it seemed, had ceased.

He clambered next up the eastern side, through pitch-black shadows, and within the hour reached the ledge upon the top whence he could see below him, like a silvered map, the sweep of the valley bed. The wind nipped keenly here again, coming over the leagues of cooling sand. Loose boulders of splintered rock, started by his climbing, crashed and boomed into the depths. He banked the rugs behind him, wrapped himself in his overcoat, and lay down to wait. Behind him was a two-foot crumbling wall against which he leaned; in front a drop of several hundred feet through space. He lay upon a platform, therefore, invisible from the Desert at his back. Below, the curving Wadi formed a natural amphitheatre in which each separate boulder fallen from the cliffs, and even the little silla shrubs the camels eat, were plainly visible. He noted all the bigger ones among them. He counted them over half aloud.

And the moving stream he had been unaware of when crossing the bed itself, now began again. The Wadi went rushing past before the broom of moonlight. Again, the enormous and the tiny combined in one single strange impression. For, through this conception of great movement, stirred also a roving, delicate touch that his imagination felt as bird-like. Behind the solid mass of the Desert's immobility flashed something swift and light and airy. Bizarre pictures interpreted it to him, like rapid snap-shots of a huge flying panorama: he thought of darting dragon-flies seen at Helouan, of children's little dancing feet, of twinkling butterflies—of birds. Chiefly, yes, of a flock of birds in flight, whose separate units formed a single entity. The idea of the Group-Soul possessed his mind once more. But it came with a sense of more than curiosity or wonder. Veneration lay behind it, a veneration touched with awe. It rose in his deepest thought that here was the first hint of a symbolical representation. A symbol, sacred and inviolable, belonging to some ancient worship that he half remembered in his soul, stirred towards interpretation through all his being.

He lay there waiting, wondering vaguely where his two companions were, yet fear all vanished because he felt attuned to a scale of things too big to mate with definite dread. There was high anticipation in him, but not anxiety. Of himself, as Felix Henriot, indeed, he hardly seemed aware. He was some one else. Or, rather, he was himself at a stage he had known once far, far away in a remote pre-existence. He watched himself from dim summits of a Past, of which no further details were as yet recoverable.

Pencil and sketching-block lay ready to his hand. The moon rose higher, tucking the shadows ever more closely against the precipices. The silver passed into a sheet of snowy whiteness, that made every boulder clearly visible. Solemnity deepened everywhere into awe. The Wadi fled silently down the stream of hours. It was almost empty now. And then, abruptly, he was aware of change. The motion altered somewhere. It moved more quietly; pace slackened; the end of the procession that evacuated the depth and length of it went trailing past and turned the distant bend.

"It's slowing up," he whispered, as sure of it as though he had watched a regiment of soldiers filing by. The wind took off his voice like a flying feather of sound.

And there was a change. It had begun. Night and the moon stood still to watch and listen. The wind dropped utterly away. The sand ceased its shifting movement. The Desert everywhere stopped still, and turned.

Some curtain, then, that for centuries had veiled the world, drew softly up, leaving a shaded vista down which the eyes of his soul peered towards long-forgotten pictures. Still buried by the sands too deep for full recovery, he yet perceived dim portions of them—things once honoured and loved passionately. For once they had surely been to him the whole of life, not merely a fragment for cheap wonder to inspect. And they were curiously familiar, even as the person of this woman who now evoked them was familiar. Henriot made no pretence to more definite remembrance; but the haunting certainty rushed over him, deeper than doubt or denial, and with such force that he felt no effort to destroy it. Some lost sweetness of spiritual ambitions, lived for with this passionate devotion, and passionately worshipped as men to-day worship fame and money, revived in him with a tempest of high glory. Centres of memory stirred from an age-long sleep, so that he could have wept at their so complete obliteration hitherto. That such majesty had departed from the world as though it never had existed, was a thought for desolation and for tears. And though the little fragment he was about to witness might be crude in itself and incomplete, yet it was part of a vast system that once explored the richest realms of deity. The reverence in him contained a holiness of the night and of the stars; great, gentle awe lay in it too; for he stood, aflame with anticipation and humility, at the gateway of sacred things.

And this was the mood, no thrill of cheap excitement or alarm to weaken in, in which he first became aware that two spots of darkness he had taken all along for boulders on the snowy valley bed, were actually something very different. They were living figures. They moved. It was not the shadows slowly following the moonlight, but the stir of human beings who all these hours had been motionless as stone. He must have passed them unnoticed within a dozen yards when he crossed the Wadi bed, and a hundred times from this very ledge his eyes had surely rested on them without recognition. Their minds, he knew full well, had not been inactive as their bodies. The important part of the ancient ritual lay, he remembered, in the powers of the evoking mind.

Here, indeed, was no effective nor theatrical approach of the principal figures. It had nothing in common with the cheap external ceremonial of modern days. In forgotten powers of the soul its grandeur lay, potent, splendid, true. Long before he came, perhaps all through the day, these two had laboured with their arduous preparations. They were there, part of the Desert, when hours ago he had crossed the plateau in the twilight. To them—to this woman's potent working of old ceremonial—had been due that singular rush of imagination he had felt. He had interpreted the Desert as alive. Here was the explanation. It was alive. Life was on the way. Long latent, her intense desire summoned it back to physical expression; and the effect upon him had steadily increased as he drew nearer to the centre where she would focus its revival and return. Those singular impressions of being watched and accompanied were explained. A priest of this old-world worship performed a genuine evocation; a Great One of Vision revived the cosmic Powers.

Henriot watched the small figures far below him with a sense of dramatic splendour that only this association of far-off Memory could account for. It was their rising now, and the lifting of their arms to form a slow revolving outline, that marked the abrupt cessation of the larger river of movement; for the sweeping of the Wadi sank into sudden stillness, and these two, with motions not unlike some dance of deliberate solemnity, passed slowly through the moonlight to and fro. His attention fixed upon them both. All other movement ceased. They fastened the flow of Time against the Desert's body.

What happened then? How could his mind interpret an experience so long denied that the power of expression, as of comprehension, has ceased to exist? How translate this symbolical representation, small detail though it was, of a transcendent worship entombed for most so utterly beyond recovery? Its splendour could never lodge in minds that conceive Deity perched upon a cloud within telephoning distance of fashionable churches. How should he phrase it even to himself, whose memory drew up pictures from so dim a past that the language fit to frame them lay unreachable and lost?

Henriot did not know. Perhaps he never yet has known. Certainly, at the time, he did not even try to think. His sensations remain his own—untranslatable; and even that instinctive description the mind gropes for automatically, floundered, halted, and stopped dead. Yet there rose within him somewhere, from depths long drowned in slumber, a reviving power by which he saw, divined and recollected—remembered seemed too literal a word—these elements of a worship he once had personally known. He, too, had worshipped thus. His soul had moved amid similar evocations in some aeonian past, whence now the sand was being cleared away. Symbols of stupendous meaning flashed and went their way across the lifting mists. He hardly caught their meaning, so long it was since, he had known them; yet they were familiar as the faces seen in dreams, and some hint of their spiritual significance left faint traces in his heart by means of which their grandeur reached towards interpretation. And all were symbols of a cosmic, deific nature; of Powers that only symbols can express—prayer-books and sacraments used in the Wisdom Religion of an older time, but to-day known only in the decrepit, literal shell which is their degradation.

Grandly the figures moved across the valley bed. The powers of the heavenly bodies once more joined them. They moved to the measure of a cosmic dance, whose rhythm was creative. The Universe partnered them.

There was this transfiguration of all common, external things. He realised that appearances were visible letters of a soundless language, a language he once had known. The powers of night and moon and desert sand married with points in the fluid stream of his inmost spiritual being that knew and welcomed them. He understood.

Old Egypt herself stooped down from her uncovered throne. The stars sent messengers. There was commotion in the secret, sandy places of the desert. For the Desert had grown Temple. Columns reared against the sky. There rose, from leagues away, the chanting of the sand.

The temples, where once this came to pass, were gone, their ruin questioned by alien hearts that knew not their spiritual meaning. But here the entire Desert swept in to form a shrine, and the Majesty that once was Egypt stepped grandly back across ages of denial and neglect. The sand was altar, and the stars were altar lights. The moon lit up the vast recesses of the ceiling, and the wind from a thousand miles brought in the perfume of her incense. For with that faith which shifts mountains from their sandy bed, two passionate, believing souls invoked the Ka of Egypt.

And the motions that they made, he saw, were definite harmonious patterns their dark figures traced upon the shining valley floor. Like the points of compasses, with stems invisible, and directed from the sky, their movements marked the outlines of great signatures of power—the sigils of the type of life they would evoke. It would come as a Procession. No individual outline could contain it. It needed for its visible expression—many. The descent of a group-soul, known to the worship of this mighty system, rose from its lair of centuries and moved hugely down upon them. The Ka, answering to the summons, would mate with sand. The Desert was its Body.

Yet it was not this that he had come to fix with block and pencil. Not yet was the moment when his skill might be of use. He waited, watched, and listened, while this river of half-remembered things went past him. The patterns grew beneath his eyes like music. Too intricate and prolonged to remember with accuracy later, he understood that they were forms of that root-geometry which lies behind all manifested life. The mould was being traced in outline. Life would presently inform it. And a singing rose from the maze of lines whose beauty was like the beauty of the constellations.

This sound was very faint at first, but grew steadily in volume. Although no echoes, properly speaking, were possible, these precipices caught stray notes that trooped in from the further sandy reaches. The figures certainly were chanting, but their chanting was not all he heard. Other sounds came to his ears from far away, running past him through the air from every side, and from incredible distances, all flocking down into the Wadi bed to join the parent note that summoned them. The Desert was giving voice. And memory, lifting her hood yet higher, showed more of her grey, mysterious face that searched his soul with questions. Had he so soon forgotten that strange union of form and sound which once was known to the evocative rituals of olden days?

Henriot tried patiently to disentangle this desert-music that their intoning voices woke, from the humming of the blood in his own veins. But he succeeded only in part. Sand was already in the air. There was reverberation, rhythm, measure; there was almost the breaking of the stream into great syllables. But was it due, this strange reverberation, to the countless particles of sand meeting in mid-air about him, or—to larger bodies, whose surfaces caught this friction of the sand and threw it back against his ears? The wind, now rising, brought particles that stung his face and hands, and filled his eyes with a minute fine dust that partially veiled the moonlight. But was not something larger, vaster these particles composed now also on the way?

Movement and sound and flying sand thus merged themselves more and more in a single, whirling torrent. But Henriot sought no commonplace explanation of what he witnessed; and here was the proof that all happened in some vestibule of inner experience where the strain of question and answer had no business. One sitting beside him need not have seen anything at all. His host, for instance, from Helouan, need not have been aware. Night screened it; Helouan, as the whole of modern experience, stood in front of the screen. This thing took place behind it. He crouched motionless, watching in some reconstructed ante-chamber of the soul's pre-existence, while the torrent grew into a veritable tempest.

Yet Night remained unshaken; the veil of moonlight did not quiver; the stars dropped their slender golden pillars unobstructed. Calmness reigned everywhere as before. The stupendous representation passed on behind it all.

But the dignity of the little human movements that he watched had become now indescribable. The gestures of the arms and bodies invested themselves with consummate grandeur, as these two strode into the caverns behind manifested life and drew forth symbols that represented vanished Powers. The sound of their chanting voices broke in cadenced fragments against the shores of language. The words Henriot never actually caught, if words they were; yet he understood their purport—these Names of Power to which the type of returning life gave answer as they approached. He remembered fumbling for his drawing materials, with such violence, however, that the pencil snapped in two between his fingers as he touched it. For now, even here, upon the outer fringe of the ceremonial ground, there was a stir of forces that set the very muscles working in him before he had become aware of it....

Then came the moment when his heart leaped against his ribs with a sudden violence that was almost pain, standing a second later still as death. The lines upon the valley floor ceased their maze-like dance. All movement stopped. Sound died away. In the midst of this profound and dreadful silence the sigils lay empty there below him. They waited to be in-formed. For the moment of entrance had come at last. Life was close.

And he understood why this return of life had all along suggested a Procession and could be no mere momentary flash of vision. From such appalling distance did it sweep down towards the present.

Upon this network, then, of splendid lines, at length held rigid, the entire Desert reared itself with walls of curtained sand, that dwarfed the cliffs, the shouldering hills, the very sky. The Desert stood on end. As once before he had dreamed it from his balcony windows, it rose upright, towering, and close against his face. It built sudden ramparts to the stars that chambered the thing he witnessed behind walls no centuries could ever bring down crumbling into dust.

He himself, in some curious fashion, lay just outside, viewing it apart. As from a pinnacle, he peered within—peered down with straining eyes into the vast picture-gallery Memory threw abruptly open. And the picture spaced its noble outline thus against the very stars. He gazed between columns, that supported the sky itself, like pillars of sand that swept across the field of vanished years. Sand poured and streamed aside, laying bare the Past.

For down the enormous vista into which he gazed, as into an avenue running a million miles towards a tiny point, he saw this moving Thing that came towards him, shaking loose the countless veils of sand the ages had swathed about it. The Ka of buried Egypt wakened out of sleep. She had heard the potent summons of her old, time-honoured ritual. She came. She stretched forth an arm towards the worshippers who evoked her. Out of the Desert, out of the leagues of sand, out of the immeasurable wilderness which was her mummied Form and Body, she rose and came. And this fragment of her he would actually see—this little portion that was obedient to the stammered and broken ceremonial. The partial revelation he would witness—yet so vast, even this little bit of it, that it came as a Procession and a host.

For a moment there was nothing. And then the voice of the woman rose in a resounding cry that filled the Wadi to its furthest precipices, before it died away again to silence. That a human voice could produce such volume, accent, depth, seemed half incredible. The walls of towering sand swallowed it instantly. But the Procession of life, needing a group, a host, an army for its physical expression, reached at that moment the nearer end of the huge avenue. It touched the Present; it entered the world of men.

X

The entire range of Henriot's experience, read, imagined, dreamed, then fainted into unreality before the sheer wonder of what he saw. In the brief interval it takes to snap the fingers the climax was thus so hurriedly upon him. And, through it all, he was clearly aware of the pair of little human figures, man and woman, standing erect and commanding at the centre—knew, too, that she directed and controlled, while he in some secondary fashion supported her—and ever watched. But both were dim, dropped somewhere into a lesser scale. It was the knowledge of their presence, however, that alone enabled him to keep his powers in hand at all. But for these two human beings there within possible reach, he must have closed his eyes and swooned.

For a tempest that seemed to toss loose stars about the sky swept round about him, pouring up the pillared avenue in front of the procession. A blast of giant energy, of liberty, came through. Forwards and backwards, circling spirally about him like a whirlwind, came this revival of Life that sought to dip itself once more in matter and in form. It came to the accurate out-line of its form they had traced for it. He held his mind steady enough to realise that it was akin to what men call a "descent" of some "spiritual movement" that wakens a body of believers into faith—a race, an entire nation; only that he experienced it in this brief, concentrated form before it has scattered down into ten thousand hearts. Here he knew its source and essence, behind the veil. Crudely, unmanageable as yet, he felt it, rushing loose behind appearances. There was this amazing impact of a twisting, swinging force that stormed down as though it would bend and coil the very ribs of the old stubborn hills. It sought to warm them with the stress of its own irresistible life-stream, to beat them into shape, and make pliable their obstinate resistance. Through all things the impulse poured and spread, like fire at white heat.

Yet nothing visible came as yet, no alteration in the actual landscape, no sign of change in things familiar to his eyes, while impetus thus fought against inertia. He perceived nothing formal. Calm and untouched himself, he lay outside the circle of evocation, watching, waiting, scarcely daring to breathe, yet well aware that any minute the scene would transfer itself from memory that was subjective to matter that was objective.

And then, in a flash, the bridge was built, and the transfer was accomplished. How or where he did not see, he could not tell. It was there before he knew it—there before his normal, earthly sight. He saw it, as he saw the hands he was holding stupidly up to shield his face. For this terrific release of force long held back, long stored up, latent for centuries, came pouring down the empty Wadi bed prepared for its reception. Through stones and sand and boulders it came in an impetuous hurricane of power. The liberation of its life appalled him. All that was free, untied, responded instantly like chaff; loose objects fled towards it; there was a yielding in the hills and precipices; and even in the mass of Desert which provided their foundation. The hinges of the Sand went creaking in the night. It shaped for itself a bodily outline.

Yet, most strangely, nothing definitely moved. How could he express the violent contradiction? For the immobility was apparent only—a sham, a counterfeit; while behind it the essential being of these things did rush and shift and alter. He saw the two things side by side: the outer immobility the senses commonly agree upon, and this amazing flying-out of their inner, invisible substance towards the vortex of attracting life that sucked them in. For stubborn matter turned docile before the stress of this returning life, taught somewhere to be plastic. It was being moulded into an approach to bodily outline. A mobile elasticity invaded rigid substance. The two officiating human beings, safe at the stationary centre, and himself, just outside the circle of operation, alone remained untouched and unaffected. But a few feet in any direction, for any one of them, meant—instantaneous death. They would be absorbed into the vortex, mere corpuscles pressed into the service of this sphere of action of a mighty Body....

How these perceptions reached him with such conviction, Henriot could never say. He knew it, because he felt it. Something fell about him from the sky that already paled towards the dawn. The stars themselves, it seemed, contributed some part of the terrific, flowing impulse that conquered matter and shaped itself this physical expression.

Then, before he was able to fashion any preconceived idea of what visible form this potent life might assume, he was aware of further change. It came at the briefest possible interval after the beginning—this certainty that, to and fro about him, as yet however indeterminate, passed Magnitudes that were stupendous as the desert. There was beauty in them too, though a terrible beauty hardly of this earth at all. A fragment of old Egypt had returned—a little portion of that vast Body of Belief that once was Egypt. Evoked by the worship of one human heart, passionately sincere, the Ka of Egypt stepped back to visit the material it once informed—the Sand.

Yet only a portion came. Henriot clearly realised that. It stretched forth an arm. Finding no mass of worshippers through whom it might express itself completely, it pressed inanimate matter thus into its service.

Here was the beginning the woman had spoken of—little opening clue. Entire reconstruction lay perhaps beyond.

And Henriot next realised that these Magnitudes in which this group-energy sought to clothe itself as visible form, were curiously familiar. It was not a new thing that he would see. Booming softly as they dropped downwards through the sky, with a motion the size of them rendered delusive, they trooped up the Avenue towards the central point that summoned them. He realised the giant flock of them—descent of fearful beauty—outlining a type of life denied to the world for ages, countless as this sand that blew against his skin. Careering over the waste of Desert moved the army of dark Splendours, that dwarfed any organic structure called a body men have ever known. He recognised them, cold in him of death, though the outlines reared higher than the pyramids, and towered up to hide whole groups of stars. Yes, he recognised them in their partial revelation, though he never saw the monstrous host complete. But, one of them, he realised, posing its eternal riddle to the sands, had of old been glimpsed sufficiently to seize its form in stone,—yet poorly seized, as a doll may stand for the dignity of a human being or a child's toy represent an engine that draws trains....

And he knelt there on his narrow ledge, the world of men forgotten. The power that caught him was too great a thing for wonder or for fear; he even felt no awe. Sensation of any kind that can be named or realised left him utterly. He forgot himself. He merely watched. The glory numbed him. Block and pencil, as the reason of his presence there at all, no longer existed....

Yet one small link remained that held him to some kind of consciousness of earthly things: he never lost sight of this—that, being just outside the circle of evocation, he was safe, and that the man and woman, being stationary in its untouched centre, were also safe. But—that a movement of six inches in any direction meant for any one of them instant death.

What was it, then, that suddenly strengthened this solitary link so that the chain tautened and he felt the pull of it? Henriot could not say. He came back with the rush of a descending drop to the realisation—dimly, vaguely, as from great distance—that he was with these two, now at this moment, in the Wadi Hof, and that the cold of dawn was in the air about him. The chill breath of the Desert made him shiver.

But at first, so deeply had his soul been dipped in this fragment of ancient worship, he could remember nothing more. Somewhere lay a little spot of streets and houses; its name escaped him. He had once been there; there were many people, but insignificant people. Who were they? And what had he to do with them? All recent memories had been drowned in the tide that flooded him from an immeasurable Past.

And who were they—these two beings, standing on the white floor of sand below him? For a long time he could not recover their names. Yet he remembered them; and, thus robbed of association that names bring, he saw them for an instant naked, and knew that one of them was evil. One of them was vile. Blackness touched the picture there. The man, his name still out of reach, was sinister, impure and dark at the heart. And for this reason the evocation had been partial only. The admixture of an evil motive was the flaw that marred complete success.

The names then flashed upon him—Lady Statham—Richard Vance.

Vance! With a horrid drop from splendour into something mean and sordid, Henriot felt the pain of it. The motive of the man was so insignificant, his purpose so atrocious. More and more, with the name, came back—his first repugnance, fear, suspicion. And human terror caught him. He shrieked. But, as in nightmare, no sound escaped his lips. He tried to move; a wild desire to interfere, to protect, to prevent, flung him forward—close to the dizzy edge of the gulf below. But his muscles refused obedience to the will. The paralysis of common fear rooted him to the rocks.

But the sudden change of focus instantly destroyed the picture; and so vehement was the fall from glory into meanness, that it dislocated the machinery of clairvoyant vision. The inner perception clouded and grew dark. Outer and inner mingled in violent, inextricable confusion. The wrench seemed almost physical. It happened all at once, retreat and continuation for a moment somehow combined. And, if he did not definitely see the awful thing, at least he was aware that it had come to pass. He knew it as positively as though his eye were glued against a magnifying lens in the stillness of some laboratory. He witnessed it.

The supreme moment of evocation was close. Life, through that awful sandy vortex, whirled and raged. Loose particles showered and pelted, caught by the draught of vehement life that moulded the substance of the Desert into imperial outline—when, suddenly, shot the little evil thing across that marred and blasted it.

Into the whirlpool flew forward a particle of material that was a human being. And the Group-Soul caught and used it.

The actual accomplishment Henriot did not claim to see. He was a witness, but a witness who could give no evidence. Whether the woman was pushed of set intention, or whether some detail of sound and pattern was falsely used to effect the terrible result, he was helpless to determine. He pretends no itemised account. She went. In one second, with appalling swiftness, she disappeared, swallowed out of space and time within that awful maw—one little corpuscle among a million through which the Life, now stalking the Desert wastes, moulded itself a troop-like Body. Sand took her.

There followed emptiness—a hush of unutterable silence, stillness, peace. Movement and sound instantly retired whence they came. The avenues of Memory closed; the Splendours all went down into their sandy tombs....

The moon had sunk into the Libyan wilderness; the eastern sky was red. The dawn drew out that wondrous sweetness of the Desert, which is as sister to the sweetness that the moonlight brings. The Desert settled back to sleep, huge, unfathomable, charged to the brim with life that watches, waits, and yet conceals itself behind the ruins of apparent desolation. And the Wadi, empty at his feet, filled slowly with the gentle little winds that bring the sunrise.

Then, across the pale glimmering of sand, Henriot saw a figure moving. It came quickly towards him, yet unsteadily, and with a hurry that was ugly. Vance was on the way to fetch him. And the horror of the man's approach struck him like a hammer in the face. He closed his eyes, sinking back to hide.

But, before he swooned, there reached him the clatter of the murderer's tread as he began to climb over the splintered rocks, and the faint echo of his voice, calling him by name—falsely and in pretence—for help.

Smith and the Pharaohs

H. Rider Haggard

I

Scientists, or some scientists, for occasionally one learned person differs from other learned persons—tell us they know all that is worth knowing about man, which statement, of course, includes woman. They trace him from his remotest origin; they show us how his bones changed and his shape modified, also how, under the influence of his needs and passions, his intelligence developed from something very humble. They demonstrate conclusively that there is nothing in man which the dissecting-table will not explain; that his aspirations towards another life have their root in the fear of death, or, say others of them, in that of earthquake or thunder; that his affinities with the past are merely inherited from remote ancestors who lived in that past, perhaps a million years ago; and that everything noble about him is but the fruit of expediency or of a veneer of civilisation, while everything base must be attributed to the instincts of his dominant and primeval nature. Man, in short, is an animal who, like every other animal, is finally subdued by his environment and takes his colour from his surroundings, as cattle do from the red soil of Devon. Such are the facts, they (or some of them) declare; all the rest is rubbish.

At times we are inclined to agree with these sages, especially after it has been our privilege to attend a course of lectures by one of them. Then perhaps something comes within the range of our experience which gives us pause and causes doubts, the old divine doubts, to arise again deep in our hearts, and with them a yet diviner hope.

Perchance when all is said, so we think to ourselves, man *is* something more than an animal. Perchance he has known the past, the far past, and will know the future, the far, far future. Perchance the dream is true, and he does indeed possess what for convenience is called an immortal soul, that may manifest itself in one shape or another; that may sleep for ages, but, waking or sleeping, still remains itself, indestructible as the matter of the Universe.

An incident in the career of Mr. James Ebenezer Smith might well occasion such reflections, were any acquainted with its details, which until this, its setting forth, was not the case. Mr. Smith is a person who knows when to be silent. Still, undoubtedly it gave cause for thought to one individual—namely, to him to whom it happened. Indeed, James Ebenezer Smith is still thinking over it, thinking very hard indeed.

J. E. Smith was well born and well educated. When he was a good-looking and able young man at college, but before he had taken his degree, trouble came to him, the particulars of which do not matter, and he was thrown penniless, also friendless, upon the rocky bosom of the world. No, not quite friendless, for he had a godfather, a gentleman connected with business whose Christian name was Ebenezer. To him, as a last resource, Smith went, feeling that Ebenezer owed him something in return for the awful appellation wherewith he had been endowed in baptism.

To a certain extent Ebenezer recognised the obligation. He did nothing heroic, but he found his godson a clerkship in a bank of which he was one of the directors—a modest clerkship, no more. Also, when he died a year later, he left him a hundred pounds to be spent upon some souvenir.

Smith, being of a practical turn of mind, instead of adorning himself with memorial jewellery for which he had no use, invested the hundred pounds in an exceedingly promising speculation. As it happened, he was not misinformed, and his talent returned to him multiplied by ten. He repeated the experiment, and, being in a position to know what he was doing, with considerable success. By the time that he was thirty he found himself possessed of a fortune of something over twenty-five thousand pounds. Then (and this shows the wise and practical nature of the man) he stopped speculating and put out his money in such a fashion that it brought him a safe and clear four per cent.

By this time Smith, being an excellent man of business, was well up in the service of his bank—as yet only a clerk, it is true, but one who drew his four hundred pounds a year, with prospects. In short, he was in a position to marry had he wished to do so. As it happened, he did not wish—perhaps because, being very friendless, no lady attracted who him crossed his path: perhaps for other reasons.

Shy and reserved in temperament, he confided only in himself. None, not even his superiors at the bank or the Board of Management, knew how well off he had become. No one visited him at the flat which he was understood to occupy somewhere in the neighbourhood of Putney; he belonged to no club, and possessed not a single intimate. The blow which the world had dealt him in his early days, the harsh repulses and the rough treatment he had then experienced, sank so deep into his sensitive soul that never again did he seek close converse with his kind. In fact, while still young, he fell into a condition of old-bachelorhood of a refined type.

Soon, however, Smith discovered—it was after he had given up speculating—that a man must have something to occupy his mind. He tried philanthropy, but found himself too sensitive for a business which so often resolves itself into rude inquiry as to the affairs of other people. After a struggle, therefore, he compromised with his conscience by setting aside a liberal portion of his income for anonymous distribution among deserving persons and objects.

While still in this vacant frame of mind Smith chanced one day, when the bank was closed, to drift into the British Museum, more to escape the vile weather that prevailed without than for any other reason. Wandering hither and thither at hazard, he found himself in the great gallery devoted to Egyptian stone objects and sculpture. The place bewildered him somewhat, for he knew nothing of Egyptology; indeed, there remained upon his mind only a sense of wonderment not unmixed with awe. It must have been a great people, he thought to himself, that executed these works, and with the thought came a desire to know more about them. Yet he was going away when suddenly his eye fell on the sculptured head of a woman which hung upon the wall.

Smith looked at it once, twice, thrice, and at the third look he fell in love. Needless to say, he was not aware that such was his condition. He knew only that a change had come over him, and never, never could he forget the face which that carven mask portrayed.

Perhaps it was not really beautiful save for its wondrous and mystic smile; perhaps the lips were too thick and the nostrils too broad. Yet to him that face was Beauty itself, beauty which drew him as with a cart-rope, and awoke within him all kinds of wonderful imaginings, some of them so strange and tender that almost they partook of the nature of memories. He stared at the image, and the image smiled back sweetly at him, as doubtless it, or rather its original—for this was but a plaster cast—had smiled at nothingness in some tomb or hiding- hole for over thirty centuries, and as the woman whose likeness it was had once smiled upon the world.

A short, stout gentleman bustled up and, in tones of authority, addressed some workmen who were arranging a base for a neighbouring statue. It occurred to Smith that he must be someone who knew about these objects. Overcoming his natural diffidence with an effort, he raised his hat and asked the gentleman if he could tell him, who was the original of the mask.

The official—who, in fact, was a very great man in the Museum—glanced at Smith shrewdly, and, seeing that his interest was genuine, answered:—

"I don't know. Nobody knows. She has been given several names, but none of them have authority. Perhaps one day the rest of the statue may be found, and then we shall learn—that is, if it is inscribed. Most likely, however, it has been burnt for lime long ago."

"Then you can't tell me anything about her?" said Smith.

"Well, only a little. To begin with, that's a cast. The original is in the Cairo Museum. Mariette found it, I believe at Karnak, and gave it a name after his fashion. Probably she was a queen—of the eighteenth dynasty, by the work. But you can see her rank for yourself from the broken *uræus*." (Smith did not stop him to explain that he had not the faintest idea what a *uræus* might be, seeing that he was utterly unfamiliar with the snake-headed crest of Egyptian royalty.) "You should go to Egypt and study the head for yourself. It is one of the most beautiful things that ever was found. Well, I must be off. Good day."

And he bustled down the long gallery.

Smith found his way upstairs and looked at mummies and other things. Somehow it hurt him to reflect that the owner of yonder sweet, alluring face must have become a mummy long, long before the Christian era. Mummies did not strike him as attractive.

He returned to the statuary and stared at his plaster cast till one of the workmen remarked to his fellow that if he were the gent he'd go and look at "a live 'un" for a change.

Then Smith retired abashed.

On his way home he called at his bookseller's and ordered "all the best works on Egyptology". When, a day or two later, they arrived in a packing-case, together with a bill for thirty-eight pounds, he was somewhat dismayed. Still, he tackled those books like a man, and, being clever and industrious, within three months had a fair working knowledge of the subject, and had even picked up a smattering of hieroglyphics.

In January—that was, at the end of those three months—Smith astonished his Board of Directors by applying for ten weeks' leave, he who had hitherto been content with a fortnight in the year. When questioned he explained that he had been suffering from bronchitis, and was advised to take a change in Egypt.

"A very good idea," said the manager; "but I'm afraid you'll find it expensive. They fleece one in Egypt."

"I know," answered Smith; "but I've saved a little and have only myself to spend it upon."

So Smith went to Egypt and saw the original of the beauteous head and a thousand other fascinating things. Indeed, he did more. Attaching himself to some excavators who were glad of his intelligent assistance, he actually dug for a month in the neighbourhood of ancient Thebes, but without finding anything in particular.

It was not till two years later that he made his great discovery, that which is known as Smith's Tomb. Here it may be explained that the state of his health had become such as to necessitate an annual visit to Egypt, or so his superiors understood.

However, as he asked for no summer holiday, and was always ready to do another man's work or to stop overtime, he found it easy to arrange for these winter excursions.

On this, his third visit to Egypt, Smith obtained from the Director-General of Antiquities at Cairo a licence to dig upon his own account. Being already well known in the country as a skilled Egyptologist, this was granted upon the usual terms—namely, that the Department of Antiquities should have a right to take any of the objects which might be found, or all of them, if it so desired.

Such preliminary matters having been arranged by correspondence, Smith, after a few days spent in the Museum at Cairo, took the night train to Luxor, where he found his head-man, an ex-dragoman named Mahomet, waiting for him and his fellaheen labourers already hired. There were but forty of them, for his was a comparatively small venture. Three hundred pounds was the amount that he had made up his mind to expend, and such a sum does not go far in excavations.

During his visit of the previous year Smith had marked the place where he meant to dig. It was in the cemetery of old Thebes, at the wild spot not far from the temple of Medinet Habu, that is known as the Valley of the Queens. Here, separated from the resting-places of their royal lords by the bold mass of the intervening hill, some of the greatest ladies of Egypt have been laid to rest, and it was their tombs that Smith desired to investigate. As he knew well, some of these must yet remain to be discovered. Who could say? Fortune favours the bold. It might be that he would find the holy grave of that beauteous, unknown Royalty whose face had haunted him for three long years!

For a whole month he dug without the slightest success. The spot that he selected had proved, indeed, to be the mouth of a tomb. After twenty-five days of laborious exploration it was at length cleared out, and he stood in a rude unfinished cave. The queen for whom it had been designed must have died quite young and been buried elsewhere, or she had chosen herself another sepulchre, or mayhap the rock had proved unsuitable for sculpture.

Smith shrugged his shoulders and moved on, sinking trial pits and trenches here and there, but still finding nothing. Two-thirds of his time and money had been spent when at last the luck turned. One day, towards evening, with some half-dozen of his best men he was returning after a fruitless morning of labour, when something seemed to attract him towards a little *wadi*, or bay, in the hillside that was filled with tumbled rocks and sand. There were scores of such places, and this one looked no more promising than any of the others had proved to be. Yet it attracted him. Thoroughly dispirited, he walked past it twenty paces or more, then turned.

"Where go you, sah?" asked his head-man, Mahomet.

He pointed to the recess in the cliff.

"No good, sah," said Mahomet. "No tomb there. Bed-rock too near top. Too much water run in there; dead queen like keep dry!"

But Smith went on, and the others followed obediently.

He walked down the little slope of sand and boulders and examined the cliff. It was virgin rock; never a tool mark was to be seen. Already the men were going, when the same strange instinct which had drawn him to the spot caused him to take a spade from one of them and begin to shovel away the sand from the face of the cliff—for here, for some unexplained reason, were no boulders or *débris*. Seeing their master, to whom they were attached, at work, they began to work too, and for twenty minutes or more dug on cheerfully enough, just to humour him, since all were sure that here there was no tomb. At length Smith ordered them to desist, for, although now they were six feet down, the rock remained of the same virgin character.

With an exclamation of disgust he threw out a last shovelful of sand. The edge of his spade struck on something that projected. He cleared away a little more sand, and there appeared a rounded ledge which seemed to be a cornice. Calling back the men, he pointed to it, and without a word all of them began to dig again. Five minutes more of work made it clear that it was a cornice, and half an hour later there appeared the top of the doorway of a tomb.

"Old people wall him up," said Mahomet, pointing to the flat stones set in mud for mortar with which the doorway had been closed, and to the undecipherable impress upon the mud of the scarab seals of the officials whose duty it had been to close the last resting-place of the royal dead for ever.

"Perhaps queen all right inside," he went on, receiving no answer to his remark.

"Perhaps," replied Smith, briefly. "Dig, man, dig! Don't waste time in talking."

So they dug on furiously till at length Smith saw something which caused him to groan aloud. There was a hole in the masonry—the tomb had been broken into. Mahomet saw it too, and examined the top of the aperture with his skilled eye.

"Very old thief," he said. "Look, he try build up wall again, but run away before he have time finish." And he pointed to certain flat stones which had been roughly and hurriedly replaced.

"Dig—dig!" said Smith.

Ten minutes more and the aperture was cleared. It was only just big enough to admit the body of a man.

By now the sun was setting. Swiftly, swiftly it seemed to tumble down the sky. One minute it was above the rough crests of the western hills behind them; the next, a great ball of glowing fire, it rested on their topmost ridge. Then it was gone. For an instant a kind of green spark shone where it had been. This too went out, and the sudden Egyptian night was upon them.

The fellaheen muttered among themselves, and one or two of them wandered off on some pretext. The rest threw down their tools and looked at Smith. "Men say they no like stop here. They afraid of ghost! Too many *afreet* live in these tomb. That what they say. Come back finish tomorrow morning when it light. Very foolish people, these common fellaheen," remarked Mahomet, in a superior tone.

"Quite so," replied Smith, who knew well that nothing that he could offer would tempt his men to go on with the opening of a tomb after sunset. "Let them go away. You and I will stop and watch the place till morning."

"Sorry, sah," said Mahomet, "but I not feel quite well inside; I think I got fever. I go to camp and lie down and pray under plenty blanket."

"All right, go," said Smith; "but if there is anyone who is not a coward, let him bring me my big coat, something to eat and drink, and the lantern that hangs in my tent. I will meet him there in the valley."

Mahomet, though rather doubtfully, promised that this should be done, and, after begging Smith to accompany them, lest the spirit of whoever slept in the tomb should work him a mischief during the night, they departed quickly enough.

Smith lit his pipe, sat down on the sand, and waited. Half an hour later he heard a sound of singing, and through the darkness, which was dense, saw lights coming up the valley.

"My brave men," he thought to himself, and scrambled up the slope to meet them.

He was right. These were his men, no less than twenty of them, for with a fewer number they did not dare to face the ghosts which they believed haunted the valley after nightfall. Presently the light from the lantern which one of them carried (not Mahomet, whose sickness had increased too suddenly to enable him to come) fell upon the tall form of Smith, who, dressed in his white working clothes, was leaning against a rock. Down went the lantern, and with a howl of terror the brave company turned and fled.

"Sons of cowards!" roared Smith after them, in his most vigorous Arabic. "It is I, your master, not an *afreet*."

They heard, and by degrees crept back again. Then he perceived that in order to account for their number each of them carried some article. Thus one had the bread, another the lantern, another a tin of sardines, another the sardine-opener, another a box of matches, another a bottle of beer, and so on. As even thus there were not enough things to go round, two of them bore his big coat between them, the first holding it by the sleeves and the second by the tail as though it were a stretcher.

"Put them down," said Smith, and they obeyed. "Now," he added, "run for your lives; I thought I heard two *afreets* talking up there just now of what they would do to any followers of the Prophet who mocked their gods, if perchance they should meet them in their holy place at night."

This kindly counsel was accepted with much eagerness. In another minute Smith was alone with the stars and the dying desert wind.

Collecting his goods, or as many of them as he wanted, he thrust them into the pockets of the greatcoat and returned to the mouth of the tomb. Here he made his simple meal by the light of the lantern, and afterwards tried to go to sleep. But sleep he could not. Something always woke him. First it was a jackal howling amongst the rocks; next a sand-fly bit him on the ankle so sharply that he thought he must have been stung by a scorpion. Then, notwithstanding his warm coat, the cold got hold of him, for the clothes beneath were wet through with perspiration, and it occurred to him that unless he did something he would probably contract an internal chill or perhaps fever. He rose and walked about.

By now the moon was up, revealing all the sad, wild scene in its every detail. The mystery of Egypt entered his soul and oppressed him. How much dead majesty lay in the hill upon which he stood? Were they all really dead, he wondered, or were those fellaheen right? Did their spirits still come forth at night and wander through the land where once they ruled? Of course that was the Egyptian faith according to which the Ka, or Double, eternally haunted the place where its earthly counterpart had been laid to rest. When one came to think of it, beneath a mass of unintelligible symbolism there was much in the Egyptian faith which it was hard for a Christian to disbelieve. Salvation through a Redeemer, for instance, and the resurrection of the body. Had he, Smith, not already written a treatise upon these points of similarity which he proposed to publish one day, not under his own name? Well, he would not think of them now; the occasion seemed scarcely fitting—they came home too pointedly to one who was engaged in violating a tomb.

His mind, or rather his imagination-of which he had plenty—went off at a tangent. What sights had this place seen thousands of years ago! Once, thousands of years ago, a procession had wound up along the roadway which was doubtless buried beneath the sand whereon he stood towards the dark door of this sepulchre. He could see it as it passed in and out between the rocks. The priests, shaven-headed and robed in leopards' skins, or some of them in pure white, bearing the mystic symbols of their office. The funeral sledge drawn by oxen, and on it the great rectangular case that contained the outer and the inner coffins, and within them the mummy of some departed Majesty; in the Egyptian formula, "the hawk that had spread its wings and flown into the bosom of Osiris," God of Death. Behind, the mourners, rending the air with their lamentations. Then those who bore the funeral furniture and offerings. Then the high officers of State and the first priests of Amen and of the other gods. Then the sister queens, leading by the hand a wondering child or two. Then the sons of Pharaoh, young men carrying the emblems of their rank.

Lastly, walking alone, Pharaoh himself in his ceremonial robes, his apron, his double crown of linen surmounted by the golden snake, his inlaid bracelets and his heavy, tinkling earrings. Pharaoh, his head bowed, his feet travelling wearily, and in his heart—what thoughts? Sorrow, perhaps, for her who had departed. Yet he had other queens and fair women without count. Doubtless she was sweet and beautiful, but sweetness and beauty were not given to her alone. Moreover, was she not wont to cross his will and to question his divinity? No, surely it is not only of her that he thinks, her for whom he had prepared this splendid tomb with all things needful to unite her with the gods. Surely he thinks also of himself and that other tomb on the farther side of the hill whereat the artists labour day by day—yes, and have laboured these many years; that tomb to which before so very long he too must travel in just this fashion, to seek his place beyond the doors of Death, who lays his equal hand on king and queen and slave.

The vision passed. It was so real that Smith thought he must have been dreaming. Well, he was awake now, and colder than ever. Moreover, the jackals had multiplied. There were a whole pack of them, and not far away. Look! One crossed in the ring of the lamplight, a slinking, yellow beast that smelt the remains of dinner. Or perhaps it smelt him. Moreover, there were bad characters who haunted these mountains, and he was alone and quite unarmed. Perhaps he ought to put out the light which advertised his whereabouts. It would be wise and yet in this particular he rejected wisdom. After all, the light was some company.

Since sleep seemed to be out of the question, he fell back upon poor humanity's other anodyne, work, which has the incidental advantage of generating warmth. Seizing a shovel, he began to dig at the doorway of the tomb, whilst the jackals howled louder than ever in astonishment. They were not used to such a sight. For thousands of years, as the old moon above could have told, no man, or at least no solitary man, had dared to rob tombs at such an unnatural hour.

When Smith had been digging for about twenty minutes something tinkled on his shovel with a noise which sounded loud in that silence.

"A stone which may come in handy for the jackals," he thought to himself, shaking the sand slowly off the spade until it appeared. There it was, and not large enough to be of much service. Still, he picked it up, and rubbed it in his hands to clear off the encrusting dirt. When he opened them he saw that it was no stone, but a bronze.

"Osiris," reflected Smith, "buried in front of the tomb to hallow the ground. No, an Isis. No, the head of a statuette, and a jolly good one, too—at any rate, in moonlight. Seems to have been gilded." And, reaching out for the lamp, he held it over the object.

Another minute, and he found himself sitting at the bottom of the hole, lamp in one hand and statuette, or rather head, in the other.

"The Queen of the Mask!" he gasped. "The same—the same! By heavens, the very same!"

Oh, he could not be mistaken. There were the identical lips, a little thick and pouted; the identical nostrils, curved and quivering, but a little wide; the identical arched eyebrows and dreamy eyes set somewhat far apart. Above all, there was the identical alluring and mysterious smile. Only on this masterpiece of ancient art was set a whole crown of uræi surrounding the entire head. Beneath the crown and pressed back behind the ears was a full-bottomed wig or royal head-dress, of which the ends descended to the breasts. The statuette, that, having been gilt, remained quite perfect and uncorroded, was broken just above the middle, apparently by a single violent blow, for the fracture was very clean.

At once it occurred to Smith that it had been stolen from the tomb by a thief who thought it to be gold; that outside of the tomb doubt had overtaken him and caused him to break it upon a stone or otherwise. The rest was clear. Finding that it was but gold-washed bronze he had thrown away the fragments, rather than be at the pains of carrying them. This was his theory, probably not a correct one, as the sequel seems to show.

Smith's first idea was to recover the other portion. He searched quite a long while, but without success. Neither then nor afterwards could it be found. He reflected that perhaps this lower half had remained in the thief's hand, who, in his vexation, had thrown it far away, leaving the head to lie where it fell. Again Smith examined this head, and more closely. Now he saw that just beneath the breasts was a delicately cut cartouche.

Being by this time a master of hieroglyphics, he read it without trouble. It ran: "Ma-Mee, Great Royal Lady. Beloved of..." Here the cartouche was broken away.

"Ma-Mé, or it might be Ma-Mi," he reflected. "I never heard of a queen called Ma-Mé, or Ma-Mi, or Ma-Mu. She must be quite new to history. I wonder of whom she was beloved? Amen, or Horus, or Isis, probably. Of some god, I have no doubt, at least I hope so!"

He stared at the beautiful portrait in his hand, as once he had stared at the cast on the Museum wall, and the beautiful portrait, emerging from the dust of ages, smiled back at him there in the solemn moonlight as once the cast had smiled from the Museum wall.

Only that had been but a cast, whereas this was real. This had slept with the dead from whose features it had been fashioned, the dead who lay, or who had lain, within.

A sudden resolution took hold of Smith. He would explore that tomb, at once and alone. No one should accompany him on this his first visit; it would be a sacrilege that anyone save himself should set foot there until he had looked on what it might contain.

Why should he not enter? His lamp, of what is called the "hurricane" brand, was very good and bright, and would burn for many hours. Moreover, there had been time for the foul air to escape through the hole that they had cleared. Lastly, something seemed to call on him to come and see. He placed the bronze head in his breast-pocket over his heart, and, thrusting the lamp through the hole, looked down. Here there was no difficulty, since sand had drifted in to the level of the bottom of the aperture. Through it he struggled, to find himself upon a bed of sand that only just left him room to push himself along between it and the roof. A little farther on the passage was almost filled with mud.

Mahomet had been right when, from his knowledge of the bed-rock, he said that any tomb made in this place must be flooded. It *had* been flooded by some ancient rain-storm, and Smith began to fear that he would find it quite filled with soil caked as hard as iron. So, indeed, it was to a certain depth, a result that apparently had been anticipated by those who hollowed it, for this entrance shaft was left quite undecorated. Indeed, as Smith found afterwards, a hole had been dug beneath the doorway to allow the mud to enter after the burial was completed. Only a miscalculation had been made. The natural level of the mud did not quite reach the roof of the tomb, and therefore still left it open.

After crawling for forty feet or so over this caked mud, Smith suddenly found himself on a rising stair. Then he understood the plan; the tomb itself was on a higher level.

Here began the paintings. Here the Queen Ma-Mee, wearing her crowns and dressed in diaphanous garments, was presented to god after god. Between her figure and those of the divinities the wall was covered with hieroglyphs as fresh today as on that when the artist had limned them. A glance told him that they were extracts from the Book of the Dead. When the thief of bygone ages had broken into the tomb, probably not very long after the interment, the mud over which Smith had just crawled was still wet. This he could tell, since the clay from the rascal's feet remained upon the stairs, and that upon his fingers had stained the paintings on the wall against which he had supported himself; indeed, in one place was an exact impression of his hand, showing its shape and even the lines of the skin.

At the top of the flight of steps ran another passage at a higher level, which the water had never reached, and to right and left were the beginnings of unfinished chambers. It was clear to him that this queen had died young. Her tomb, as she or the king had designed it, was never finished. A few more paces, and the passage enlarged itself into a hall about thirty feet square. The ceiling was decorated with vultures, their wings outspread, the looped Cross of Life hanging from their talons. On one wall her Majesty Ma-Mee stood expectant while Anubis weighed her heart against the feather of truth, and Thoth, the Recorder, wrote down the verdict upon his tablets. All her titles were given to her here, such as "Great Royal Heiress, Royal Sister, Royal Wife, Royal Mother, Lady of the Two Lands, Palm-branch of Love, Beautiful exceedingly."

Smith read them hurriedly and noted that nowhere could he see the name of the king who had been her husband. It would almost seem as though this had been purposely omitted. On the other walls Ma-Mee, accompanied by her Ka, or Double, made offerings to the various gods, or uttered propitiatory speeches to the hideous demons of the underworld, declaring their names to them and forcing them to say: "Pass on. Thou art pure!"

Lastly, on the end wall, triumphant, all her trials done, she, the justified Osiris, or Spirit, was received by the god Osiris, Saviour of Spirits.

All these things Smith noted hurriedly as he swung the lamp to and fro in that hallowed place. Then he saw something else which filled him with dismay. On the floor of the chamber where the coffins had been—for this was the burial chamber—lay a heap of black fragments charred with fire. Instantly he understood. After the thief had done his work he had burned the mummy-cases, and with them the body of the queen. There could be no doubt that this was so, for look! among the ashes lay some calcined human bones, while the roof above was blackened with the smoke and cracked by the heat of the conflagration. There was nothing left for him to find!

Oppressed with the closeness of the atmosphere, he sat down upon a little bench or table cut in the rock that evidently had been meant to receive offerings to the dead. Indeed, on it still lay the scorched remains of some votive flowers. Here, his lamp between his feet, he rested a while, staring at those calcined bones. See, yonder was the lower jaw, and in it some teeth, small, white, regular, and but little worn. Yes, she had died young. Then he turned to go, for disappointment and the holiness of the place overcame him; he could endure no more of it that night.

Leaving the burial hall, he walked along the painted passage, the lamp swinging and his eyes fixed upon the floor. He was disheartened, and the paintings could wait till the morrow. He descended the steps and came to the foot of the mud slope. Here suddenly he perceived, projecting from some sand that had drifted down over the mud, what seemed to be the corner of a reed box or basket. To clear away the sand was easy, and—yes, it was a basket, a foot or so in length, such a basket as the old Egyptians used to contain the funeral figures which are called *ushaptis*, or other objects connected with the dead. It looked as though it had been dropped, for it lay upon its side. Smith opened it—not very hopefully, for surely nothing of value would have been abandoned thus.

The first thing that met his eyes was a mummied hand, broken off at the wrist, a woman's little hand, most delicately shaped. It was withered and paper-white, but the contours still remained; the long fingers were perfect, and the almond- shaped nails had been stained with henna, as was the embalmers' fashion. On the hand were two gold rings, and for those rings it had been stolen. Smith looked at it for a long while, and his heart swelled within him, for here was the hand of that royal lady of his dreams.

Indeed, he did more than look; he kissed it, and as his lips touched the holy relic it seemed to him as though a wind, cold but scented, blew upon his brow. Then, growing fearful of the thoughts that arose within him, he hurried his mind back to the world, or rather to the examination of the basket.

Here he found other objects roughly wrapped in fragments of mummy-cloth that had been torn from the body of the queen. These it is needless to describe, for are they not to be seen in the gold room of the Museum, labelled "Bijouterie de la Reine Ma-Mé, XVIIIème Dynastie. Thebes (Smith's Tomb)"? It may be mentioned, however, that the set was incomplete. For instance, there was but one of the great gold ceremonial ear-rings fashioned like a group of pomegranate blooms, and the most beautiful of the necklaces had been torn in two- -half of it was missing.

It was clear to Smith that only a portion of the precious objects which were buried with the mummy had been placed in this basket. Why had these been left where he found them? A little reflection made that clear also. Something had prompted the thief to destroy the desecrated body and its coffin with fire, probably in the hope of hiding his evil handiwork. Then he fled with his spoil. But he had forgotten how fiercely mummies and their trappings can burn. Or perhaps the thing was an accident. He must have had a lamp, and if its flame chanced to touch this bituminous tinder!

At any rate, the smoke overtook the man in that narrow place as he began to climb the slippery slope of clay. In his haste he dropped the basket, and dared not return to search for it. It could wait till the morrow, when the fire would be out and the air pure. Only for this desecrator of the royal dead that morrow never came, as was discovered afterwards.

When at length Smith struggled into the open air the stars were paling before the dawn. An hour later, after the sky was well up, Mahomet (recovered from his sickness) and his myrmidons arrived.

"I have been busy while you slept," said Smith, showing them the mummied hand (but not the rings which he had removed from the shrunk fingers), and the broken bronze, but not the priceless jewellery which was hidden in his pockets.

For the next ten days they dug till the tomb and its approach were quite clear. In the sand, at the head of a flight of steps which led down to the doorway, they found the skeleton of a man, who evidently had been buried there in a hurried fashion. His skull was shattered by the blow of an axe, and the shaven scalp that still clung to it suggested that he might have been a priest.

Mahomet thought, and Smith agreed with him, that this was the person who had violated the tomb. As he was escaping from it the guards of the holy place surprised him after he had covered up the hole by which he had entered and purposed to return. There they executed him without trial and divided up the plunder, thinking that no more was to be found. Or perhaps his confederates killed him.

Such at least were the theories advanced by Mahomet. Whether they were right or wrong none will ever know. For instance, the skeleton may not have been that of the thief, though probability appears to point the other way.

Nothing more was found in the tomb, not even a scarab or a mummy-bead. Smith spent the remainder of his time in photographing the pictures and copying the inscriptions, which for various reasons proved to be of extraordinary interest. Then, having reverently buried the charred bones of the queen in a secret place of the sepulchre, he handed it over to the care of the local Guardian of Antiquities, paid off Mahomet and the fellaheen, and departed for Cairo. With him went the wonderful jewels of which he had breathed no word, and another relic to him yet more precious—the hand of her Majesty Ma-Mee, Palm-branch of Love.

II

Smith was seated in the sanctum of the distinguished Director-General of Antiquities at the new Cairo Museum. It was a very interesting room. Books piled upon the floor; objects from tombs awaiting examination, lying here and there; a hoard of Ptolemaic silver coins, just dug up at Alexandria, standing on the table in the pot that had hidden them for two thousand years; in the corner the mummy of a royal child, aged six or seven, not long ago discovered, with some inscription scrawled upon the wrappings (brought here to be deciphered by the Master), and the withered lotus-bloom, love's last offering, thrust beneath one of the pink retaining bands.

"A touching object," thought Smith to himself. "Really, they might have left the dear little girl in peace."

Smith had a tender heart, but even as he reflected he became aware that some of the jewellery hidden in an inner pocket of his waistcoat (designed for bank notes) was fretting his skin. He had a tender conscience also.

Just then the Director, a French savant, bustled in, alert, vigorous, full of interest.

"Ah, my dear Mr. Smith!" he said, in his excellent English. "I am indeed glad to see you back again, especially as I understand that you are come rejoicing and bringing your sheaves with you. They tell me you have been extraordinarily successful. What do you say is the name of this queen whose tomb you have found—Ma-Mee? A very unusual name. How do you get the extra vowel? Is it for euphony—eh? Did I not know how good a scholar you are, I should be tempted to believe that you had misread it. Me-Mee, Ma-Mee! That would be pretty in French, would it not? *Ma mie*—my darling! Well, I dare say she was somebody's *mie* in her time. But tell me the story."

Smith told him shortly and clearly; also he produced his photographs and copies of inscriptions.

"This is interesting—interesting truly," said the Director, when he had glanced through them. "You must leave them with me to study. Also you will publish them, is it not so? Perhaps one of the Societies would help you with the cost, for it should be done in facsimile. Look at this vignette! Most unusual. Oh, what a pity that scoundrelly priest got off with the jewellery and burnt her Majesty's body!"

"He didn't get off with all of it."

"What, Mr. Smith? Our inspector reported to me that you found nothing."

"I dare say, sir; but your inspector did not know what I found."

"Ah, you are a discreet man! Well, let us see."

Slowly Smith unbuttoned his waistcoat. From its inner pocket and elsewhere about his person he extracted the jewels wrapped in mummy-cloth as he had found them. First he produced a sceptre-head of gold, in the shape of a pomegranate fruit and engraved with the throne name and titles of Ma-Mee.

"What a beautiful object!" said the Director. "Look! the handle was of ivory, and that sacré thief of a priest smashed it out at the socket. It was fresh ivory then; the robbery must have taken place not long after the burial. See, this magnifying-glass shows it. Is that all?"

Smith handed him the surviving half of the marvellous necklace that had been torn in two.

"I have re-threaded it," he muttered, "but every bead is in its place."

"Oh, heavens! How lovely! Note the cutting of those cornelian heads of Hathor and the gold lotus-blooms between—yes, and the enamelled flies beneath. We have nothing like it in the Museum."

So it went on.

"Is that all?" gasped the Director at last, when every object from the basket glittered before them on the table.

"Yes," said Smith. "That is—no. I found a broken statuette hidden in the sand outside the tomb. It is of the queen, but I thought perhaps you would allow me to keep this."

"But certainly, Mr. Smith; it is yours indeed. We are not niggards here. Still, if I might see it—"

From yet another pocket Smith produced the head. The Director gazed at it, then he spoke with feeling.

"I said just now that you were discreet, Mr. Smith, and I have been reflecting that you are honest. But now I must add that you are very clever. If you had not made me promise that this bronze should be yours before you showed it to me—well, it would never have gone into that pocket again. And, in the public interest, won't you release me from the promise?"

"*No*," said Smith.

"You are perhaps not aware," went on the Director, with a groan, "that this is a portrait of Mariette's unknown queen whom we are thus able to identify. It seems a pity that the two should be separated; a replica we could let you have."

"I am quite aware," said Smith, "and I will be sure to send you a replica, with photographs. Also I promise to leave the original to some museum by will."

The Director clasped the image tenderly, and, holding it to the light, read the broken cartouche beneath the breasts.

"'Ma-Mé, Great Royal Lady. Beloved of—' Beloved of whom? Well, of Smith, for one. Take it, monsieur, and hide it away at once, lest soon there should be another mummy in this collection, a modern mummy called Smith; and, in the name of Justice, let the museum which inherits it be not the British, but that of Cairo, for this queen belongs to Egypt. By the way, I have been told that you are delicate in the lungs. How is your health now? Our cold winds are very trying. Quite good? Ah, that is excellent! I suppose that you have no more articles that you can show me?"

"I have nothing more except a mummied hand, which I found in the basket with the jewels. The two rings off it lie there. Doubtless it was removed to get at that bracelet. I suppose you will not mind my keeping the hand—"

"Of the beloved of Smith," interrupted the Director drolly. "No, I suppose not, though for my part I should prefer one that was not quite so old. Still, perhaps *you* will not mind my seeing it. That pocket of yours still looks a little bulky; I thought that it contained books!"

Smith produced a cigar-box; in it was the hand wrapped in cotton wool.

"Ah," said the Director, "a pretty, well-bred hand. No doubt this Ma-Mee was the real heiress to the throne, as she describes herself. The Pharaoh was somebody of inferior birth, half-brother—she is called 'Royal Sister', you remember—son of one of the Pharaoh's slave-women, perhaps. Odd that she never mentioned him in the tomb. It looks as though they didn't get on in life, and that she was determined to have done with him in death. Those were the rings upon that hand, were they not?"

He replaced them on the fingers, then took off one, a royal signet in a cartouche, and read the inscription on the other: "'Bes Ank, Ank Bes.' 'Bes the Living, the living Bes.'

"Your Ma-Mee had some human vanity about her," he added. "Bes, among other things, as you know, was the god of beauty and of the adornments of women. She wore that ring that she might remain beautiful, and that her dresses might always fit, and her rouge never cake when she was dancing before the gods. Also it fixes her period pretty closely, but then so do other things. It seems a pity to rob Ma-Mee of her pet ring, does it not? The royal signet will be enough for us."

With a little bow he gave the hand back to Smith, leaving the Bes ring on the finger that had worn it for more than three thousand years. At least, Smith was so sure it was the Bes ring that at the time he did not look at it again.

Then they parted, Smith promising to return upon the morrow, which, owing to events to be described, he did not do.

"Ah!" said the Master to himself, as the door closed behind his visitor. "He's in a hurry to be gone. He has fear lest I should change my mind about that ring. Also there is the bronze. Monsieur Smith was *rusé* there. It is worth a thousand pounds, that bronze. Yet I do not believe he was thinking of the money. I believe he is in love with that Ma-Mee and wants to keep her picture. *Mon Dieu!* A well-established affection. At least he is what the English call an odd fish, one whom I could never make out, and of whom no one seems to know anything. Still, honest, I am sure—quite honest. Why, he might have kept every one of those jewels and no one have been the wiser. And what things! What a find! *Ciel!* what a find! There has been nothing like it for years. Benedictions on the head of Odd-fish Smith!"

Then he collected the precious objects, thrust them into an inner compartment of his safe, which he locked and double-locked, and, as it was nearly five o'clock, departed from the Museum to his private residence in the grounds, there to study Smith's copies and photographs, and to tell some friends of the great things that had happened.

When Smith found himself outside the sacred door, and had presented its venerable guardian with a baksheesh of five piastres, he walked a few paces to the right and paused a while to watch some native labourers who were dragging a huge sarcophagus upon an improvised tramway. As they dragged they sang an echoing rhythmic song, whereof each line ended with an invocation to Allah.

Just so, reflected Smith, had their forefathers sung when, millenniums ago, they dragged that very sarcophagus from the quarries to the Nile, and from the Nile to the tomb whence it reappeared today, or when they slid the casing blocks of the pyramids up the great causeway and smooth slope of sand, and laid them in their dizzy resting-places. Only then each line of the immemorial chant of toil ended with an invocation to Amen, now transformed to Allah. The East may change its masters and its gods, but its customs never change, and if today Allah wore the feathers of Amen one wonders whether the worshippers would find the difference so very great.

Thus thought Smith as he hurried away from the sarcophagus and those blue-robed, dark-skinned fellaheen, down the long gallery that is filled with a thousand sculptures. For a moment he paused before the wonderful white statue of Queen Amenartas, then, remembering that his time was short, hastened on to a certain room, one of those which opened out of the gallery.

In a corner of this room, upon the wall, amongst many other beautiful objects, stood that head which Mariette had found, whereof in past years the cast had fascinated him in London. Now he knew whose head it was; to him it had been given to find the tomb of her who had sat for that statue. Her very hand was in his pocket—yes, the hand that had touched yonder marble, pointing out its defects to the sculptor, or perhaps swearing that he flattered her. Smith wondered who that sculptor was; surely he must have been a happy man. Also he wondered whether the statuette was also this master's work. He thought so, but he wished to make sure.

Near to the end of the room he stopped and looked about him like a thief. He was alone in the place; not a single student or tourist could be seen, and its guardian was somewhere else. He drew out the box that contained the hand. From the hand he slipped the ring which the Director-General had left there as a gift to himself. He would much have preferred the other with the signet, but how could he say so, especially after the episode of the statuette?

Replacing the hand in his pocket without looking at the ring—for his eyes were watching to see whether he was observed he set it upon his little finger, which it exactly fitted. (Ma-Mee had worn both of them upon the third finger of her left hand, the Bes ring as a guard to the signet.) He had the fancy to approach the effigy of Ma-Mee wearing a ring which she had worn and that came straight from her finger to his own.

Smith found the head in its accustomed place. Weeks had gone by since he looked upon it, and now, to his eyes, it had grown more beautiful than ever, and its smile was more mystical and loving.

He drew out the statuette and began to compare them point by point. Oh, no doubt was possible! Both were likenesses of the same woman, though the statuette might have been executed two or three years later than the statue. To him the face of it looked a little older and more spiritual. Perhaps illness, or some premonition of her end had then thrown its shadow on the queen. He compared and compared. He made some rough measurements and sketches in his pocket-book, and set himself to work out a canon of proportions.

So hard and earnestly did he work, so lost was his mind that he never heard the accustomed warning sound which announces that the Museum is about to close. Hidden behind an altar as he was, in his distant, shadowed corner, the guardian of the room never saw him as he cast a last perfunctory glance about the place before departing till the Saturday morning; for the morrow was Friday, the Mohammedan Sabbath, on which the Museum remains shut, and he would not be called upon to attend. So he went. Everybody went. The great doors clanged, were locked and bolted, and, save for a watchman outside, no one was left in all that vast place except Smith in his corner, engaged in sketching and in measurements.

The difficulty of seeing, owing to the increase of shadow, first called his attention to the fact that time was slipping away. He glanced at his watch and saw that it was ten minutes to the hour.

"Soon be time to go," he thought to himself, and resumed his work. How strangely silent the place seemed! Not a footstep to be heard or the sound of a human voice. He looked at his watch again, and saw that it was six o'clock, not five, or so the thing said. But that was impossible, for the Museum shut at five; evidently the desert sand had got into the works. The room in which he stood was that known as Room I, and he had noticed that its Arab custodian often frequented Room K or the gallery outside. He would find him and ask what was the real time.

Passing round the effigy of the wonderful Hathor cow, perhaps the finest example of an ancient sculpture of a beast in the whole world, Smith came to the doorway and looked up and down the gallery. Not a soul to be seen. He ran to Room K, to Room H, and others. Still not a soul to be seen. Then he made his way as fast as he could go to the great entrance. The doors were locked and bolted.

"Watch must be right after all. I'm shut in," he said to himself. "However, there's sure to be someone about somewhere. Probably the *salle des ventes* is still open. Shops don't shut till they are obliged."

Thither he went, to find its door as firmly closed as a door can be. He knocked on it, but a sepulchral echo was the only answer.

"I know," he reflected. "The Director must still be in his room. It will take him a long while to examine all that jewellery and put it away."

So for the room he headed, and, after losing his path twice, found it by help of the sarcophagus that the Arabs had been dragging, which now stood as deserted as it had done in the tomb, a lonesome and impressive object in the gathering shadows. The Director's door was shut, and again his knockings produced nothing but an echo. He started on a tour round the Museum, and, having searched the ground floors, ascended to the upper galleries by the great stairway.

Presently he found himself in that devoted to the royal mummies, and, being tired, rested there a while. Opposite to him, in a glass case in the middle of the gallery, reposed Rameses II. Near to, on shelves in a side case, were Rameses's son, Meneptah, and above, his son, Seti II, while in other cases were the mortal remains of many more of the royalties of Egypt. He looked at the proud face of Rameses and at the little fringe of white locks turned yellow by the embalmer's spices, also at the raised left arm. He remembered how the Director had told him that when they were unrolling this mighty monarch they went away to lunch, and that presently the man who had been left in charge of the body rushed into the room with his hair on end, and said that the dead king had lifted his arm and pointed at him.

Back they went, and there, true enough, was the arm lifted; nor were they ever able to get it quite into its place again. The explanation given was that the warmth of the sun had contracted the withered muscles, a very natural and correct explanation.

Still, Smith wished that he had not recollected the story just at this moment, especially as the arm seemed to move while he contemplated it—a very little, but still to move.

He turned round and gazed at Meneptah, whose hollow eyes stared at him from between the wrappings carelessly thrown across the parchment-like and ashen face. There, probably, lay the countenance that had frowned on Moses. There was the heart which God had hardened. Well, it was hard enough now, for the doctors said he died of ossification of the arteries, and that the vessels of the heart were full of lime!

Smith stood upon a chair and peeped at Seti II above. His weaker countenance was very peaceful, but it seemed to wear an air of reproach. In getting down Smith managed to upset the heavy chair. The noise it made was terrific. He would not have thought it possible that the fall of such an article could produce so much sound. Satisfied with his inspection of these particular kings, who somehow looked quite different now from what they had ever done before—more real and imminent, so to speak—he renewed his search for a living man.

On he went, mummies to his right, mummies to his left, of every style and period, till be began to feel as though he never wished to see another dried remnant of mortality. He peeped into the room where lay the relics of Iouiya and Touiyou, the father and mother of the great Queen Taia. Cloths had been drawn over these, and really they looked worse and more suggestive thus draped than in their frigid and unadorned blackness. He came to the coffins of the priest-kings of the twentieth dynasty, formidable painted coffins with human faces. There seemed to be a vast number of these priest-kings, but perhaps they were better than the gold masks of the great Ptolemaic ladies which glinted at him through the gathering gloom.

Really, he had seen enough of the upper floors. The statues downstairs were better than all these dead, although it was true that, according to the Egyptian faith, every one of those statues was haunted eternally by the Ka or Double, of the person whom it represented. He descended the great stairway. Was it fancy, or did something run across the bottom step in front of him—an animal of some kind, followed by a swift-moving and indefinite shadow? If so, it must have been the Museum cat hunting a Museum mouse. Only then what on earth was that very peculiar and unpleasant shadow?

He called, "Puss! puss! puss!" for he would have been quite glad of its company; but there came no friendly "miau" in response. Perhaps it was only the *Ka* of a cat and the shadow was—oh! never mind what. The Egyptians worshipped cats, and there were plenty of their mummies about on the shelves. But the shadow!

Once he shouted in the hope of attracting attention, for there were no windows to which he could climb. He did not repeat the experiment, for it seemed as though a thousand voices were answering him from every corner and roof of the gigantic edifice.

Well, he must face the thing out. He was shut in a museum, and the question was in what part of it he should camp for the night. Moreover, as it was growing rapidly dark, the problem must be solved at once. He thought with affection of the lavatory, where, before going to see the Director, only that afternoon he had washed his hands with the assistance of a kindly Arab who watched the door and gracefully accepted a piastre. But there was no Arab there now, and the door, like every other in this confounded place, was locked. He marched on to the entrance.

Here, opposite to each other, stood the red sarcophagi of the great Queen Hatshepu and her brother and husband, Thotmes III. He looked at them. Why should not one of these afford him a night's lodging? They were deep and quiet, and would fit the human frame very nicely. For a while Smith wondered which of these monarchs would be the more likely to take offence at such a use of a private sarcophagus, and, acting on general principles, concluded that he would rather throw himself on the mercy of the lady.

Already one of his legs was over the edge of that solemn coffer, and he was squeezing his body beneath the massive lid that was propped above it on blocks of wood, when he remembered a little, naked, withered thing with long hair that he had seen in a side chamber of the tomb of Amenhotep II in the Valley of Kings at Thebes. This caricature of humanity many thought, and he agreed with them, to be the actual body of the mighty Hatshepu as it appeared after the robbers had done with it.

Supposing now, that when he was lying at the bottom of that sarcophagus, sleeping the sleep of the just, this little personage should peep over its edge and ask him what he was doing there! Of course the idea was absurd; he was tired, and his nerves were a little shaken. Still, the fact remained that for centuries the hallowed dust of Queen Hatshepu had slept where he, a modern man, was proposing to sleep.

He scrambled down from the sarcophagus and looked round him in despair. Opposite to the main entrance was the huge central hall of the Museum. Now the cement roof of this hall had, he knew, gone wrong, with the result that very extensive repairs had become necessary. So extensive were they, indeed, that the Director-General had informed him that they would take several years to complete. Therefore this hall was boarded up, only a little doorway being left by which the workmen could enter. Certain statues, of Seti II and others, too large to be moved, were also roughly boarded over, as were some great funeral boats on either side of the entrance. The rest of the place, which might be two hundred feet long with a proportionate breadth, was empty save for the colossi of Amenhotep III and his queen Taia that stood beneath the gallery at its farther end.

It was an appalling place in which to sleep, but better, reflected Smith, than a sarcophagus or those mummy chambers. If, for instance, he could creep behind the deal boards that enclosed one of the funeral boats he would be quite comfortable there. Lifting the curtain, he slipped into the hall, where the gloom of evening had already settled. Only the sky-lights and the outline of the towering colossi at the far end remained visible. Close to him were the two funeral boats which he had noted when he looked into the hall earlier on that day, standing at the head of a flight of steps which led to the sunk floor of the centre. He groped his way to that on the right. As he expected, the projecting planks were not quite joined at the bow. He crept in between them and the boat and laid himself down.

Presumably, being altogether tired out, Smith did ultimately fall asleep, for how long he never knew. At any rate, it is certain that, if so, he woke up again. He could not tell the time, because his watch was not a repeater, and the place was as black as the pit. He had some matches in his pocket, and might have struck one and even have lit his pipe. To his credit be it said, however, he remembered that he was the sole tenant of one of the most valuable museums in the world, and his responsibilities with reference to fire. So he refrained from striking that match under the keel of a boat which had become very dry in the course of five thousand years.

Smith found himself very wide awake indeed. Never in all his life did he remember being more so, not even in the hour of its great catastrophe, or when his godfather, Ebenezer, after much hesitation, had promised him a clerkship in the bank of which he was a director. His nerves seemed strung tight as harp-strings, and his every sense was painfully acute. Thus he could even smell the odour of mummies that floated down from the upper galleries and the earthly scent of the boat which had been buried for thousands of years in sand at the foot of the pyramid of one of the fifth dynasty kings.

Moreover, he could hear all sorts of strange sounds, faint and far-away sounds which at first he thought must emanate from Cairo without. Soon, however, he grew sure that their origin was more local. Doubtless the cement work and the cases in the galleries were cracking audibly, as is the unpleasant habit of such things at night.

Yet why should these common manifestations be so universal and affect him so strangely? Really, it seemed as though people were stirring all about him. More, he could have sworn that the great funeral boat beneath which he lay had become re-peopled with the crew that once it bore.

He heard them at their business above him. There were trampings and a sound as though something heavy were being laid on the deck, such, for instance, as must have been made when the mummy of Pharaoh was set there for its last journey to the western bank of the Nile. Yes, and now he could have sworn again that the priestly crew were getting out the oars.

Smith began to meditate flight from the neighbourhood of that place when something occurred which determined him to stop where he was.

The huge hall was growing light, but not, as at first he hoped, with the rays of dawn. This light was pale and ghostly, though very penetrating. Also it had a blue tinge, unlike any other he had ever seen. At first it arose in a kind of fan or fountain at the far end of the hall, illumining the steps there and the two noble colossi which sat above.

But what was this that stood at the head of the steps, radiating glory? By heavens! it was Osiris himself or the image of Osiris, god of the Dead, the Egyptian saviour of the world!

There he stood, in his mummy-cloths, wearing the feathered crown, and holding in his hands, which projected from an opening in the wrappings, the crook and the scourge of power. Was he alive, or was he dead? Smith could not tell, since he never moved, only stood there, splendid and fearful, his calm, benignant face staring into nothingness.

Smith became aware that the darkness between him and the vision of this god was peopled; that a great congregation was gathering, or had gathered there. The blue light began to grow; long tongues of it shot forward, which joined themselves together, illumining all that huge hall.

Now, too, he saw the congregation. Before him, rank upon rank of them, stood the kings and queens of Egypt. As though at a given signal, they bowed themselves to the Osiris, and ere the tinkling of their ornaments had died away, lo! Osiris was gone. But in his place stood another, Isis, the Mother of Mystery, her deep eyes looking forth from beneath the jewelled vulture-cap. Again the congregation bowed, and, lo! she was gone. But in her place stood yet another, a radiant, lovely being, who held in her hand the Sign of Life, and wore upon her head the symbol of the shining disc—Hathor, Goddess of Love. A third time the congregation bowed, and she, too, was gone; nor did any other appear in her place.

The Pharaohs and their queens began to move about and speak to each other; their voices came to his ears in one low, sweet murmur.

In his amaze Smith had forgotten fear. From his hiding-place he watched them intently. Some of them he knew by their faces. There, for instance, was the long-necked Khu-en-aten, talking somewhat angrily to the imperial Rameses II. Smith could understand what he said, for this power seemed to have been given to him. He was complaining in a high, weak voice that on this, the one night of the year when they might meet, the gods, or the magic images of the gods who were put up for them to worship, should not include *his* god, symbolized by the "Aten", or the sun's disc.

"I have heard of your Majesty's god," replied Rameses; "the priests used to tell me of him, also that he did not last long after your Majesty flew to heaven. The Fathers of Amen gave you a bad name; they called you 'the heretic' and hammered out your cartouches. They were quite rare in my time. Oh, do not let your Majesty be angry! So many of us have been heretics. My grandson, Seti, there," —and he pointed to a mild, thoughtful-faced man— "for example. I am told that he really worshipped the god of those Hebrew slaves whom I used to press to build my cities. Look at that lady with him. Beautiful, isn't she? Observe her large, violet eyes! Well, she was the one who did the mischief, a Hebrew herself. At least, they tell me so."

"I will talk with him," answered Khu-en-aten. "It is more than possible that we may agree on certain points. Meanwhile, let me explain to your Majesty—"

"Oh, I pray you, not now. There is my wife."

"Your wife?" said Khu-en-aten, drawing himself up. "Which wife? I am told that your Majesty had many and left a large family;

indeed, I see some hundreds of them here tonight. Now, I—but let me introduce Nefertiti to your Majesty. I may explain that she was my *only* wife."

"So I have understood. Your Majesty was rather an invalid, were you not? Of course, in those circumstances, one prefers the nurse whom one can trust. Oh, pray, no offence! Nefertari, my love—oh, I beg pardon!—Astnefert—Nefertari has gone to speak to some of her children—let me introduce you to your predecessor, the Queen Nefertiti, wife of Amenhotep IV—I mean Khu-en-aten (he changed his name, you know, because half of it was that of the father of the gods). She is interested in the question of plural marriage. Goodbye! I wish to have a word with my grandfather, Rameses I. He was fond of me as a little boy."

At this moment Smith's interest in that queer conversation died away, for of a sudden he beheld none other than the queen of his dreams, Ma-Mee. Oh! there she stood, without a doubt, only ten times more beautiful than he had ever pictured her. She was tall and somewhat fair-complexioned, with slumbrous, dark eyes, and on her face gleamed the mystic smile he loved. She wore a robe of simple white and a purple-broidered apron, a crown of golden *uræi* with turquoise eyes was set upon her dark hair as in her statue, and on her breast and arms were the very necklace and bracelets that he had taken from her tomb. She appeared to be somewhat moody, or rather thoughtful, for she leaned by herself against a balustrade, watching the throng without much interest.

Presently a Pharaoh, a black-browed, vigorous man with thick lips, drew near.

"I greet your Majesty," he said.

She started, and answered:

"Oh, it is you! I make my obeisance to your Majesty," and she curtsied to him, humbly enough, but with a suggestion of mockery in her movements.

"Well, you do not seem to have been very anxious to find me, Ma-Mee, which, considering that we meet so seldom—"

"I saw that your Majesty was engaged with my sister queens," she interrupted, in a rich, low voice, "and with some other ladies in the gallery there, whose faces I seem to remember, but who I think were *not* queens. Unless, indeed, you married them after I was drawn away.

"One must talk to one's relations," replied the Pharaoh.

"Quite so. But, you see, I have no relations—at least, none whom I know well. My parents, you will remember, died when I was young, leaving me Egypt's heiress, and they are still vexed at the marriage which I made on the advice of my counsellors. But, is it not annoying? I have lost one of my rings, that which had the god Bes on it. Some dweller on the earth must be wearing it today, and that is why I cannot get it back from him."

"Him! Why 'him'? Hush; the business is about to begin."

"What business, my lord?"

"Oh, the question of the violation of our tombs, I believe."

"Indeed! That is a large subject, and not a very profitable one, I should say. Tell me, who is that?" And she pointed to a lady who had stepped forward, a very splendid person, magnificently arrayed.

"Cleopatra the Greek," he answered, "the last of Egypt's Sovereigns, one of the Ptolemys. You can always know her by that Roman who walks about after her."

"Which?" asked Ma-Mee. "I see several—also other men. She was the wretch who rolled Egypt in the dirt and betrayed her. Oh, if it were not for the law of peace by which we abide when we meet thus!"

"You mean that she would be torn to shreds, Ma-Mee, and her very soul scattered like the limbs of Osiris? Well, if it were not for that law of peace, so perhaps would many of us, for never have I heard a single king among these hundreds speak altogether well of those who went before or followed after him."

"Especially of those who went before if they happen to have hammered out their cartouches and usurped their monuments," said the queen, dryly, and looking him in the eyes.

At this home-thrust the Pharaoh seemed to wince. Making no answer, he pointed to the royal woman who had mounted the steps at the end of the hall.

Queen Cleopatra lifted her hand and stood thus for a while. Very splendid she was, and Smith, on his hands and knees behind the boarding of the boat, thanked his stars that alone among modern men it had been his lot to look upon her rich and living loveliness. There she shone, she who had changed the fortunes of the world, she who, whatever she did amiss, at least had known how to die.

Silence fell upon that glittering galaxy of kings and queens and upon all the hundreds of their offspring, their women, and their great officers who crowded the double tier of galleries around the hall.

"Royalties of Egypt," she began, in a sweet, clear voice which penetrated to the farthest recesses of the place, "I, Cleopatra, the sixth of that name and the last monarch who ruled over the Upper and the Lower Lands before Egypt became a home of slaves, have a word to say to your Majesties, who, in your mortal days, all of you more worthily filled the throne on which once I sat. I do not speak of Egypt and its fate, or of our sins—whereof mine were not the least—that brought her to the dust. Those sins I and others expiate elsewhere, and of them, from age to age, we hear enough. But on this one night of the year, that of the feast of him whom we call Osiris, but whom other nations have known and know by different names, it is given to us once more to be mortal for an hour, and, though we be but shadows, to renew the loves and hates of our long-perished flesh. Here for an hour we strut in our forgotten pomp; the gems that were ours still adorn our brows, and once more we seem to listen to our people's praise. Our hopes are the hopes of mortal life, our foes are the foes we feared, our gods grow real again, and our lovers whisper in our ears. Moreover, this joy is given to us—to see each other as we are, to know as the gods know, and therefore to forgive, even where we despise and hate. Now I have done, and I, the youngest of the rulers of ancient Egypt, call upon him who was the first of her kings to take my place."

She bowed, and the audience bowed back to her. Then she descended the steps and was lost in the throng. Where she had been appeared an old man, simply-clad, long-bearded, wise-faced, and wearing on his grey hair no crown save a plain band of gold, from the centre of which rose the snake-headed *uræus* crest.

"Your Majesties who came after me," said the old man, "I am Menes, the first of the accepted Pharaohs of Egypt, although many of those who went before me were more truly kings than I. Yet as the first who joined the Upper and the Lower Lands, and took the royal style and titles, and ruled as well as I could rule, it is given to me to talk with you for a while this night whereon our spirits are permitted to gather from the uttermost parts of the uttermost worlds and see each other face to face. First, in darkness and in secret, let us speak of the mystery of the gods and of its meanings. Next, in darkness and in secret, let us speak of the mystery of our lives, of whence they come, of where they tarry by the road, and whither they go at last. And afterwards, let us speak of other matters face to face in light and openness, as we were wont to do when we were men. Then hence to Thebes, there to celebrate our yearly festival. Is such your will?"

"Such is our will," they answered.

It seemed to Smith that dense darkness fell upon the place, and with it a silence that was awful. For a time that he could not reckon, that might have been years or might have been moments, he sat there in the utter darkness and the utter silence.

At length the light came again, first as a blue spark, then in upward pouring rays, and lastly pervading all. There stood Menes on the steps, and there in front of him was gathered the same royal throng.

"The mysteries are finished," said the old king. "Now, if any have aught to say, let it be said openly."

A young man dressed in the robes and ornaments of an early dynasty came forward and stood upon the steps between the Pharaoh Menes and all those who had reigned after him. His face seemed familiar to Smith, as was the side lock that hung down behind his right ear in token of his youth. Where had he seen him? Ah, he remembered. Only a few hours ago lying in one of the cases of the Museum, together with the bones of the Pharaoh Unas.

"Your Majesties," he began, "I am the King Metesuphis. The matter that I wish to lay before you is that of the violation of our sepulchres by those men who live upon the earth. The mortal bodies of many who are gathered here tonight lie in this place to be stared at and mocked by the curious. I myself am one of them, jawless, broken, hideous to behold. Yonder, day by day, must my Ka sit watching my desecrated flesh, torn from the pyramid that, with cost and labour, I raised up to be an eternal house wherein I might hide till the hour of resurrection. Others of us lie in far lands. Thus, as he can tell you, my predecessor, Man-kau-ra, he who built the third of the great pyramids, the Pyramid of Her, sleeps, or rather wakes in a dark city, called London, across the seas, a place of murk where no sun shines. Others have been burnt with fire, others are scattered in small dust. The ornaments that were ours are stole away and sold to the greedy; our sacred writings and our symbols are their jest. Soon there will not be one holy grave in Egypt that remains undefiled."

"That is so," said a voice from the company. "But four months gone the deep, deep pit was opened that I had dug in the shadow of the Pyramid of Cephren, who begat me in the world. There in my chamber I slept alone, two handfuls of white bones, since when I died they did not preserve the body with wrappings and with spices. Now I see those bones of mine, beside which my Double has watched for these five thousand years, hid in the blackness of a great ship and tossing on a sea that is strewn with ice."

"It is so," echoed a hundred other voices.

"Then," went on the young king, turning to Menes, "I ask of your Majesty whether there is no means whereby we may be avenged on those who do us this foul wrong."

"Let him who has wisdom speak," said the old Pharaoh.

A man of middle age, short in stature and of a thoughtful brow, who held in his hand a wand and wore the feathers and insignia of the heir to the throne of Egypt and of a high priest of Amen, moved to the steps. Smith knew him at once from his statues. He was Khaemuas, son of Rameses the Great, the mightiest magician that ever was in Egypt, who of his own will withdrew himself from earth before the time came that he should sit upon the throne.

"I have wisdom, your Majesties, and I will answer," he said. "The time draws on when, in the land of Death which is Life, the land that we call Amenti, it will be given to us to lay our wrongs as to this matter before Those who judge, knowing that they will be avenged. On this night of the year also, when we resume the shapes we were, we have certain powers of vengeance, or rather of executing justice. But our time is short, and there is much to say and do before the sun-god Ra arises and we depart each to his place. Therefore it seems best that we should leave these wicked ones in their wickedness till we meet them face to face beyond the world."

Smith, who had been following the words of Khaemuas with the closest attention and considerable anxiety, breathed again, thanking Heaven that the engagements of these departed monarchs were so numerous and pressing. Still, as a matter of precaution, he drew the cigar-box which contained Ma-Mee's hand from his pocket, and pushed it as far away from him as he could. It was a most unlucky act. Perhaps the cigar-box grated on the floor, or perhaps the fact of his touching the relic put him into psychic communication with all these spirits. At any rate, he became aware that the eyes of that dreadful magician were fixed upon him, and that a bone had a better chance of escaping the search of a Röntgen ray than he of hiding himself from their baleful glare.

"As it happens, however," went on Khaemuas, in a cold voice, "I now perceive that there is hidden in this place, and spying on us, one of the worst of these vile thieves. I say to your Majesties that I see him crouched beneath your funeral barge, and that he has with him at this moment the hand of one of your Majesties, stolen by him from her tomb at Thebes."

Now every queen in the company became visibly agitated (Smith, who was watching Ma-Mee, saw her hold up her hands and look at them), while all the Pharaohs pointed with their fingers and exclaimed together, in a voice that rolled round the hall like thunder:—

"Let him be brought forth to judgment!"

Khaemuas raised his wand and, holding it towards the boat where Smith was hidden, said:—

"Draw near, Vile One, bringing with thee that thou hast stolen."

Smith tried hard to remain where he was. He sat himself down and set his heels against the floor. As the reader knows, he was always shy and retiring by disposition, and never had these weaknesses oppressed him more than they did just then. When a child his favourite nightmare had been that the foreman of a jury was in the act of proclaiming him guilty of some dreadful but unstated crime. Now he understood what that nightmare foreshadowed. He was about to be convicted in a court of which all the kings and queens of Egypt were the jury, Menes was Chief Justice, and the magician Khaemuas played the *rôle* of Attorney-General.

In vain did he sit down and hold fast. Some power took possession of him which forced him first to stretch out his arm and pick up the cigar-box containing the hand of Ma-Mee, and next drew him from the friendly shelter of the deal boards that were about the boat.

Now he was on his feet and walking down the flight of steps opposite to those on which Menes stood far away. Now he was among all that throng of ghosts, which parted to let him pass, looking at him as he went with cold and wondering eyes. They were very majestic ghosts; the ages that had gone by since they laid down their sceptres had taken nothing from their royal dignity. Moreover, save one, none of them seemed to have any pity for his plight. She was a little princess who stood by her mother, that same little princess whose mummy he had seen and pitied in the Director's room with a lotus flower thrust beneath her bandages. As he passed Smith heard her say:

"This Vile One is frightened. Be brave, Vile One!"

Smith understood, and pride come to his aid. He, a gentleman of the modern world, would not show the white feather before a crowd of ancient Egyptian ghosts. Turning to the child, he smiled at her, them drew himself to his full height and walked on quietly. Here it may be stated that Smith was a tall man, still comparatively young, and very good-looking, straight and spare in frame, with dark, pleasant eyes and a little black beard.

"At least he is a well-favoured thief," said one of the queens to another.

"Yes," answered she who had been addressed. "I wonder that a man with such a noble air should find pleasure in disturbing graves and stealing the offerings of the dead," words that gave Smith much cause for thought. He had never considered the matter in this light.

Now he came to the place where Ma-Mee stood, the black-browed Pharaoh who had been her husband at her side. On his left hand which held the cigar-box was the gold Bes ring, and that box he felt constrained to carry pressed against him just over his heart.

As he went by he turned his head, and his eyes met those of Ma-Mee. She started violently. Then she saw the ring upon his hand and again started still more violently.

"What ails your Majesty?" asked the Pharaoh.

"Oh, naught," she answered. "Yet does this earth-dweller remind you of anyone?"

"Yes, he does," answered the Pharaoh. "He reminds me very much of that accursed sculptor about whom we had words."

"Do you mean a certain Horu, the Court artist; he who worked the image that was buried with me, and whom you sent to carve your statues in the deserts of Kush, until he died of fevers—or was it poison?"

"Aye; Horu and no other, may Set take and keep him!" growled the Pharaoh.

Then Smith passed on and heard no more. Now he stood before the venerable Menes. Some instinct caused him to bow to bowed to the royal company, and they also bowed back to him, coldly, but very gravely and courteously.

"Dweller on the world where once we had our place, and therefore brother of us, the dead," began Menes, "this divine priest and magician" —and he pointed to Khaemuas— "declares that you are one of those who foully violate our sepulchres and desecrate our ashes. He declares, moreover, that at this very moment you have with you a portion of the mortal flesh of a certain Majesty whose spirit is present here. Say, now, are these things true?"

To his astonishment Smith found that he had not the slightest difficulty in answering in the same sweet tongue.

"O King, they are true, and not true. Hear me, rulers of Egypt. It is true that I have searched in your graves, because my heart has been drawn towards you, and I would learn all that I could concerning you, for it comes to me now that once I was one of you—no king, indeed, yet perchance of the blood of kings. Also—for I would hide nothing even if I could—I searched for one tomb above all others."

"Why, O man?" asked the Judge.

"Because a face drew me, a lovely face that was cut in stone."

Now all that great audience turned their eyes towards him and listened as though his words moved them.

"Did you find that holy tomb?" asked Menes. "If so, what did you find therein?"

"Aye, Pharaoh, and in it I found these," and he took from the box the withered hand, from his pocket the broken bronze, and from his finger the ring.

"Also I found other things which I delivered to the keeper of this place, articles of jewellery that I seem to see tonight upon one who is present here among you."

"Is the face of this figure the face you sought?" asked the Judge.

"It is the lovely face," he answered.

Menes took the effigy in his hand and read the cartouche that was engraved beneath its breast.

"If there be here among us," he said, presently, "one who long after my day ruled as queen in Egypt, one who was named Ma-Mé, let her draw near."

Now from where she stood glided Ma-Mee and took her place opposite to Smith.

"Say, O Queen," asked Menes, "do you know aught of this matter?"

"I know that hand; it was my own hand," she answered. "I know that ring; it was my ring. I know that image in bronze; it was my image. Look on me and judge for yourselves whether this be so. A certain sculptor fashioned it, the son of a king's son, who was named Horu, the first of sculptors and the head artist of my Court. There, clad in strange garments, he stands before you. Horu, or the Double of Horu, he who cut the image when I ruled in Egypt, is he who found the image and the man who stands before you; or, mayhap, his Double cast in the same mould."

The pharaoh Menes turned to the magician Khaemuas and said:—

"Are these things so, O Seer?"

"They are so," answered Khaemuas. "This dweller on the earth is he who, long ago, was the sculptor Horu. But what shall that avail? He, once more a living man, is a violator of the hallowed dead. I say, therefore, that judgment should be executed on his flesh, so that when the light comes here tomorrow he himself will again be gathered to the dead."

Menes bent his head upon his breast and pondered. Smith said nothing. To him the whole play was so curious that he had no wish to interfere with its development. If these ghosts wished to make him of their number, let them do so. He had no ties on earth, and now when he knew full surely that there was a life beyond this of earth he was quite prepared to explore its mysteries. So he folded his arms upon his breast and awaited the sentence.

But Ma-Mee did not wait. She raised her hand so swiftly that the bracelets jingled on her wrists, and spoke out with boldness.

"Royal Khaemuas, prince and magician," she said, "hearken to one who, like you, was Egypt's heir centuries before you were born, one also who ruled over the Two Lands, and not so ill—which, Prince, never was your lot. Answer me! Is all wisdom centred in your breast? Answer me! Do you alone know the mysteries of Life and Death? Answer me! Did your god Amen teach you that vengeance went before mercy? Answer me! Did he teach you that men should be judged unheard? That they should be hurried by violence to Osiris ere their time, and thereby separated from the dead ones whom they loved and forced to return to live again upon this evil Earth?

"Listen: when the last moon was near her full my spirit sat in my tomb in the burying-place of queens. My spirit saw this man enter into my tomb, and what he did there. With bowed head he looked upon my bones that a thief of the priesthood of Amen had robbed and burnt within twenty years of their burial, in which he himself had taken part. And what did this man with those bones, he who was once Horu? I tell you that he hid them away there in the tomb where he thought they could not be found again. Who, then, was the thief and the violator? He who robbed and burnt my bones, or he who buried them with reverence? Again, he found the jewels that the priest of your brotherhood had dropped in his flight, when the smoke of the burning flesh and spices overpowered him, and with them the hand which that wicked one had broken off from the body of my Majesty. What did this man then? He took the jewels. Would you have had him leave them to be stolen by some peasant? And the hand? I tell you that he kissed that poor dead hand which once had been part of the body of my Majesty, and that now he treasures it as a holy relic. My spirit saw him do these things and made report thereof to me. I ask you, therefore, Prince, I ask you all, Royalties of Egypt—whether for such deeds this man should die?"

Now Khaemuas, the advocate of vengeance, shrugged his shoulders and smiled meaningly, but the congregation of kings and queens thundered an answer, and it was: "*No!*"

Ma-Mee looked to Menes to give judgment. Before he could speak the dark-browed Pharaoh who had named her wife strode forward and addressed them.

"Her Majesty, Heiress of Egypt, Royal Wife, Lady of the Two Lands, has spoken," he cried. "Now let me speak who was the husband of her Majesty. Whether this man was once Horu the sculptor I know not. If so he was also an evil-doer who, by my decree, died in banishment in the land of Kush. Whatever be the truth as to that matter, he admits that he violated the tomb of her Majesty and stole what the old thieves had left. Her Majesty says also—and he does not deny it—that he dared to kiss her hand, and for a man to kiss the hand of a wedded Queen of Egypt the punishment is death. I claim that this man should die to the World before his time, that in a day to come again he may live and suffer in the World. Judge, O Menes."

Menes lifted his head and spoke, saying:—

"Repeat to me the law, O Pharaoh, under which a living man must die for the kissing of a dead hand. In my day and in that of those who went before me there was no such law in Egypt. If a living man, who was not her husband, or of her kin, kissed the living hand of a wedded Queen of Egypt, save in ceremony, then perchance he might be called upon to die. Perchance for such a reason a certain Horu once was called upon to die. But in the grave there is no marriage, and therefore even if he had found her alive within the tomb and kissed her hand, or even her lips, why should he die for the crime of love?

"Hear me, all; this is my judgment in the matter. Let the soul of that priest who first violated the tomb of the royal Ma-Mee be hunted down and given to the jaws of the Destroyer, that he may know the last depths of Death, if so the gods declare. But let this man go from among us unharmed, since what he did he did in reverent ignorance and because Hathor, Goddess of Love, guided him from of old. Love rules this world wherein we meet tonight, with all the worlds whence we have gathered or whither we still must go. Who can defy its power? Who can refuse its rites? Now hence to Thebes!"

There was a rushing sound as of a thousand wings, and all were gone.

No, not all, since Smith yet stood before the draped colossi and the empty steps, and beside him, glorious, unearthly, gleamed the vision of Ma-Mee.

"I, too, must away," she whispered; "yet ere I go a word with you who once were a sculptor in Egypt. You loved me then, and that love cost you your life, you who once dared to kiss this hand of mine that again you kissed in yonder tomb. For I was Pharaoh's wife in name only; understand me well, in name only; since that title of Royal Mother, which they gave me is but a graven lie. Horu, I never was a wife, and when you died, swiftly I followed you to the grave. Oh, you forget, but I remember! I remember many things. You think that the priestly thief broke this figure of me which you found in the sand outside my tomb. Not so. *I* broke it, because, daring greatly, you had written thereon, 'Beloved' not 'of *Horus* the God' as you should have done, but of '*Horu* the Man'. So when I came to be buried, Pharaoh, knowing all, took the image from my wrappings and hurled it away. I remember, too, the casting of that image, and how you threw a gold chain I had given you into the crucible with the bronze, saying that gold alone was fit to fashion me. And this signet that I bear—it was you who cut it. Take it, take it, Horu, and in its place give me back that which is on your hand, the Bes ring that I also wore. Take it and wear it ever till you die again, and let it go to the grave with you as once it went to the grave with me.

"Now hearken. When Ra the great sun arises again and you awake you will think that you have dreamed a dream. You will think that in this dream you saw and spoke with a lady of Egypt who died more than three thousand years ago, but whose beauty, carved in stone and bronze, has charmed your heart today. So let it be, yet know, O man, who once was named Horu, that such dreams are oft-times a shadow of the truth. Know that this Glory which shines before you is mine indeed in the land that is both far and near, the land wherein I dwell eternally, and that what is mine has been, is, and shall be yours for ever. Gods may change their kingdoms and their names; men may live and die, and live again once more to die; empires may fall and those who ruled them be turned to forgotten dust. Yet true love endures immortal as the souls in which it was conceived, and from it for you and me, the night of woe and separation done, at the daybreak which draws on, there shall be born the splendour and the peace of union. Till that hour foredoomed seek me no more, though I be ever near you, as I have ever been. Till that most blessed hour, Horu, farewell."

She bent towards him; her sweet lips touched his brow; the perfume from her breath and hair beat upon him; the light of her wondrous eyes searched out his very soul, reading the answer that was written there.

He stretched out his arms to clasp her, and lo! she was gone.

It was a very cold and a very stiff Smith who awoke on the following morning, to find himself exactly where he had lain down—namely, on a cement floor beneath the keel of a funeral boat in the central hall of the Cairo Museum. He crept from his shelter shivering, and looked at this hall, to find it quite as empty as it had been on the previous evening. Not a sign or a token was there of Pharaoh Menes and all those kings and queens of whom he had dreamed so vividly.

Reflecting on the strange fantasies that weariness and excited nerves can summon to the mind in sleep, Smith made his way to the great doors and waited in the shadow, praying earnestly that, although it was the Mohammedan Sabbath, someone might visit the Museum to see that all was well.

As a matter of fact, someone did, and before he had been there a minute—a watchman going about his business. He unlocked the place carelessly, looking over his shoulder at a kite fighting with two nesting crows. In an instant Smith, who was not minded to stop and answer questions, had slipped past him and was gliding down the portico, from monument to monument, like a snake between boulders, still keeping in the shadow as he headed for the gates.

The attendant caught sight of him and uttered a yell of fear; then, since it is not good to look upon an *afreet*, appearing from whence no mortal man could be, he turned his head away. When he looked again Smith was through those gates and had mingled with the crowd in the street beyond.

The sunshine was very pleasant to one who was conscious of having contracted a chill of the worst Egyptian order from long contact with a damp stone floor. Smith walked on through it towards his hotel—it was Shepheard's, and more than a mile away—making up a story as he went to tell the hall-porter of how he had gone to dine at Mena House by the Pyramids, missed the last tram, and stopped the night there.

Whilst he was thus engaged his left hand struck somewhat sharply against the corner of the cigar-box in his pocket, that which contained the relic of the queen Ma-Mee. The pain caused him to glance at his fingers to see if they were injured, and to perceive on one of them the ring he wore. Surely, surely it was not the same that the Director-General had given him! *That* ring was engraved with the image of the god Bes. On *this* was cut the cartouche of her Majesty Ma-Mee! And he had dreamed—oh, he had dreamed—!

To this day Smith is wondering whether, in the hurry of the moment, he made a mistake as to which of those rings the Director-General had given him as part of his share of the spoil of the royal tomb he discovered in the Valley of Queens. Afterwards Smith wrote to ask, but the Director-General could only remember that he gave him one of the two rings, and assured him that that inscribed "*Bes Ank, Ank Bes*," was with Ma-Mee's other jewels in the Gold Room of the Museum.

Also Smith is wondering whether any other bronze figure of an old Egyptian royalty shows so high a percentage of gold as, on analysis, the broken image of Ma-Mee was proved to do. For had she not seemed to tell him a tale of the melting of a golden chain when that effigy was cast?

Was it all only a dream, or was it—something more—by day and by night he asks of Nothingness?

But, be she near or far, no answer comes from the Queen Ma-Mee, whose proud titles were "Her Majesty the Good God, the justified

Dweller in Osiris; Daughter of Amen, Royal Heiress, Royal Sister, Royal Wife, Royal Mother; Lady of the Two Lands; Wearer of the Double Crown; of the White Crown, of the Red Crown; Sweet Flower of Love, Beautiful Eternally."

So, like the rest of us, Smith must wait to learn the truth concerning many things, and more particularly as to which of those two circles of ancient gold the Director-General gave him yonder at Cairo.

It seems but a little matter, yet it is more than all the worlds to him!

To the astonishment of his colleagues in antiquarian research, Smith has never returned to Egypt. He explains to them that his health is quite restored, and that he no longer needs this annual change to a more temperate clime.

Now, *which* of the two royal rings did the Director-General return to Smith on the mummied hand of her late Majesty Ma-Mee?

In the Valley of the Sorceress

Sax Rohmer

I

Condor wrote to me three times before the end (said Neville, Assistant-Inspector of Antiquities, staring vaguely from his open window at a squad drilling before the Kasr-en-Nîl Barracks). He dated his letters from the camp at Deir-el-Bahari. Judging from these, success appeared to be almost within his grasp. He shared my theories, of course, respecting Queen Hatasu, and was devoting the whole of his energies to the task of clearing up the great mystery of Ancient Egypt which centres around that queen.

For him, as for me, there was a strange fascination about those defaced walls and roughly obliterated inscriptions. That the queen under whom Egyptian art came to the apogee of perfection should thus have been treated by her successors; that no perfect figure of the wise, famous, and beautiful Hatasu should have been spared to posterity; that her very cartouche should have been ruthlessly removed from every inscription upon which it appeared, presented to Condor's mind a problem only second in interest to the immortal riddle of Gîzeh.

You know my own views upon the matter? My monograph, "Hatasu, the Sorceress," embodies my opinion. In short, upon certain evidences, some adduced by Theodore Davis, some by poor Condor, and some resulting from my own inquiries, I have come to the conclusion that the source—real or imaginary—of this queen's power was an intimate acquaintance with what nowadays we term, vaguely, magic. Pursuing her studies beyond the limit which is lawful, she met with a certain end, not uncommon, if the old writings are to be believed, in the case of those who penetrate too far into the realms of the Borderland.

For this reason—the practice of black magic—her statues were dishonored, and her name erased from the monuments. Now, I do not propose to enter into any discussion respecting the reality of such practices; in my monograph I have merely endeavored to show that, according to contemporary belief, the queen was a sorceress. Condor was seeking to prove the same thing; and when I took up the inquiry, it was in the hope of completing his interrupted work.

He wrote to me early in the winter of 1908, from his camp by the Rock Temple. Davis's tomb, at Bibân el-Mulûk, with its long, narrow passage, apparently had little interest for him; he was at work on the high ground behind the temple, at a point one hundred yards or so due west of the upper platform. He had an idea that he should find there the mummies of Hatasu—and another; the latter, a certain Sen-Mût, who appears in the inscriptions of the reign as an architect high in the queen's favor. The archaeological points of the letter do not concern us in the least, but there was one odd little paragraph which I had cause to remember afterwards.

"A girl belonging to some Arab tribe," wrote Condor, "came racing to the camp two nights ago to claim my protection. What crime she had committed, and what punishment she feared, were far from clear; but she clung to me, trembling like a leaf, and positively refused to depart. It was a difficult situation, for a camp of fifty native excavators, and one highly respectable European enthusiast, affords no suitable quarters for an Arab girl—and a very personable Arab girl. At any rate, she is still here; I have had a sort of lean-to rigged up in a little valley east of my own tent, but it is very embarrassing."

Nearly a month passed before I heard from Condor again; then came a second letter, with the news that on the eve of a great discovery—as he believed—his entire native staff—the whole fifty—had deserted one night in a body! "Two days' work," he wrote, "would have seen the tomb opened—for I am more than ever certain that my plans are accurate. Then I woke up one morning to find every man Jack of my fellows missing! I went down into the village where a lot of them live, in a towering rage, but not one of the brutes was to be found, and their relations professed entire ignorance respecting their whereabouts. What caused me almost as much anxiety as the check in my work was the fact that Mahâra—the Arab girl—had vanished also. I am wondering if the thing has any sinister significance."

Condor finished with the statement that he was making tremendous efforts to secure a new gang. "But," said he, "I shall finish the excavation, if I have to do it with my own hands."

His third and last letter contained even stranger matters than the two preceding it. He had succeeded in borrowing a few men from the British Archaeological camp in the Fáyûm. Then, just as the work was restarting, the Arab girl, Mahâra, turned up again, and entreated him to bring her down the Nile, "at least as far as Dendera. For the vengeance of her tribesmen," stated Condor, "otherwise would result not only in her own death, but in mine! At the moment of writing I am in two minds what to do. If Mahâra is to go upon this journey, I do not feel justified in sending her alone, and there is no one here who could perform the duty," etc.

I began to wonder, of course; and I had it in mind to take the train to Luxor merely in order to see this Arab maiden, who seemed to occupy so prominent a place in Condor's mind. However, Fate would have it otherwise; and the next thing I heard was that Condor had been brought into Cairo, and was at the English hospital.

He had been bitten by a cat—presumably from the neighboring village; and although the doctor at Luxor dealt with the bite at once, traveled down with him, and placed him in the hand of the Pasteur man at the hospital, he died, as you remember, in the night of his arrival, raving mad; the Pasteur treatment failed entirely.

I never saw him before the end, but they told me that his howls were horribly like those of a cat. His eyes changed in some way, too, I understand; and, with his fingers all contracted, he tried to *scratch* everyone and everything within reach.

They had to strap the poor beggar down, and even then he tore the sheets into ribbons.

Well, as soon as possible, I made the necessary arrangements to finish Condor's inquiry. I had access to his papers, plans, etc., and in the spring of the same year I took up my quarters near Deir-el-Bahari, roped off the approaches to the camp, stuck up the usual notices, and prepared to finish the excavation, which, I gathered, was in a fairly advanced state.

My first surprise came very soon after my arrival, for when, with the plan before me, I started out to find the shaft, I found it, certainly, but only with great difficulty.

It had been filled in again with sand and loose rock right to the very top!

II

All my inquiries availed me nothing. With what object the excavation had been thus closed I was unable to conjecture. That Condor had not reclosed it I was quite certain, for at the time of his mishap he had actually been at work at the bottom of the shaft, as inquiries from a native of Suefee, in the Fáyûm, who was his only companion at the time, had revealed.

In his eagerness to complete the inquiry, Condor, by lantern light, had been engaged upon a solitary night-shift below, and the rabid cat had apparently fallen into the pit; probably in a frenzy of fear, it had attacked Condor, after which it had escaped.

Only this one man was with him, and he, for some reason that I could not make out, had apparently been sleeping in the temple—quite a considerable distance from Condor's camp. The poor fellow's cries had aroused him, and he had met Condor running down the path and away from the shaft.

This, however, was good evidence of the existence of the shaft at the time, and as I stood contemplating the tightly packed rubble which alone marked its site, I grew more and more mystified, for this task of reclosing the cutting represented much hard labor.

Beyond perfecting my plans in one or two particulars, I did little on the day of my arrival. I had only a handful of men with me, all of whom I knew, having worked with them before, and beyond clearing Condor's shaft I did not intend to excavate further.

Hatasu's Temple presents a lively enough scene in the daytime during the winter and early spring months, with the streams of tourists constantly passing from the white causeway to Cook's Rest House on the edge of the desert. There had been a goodly number of visitors that day to the temple below, and one or two of the more curious and venturesome had scrambled up the steep path to the little plateau which was the scene of my operations. None had penetrated beyond the notice boards, however, and now, with the evening sky passing through those innumerable shades which defy palette and brush, which can only be distinguished by the trained eye, but which, from palest blue melt into exquisite pink, and by some magical combination form that deep violet which does not exist to perfection elsewhere than in the skies of Egypt, I found myself in the silence and the solitude of "the Holy Valley."

I stood at the edge of the plateau, looking out at the rosy belt which marked the course of the distant Nile, with the Arabian hills vaguely sketched beyond. The rocks stood up against that prospect as great black smudges, and what I could see of the causeway looked like a gray smear upon a drab canvas. Beneath me were the chambers of the Rock Temple, with those wall paintings depicting events in the reign of Hatasu which rank among the wonders of Egypt.

Not a sound disturbed my reverie, save a faint clatter of cooking utensils from the camp behind me—a desecration of that sacred solitude. Then a dog began to howl in the neighboring village. The dog ceased, and faintly to my ears came the note of a reed pipe. The breeze died away, and with it the piping.

I turned back to the camp, and, having partaken of a frugal supper, turned in upon my campaigner's bed, thoroughly enjoying my freedom from the routine of official life in Cairo, and looking forward to the morrow's work pleasurably.

Under such circumstances a man sleeps well; and when, in an uncanny gray half-light, which probably heralded the dawn, I awoke with a start, I knew that something of an unusual nature alone could have disturbed my slumbers.

Firstly, then, I identified this with a concerted howling of the village dogs. They seemed to have conspired to make night hideous; I have never heard such an eerie din in my life. Then it gradually began to die away, and I realized, secondly, that the howling of the dogs and my own awakening might be due to some common cause. This idea grew upon me, and as the howling subsided, a sort of disquiet possessed me, and, despite my efforts to shake it off, grew more urgent with the passing of every moment.

In short, I fancied that the thing which had alarmed or enraged the dogs was passing from the village through the Holy Valley, upward to the Temple, upward to the plateau, and was approaching *me*.

I have never experienced an identical sensation since, but I seemed to be audient of a sort of psychic patrol, which, from a remote *pianissimo*, swelled *fortissimo*, to an intimate but silent clamor, which beat in some way upon my brain, but not through the faculty of hearing, for now the night was deathly still.

Yet I was persuaded of some *approach*—of the coming of something sinister, and the suspense of waiting had become almost insupportable, so that I began to accuse my Spartan supper of having given me nightmare, when the tent-flap was suddenly raised, and, outlined against the paling blue of the sky, with a sort of reflected elfin light playing upon her face, I saw an Arab girl looking in at me!

By dint of exerting all my self-control I managed to restrain the cry and upward start which this apparition prompted. Quite still, with my fists tightly clenched, I lay and looked into the eyes which were looking into mine.

The style of literary work which it has been my lot to cultivate fails me in describing that beautiful and evil face. The features were severely classical and small, something of the Bisharîn type, with a cruel little mouth and a rounded chin, firm to hardness. In the eyes alone lay the languor of the Orient; they were exceedingly—indeed, excessively—long and narrow. The ordinary ragged, picturesque finery of a desert girl bedecked this midnight visitant, who, motionless, stood there watching me.

I once read a work by Pierre de l'Ancre, dealing with the Black Sabbaths of the Middle Ages, and now the evil beauty of this Arab face threw my memory back to those singular pages, for, perhaps owing to the reflected light which I have mentioned, although the explanation scarcely seemed adequate, those long, narrow eyes shone catlike in the gloom.

Suddenly I made up my mind. Throwing the blanket from me, I leapt to the ground, and in a flash had gripped the girl by the wrists. Confuting some lingering doubts, she proved to be substantial enough. My electric torch lay upon a box at the foot of the bed, and, stooping, I caught it up and turned its searching rays upon the face of my captive.

She fell back from me, panting like a wild creature trapped, then dropped upon her knees and began to plead—began to plead in a voice and with a manner which touched some chord of consciousness that I could swear had never spoken before, and has never spoken since.

She spoke in Arabic, of course, but the words fell from her lips as liquid music in which lay all the beauty and all the deviltry of the "Siren's Song." Fully opening her astonishing eyes, she looked up at me, and, with her free hand pressed to her bosom, told me how she had fled from an unwelcome marriage; how, an outcast and a pariah, she had hidden in the desert places for three days and three nights, sustaining life only by means of a few dates which she had brought with her, and quenching her thirst with stolen water-melons.

"I can bear it no longer, *effendim*. Another night out in the desert, with the cruel moon beating, beating, beating upon my brain, with creeping things coming out from the rocks, wriggling, wriggling, their many feet making whisperings in the sand—ah, it will kill me! And I am for ever outcast from my tribe, from my people.

"No tent of all the Arabs, though I fly to the gates of Damascus, is open to me, save I enter in shame, as a slave, as a plaything, as a toy. My heart" —furiously she beat upon her breast— "is empty and desolate, *effendim*. I am meaner than the lowliest thing that creeps upon the sand; yet the God that made that creeping thing made me also—and you, you, who are merciful and strong, would not crush any creature because it was weak and helpless."

I had released her wrist now, and was looking down at her in a sort of stupor. The evil which at first I had seemed to perceive in her was effaced, wiped out as an artist wipes out an error in his drawing. Her dark beauty was speaking to me in a language of its own; a strange language, yet one so intelligible that I struggled in vain to disregard it. And her voice, her gestures, and the witch-fire of her eyes were whipping up my blood to a fever heat of passionate sorrow—of despair. Yes, incredible as it sounds, despair!

In short, as I see it now, this siren of the wilderness was playing upon me as an accomplished musician might play upon a harp, striking this string and that at will, and sounding each with such full notes as they had rarely, if ever, emitted before.

Most damnable anomaly of all, I—Edward Neville, archaeologist, most prosy and matter-of-fact man in Cairo, perhaps—*knew* that this nomad who had burst into my tent, upon whom I had set eyes for the first time scarce three minutes before, held me enthralled; and yet, with her wondrous eyes upon me, I could summon up no resentment, and could offer but poor resistance.

"In the Little Oasis, *effendim*, I have a sister who will admit me into her household, if only as a servant. There I can be safe, there I can rest. O *Inglîsi*, at home in England you have a sister of your own! Would you see her pursued, a hunted thing from rock to rock, crouching for shelter in the lair of some jackal, stealing that she might live—and flying always, never resting, her heart leaping for fear, flying, flying, with nothing but dishonor before her?"

She shuddered and clasped my left hand in both her own convulsively, pulling it down to her bosom.

"There can be only one thing, *effendim*," she whispered. "Do you not see the white bones bleaching in the sun?"

Throwing all my resolution into the act, I released my hand from her clasp, and, turning aside, sat down upon the box which served me as chair and table, too.

A thought had come to my assistance, had strengthened me in the moment of my greatest weakness; it was the thought of that Arab girl mentioned in Condor's letters. And a scheme of things, an incredible scheme, that embraced and explained some, if not all, of the horrible circumstances attendant upon his death, began to form in my brain.

Bizarre it was, stretching out beyond the realm of things natural and proper, yet I clung to it, for there, in the solitude, with this wildly beautiful creature kneeling at my feet, and with her uncanny powers of fascination yet enveloping me like a cloak, I found it not so improbable as inevitably it must have seemed at another time.

I turned my head, and through the gloom sought to look into the long eyes. As I did so they closed and appeared as two darkly luminous slits in the perfect oval of the face.

"You are an impostor!" I said in Arabic, speaking firmly and deliberately. "To Mr. Condor" —I could have sworn that she started slightly at sound of the name— "you called yourself Mahâra. I know you, and I will have nothing to do with you."

But in saying it I had to turn my head aside, for the strangest, maddest impulses were bubbling up in my brain in response to the glances of those half-shut eyes.

I reached for my coat, which lay upon the foot of the bed, and, taking out some loose money, I placed fifty piastres in the nerveless brown hand.

"That will enable you to reach the Little Oasis, if such is your desire," I said. "It is all I can do for you, and now—you must go."

The light of the dawn was growing stronger momentarily, so that I could see my visitor quite clearly. She rose to her feet, and stood before me, a straight, slim figure, sweeping me from head to foot with such a glance of passionate contempt as I had never known or suffered. She threw back her head magnificently, dashed the money on the ground at my feet, and, turning, leaped out of the tent.

For a moment I hesitated, doubting, questioning my humanity, testing my fears; then I took a step forward, and peered out across the plateau. Not a soul was in sight. The rocks stood up gray and eerie, and beneath lay the carpet of the desert stretching unbroken to the shadows of the Nile Valley.

III

We commenced the work of clearing the shaft at an early hour that morning. The strangest ideas were now playing in my mind, and in some way I felt myself to be in opposition to definite enmity. My excavators labored with a will, and, once we had penetrated below the first three feet or so of tightly packed stone, it became a mere matter of shoveling, for apparently the lower part of the shaft had been filled up principally with sand.

I calculated that four days' work at the outside would see the shaft clear to the base of Condor's excavation. There remained, according to his own notes, only another six feet or so; but it was solid limestone—the roof of the passage, if his plans were correct, communicating with the tomb of Hatasu.

With the approach of night, tired as I was, I felt little inclination for sleep. I lay down on my bed with a small Browning pistol under the pillow, but after an hour or so of nervous listening drifted off into slumber. As on the night before, I awoke shortly before the coming of dawn.

Again the village dogs were raising a hideous outcry, and again I was keenly conscious of some ever-nearing menace. This consciousness grew stronger as the howling of the dogs grew fainter, and the sense of *approach* assailed me as on the previous occasion.

I sat up immediately with the pistol in my hand, and, gently raising the tent flap, looked out over the darksome plateau. For a long time I could perceive nothing; then, vaguely outlined against the sky, I detected something that moved above the rocky edge.

It was so indefinite in form that for a time I was unable to identify it, but as it slowly rose higher and higher, two luminous eyes—obviously feline eyes, since they glittered greenly in the darkness—came into view. In character and in shape they were the eyes of a cat, but in point of size they were larger than the eyes of any cat I had ever seen. Nor were they jackal eyes. It occurred to me that some predatory beast from the Sûdan might conceivably have strayed thus far north.

The presence of such a creature would account for the nightly disturbance amongst the village dogs; and, dismissing the superstitious notions which had led me to associate the mysterious Arab girl with the phenomenon of the howling dogs, I seized upon this new idea with a sort of gladness.

Stepping boldly out of the tent, I strode in the direction of the gleaming eyes. Although my only weapon was the Browning pistol, it was a weapon of considerable power, and, moreover, I counted upon the well-known cowardice of nocturnal animals. I was not disappointed in the result.

The eyes dropped out of sight, and as I leaped to the edge of rock overhanging the temple a lithe shape went streaking off in the greyness beneath me. Its coloring appeared to be black, but this appearance may have been due to the bad light. Certainly it was no cat, was no jackal; and once, twice, thrice my Browning spat into the darkness.

Apparently I had not scored a hit, but the loud reports of the weapon aroused the men sleeping in the camp, and soon I was surrounded by a ring of inquiring faces.

But there I stood on the rock-edge, looking out across the desert in silence. Something in the long, luminous eyes, something in the sinuous, flying shape had spoken to me intimately, horribly.

Hassan es-Sugra, the headman, touched my arm, and I knew that I must offer some explanation.

"Jackals," I said shortly. And with no other word I walked back to my tent.

The night passed without further event, and in the morning we addressed ourselves to the work with such a will that I saw, to my satisfaction, that by noon of the following day the labor of clearing the loose sand would be completed.

During the preparation of the evening meal I became aware of a certain disquiet in the camp, and I noted a disinclination on the part of the native laborers to stray far from the tents. They hung together in a group, and whilst individually they seemed to avoid meeting my eye, collectively they watched me in a furtive fashion.

A gang of Moslem workmen calls for delicate handling, and I wondered if, inadvertently, I had transgressed in some way their iron-bound code of conduct. I called Hassan es-Sugra aside.

"What ails the men?" I asked him. "Have they some grievance?"

Hassan spread his palms eloquently.

"If they have," he replied, "they are secret about it, and I am not in their confidence. Shall I thrash three or four of them in order to learn the nature of this grievance?"

"No thanks all the same," I said, laughing at this characteristic proposal. "If they refuse to work to-morrow, there will be time enough for you to adopt those measures."

On this, the third night of my sojourn in the Holy Valley by the Temple of Hatasu, I slept soundly and uninterruptedly. I had been looking forward with the keenest zest to the morrow's work, which promised to bring me within sight of my goal, and when Hassan came to awaken me, I leaped out of bed immediately.

Hassan es-Sugra, having performed his duty, did not, as was his custom, retire; he stood there, a tall, angular figure, looking at me strangely.

"Well?" I said.

"There is trouble," was his simple reply. "Follow me, Neville Effendi."

Wondering greatly, I followed him across the plateau and down the slope to the excavation. There I pulled up short with a cry of amazement.

Condor's shaft was filled in to the very top, and presented, to my astonished gaze, much the same aspect that had greeted me upon my first arrival!

"The men—" I began.

Hassan es-Sugra spread wide his palms. "Gone!" he replied. "Those Coptic dogs, those eaters of carrion, have fled in the night."

"And this" —I pointed to the little mound of broken granite and sand— "is their work?"

"So it would seem," was the reply; and Hassan sniffed his sublime contempt.

I stood looking bitterly at this destruction of my toils. The strangeness of the thing at the moment did not strike me, in my anger; I was only concerned with the outrageous impudence of the missing workmen, and if I could have laid hands upon one of them it had surely gone hard with him.

As for Hassan es-Sugra, I believe he would cheerfully have broken the necks of the entire gang. But he was a man of resource.

"It is so newly filled in," he said, "that you and I, in three days, or in four, can restore it to the state it had reached when those nameless dogs, who regularly prayed with their shoes on, those devourers of pork, began their dirty work."

His example was stimulating. I was not going to be beaten, either.

After a hasty breakfast, the pair of us set to work with pick and shovel and basket. We worked as those slaves must have worked whose toil was directed by the lash of the Pharaoh's overseer. My back acquired an almost permanent crook, and every muscle in my body seemed to be on fire. Not even in the midday heat did we slacken or stay our toils; and when dusk fell that night a great mound had arisen beside Condor's shaft, and we had excavated to a depth it had taken our gang double the time to reach.

When at last we threw down our tools in utter exhaustion, I held out my hand to Hassan, and wrung his brown fist enthusiastically. His eyes sparkled as he met my glance.

"Neville Effendi," he said, "you are a true Moslem!"

And only the initiated can know how high was the compliment conveyed.

That night I slept the sleep of utter weariness, yet it was not a dreamless sleep, or perhaps it was not so deep as I supposed, for blazing cat-eyes encircled me in my dreams, and a constant feline howling seemed to fill the night.

When I awoke the sun was blazing down upon the rock outside my tent, and, springing out of bed, I perceived, with amazement, that the morning was far advanced. Indeed, I could hear the distant voices of the donkey-boys and other harbingers of the coming tourists.

Why had Hassan es-Sugra not awakened me? I stepped out of the tent and called him in a loud voice. There was no reply. I ran across the plateau to the edge of the hollow.

Condor's shaft had been reclosed to the top!

Language fails me to convey the wave of anger, amazement, incredulity, which swept over me. I looked across to the deserted camp and back to my own tent; I looked down at the mound, where but a few hours before had been a pit, and seriously I began to question whether I was mad or whether madness had seized upon all who had been with me. Then, pegged down upon the heap of broken stones, I perceived, fluttering, a small piece of paper.

Dully I walked across and picked it up. Hassan, a man of some education, clearly was the writer. It was a pencil scrawl in doubtful Arabic, and, not without difficulty, I deciphered it as follows:

"Fly, Neville Effendi! This is a haunted place!"

Standing there by the mound, I tore the scrap of paper into minute fragments, bitterly casting them from me upon the ground. It was incredible; it was insane.

The man who had written that absurd message, the man who had undone his own work, had the reputation of being fearless and honorable. He had been with me before a score of times, and had quelled petty mutinies in the camp in a manner which marked him a born overseer. I could not understand; I could scarcely believe the evidence of my own senses.

What did I do?

I suppose there are some who would have abandoned the thing at once and for always, but I take it that the national traits are strong within me. I went over to the camp and prepared my own breakfast; then, shouldering pick and shovel, I went down into the valley and set to work. What ten men could not do, what two men had failed to do, one man was determined to do.

It was about half an hour after commencing my toils, and when, I suppose, the surprise and rage occasioned by the discovery had begun to wear off, that I found myself making comparisons between my own case and that of Condor. It became more and more evident to me that events—mysterious events—were repeating themselves.

The frightful happenings attendant upon Condor's death were marshaling in my mind. The sun was blazing down upon me, and distant voices could be heard in the desert stillness. I knew that the plain below was dotted with pleasure-seeking tourists, yet nervous tremors shook me. Frankly, I dreaded the coming of the night.

Well, tenacity or pugnacity conquered, and I worked on until dusk. My supper despatched, I sat down on my bed and toyed with the Browning.

I realized already that sleep, under existing conditions, was impossible. I perceived that on the morrow I must abandon my one-man enterprise, pocket my pride, in a sense, and seek new assistants, new companions.

The fact was coming home to me conclusively that a menace, real and not mythical, hung over that valley. Although, in the morning sunlight and filled with indignation, I had thought contemptuously of Hassan es-Sugra, now, in the mysterious violet dusk so conducive to calm consideration, I was forced to admit that he was at least as brave a man as I. And he had fled! What did that night hold in keeping for me?

I will tell you what occurred, and it is the only explanation I have to give of why Condor's shaft, said to communicate with the real tomb of Hatasu, to this day remains unopened.

There, on the edge of my bed, I sat far into the night, not daring to close my eyes. But physical weariness conquered in the end, and, although I have no recollection of its coming, I must have succumbed to sleep, since I remember—can never forget—a repetition of the dream, or what I had assumed to be a dream, of the night before.

A ring of blazing green eyes surrounded me. At one point this ring was broken, and in a kind of nightmare panic I leaped at that promise of safety, and found myself outside the tent.

Lithe, slinking shapes hemmed me in—cat shapes, ghoul shapes, veritable figures of the pit. And the eyes, the shapes, although they were the eyes and shapes of cats, sometimes changed elusively, and became the wicked eyes and the sinuous, writhing shapes of women. Always the ring was incomplete, and always I retreated in the only direction by which retreat was possible. I retreated from those cat-things.

In this fashion I came at last to the shaft, and there I saw the tools which I had left at the end of my day's toil.

Looking around me, I saw also, with such a pang of horror as I cannot hope to convey to you, that the ring of green eyes was now unbroken about me.

And it was closing in.

Nameless feline creatures were crowding silently to the edge of the pit, some preparing to spring down upon me where I stood. A voice seemed to speak in my brain; it spoke of capitulation, telling me to accept defeat, lest, resisting, my fate be the fate of Condor.

Peals of shrill laughter rose upon the silence. The laughter was mine.

Filling the night with this hideous, hysterical merriment, I was working feverishly with pick and with shovel filling in the shaft.

The end? The end is that I awoke, in the morning, lying, not on my bed, but outside on the plateau, my hands torn and bleeding and every muscle in my body throbbing agonisingly. Remembering my dream—for even in that moment of awakening I thought I had dreamed—I staggered across to the valley of the excavation.

Condor's shaft was reclosed to the top.

The Death-Ring of Sneferu

Sax Rohmer

I

The orchestra had just ceased playing; and, taking advantage of the lull in the music, my companion leaned confidentially forward, shooting suspicious glances all around him, although there was nothing about the well-dressed after-dinner throng filling Shepheard's that night to have aroused misgiving in the mind of a cinema anarchist.

"I have a very big thing in view," he said, speaking in a husky whisper. "I shall be one up on you, Kernaby, if I pull it off."

He glanced sideways, in the manner of a pantomime brigand, at a party of New York tourists, our immediate neighbors, and from them to an elderly peer with whom I was slightly acquainted and who, in addition to his being stone deaf, had never noticed anything in his life, much less attempted so fatiguing an operation as intrigue.

"Indeed," I commented; and rang the bell with the purpose in view of ordering another cooling beverage.

True, I might be the Egyptian representative of a Birmingham commercial enterprise, but I did not gladly suffer the society of this individual, whose only claim to my acquaintance lay in the fact that he was in the employ of a rival house. My lack of interest palpably disappointed him; but I thought little of the man's qualities as a connoisseur and less of his company. His name was Theo Bishop and I fancy that his family was associated with the tanning industry. I have since thought more kindly of poor Bishop, but at the time of which I write nothing could have pleased me better than his sudden dissolution.

Perhaps unconsciously I had allowed my boredom to become rudely apparent; for Bishop slightly turned his head aside, and—

"Right-o, Kernaby," he said; "I know you think I am an ass, so we will say no more about it. Another cocktail?"

And now I became conscience-stricken; for mingled with the disappointment in Bishop's tone and manner was another note. Vaguely it occurred to me that the man was yearning for sympathy of some kind, that he was bursting to unbosom himself, and that the vanity of a successful rival was by no means wholly responsible. I have since placed that ambiguous note and recognized it for a note of tragedy. But at the time I was deaf to its pleading.

We chatted then for some while longer on indifferent topics, Bishop being, as I have indicated, a man difficult to offend; when, having correspondence to deal with, I retired to my own room. I suppose I had been writing for about an hour, when a servant came to announce a caller. Taking an ordinary visiting-card from the brass salver, I read—

Abû Tabâh.

No title preceded the name, no address followed, but I became aware of something very like a nervous thrill as I stared at the name of my visitor. Personality is one of the profoundest mysteries of our being. Of the person whose card I hold in my hand I knew little, practically nothing; his actions, if at times irregular, had never been wantonly violent; his manner was gentle as that of a mother to a baby and his singular reputation among the natives I thought I could afford to ignore; for the Egyptian, like the Celt, with all his natural endowments, is yet a child at heart. Therefore I cannot explain why, sitting there in my room in Shepheard's Hotel, I knew and recognized, at the name of Abû Tabâh, the touch of fear.

"I will see him downstairs," I said. Then, as the servant was about to depart, recognizing that I had made a concession to that strange sentiment which the Imám Abû Tabâh had somehow inspired in me—

"No," I added; "show him up here to my room."

A few moments later the man returned again, carrying the brass salver, upon which lay a sealed envelope. I took it up in surprise, noting that it was one belonging to the hotel, and, ere opening it—

"Where is my visitor?" I said in Arabic.

"He regrets that he cannot stay," replied the man; "but he sends you this letter."

Greatly mystified, I dismissed the servant and tore open the envelope. Inside, upon a sheet of hotel notepaper I found this remarkable message—

> Kernaby Pasha—
>
> There are reasons why I cannot stay to see you personally, but I would have you believe that this warning is dictated by nothing but friendship. Grave peril threatens. It is associated with the hieroglyphic—

> If you would avert it, and if you value your life, avoid all contact with anything bearing this figure.
>
> Abû Tabâh.

The mystery deepened. There had been something incongruous about the modern European visiting-card used by this representative of Islam, this living illustration of the *Arabian Nights*; now, his incomprehensible "warning" plunged me back again into the mediæval Orient to which be properly belonged. Yet I knew Abû Tabâh, for all his romantic aspect, to be eminently practical, and I could not credit him with descending to the methods of melodrama.

As I studied the precise wording of the note, I seemed to see the slim figure of its author before me, black-robed, white-turbaned, and urbane, his delicate ivory hands crossed and resting upon the head of the ebony cane without which I had never seen him. Almost, I succumbed to a sort of subjective hallucination; Abû Tabâh became a veritable presence, and the poetic beauty of his face struck me anew, as, fixing upon me his eyes, which were like the eyes of a gazelle, he spoke the strange words cited above, in the pure and polished English which he held at command, and described in the air, with a long nervous forefinger, the queer device which symbolized the Ancient Egyptian god, Set, the Destroyer.

Of course, it was the aura of a powerful personality, clinging even to the written message; but there was something about the impression made upon me which argued for the writer's sincerity.

That Abû Tabâh was some kind of agent, recognized—at any rate unofficially—by the authorities, I knew or shrewdly surmised; but the exact nature of his activities, and how be reconciled them with his religious duties, remained profoundly mysterious. The episode had rendered further work impossible, and I descended to the terrace, with no more definite object in view than that of finding a quiet corner where I might meditate in the congenial society of my briar, and at the same the seek inspiration from the ever-changing throng in the Shâria Kâmel Pasha.

I had scarcely set my foot upon the terrace, however, ere a hand was laid upon my arm.

Turning quickly I recognized, in the dusk, Hassan es-Sugra, for many years a trusted employee of the British Archæological Society.

His demeanor was at once excited and furtive, and I recognized with something akin to amazement that he, also, had a story to unfold. I mentally catalogued this eventful evening "the night of strange confidences."

Seated at a little table on the deserted balcony (for the evening was very chilly) and directly facing the shop of Philip, the dealer in Arab woodwork, Hassan es-Sugra told his wonder tale; and as he told it I knew that Fate had cast me, willy-nilly, for a part in some comedy upon which the curtain had already risen here in Cairo, and whereof the second act should be played in perhaps the most ancient setting which the hand of man has builded. As the narrative unrolled itself before me, I perceived wheels within wheels; I was wholly absorbed, yet half incredulous.

"... When the professor abandoned work on the pyramid, Kernaby Pasha," he said, bending eagerly forward and laying his muscular brown hand upon my sleeve, "it was not because there was no more to learn there."

"I am aware of this, O Hassan," I interrupted, "it was in order that they might carry on the work at the Pyramid of Illahûn, which resulted in a find of jewelery almost unique in the annals of Egyptology."

"Do I not know all this!" exclaimed Hassan impatiently; "and was not mine the hand that uncovered the golden uræus? But the work projected at the Pyramid of Méydûm was never completed, and I can tell you why."

I stared at him through the gloom; for I had already some idea respecting the truth of this matter.

"It was that, the men, over two hundred of them, refused to enter the passage again," he whispered dramatically, "it was because misfortune and disaster visited more than one who had penetrated to a certain place therein." He bent further forward. "The Pyramid of Méydûm is the home of a powerful *Efreet*, Kernaby Pasha! But I who was the last to leave it, know what is concealed there. In a certain place, low down in the corner of the King's Chamber, is a ring of gold, bearing a cartouche. It is the royal ring of the Pharaoh who built the pyramid."

He ceased, watching me intently. I did not doubt Hassan's word, for I had always counted him a man of integrity; but there was much that was obscure and much that was mysterious in his story.

"Why did you not bring it away?" I asked.

"I feared to touch it, Kernaby Pasha; it is an evil talisman. Until to-day I have feared to speak of it."

"And to-day?"

Hassan extended his hands, palms upward.

"I am threatened with the loss of my house," he said simply, "if I do not find a certain sum of money within a period of twelve days."

I sat resting my chin on my hand and staring into the face of Hassan es-Sugra. Could it be that from superstitious motives such a treasure had indeed been abandoned? Could it be that Fate had delivered into my hands a relic so priceless as the signet-ring of Sneferu, one of the earliest Memphite Pharaohs? Since I had recently incurred the displeasure of my principals, Messrs. Moses, Murphy Co., of Birmingham, the mere anticipation of such a "find" was sufficient to raise my professional enthusiasm to white heat, and in those few moments of silence I had decided upon instant action.

"Meet me at Rikka Station, to-morrow morning at nine o'clock," I said, "and arrange for donkeys to carry us to the pyramid."

II

On my arrival at Rikka, and therefore at the very outset of my inquiry, I met with what one slightly prone to superstition might have regarded as an unfortunate omen. A native funeral was passing out of the town and the wailing of women and the chanting by the *Yemeneeyeh*, of the Profession of the Faith, with its queer monotonous cadences, a performance which despite its familiarity in the Near East never failed to affect me unpleasantly. By the token of the *tarbûsh* upon the bier, I knew that this was a man who was being hurried to his lonely resting-place on the fringe of the desert.

As the procession wound its way out across the sands, I saw to the removal of my baggage and joined Hassan es-Sugra, who awaited me by the wooden barrier. I perceived immediately that something was wrong within the man; he was palpably laboring under the influence of some strong excitement, and his dark eyes regarded me almost fearfully, he was muttering to himself like one suffering from an over-indulgence in *Hashish*, and I detected the words "*Allahu akbar!*" (God is most great) several times repeated.

"What ails you, Hassan, my friend?" I said; and noting mow his gaze persistently returned to the melancholy procession wending its way towards the little Moslem cemetery:— "Was the dead man some relation of yours?"

"No, no, Kernaby Pasha," he muttered gutturally, and moistened his lips with his tongue; "I was but slightly acquainted with him."

"Yet you are much disturbed."

"Not at all, Kernaby Pasha," he assured me; "not in the slightest."

By which familiar formula I knew that Hassan es-Sugra would conceal from me the cause of his distress, and therefore, since I had no appetite for further mysteries, I determined to learn it from another source.

"See to the loading of the donkey," I directed him—for three sleek little animals were standing beside him, patiently awaiting the toil of the day.

Hassan setting about the task with a cheerful alacrity obviously artificial, I approached the native station master, with whom I was acquainted, and put to him a number of questions respecting his important functions—in which I was not even mildly interested. But to the Oriental mind a direct inquiry is an affront, almost an insult; and to have inquired bluntly the name of the deceased and the manner of his death would have been the best way to have learned nothing whatever about the matter. Therefore having discussed in detail the slothful incompetence of Arab ticket collectors and the lazy condition and innate viciousness of Egyptian porters as a class, I mentioned incidentally that I had observed a funeral leaving Rikka.

The station master (who was bursting to talk about this very matter, but who would have declined on principle to do so had I definitely questioned him) now unfolded to me the strange particulars respecting the death of one, Ahmed Abdulla, who had been a retired dragoman though some the employed as an excavator.

"He rode out one night upon his white donkey," said my informant, "and no man knows whither he went. But it is believed, Kernaby Pasha, that it was to the Haram el-Kaddâb" (the False Pyramid)—extending his hand to where, beyond the belt of fertility, the tomb of Sneferu up-reared its three platforms from the fringe of the desert. "To enter the pyramid even in day the is to court misfortune; to enter at night is to fall into the hands of the powerful *Efreet* who dwells there. His donkey returned without him, and therefore search was made for Ahmed Abdulla. He was found the next day"—again the long arm shot out towards the desert— "dead upon the sands, near the foot of the pyramid."

I looked into the face of the speaker; beyond doubt he was in deadly earnest.

"Why should Ahmed Abdulla have wanted to visit such a place at night?" I asked.

My acquaintance lowered his voice, muttered "*Sahâm Allah fee'adoo ed—dîn!*" (May God transfix the enemies of the religion) and touched his forehead, his mouth, and his breast with the iron ring which he wore.

"There is a great treasure concealed there, Kernaby Pasha," he replied: "a treasure hidden from the world in the days of Suleyman the Great, sealed with his seal, and guarded by the servants of Gánn Ibn-Gánn."

"So you think the guardian *ginn* killed Ahmed Abdulla?"

The station master muttered invocations, and—

"There are things which may not be spoken of," he said; "but those who saw him dead say that he was terrible to look upon. A great *Welee*, a man of wisdom famed throughout Egypt, has been summoned to avert the evil; for if the anger of the *ginn* is aroused they may visit the most painful and unfortunate penalties upon all Rikka..."

Half an hour later I set out, having confidentially informed the station master that I sought to obtain a fine turquoise necklet which I knew to be in the possession of the Sheikh of Méydûm.

Little did I suspect how it was written that I should indeed visit the house of the venerable Sheikh. Out through the fields of young green corn, the palm groves and the sycamore orchards I rode, Hassan plodding silently behind me and leading the donkey who bore the baggage. Curious eyes watched our passage, from field, doorway, and *shadûf*; but nothing of note marked our journey save the tremendous heat of the sun at noon, beneath which I knew myself a fool to travel.

I camped on the western side of the pyramid, but well clear of the marshes, which arc the home of countless wild-fowl. I had no idea how long it would take me to extract the coveted ring from its hiding-place (which Hassan had closely described to me); and, remembering the speculative glances of the villagers, I had no intention of exposing myself against the face of the pyramid until dusk should have come to cloak my operations.

Hassan es-Sugra, whose new taciturnity was remarkable and whose behavior was distinguished by an odd disquiet, set out with his gun to procure our dinner, and I mounted the sandy slope on the southwest of the pyramid, where from my cover behind a mound of rubbish, I studied through my field-glasses the belt of vegetation marking the course of the Nile. I could detect no sign of surveillance, but in view of the fact that the smuggling of relics out of Egypt is a punishable offence my caution was dictated by wisdom.

We dined excellently, Hassan the Silent and I, upon quail, tinned tomatoes, fresh dates, bread, and Vichy-water (to which in my own case was added a stiff three fingers of whisky).

When the newly risen moon cast an ebon shadow of the Pyramid of Sneferu upon the carpet of the sands, I made my way around the angle of the ancient building towards the mound on the northern side whereby one approaches the entrance. Three paces from the shadow's edge, I paused, transfixed, because of that which confronted me.

Outlined against the moon-bright sky upon a ridge of the desert behind and to the north of the great structure, stood the motionless figure of a man!

For a moment I thought that my mind had conjured up this phantasmal watcher, that he was a thing of moon-magic and not of flesh and blood. But as I stood regarding him, he moved, seemed to raise his head, then turned and disappeared beyond the crest.

How long I remained staring at the spot where he had been I know not; but I was aroused from my useless contemplation by the jingling of camel bells. The sound came from behind me, stealing sweetly through the stillness from a great distance. I turned in a flash, whipped out my glasses and searched the remote fringe of the Fáyûm. Stately across the jeweled curtain of the night moved a caravan, blackly marked against that wondrous background. Three walking figures I counted, three laden donkeys, and two camels. Upon the first of the camels a man was mounted, upon the second was a *shibreeyeh*, a sort of covered litter, which I knew must conceal a woman. The caravan passed out of sight into the palm grove which conceals the village of Méydûm.

I returned my glasses to their case, and stood for some moments deep in reflection; then I descended the slope, to the tiny encampment where I had left Hassan es-Sugra. He was nowhere to be seen; and having waited some ten minutes I grew impatient, and raising my voice:

"Hassan!" I cried; "Hassan es-Sugra!"

No answer greeted me, although in the desert stillness the call must have been audible for miles. A second and a third time I called his name and the only reply was the shrill note of a pyramid bat that swooped low above my head; the vast solitude of the sands swallowed up my voice and the walls of the Tomb of Sneferu mocked me with their echo, crying eerily:

"Hassan! Hassan es-Sugra.... Hassan! ..."

III

This mysterious episode affected me unpleasantly, but did not divert me from my purpose: I succeeded in casting out certain demons of superstition who had sought to lay hold upon me; and a prolonged scrutiny of the surrounding desert somewhat allayed my fears of human surveillance. For my visit to the chamber in the heart of the ancient building I had arrayed myself in rubber-soled shoes, an old pair of drill trousers, and a pyjama jacket. A Colt repeater was in my hip pocket, and, in addition to several instruments which I thought might be useful in extracting the ring from its setting, I carried a powerful electric torch.

Seated on the threshold of the entrance, fifty feet above the desert level, I cast a final glance backward towards the Nile valley, then, the lighted torch carried in my jacket pocket, I commenced the descent of the narrow, sloping passage. Periodically, when some cranny between the blocks offered a foothold, I checked my progress, and inspected the steep path below for snake tracks.

Some two hundred and forty feet of labored descent discovered me in a sort of shallow cavern little more than a yard high and partly hewn out of the living rock which formed the foundation of the pyramid. In this place I found the heat to be almost insufferable, and the smell of remote mortality which assailed my nostrils from the sand-strewn floor threatened to choke me. For five minutes or more I lay there, bathed in perspiration, my nerves at high tension, listening for the slightest sound within or without. I cannot pretend that I was entirely master of myself. The stuff that fear is made of seemed to rise from the ancient dust; and I had little relish for the second part of my journey, which lay through a long horizontal passage rarely exceeding fourteen inches in height. The mere memory of that final crawl of forty feet or so is sufficient to cause me to perspire profusely; therefore let it suffice that I reached the end of the second passage, and breathing with difficulty the deathful, poisonous atmosphere of the place, found myself at the foot of the rugged shaft which gives access to the King's Chamber. Resting my torch upon a convenient ledge, I climbed up, and knew myself to be in one of the oldest chambers fashioned by human handiwork.

The journey had been most exhausting, but, allowing myself only a few moments' rest, I crossed to the eastern corner of the place and directed a ray of light upon the crevice which, from Hassan's description, I believed to conceal the ring. His account having been detailed, I experienced little difficulty in finding the cavity; but in the very moment of success the light of the torch grew dim ... and I recognized with a mingling of chagrin and fear that it was burnt out and that I had no means of recharging it.

Ere the light expired, I had the to realize two things: that the cavity was empty ... and that someone or something was approaching the foot of the shaft along the horizontal passage below!

Strictly though I have schooled my emotions, my heart was beating in a most uncomfortable fashion as, crouching near the edge of the shaft, I watched the red glow fade from the delicate filament of the lamp. Retreat was impossible; there is but one entrance to the pyramid; and the darkness which now descended upon me was indescribable; it possessed horrific qualities; it seemed palpably to enfold me like the wings of some monstrous bat. The air of the King's Chamber I found to be almost unbearable, and it was no steady hand with which I gripped my pistol.

The sounds of approach continued. The suspense was becoming intolerable—when, into the Memphian gloom below me, there suddenly intruded a faint but ever-growing light. Between excitement and insufficient air, I regarded suffocation as imminent. Then, out into view beneath me, was thrust a slim ivory hand which held an electric pocket lamp. Fascinatedly I watched it, saw it joined by its fellow, then observed a white-turbaned head and a pair of black-robed shoulders follow. In my surprise I almost dropped the weapon which I held. The new arrival now standing upright and raising his bead, I found myself looking into the face of *Abû Tabâh*!

"To Allah, the Great, the Compassionate, be all praise that I have found you alive," he said simply.

He exhibited little evidence of the journey which I had found so fatiguing, but an expression strongly like that of real anxiety rested upon his ascetic face.

"If life is dear to you," be continued, "answer me this, Kernaby Pasha; have you found the ring?"

"I have not," I replied; "my lamp failed me; but I think the ring is gone."

And now, as I spoke the words, the strangeness of his question came home to me, bringing with it an acute suspicion.

"What do you know of this ring, O my friend?" I asked.

Abû Tabâh shrugged his shoulders.

"I know much that is evil," he replied; "and because you doubt the purity of my motives, all that I have learned you shall learn also; for Allah the Great, the Merciful, this night has protected you from danger and spared you a frightful death. Follow me, Kernaby Pasha, in order that these things may be made manifest to you."

IV

A pair of fleet camels were kneeling at the foot of the slope below the entrance to the pyramid, and having recovered somewhat from the effect of the fatiguing climb out from the King's Chamber—

"It might be desirable," I said, "that I adopt a more suitable raiment for camel riding?"

Abû Tabâh slowly shook his head in that dignified manner which never deserted him, he had again taken up his ebony walking-stick and was now resting his crossed hands upon it and regarding me with his strange, melancholy eyes.

"To delay would be unwise," be replied. "You have mercifully been spared a painful and unfortunate end (all praise to Him who averted the peril); but the ring, which bears an ancient curse, is gone: for me there is no rest until I have found and destroyed it."

He spoke with a solemn conviction which bore the seal of verity.

"Your destructive theory may be perfectly sound," I said; "but as one professionally interested in relics of the past, I feel called upon to protest. Perhaps before we proceed any further you will enlighten me respecting this most obscure matter. Can you inform me, for example, what became of Hassan es-Sugra?"

"He observed my approach from a distance, and fled, being a man of little virtue. Respecting the other matters you shall be fully enlightened, to-night. The white camel is for you."

There was a gentle finality in his manner to which I succumbed. My feelings towards this mysterious being had undergone a slight change; and whilst I cannot truthfully say that I loved him as a brother, a certain respect for Abû Tabâh was taking possession of my mind. I began to understand his reputation with the natives; beyond doubt his uncanny wisdom was impressive; his lofty dignity awed. And no man is at his best arrayed in canvas shoes, very dirty drill trousers, and a pyjama jacket.

As I had anticipated, the village of Méydûm proved to be our destination, and the gait of the magnificent creatures upon which we were mounted was exhausting. I shall always remember that moonlight ride across the desert to the palm groves of Méydûm. I entered the house of the Sheikh with misgivings; for my attire fell short of the ideal to which every representative of protective Britain looks up, but often fails to realize.

In a *mandarah*, part of it inlaid with fine mosaic and boasting a pretty fountain, I was presented to the imposing old man who was evidently the host of Abû Tabâh. Ere taking my seat upon the dîwan, I shed my canvas shoes, in accordance with custom, accepted a pipe and a cup of excellent coffee, and awaited with much curiosity the next development. A brief colloquy between Abû Tabâh and the Sheikh, at the further end of the apartment resulted in the disappearance of the Sheikh and the approach of my mysterious friend.

"Because, although you are not a Moslem, you are a man of culture and understanding," said Abû Tabâh, "I have ordered that my sister shall be brought into your presence."

"That is exceedingly good of you," I said, but indeed I knew it to be an honor which spoke volumes at once for Abû Tabâh's enlightenment and good opinion of myself.

"She is a virgin of great beauty," he continued; "and the excellence of her mind exceeds the perfection of her person."

"I congratulate you," I answered politely, "upon the possession of a sister in every way so desirable."

Abû Tabâh inclined his head in a characteristic gesture of gentle courtesy.

"Allah has indeed blessed my house," he admitted; "and because your mind is filled with conjectures respecting the source of certain information which you know me to possess, I desire that the matter shall be made clear to you."

How I should have answered this singular man I know not; but as he spoke the words, into the *mandarah* came the Sheikh, followed by a girl robed and veiled entirely in white. With gait slow and graceful she approached the *dîwan*. She wore a white *yelek* so closely wrapped about her that it concealed the rest of her attire, and a white *tarbar*, or head-veil, decorated with gold embroidery, almost entirely concealed her hair, save for one jet-black plait in which little gold ornaments were entwined and which hung down on the left of her forehead. A white *yashmak* reached nearly to her feet, which were clad in little red leather slippers.

As she approached me I was impressed, not so much with the details of her white attire, nor with the fine lines of a graceful figure which the gossamer robe quite failed to conceal, but with her wonderful gazelle-like eyes, which were uncannily like those of her brother, save that their bordering of *kohl* lent them an appearance of being larger and more luminous.

No form of introduction was observed; with modestly lowered eyes the girl saluted me and took her seat upon a heap of cushions before a small coffee table set at one end of the *dîwan*. The Sheikh seated himself beside me, and Abû Tabâh, with a reed pen, wrote something rapidly on a narrow strip of paper. The Sheikh clapped his hands, a man entered bearing a brazier containing live charcoal, and, having placed it upon the floor, immediately withdrew. The *dîwan* was lighted by a lantern swung from the ceiling, and its light, pouring fully down upon the white figure of the girl, and leaving the other persons and objects in comparative shadow, produced a picture which I am unlikely to forget.

Amid a tense silence, Abû Tabâh took from a box upon the table some resinous substance. This he sprinkled upon the fire in the brazier; and the girl extending a small hand and round soft arm across the table, he again dipped his pen in the ink and drew upon the upturned palm a rough square which he divided into nine parts, writing in each an Arabic figure. Finally, in the centre he poured a small drop of ink, upon which, in response to words rapidly spoken, the girl fixed an intent gaze.

Into the brazier Abû Tabâh dropped one by one fragments of the paper upon which he had written what I presumed to be a form of invocation. Immediately, standing between the smoking brazier and the girl, he commenced a subdued muttering. I recognized that I was about to be treated to an exhibition of *darb el-mendel*, Abû Tabâh being evidently a *sahhar*, or adept in the art called *er-roohânee*. Save for this indistinct muttering, no other sound disturbed the silence of the apartment, until suddenly the girl began to speak Arabic and in a sweet but monotonous voice.

"Again I see the ring," she said, "a hand is holding it before me. The ring bears a green scarab, upon which is written the name of a king of Egypt. ... The ring is gone. I can see it no more."

"Seek it," directed Abû Tabâh in a low voice, and threw more incense upon the fire. "Are you seeking it?"

"Yes," replied the girl, who now began to tremble violently, "I am in a low passage which slopes downwards so steeply that I am afraid."

"Fear nothing," said Abû Tabâh; "follow the passage."

With marvelous fidelity the girl described the passage and the shaft leading to the King's Chamber in the Pyramid of Méydûm. She described the cavity in the wall where once (if Hassan es-Sugra was worthy of credence) the ring had been concealed.

"There is a freshly made hole in the stonework," she said. "The picture has gone; I am standing in some dark place and the same hand again holds the ring before me."

"Is it the hand of an Oriental," asked Abû Tabâh, "or of a European?"

"It is the hand of a European. It has disappeared; I see a funeral procession winding out from Rikka into the desert."

"Follow the ring," directed Abû Tabâh, a queer, compelling note in his voice.

Again he sprinkled perfume upon the fire and—

"I see a Pharaoh upon his throne," continued the monotonous voice, "upon the first finger of his left hand he wears the ring with the green scarab. A prisoner stands before him in chains; a woman pleads with the king, but he is deaf to her. He draws the ring from his finger and hands it to one standing behind the throne—one who has a very evil face. Ah! ..."

The girl's voice died away in a low wail of fear or horror. But—

"What do you see?" demanded Abû Tabâh.

"The death-ring of Pharaoh!" whispered the soft voice tremulously; "it is the death-ring!"

"Return from the past to the present," ordered Abû Tabâh. "Where is the ring now?"

He continued his weird muttering, whilst the girl, who still shuddered violently, peered again into the pool of ink. Suddenly—

"I see a long line of dead men," she whispered, speaking in a kind of chant; "they are of all the races of the East, and some are swathed in mummy wrappings; the wrappings are sealed with the death-ring of Pharaoh. They are passing me slowly, on their way across the desert from the Pyramid of Méydûm to a narrow ravine where a tent is erected. They go to summon one who is about to join their company...."

I suppose the suffocating perfume of the burning incense was chiefly responsible, but at this point I realized that I was becoming dizzy and that immediate departure into a cooler atmosphere was imperative. Quietly, in order to avoid disturbing the séance, I left the *mandarah*. So absorbed were the three in their weird performance that my departure was apparently unnoticed.

Out in the coolness of the palm grove I soon recovered. I doubt if I possess the temperament which enables one to contemplate with equanimity a number of dead men promenading in their shrouds.

V

"The truth is now wholly made manifest," said Abû Tabâh; "the revelation is complete."

Once more I was mounted upon the white camel and the mysterious *imám* rode beside me upon its fellow, which was of less remarkable color.

"I hear your words," I replied.

"The poor Ahmed Abdulla," he continued, "who was of little wisdom, knew, as Hassan es-Sugra knew, of the hidden ring; for he was one of those who fled from the pyramid refusing to enter it again. Greed spoke to him, however, and he revealed the secret to a certain Englishman, called Bishop, contracting to aid him in recovering the ring."

At last enlightenment was mine ... and it brought in its train a dreadful premonition.

"Something I knew of the peril," said Abû Tabâh, "but not, at first, all. The Englishman I warned, but he neglected my warning. Already Ahmed Abdulla was dead, having been despatched by his employer to the pyramid; and the people of Rikka had sent for me. Now, by means known to you, I learned that evil powers threatened your life also, in what form I knew not at that time save that the sign of Set had been revealed to me in conjunction with your death."

I shuddered.

"That the secret of the pyramid was a Pharaoh's ring I did not learn until later; but now it is made manifest that the thing of power is the death-ring of Sneferu...."

The huge bulk of the Pyramid of Méydûm loomed above us as he spoke the words, for we were nearly come to our destination; and its proximity occasioned within me a physical chill. I do not think an open check for a thousand pounds would have tempted me to enter the place again. The death-ring of Sneferu possessed uncomfortable and supernatural properties. So far as I was aware, no example of such a ring (the *lettre de cachet* of the period) was included in any known collection. One dating much after Sneferu, and bearing the cartouche of Apepi II (one of the Hyksos, or Shepherd Kings) came to light late in the nineteenth century; it was reported to be the ring which, traditionally, Joseph wore as emblematical of the power vested in him by Pharaoh. Sir Gaston Maspero and other authorities considered it to be a forgery and it vanished from the ken of connoisseurs. I never learned by what firm it was manufactured.

A mile to the west of the pyramid we found Theo Bishop's encampment. I thought it to be deserted-until I entered the little tent....

An oil-lamp stood upon a wooden box; and its rays made yellow the face of the man stretched upon the camp-bed. My premonition was realized; Bishop must have entered the pyramid less than an hour ahead of me; he it was who had stood upon the mound, silhouetted against the sky, when I had first approached the slope, he had met with the fate of Ahmed Abdulla.

He had been dead for at least two hours, and by the token of certain hideous glandular swellings, I knew that he had met his end by the bite of an Egyptian viper.

"Abû Tabâh!" I cried, my voice hoarsely unnatural— "the recess in the King's Chamber is a viper's nest!"

"You speak wisdom, Kernaby Pasha; the viper is the servant of the *ginn*."

Upon the third finger of his swollen right hand Bishop wore the ring of ghastly history; and the mysterious significance of the Sign of Set became apparent. For added to the usual cartouche of the Pharaoh was the symbol of the god of destruction, thus:

We buried him deeply, piling stones upon the grave, that the jackals of the desert might never disturb the last holder of the death-ring of Sneferu.

The Wings of Horus

Algernon Blackwood

Binovitch had the bird in him somewhere: in his features, certainly, with his piercing eye and hawk-like nose; in his movements, with his quick way of flitting, hopping, darting; in the way he perched on the edge of a chair; in the manner he pecked at his food; in his twittering, high-pitched voice as well; and, above all, in his mind. He skimmed all subjects and picked their heart out neatly, as a bird skims lawn or air to snatch its prey. He had the bird's-eye view of everything. He loved birds and understood them instinctively; could imitate their whistling notes with astonishing accuracy. Their one quality he had not was poise and balance. He was a nervous little man; he was neurasthenic. And he was in Egypt by doctor's orders.

Such imaginative, unnecessary ideas he had! Such uncommon beliefs!

"The old Egyptians," he said laughingly, yet with a touch of solemn conviction in his manner, "were a great people. Their consciousness was different from ours. The bird idea, for instance, conveyed a sense of deity to them—of bird deity, that is: they had sacred birds—hawks, ibis, and so forth—and worshipped them." And he put his tongue out as though to say with challenge, "Ha, ha!"

"They also worshipped cats and crocodiles and cows," grinned Palazov. Binovitch seemed to dart across the table at his adversary. His eyes flashed; his nose pecked the air. Almost one could imagine the beating of his angry wings.

"Because everything alive," he half screamed, "was a symbol of some spiritual power to them. Your mind is as literal as a dictionary and as incoherent. Pages of ink without connected meaning! Verb always in the infinitive! If you were an old Egyptian, you—you"—he flashed and spluttered, his tongue shot out again, his keen eyes blazed— "you might take all those words and spin them into a great interpretation of life, a cosmic romance, as they did. Instead, you get the bitter, dead taste of ink in your mouth, and spit it over us like that"—he made a quick movement of his whole body as a bird that shakes itself "in empty phrases."

Khilkoff ordered another bottle of champagne, while Vera, his sister, said half nervously, "Let's go for a drive; it's moonlight." There was enthusiasm at once. Another of the party called the head waiter and told him to pack food and drink in baskets. It was only eleven o'clock. They would drive out into the desert, have a meal at two in the morning, tell stories, sing, and see the dawn.

It was in one of those cosmopolitan hotels in Egypt which attract the ordinary tourists as well as those who are doing a "cure," and all these Russians were ill with one thing or another. All were ordered out for their health, and all were the despair of their doctors. They were as unmanageable as a bazaar and as incoherent. Excess and bed were their routine. They lived, but none of them got better. Equally, none of them got angry. They talked in this strange personal way without a shred of malice or offence. The English, French, and Germans in the hotel watched them with remote amazement, referring to them as "that Russian lot." Their energy was elemental. They never stopped. They merely disappeared when the pace became too fast, then reappeared again after a day or two, and resumed their "living" as before. Binovitch, despite his neurasthenia, was the life of the party. He was also a special patient of Dr. Plitzinger, the famous psychiatrist, who took a peculiar interest in his case. It was not surprising. Binovitch was a man of unusual ability and of genuine, deep culture. But there was something more about him that stimulated curiosity. There was this striking originality. He said and did surprising things.

"I could fly if I wanted to," he said once when the airmen came to astonish the natives with their biplanes over the desert, "but without all that machinery and noise. It's only a question of believing and understanding "

"Show us!" they cried. "Let's see you fly!"

"He's got it! He's off again! One of his impossible moments."

These occasions when Binovitch let himself go always proved wildly entertaining. He said monstrously incredible things as though he really did believe them. They loved his madness, for it gave them new sensations.

"It's only levitation, after all, this flying," he exclaimed, shooting out his tongue between the words, as his habit was when excited; "and what is levitation but a power of the air? None of you can hang an orange in space for a second, with all your scientific knowledge; but the moon is always levitated perfectly. And the stars. D'you think they swing on wires? What raised the enormous stones of ancient Egypt? D'you really believe it was heaped-up sand and ropes and clumsy leverage and all our weary and laborious mechanical contrivances? Bah! It was levitation. It was the powers of the air. Believe in those powers, and gravity becomes a mere nursery trick—true where it is, but true nowhere else. To know the fourth dimension is to step out of a locked room and appear instantly on the roof or in another country altogether. To know the powers of the air, similarly, is to annihilate what you call weight and fly."

"Show us, show us!" they cried, roaring with delighted laughter.

"It's a question of belief," he repeated, his tongue appearing and disappearing like a pointed shadow. "It's in the heart; the power of the air gets into your whole being. Why should I show you? Why should I ask my deity to persuade your scoffing little minds by any miracle? For it is deity, I tell you, and nothing else. I know it. Follow one idea like that, as I follow my bird idea follow it with the impetus and undeviating concentration of a projectile and you arrive at power. You know deity—the bird idea of deity, that is. They knew that. The old Egyptians knew it."

"Oh, show us, show us!" they shouted impatiently, wearied of his nonsense-talk. "Get up and fly! Levitate yourself, as they did! Become a star!"

Binovitch turned suddenly very pale, and an odd light shone in his keen brown eyes. He rose slowly from the edge of the chair where he was perched. Something about him changed. There was silence instantly.

"I will show you," he said calmly, to their intense amazement; "not to convince your disbelief, but to prove it to myself. For the powers of the air are with me here. I believe. And Horus, great falcon-headed symbol, is my patron god."

The suppressed energy in his voice and manner' was indescribable. There was a sense of lifting, upheaving power about him. He raised his arms; his face turned upward; he inflated his lungs with a deep, long breath, and his voice broke into a kind of singing cry, half prayer, half chant:

> "O Horus,
> Bright-eyed deity of wind,
> Feather my soul
> Though earth's thick air,
> To know thy awful swiftness"

He broke off suddenly. He climbed lightly and swiftly upon the nearest table—it was in a deserted card-room, after a game in which he had lost more pounds than there are days in the year and leaped into the air. He hovered a second, spread his arms and legs in space, appeared to float a moment, then buckled, rushed down and forward, and dropped in a heap upon the floor, while every one roared with laughter.

But the laughter died out quickly, for there was something in his wild performance that was peculiar and unusual. It was uncanny, not quite natural. His body had seemed, as with Mordkin and Nijinski, literally to hang upon the air a moment. For a second he gave the distressing impression of overcoming gravity. There was a touch in it of that faint horror which appalls by its very vagueness. He picked himself up unhurt, and his face was as grave as a portrait in the academy, but with a new expression in it that everybody noticed with this strange, half-shocked amazement. And it was this expression that extinguished the claps of laughter as wind that takes away the sound of bells. Like many ugly men, he was an inimitable actor, and his facial repertory was endless and incredible. But this was neither acting nor clever manipulation of expressive features. There was something in his curious Russian physiognomy that made the heart beat slower. And that was why the laughter died away so suddenly.

"You ought to have flown farther," cried some one. It expressed what all had felt.

"Icarus didn't drink champagne," another replied, with a laugh; but nobody laughed with him.

"You went too near to Vera," said Palazov, "and passion melted the wax." But his face twitched oddly as he said it. There was something he did not understand, and so heartily disliked.

The strange expression on the features deepened. It was arresting in a disagreeable, almost in a horrible, way. The talk stopped dead;

all stared; there was a feeling of dismay in everybody's heart, yet unexplained. Some lowered their eyes, or else looked stupidly elsewhere; but the women of the party felt a kind of fascination. Vera, in particular, could not move her sight away. The joking reference to his passionate admiration for her passed unnoticed. There was a general and individual sense of shock. And a chorus of whispers rose instantly:

"Look at Binovitch! What's happened to his face?"

"He's changed he's changing!"

"God! Why he looks like a bird!"

But no one laughed. Instead, they chose the names of birds—hawk, eagle, even owl. The figure of a man leaning against the edge of the door, watching them closely, they did not notice. He had been passing down the corridor, had looked in unobserved, and then had paused. He had seen the whole performance. He watched Binovitch narrowly, now with calm, discerning eyes. It was Dr. Plitzinger, the great psychiatrist.

For Binovitch had picked himself up from the floor in a way that was oddly self-possessed, and precluded the least possibility of the ludicrous. He looked neither foolish nor abashed. He looked surprised, but also he looked half angry and half frightened. As some one had said, he "ought to have flown farther." That was the incredible impression his acrobatics had produced—incredible, yet somehow actual. This uncanny idea prevailed, as at a séance where nothing genuine is expected to happen, and something genuine, after all, does happen. There was no pretence in this: Binovitch had flown.

And now he stood there, white in the face with terror and with anger white. He looked extraordinary, this little, neurasthenic Russian, but he looked at the same time half terrific. Another thing, not commonly experienced by men, was in him, breaking out of him, affecting directly the minds of his companions. His mouth opened; blood and fury shone in his blazing eyes; his tongue shot out like an ant-eater's, though even in that the comic had no place. His arms were spread like flapping wings, and his voice rose dreadfully:

"He failed me, he failed me!" he tried to bellow. "Horus, my falcon-headed deity, my power of the air, deserted me! Hell take him! Hell burn his wings and blast his piercing sight! Hell scorch him into dust for his false prophecies! I curse him—I curse Horus!"

The voice that should have roared across the silent room emitted, instead, this high-pitched, bird-like scream. The added touch of sound, the reality it lent, was ghastly. Yet it was marvellously done and acted. The entire thing was a bit of instantaneous inspiration—his voice, his words, his gestures, his whole wild appearance. Only—here was the reality that caused the sense of shock—the expression on his altered features was genuine. That was not assumed. There was something new and alien in him, something cold and difficult to human life, something alert and swift and cruel, of another element than earth. A strange, rapacious grandeur had leaped upon the struggling features. The face looked hawk-like.

And he came forward suddenly and sharply toward Vera, whose fixed, staring eyes had never once ceased watching him with a kind of anxious and devouring pain in them. She was both drawn and beaten back. Binovitch advanced on tiptoe. No doubt he still was acting, still pretending this mad nonsense that he worshipped Horus, the falcon-headed deity of forgotten days, and that Horus had failed him in his hour of need; but somehow there was just a hint of too much reality in the way he moved and looked. The girl, a little creature, with fluffy golden hair, opened her lips; her cigarette fell to the floor; she shrank back; she looked for a moment like some smaller, coloured bird trying to escape from a great pursuing hawk; she screamed. Binovitch, his arms wide, his bird-like face thrust forward, had swooped upon her. He leaped. Almost he caught her.

No one could say exactly what happened. Play, become suddenly and unexpectedly too real, confuses the emotions. The change of key was swift. From fun to terror is a dislocating jolt upon the mind. Some one—it was Khilkoff, the brother—upset a chair; everybody spoke at once; everybody stood up. An unaccountable feeling of disaster was in the air, as with those drinkers' quarrels that blaze out from nothing, and end in a pistol-shot and death, no one able to explain clearly how it came about. It was the silent, watching figure in the doorway who saved the situation. Before any one had noticed his approach, there he was among the group, laughing, talking, applauding between Binovitch and Vera. He was vigorously patting his patient on the back, and his voice rose easily above the general clamour. He was a strong, quiet personality; even in his laughter there was authority. And his laughter now was the only sound in the room, as though by his mere presence peace and harmony were restored. Confidence came with him. The noise subsided; Vera was in her chair again. Khilkoff poured out a glass of wine for the great man.

"The Czar!" said Plitzinger, sipping his champagne, while all stood up, delighted with his compliment and tact. "And to your opening night with the Russian ballet," he added quickly a second toast, "or to your first performance at the Moscow Theatre des Arts!" Smiling significantly, he glanced at Binovitch; he clinked glasses with him. Their arms were already linked, but it was Palazov who noticed that the doctor's fingers seemed rather tight upon the creased black coat. All drank, looking with laughter, yet with a touch of respect, toward Binovitch, who stood there dwarfed beside the stalwart Austrian, and suddenly as meek and subdued as any mole. Apparently the abrupt change of key had taken his mind successfully off something else.

"Of course—'The Fire-Bird,'" exclaimed the little man, mentioning the famous Russian ballet. "The very thing!" he exclaimed. "For us," he added, looking with devouring eyes at Vera. He was greatly pleased. He began talking vociferously about dancing and the rationale of dancing. They told him he was an undiscovered master. He was delighted. He winked at Vera and touched her glass again with his. "We'll make our debut together," he cried. "We'll begin at Covent Garden, in London. I'll design the dresses and the posters 'The Hawk and the Dove!' Magnifique! I in dark grey, and you in blue and gold! Ah, dancing, you know, is sacred. The little self is lost, absorbed. It is ecstasy, it is divine. And dancing in air the passion of the birds and stars—ah! they are the movements of the gods. You know deity that way by living it."

He went on and on. His entire being had shifted with a leap upon this new subject. The idea of realising divinity by dancing it absorbed him. The party discussed it with him as though nothing else existed in the world, all sitting now and talking eagerly together. Vera took the cigarette he offered her, lighting it from his own; their fingers touched; he was as harmless and normal as a retired diplomat in a drawing-room. But it was Plitzinger whose subtle manoeuvring had accomplished the change so cleverly, and it was Plitzinger who presently suggested a game of billiards, and led him off, full now of a fresh enthusiasm for cannons, balls, and pockets, into another room. They departed arm in arm, laughing and talking together.

Their departure, it seemed, made no great difference at first. Vera's eyes watched him out of sight, then turned to listen to Baron Minski, who was describing with gusto how he caught wolves alive for coursing purposes. The speed and power of the wolf, he said, was impossible to realise; the force of their awful leap, the strength of their teeth, which could bite through metal stirrup-fastenings. He showed a scar on his arm and another on his lip. He was telling truth, and everybody listened with deep interest. The narrative lasted perhaps ten minutes or more, when Minski abruptly stopped. He had come to an end; he looked about him; he saw his glass, and emptied it. There was a general pause. Another subject did not at once present itself. Sighs were heard; several fidgeted; fresh cigarettes were lighted. But there was no sign of boredom, for where one or two Russians are gathered together there is always life. They produce gaiety and enthusiasm as wind produces waves. Like great children, they plunge whole-heartedly into whatever interest presents itself at the moment. There is a kind of uncouth gambolling in their way of taking life. It seems as if they are always fighting that deep, underlying, national sadness which creeps into their very blood.

"Midnight!" then exclaimed Palazov, abruptly, looking at his watch; and the others fell instantly to talking about that watch, admiring it and asking questions. For the moment that very ordinary timepiece became the centre of observation. Palazov mentioned the price. "It never stops," he said proudly, "not even under water." He looked up at everybody, challenging admiration. And he told how, at a country house, he made a bet that he would swim to a certain island in the lake, and won the bet. He and a girl were the winners, but as it was a horse they had bet, he got nothing out of it for himself, giving the horse to her. It was a genuine grievance in him. One felt he could have cried as he spoke of it. "But the watch went all the time," he said delightedly, holding the gun-metal object in his hand to show, "and I was twelve minutes in the water with my clothes on."

Yet this fragmentary talk was nothing but pretence. The sound of clicking billiard-balls was audible from the room at the end of the corridor. There was another pause. The pause, however, was intentional. It was not vacuity of mind or absence of ideas that caused it. There was another subject, an unfinished subject that each member of the group was still considering. Only no one cared to begin about it till at last, unable to resist the strain any longer,

Palazov turned to Khilkoff, who was saying he would take a "whisky-soda," as the champagne was too sweet, and whispered something beneath his breath; whereupon Khilkoff, forgetting his drink, glanced at his sister, shrugged his shoulders, and made a curious grimace. "He's all right now" his reply was just audible "he's with Plitzinger." He cocked his head sidewise to indicate that the clicking of the billiard-balls still was going on.

The subject was out: all turned their heads; voices hummed and buzzed; questions were asked and answered or half answered; eyebrows were raised, shoulders shrugged, hands spread out expressively. There came into the atmosphere a feeling of presentiment, of mystery, of things half understood; primitive, buried instinct stirred a little, the kind of racial dread of vague emotions that might gain the upper hand if encouraged. They shrank from looking something in the face, while yet this unwelcome influence drew closer round them all. They discussed Binovitch and his astonishing performance. Pretty little Vera listened with large and troubled eyes, though saying nothing. The Arab waiter had put out the lights in the corridor, and only a solitary cluster burned now above their heads, leaving their faces in shadow. In the distance the clicking of the billiard-balls still continued.

"It was not play; it was real," exclaimed Minski vehemently. "I can catch wolves," he blurted; "but birds ugh! and human birds!" He was half inarticulate. He had witnessed something he could not understand, and it had touched instinctive terror in him. "It was the way he leaped that put the wolf first into my mind, only it was not a wolf at all." The others agreed and disagreed. "It was play at first, but it was reality at the end," another whispered; "and it was no animal he mimicked, but a bird, and a bird of prey at that!"

Vera thrilled. In the Russian woman hides that touch of savagery which loves to be caught, mastered, swept helplessly away, captured utterly and deliciously by the one strong enough to do it thoroughly. She left her chair and sat down beside an older woman in the party, who took her arm quietly at once. Her little face wore a perplexed expression, mournful, yet somehow wild. It was clear that Binovitch was not indifferent to her.

"It's become an *idée fixe* with him," this older woman said. "The bird idea lives in his mind. He lives it in his imagination. Ever since that time at Edfu, when he pretended to worship the great stone falcons outside the temple—the Horus figures—he's been full of it." She stopped. The way Binovitch had behaved at Edfu was better left unmentioned at the moment, perhaps. A slight shiver ran round the listening group, each one waiting for some one else to focus their emotion, and so explain it by saying the convincing thing. Only no one ventured. Then Vera abruptly gave a little jump.

"Hark!" she exclaimed, in a staccato whisper, speaking for the first time. She sat bolt upright. She was listening. "Hark!" she repeated. "There it is again, but nearer than before. It's coming closer. I hear it." She trembled. Her voice, her manner, above all her great staring eyes, startled everybody. No one spoke for several seconds; all listened. The clicking of the billiard-balls had ceased. The halls and corridors lay in darkness, and gloom was over the big hotel. Everybody was in bed.

"Hear what?" asked the older woman soothingly, yet with a perceptible quaver in her voice, too. She was aware that the girl's arm shook upon her own.

"Do you not hear it, too?" the girl whispered.

All listened without speaking. All watched her paling face. Something wonderful, yet half terrible, seemed in the air about them. There was a dull murmur, audible, faint, remote, its direction hard to tell. It had come suddenly from nowhere. They shivered. That strange racial thrill again passed into the group, unwelcome, unexplained. It was aboriginal; it belonged to the unconscious primitive mind, half childish, half terrifying.

"What do you hear?" her brother asked angrily the irritable anger of nervous fear.

"When he came at me," she answered very low, "I heard it first. I hear it now again. Listen! He's coming."

And at that minute, out of the dark mouth of the corridor, emerged two human figures, Plitzinger and Binovitch. Their game was over; they were going up to bed. They passed the open door of the card-room. But Binovitch was being half dragged, half restrained, for he was apparently attempting to run down the passage with flying, dancing leaps. He bounded. It was like a huge bird trying to rise for flight, while his companion kept him down by force upon the earth. As they entered the strip of light, Plitzinger changed his own position, placing himself swiftly between his companion and the group in the dark corner of the room. He hurried Binovitch along as though he sheltered him from view. They passed into the shadows down the passage. They disappeared. And every one looked significantly, questioningly, at his neighbour, though at first saying no word. It seemed that a curious disturbance of the air had followed them audibly.

Vera was the first to Open her lips. "You heard it then" she said breathlessly, her face whiter than the ceiling.

"Damn!" exclaimed her brother furiously. "It was wind against the outside walls—wind in the desert. The sand is driving."

Vera looked at him. She shrank closer against the side of the older woman, whose arm was tight about her.

"It was not wind," she whispered simply. She paused. All waited uneasily for the completion of her sentence. They stared into her face like peasants who expected a miracle.

"Wings," she whispered. "It was the sound of enormous wings."

And at four o'clock in the morning, when they all returned exhausted from their excursion into the desert, little Binovitch was sleeping soundly and peacefully in his bed. They passed his door on tiptoe. But he did not hear them. He was dreaming. His spirit was at Edfu, experiencing with that ancient deity who was master of all flying life those strange enjoyments upon which his own troubled human heart was passionately set. Safe with that mighty falcon whose powers his lips had scorned a few hours before, his soul, released in vivid dream, went sweetly flying. It was amazing, it was gorgeous. He skimmed the Nile at lightning speed. Dashing down headlong from the height of the great Pyramid, he chased with faultless accuracy a little dove that sought vainly to hide from his terrific pursuit beneath the palm trees. For what he loved must worship where he worshipped, and the majesty of those tremendous effigies had fired his imagination to the creative point where expression was imperative.

Then suddenly, at the very moment of delicious capture, the dream turned horrible, becoming awful with the nightmare touch. The sky lost all its blue and sunshine. Far, far below him the little dove enticed him into nameless depths, so that he flew faster and faster, yet never fast enough to overtake it. Behind him came a great thing down the air, black, hovering, with gigantic wings outstretched. It had terrific eyes, and the beating of its feathers stole his wind away. It followed him, crowding space. He was aware of a colossal beak, curved like a scimitar and pointed wickedly like a tooth of iron. He dropped. He faltered. He tried to scream.

Through empty space he fell, caught by the neck. The huge spectral falcon was upon him. The talons were in his heart. And in sleep he remembered then that he had cursed. He recalled his reckless language. The curse of the ignorant is meaningless; that of the worshipper is real. This attack was on his soul. He had invoked it. He realised next, with a touch of ghastly horror, that the dove he chased was, after all, the bait that had lured him purposely to destruction, and awoke with a suffocating terror upon him, and his entire body bathed in icy perspiration. Outside the open window he heard a sound of wings retreating with powerful strokes into the surrounding darkness of the sky.

The nightmare made its impression upon Binovitch's impressionable and dramatic temperament. It aggravated his tendencies. He related it next day to Mme. de Drühn, the friend of Vera, telling it with that somewhat boisterous laughter some minds use to disguise less kind emotions. But he received no encouragement. The mood of the previous night was not recoverable; it was already ancient history. Russians never make the banal mistake of repeating a sensation till it is exhausted; they hurry on to novelties. Life flashes and rushes with them, never standing still for exposure before the cameras of their minds. Mme. de Drühn, however, took the trouble to mention the matter to Plitzinger, for Plitzinger, like Freud of Vienna, held that dreams revealed subconscious tendencies which sooner or later must betray themselves in action.

"Thank you for telling me," he smiled politely, "but I have already heard it from him." He watched her eyes for a moment, really examining her soul. "Binovitch, you see," he continued, apparently satisfied with what he saw, "I regard as that rare phenomenon—'a genius without an outlet!' His spirit, intensely creative, finds no adequate expression. His power of production is enormous and prolific; yet he accomplishes nothing." He paused an instant. "Binovitch, therefore, is in danger of poisoning himself." He looked steadily into her face, as a man who weighs how much he may confide. "Now," he continued, "if we can find an outlet for him, a field wherein his bursting imaginative genius can produce results—above all, visible results" he shrugged his shoulders "the man is saved. Otherwise"—he looked extraordinarily impressive— "there is bound to be sooner or later—"

"Madness?" she asked very quietly.

"An explosion, let us say," he replied gravely. "For instance, take this Horus obsession of his, quite wrong archaeologically though it is. As fond it is megalomania of a most unusual kind. His passionate interest, his love, his worship of birds, wholesome enough in itself, finds no satisfying outlet. A man who really loves birds neither keeps them in cages nor shoots them nor stuffs them. What, then, can he do? The commonplace bird-lover observes them through glasses, studies their habits, then writes a book about them. But a man like Binovitch, overflowing with this intense creative power of mind and imagination, is not content with that. He wants to know them from within. He wants to feel what they feel, to live their life. He wants to become them. You follow me? Not quite. Well, he seeks to be identified with the object of his sacred, passionate adoration. All genius seeks to know the thing itself from its own point of view. It desires union. That tendency, unrecognised by himself, perhaps, and therefore subconscious, hides in his very soul." He paused a moment. "And the sudden sight of those majestic figures at Edfu that crystallisation of his *idée fixe* in granite took hold of this excess in him, so to speak and is now focusing it toward some definite act. Binovitch sometimes feels himself a bird! You noticed what occurred last night?"

She nodded; a slight shiver passed over her.

"A most curious performance," she murmured; "an exhibition I never want to see again."

"The most curious part," replied the doctor coolly, "was its truth."

"Its truth!" she exclaimed beneath her breath. She was frightened by something in his voice and by the uncommon gravity in his eyes. It seemed to arrest her intelligence. She felt upon the edge of things beyond her. "You mean that Binovitch did for a moment hang in the air?" The other verb, the right one, she could not bring herself to use.

The great man's face was enigmatical. He talked to her sympathy, perhaps, rather than to her mind.

"Real genius," he said smilingly, "is as rare as talent, even great talent, is common. It means that the personality, if only for one second, becomes everything; becomes the universe; becomes the soul of the world. It gets the flash. It is identified with the universal life. Being everything and everywhere, all is possible to it in that second of vivid realisation. It can brood with the crystal, grow with the plant, leap with the animal, fly with the bird: genius unifies all three. That is the meaning of 'creative.' It is faith. Knowing it, you can pass through fire and not be burned, walk on water and not sink, move a mountain, fly. Because you are fire, water, earth, air. Genius, you see, is madness in the magnificent sense of being superhuman. Binovitch has it."

He broke off abruptly, seeing he was not understood. Some great enthusiasm in him he deliberately suppressed.

"The point is," he resumed, speaking more carefully, "that we must try to lead this passionate constructive genius of the man into some human channel that will absorb it, and therefore render it harmless."

"He loves Vera," the woman said, bewildered, yet seizing this point correctly.

"But would he marry her?" asked Plitzinger at once.

"He is already married."

The doctor looked steadily at her a moment, hesitating whether he should utter all his thought.

"In that case," he said slowly after a pause, "it is better he or she should leave."

His tone and manner were exceedingly impressive.

"You mean there's danger?" she asked.

"I mean, rather," he replied earnestly, "that this great creative flood in him, so curiously focused now upon his Horus-falcon-bird idea, may result in some act of violence."

"Which would be madness," she said, looking hard at him.

"Which would be disastrous," he corrected her. And then he added slowly: "Because in the mental moment of immense creation he might overlook material laws."

The costume ball two nights later was a great success. Palazov was a Bedouin, and Khilkoff an Apache; Mme. de Drühn wore a national head-dress; Minski looked almost natural as Don Quixote; and the entire Russian "set" was cleverly, if somewhat extravagantly, dressed. But Binovitch and Vera were the most successful of all the two hundred dancers who took part. Another figure, a big man dressed as a Pierrot, also claimed exceptional attention, for though the costume was commonplace enough, there was something of dignity in his appearance that drew the eyes of all upon him. But he wore a mask, and his identity was not discoverable.

It was Binovitch and Vera, however, who must have won the prize, if prize there had been, for they not only looked their parts, but acted them as well. The former in his dark grey feather tunic, and his falcon mask, complete even to the brown hooked beak and tufted talons, looked fierce and splendid. The disguise was so admirable, yet so entirely natural, that it was uncommonly seductive. Vera, in blue and gold, a charming head-dress of a dove upon her loosened hair, and a pair of little dove-pale wings fluttering from her shoulders, her tiny twinkling feet and slender ankles well visible, too, was equally successful and admired. Her large and timid eyes, her flitting movements, her light and dainty way of dancing all added touches that made the picture perfect.

How Binovitch contrived his dress remained a mystery, for the layers of wings upon his back were real; the large black kites that haunt the Nile, soaring in their hundreds over Cairo and the bleak Mokattam Hills, had furnished them. He had procured them none knew how. They measured four feet across from tip to tip; they swished and rustled as he swept along; they were true falcons' wings. He danced with Nautch-girls and Egyptian princesses and Rumanian Gipsies; he danced well, with beauty, grace, and lightness. But with Vera he did not dance at all; with her he simply flew. A kind of passionate abandon was in him as he skimmed the floor with her in a way that made everybody turn to watch them. They seemed to leave the ground together. It was delightful, an amazing sight; but it was peculiar. The strangeness of it was on many lips. Somehow its queer extravagance communicated itself to the entire ball-room. They became the centre of observation. There were whispers.

"There's that extraordinary bird-man! Look! He goes by like a hawk. And he's always after that dove-girl. How marvellously he does it! It's rather awful. Who is he? I don't envy her."

People stood aside when he rushed past. They got out of his way. He seemed forever pursuing Vera, even when dancing with another partner. Word passed from mouth to mouth. A kind of telepathic interest was established everywhere. It was a shade too real sometimes—something unduly earnest in the chasing wildness, something unpleasant. There was even alarm.

"It's rowdy; I'd rather not see it; it's quite disgraceful," was heard. "I think it's horrible; you can see she's terrified."

And once there was a little scene, trivial enough, yet betraying this reality that many noticed and disliked. Binovitch came up to claim a dance, programme clutched in his great tufted claws, and at the same moment the big Pierrot appeared abruptly round the corner with a similar claim. Those who saw it assert he had been waiting, and came on purpose, and that there was something protective and authoritative in his bearing. The misunderstanding was ordinary enough both men had written her name against the dance but "No. 13, Tango" also included the supper interval, and neither Hawk nor Pierrot would give way. They were very obstinate. Both men wanted her. It was awkward.

"The Dove shall decide between us," smiled the Hawk politely, yet his taloned fingers working nervously. Pierrot, however, more experienced in the ways of dealing with women, or more bold, said suavely:

"I am ready to abide by her decision" his voice poorly cloaked this aggravating authority, as though he had the right to her "only I engaged this dance before his Majesty Horus appeared upon the scene at all, and therefore it is clear that Pierrot has the right of way."

At once, with a masterful air, he took her off. There was no withstanding him. He meant to have her and he got her. She yielded meekly. They vanished among the maze of coloured dancers, leaving the Hawk, disconsolate and vanquished, amid the titters of the onlookers. His swiftness, as against this steady power, was of no avail.

It was then that the singular phenomenon was witnessed first. Those who saw it affirm that he changed absolutely into the part he played. It was dreadful; it was wicked. A frightened whisper ran about the rooms and corridors:

"An extraordinary thing is in the air!"

Some shrank away, while others flocked to see. There were those who swore that a curious, rushing sound was audible, the atmosphere visibly disturbed and shaken; that a shadow fell upon the spot the couple had vacated; that a cry was heard, a high, wild, searching cry: "Horus! bright deity of wind," it began, then died away. One man was positive that the windows had been opened and that something had flown in. It was the obvious explanation. The thing spread horribly. As in a fire-panic, there was consternation and excitement. Confusion caught the feet of all the dancers. The music fumbled and lost time. The leading pair of tango dancers halted and looked round. It seemed that everybody pressed back, hiding, shuffling, eager to see, yet more eager not to be seen, as though something dangerous, hostile, terrible, had broken loose. In rows against the wall they stood. For a great space had made itself in the middle of the ball-room, and into this empty space appeared suddenly the Pierrot and the Dove.

It was like a challenge. A sound of applause, half voices, half clapping of gloved hands, was heard. The couple danced exquisitely into the arena. All stared. There was an impression that a set piece had been prepared, and that this was its beginning. The music again took heart. Pierrot was strong and dignified, no whit nonplussed by this abrupt publicity. The Dove, though faltering, was deliciously obedient. They danced together like a single outline. She was captured utterly. And to the man who needed her the sight was naturally agonizing—the protective way the Pierrot held her, the right and strength of it, the mastery, the complete possession.

"He's got her!" some one breathed too loud, uttering the thought of all. "Good thing it's not the Hawk!" And, to the absolute amazement of the throng, this sight was then apparent. A figure dropped through space. That high, shrill cry again was heard:

"Feather my soul ... to know thy awful swiftness!"

Its singing loveliness touched the heart, its appealing, passionate sweetness was marvellous, as from the gallery this figure of a man, dressed as a strong, dark bird, shot down with splendid grace and ease. The feathers swept; the swings spread out as sails that take the wind. Like a hawk that darts with unerring power and aim upon its prey, this thing of mighty wings rushed down into the empty space where the two danced. Observed by all, he entered, swooping beautifully, stretching his wings like any eagle. He dropped. He fixed his point of landing with consummate skill close beside the astonished dancers. He landed.

It happened with such swiftness it brought the dazzle and blindness as when lightning strikes. People in different parts of the room saw different details; a few saw nothing at all after the first startling shock, closing their eyes, or holding their arms before their faces as in self-protection. The touch of panic fear caught the entire room. The nameless thing that all the evening had been vaguely felt was come. It had suddenly materialised.

For this incredible thing occurred in the full blaze of light upon the open floor. Binovitch, grown in some sense formidable, opened his dark, big wings about the girl. The long grey feathers moved, causing powerful draughts of wind that made a rushing sound. An aspect of the terrible was about him, like an emanation. The great beaked head was poised to strike, the tufted claws were raised like fingers that shut and opened, and the whole presentment of his amazing figure focused in an attitude of attack that was magnificent and terrible. No one who saw it doubted. Yet there were those who swore that it was not Binovitch at all, but that another outline, monstrous and shadowy, towered above him, draping his lesser proportions with two colossal wings of darkness. That some touch of strange divinity lay in it may be claimed, however confused the wild descriptions afterward. For many lowered their heads and bowed their shoulders. There was terror. There was also awe. The onlookers swayed as though some power passed over them through the air. A sound of wings was certainly in the room.

Then some one screamed; a shriek broke high and clear; and emotion, ordinary human emotion, unaccustomed to terrific things, swept loose. The Hawk and Vera flew. Beaten back against the wall as by a stroke of whirlwind, the Pierrot staggered. He watched them go. Out of the lighted room they flew, out of the crowded human atmosphere, out of the heat and artificial light, the walled-in, airless halls that were a cage. All this they left behind. They seemed things of wind and air, made free happily of another element. Earth held them not. Toward the open night they raced with this extraordinary lightness as of birds, down the long corridor and on to the southern terrace, where great coloured curtains were hung suspended from the columns. A moment they were visible. Then the fringe of one huge curtain, lifted by the wind, showed their dark outline for a second against the starry sky. There was a cry, a leap. The curtain flapped again and closed. They vanished. And into the ball-room swept the cold draught of night air from the desert.

But three figures instantly were close upon their heels. The throng of half-dazed, half-stupefied onlookers, it seemed, projected them as though by some explosive force. The general mass held back, but, like projectiles, these three flung themselves after the fugitives down the corridor at high speed the Apache, Don Quixote, and, last of them, the Pierrot. For Khilkoff, the brother, and Baron Minski, the man who caught wolves alive, had been for some time keenly on the watch, while Dr. Plitzinger, reading the symptoms clearly, never far away, had been faithfully observant of every movement. His mask tossed aside, the great psychiatrist was now recognised by all. They reached the parapet just as the curtain flapped back heavily into place; the next second all three were out of sight behind it. Khilkoff was first, however, urged forward at frantic speed by the warning words the doctor had whispered as they ran. Some thirty yards beyond the terrace was the brink of the crumbling cliff on which the great hotel was built, and there was a drop of sixty feet to the desert floor below. Only a low stone wall marked the edge.

Accounts varied. Khilkoff, it seems, arrived in time in the nick of time to seize his sister, virtually hovering on the brink. He heard the loose stones strike the sand below. There was no struggle, though it appears she did not thank him for his interference at first. In a sense she was beside outside herself. And he did a characteristic thing: he not only brought her back into the ball-room, but he danced her back. It was admirable. Nothing could have calmed the general excitement better. The pair of them danced in together as though nothing was amiss. Accustomed to the strenuous practice of his Cossack regiment, this young cavalry officer's muscles were equal to the semi-dead weight in his arms. At most the onlookers thought her tired, perhaps. Confidence was restored such is the psychology of a crowd and in the middle of a thrilling Viennese waltz he easily smuggled her out of the room, administered brandy, and got her up to bed. The absence of the Hawk, meanwhile, was hardly noticed; comments were made and then forgotten; it was Vera in whom the strange, anxious sympathy had centred. And, with her obvious safety, the moment of primitive, childish panic passed away. Don Quixote, too, was presently seen dancing gaily as though nothing untoward had happened; supper intervened; the incident was over; it had melted into the general wildness of the evening's irresponsibility. The fact that Pierrot did not appear again was noticed by no single person.

But Dr. Plitzinger was otherwise engaged, his heart and mind and soul all deeply exercised. A death-certificate is not always made out quite so simply as the public thinks. That Binovitch had died of suffocation in his swift descent through merely sixty feet of air was not conceivable; yet that his body lay so neatly placed upon the desert after such a fall was stranger still. It was not crumpled, it was not torn; no single bone was broken, no muscle wrenched; there was no bruise. There was no indenture in the sand. The figure lay sidewise as though in sleep, no sign of violence visible anywhere, the dark wings folded as a great bird folds them when it creeps away to die in loneliness. Beneath the Horus mask the face was smiling. It seemed he had floated into death upon the element he loved. And only Vera had seen the enormous wings that, hovering invitingly above the dark abyss, bore him so softly into another world. Plitzinger, that is, saw them, too, but he said firmly that they belonged to the big black falcons that haunt the Mokattam Hills and roost upon these ridges, close beside the hotel, at night. Both he and Vera, however, agreed on one thing: the high, sharp cry in the air above them, wild and plaintive, was certainly the black kite's cry—the note of the falcon that passionately seeks its mate. It was the pause of a second, when she stood to listen, that made her rescue possible. A moment later and she, too, would have flown to death with Binovitch.

LORD OF THE JACKALS

SAX ROHMER

In those days, of course (said the French agent, looking out across the sea of Yûssuf Effendis which billowed up against the balcony to where, in the moonlight, the minarets of Cairo pointed the way to God), I did not occupy the position which I occupy today. No, I was younger, and more ambitious; I thought to carve in the annals of Egypt a name for myself such as that of De Lesseps.

I had a scheme—and there were those who believed in it—for extending the borders of Egypt. Ah! my friends, Egypt after all is but a double belt of mud following the Nile, and terminated east and west by the desert. The desert! It was the dream of my life to exterminate that desert, that hungry gray desert; it was my plan—a foolish plan as I know now—to link the fertile Fáyûm to the Oases! How was this to be done?

Ah! Why should I dig up those buried skeletons? It was not done; it never could be done; therefore, let me not bore you with how I had proposed to do it. Suffice it that my ambitions took me far off the beaten tracks, far, even, from the caravan roads—far into the gray heart of the desert.

But I was ambitious, and only nineteen—or scarcely twenty. At nineteen, a man who comes from St. Rémy fears no obstacle which Fate can place in his way, and looks upon the world as a grape-fruit to be sweetened with endeavor and sucked empty.

It was in those days, then, that I learned as your Rudyard Kipling has also learned that "East is East"; it was in those days that I came face to face with that "mystery of Egypt" about which so much is written, has always been written, and always will be written, but concerning which so few people, so very few people, know anything whatever.

Yes, I, René de Flassans, saw with my own eyes a thing that I knew to be magic, a thing whereat my reason rebelled—a thing which my poor European intelligence could not grapple, could not begin to explain.

It was this which you asked me to tell you, was it not? I will do so with pleasure, because I know that I speak to men of honor, and because it is good for me, now that I cannot count the gray hairs in my beard, to confess how poor a thing I was when I could count every hair upon my chin—and how grand a thing I thought myself.

One evening, at the end of a dreadful day in the saddle—beneath a sky which seemed to reflect all the fires of hell, a day passed upon sands simply smoking in that merciless sun—I and my native companions came to an encampment of Arabs.

They were Bedouins—the tribe does not matter at the moment—and, as you may know, the Bedouin is the most hospitable creature whom God has yet created. The tent of the Sheikh is open to any traveller who cares to rest his weary limbs therein. Freely he may partake of all that the tribe has to offer, food and drink and entertainment; and to seek to press payment upon the host would be to insult a gentleman.

That is desert hospitality. A spear that stands thrust upright in the sand before the tent door signifies that whosoever would raise his hand against the guest has first to reckon with the Sheikh. Equally it would be an insult to erect one's own tent in the neighborhood of a Bedouin encampment.

Well, my friends, I knew this well, for I was no stranger to the nomadic life, and accordingly, without fear of the fierce-eyed throng who came forth to meet us, I made my respects to the Sheikh Saïd Mohammed, and was reckoned by him as a friend and a brother. His tent was placed at my disposal and provisions were made for the suitable entertainment of those who were with me.

You know how dusk falls in Egypt? At one moment the sky is a brilliant canvas, glorious with every color known to art, at the next the curtain—the wonderful veil of deepest violet—has fallen; the stars break through it like diamonds through the finest gauze; it is night, velvet, violet night. You see it here in this noisy modern Cairo. In the lonely desert it is ten thousand times grander, ten thousand times more impressive; it speaks to the soul with the voice of the silence. Ah, those desert nights!

So was the night of which I speak; and having partaken of the fare which the Sheikh caused to be set before me—and Bedouin fare is not for the squeamish stomach—I sipped that delicious coffee which, though an acquired taste, is the true nectar, and looked out beyond the four or five palm trees of this little oasis to where the gray carpet of the desert grew black as ebony and met the violet sweep of the sky.

Perhaps I was the first to see him; I cannot say; but certainly he was not perceived by the Bedouins, although one stood on guard at the entrance to the camp.

How can I describe him? At the time, as he approached in the moonlight with a shambling, stooping gait, I felt that I had never seen his like before. Now I know the reason of my wonder, and the reason of my doubt. I know what it was about him which inspired a kind of horror and a revulsion—a dread.

Elfin locks he had, gray and matted, falling about his angular face, shading his strange, yellow eyes. His was dressed in rags, in tatters; he was furtive, and he staggered as one who is very weak, slowly approaching out of the vastness.

Then it appeared as though every dog in the camp knew of his coming. Out from the shadows of the tents they poured, those yapping mongrels. Never have I seen such a thing. In the midst of the yellowish, snarling things, at the very entrance to the camp, the wretched old man fell, uttering a low cry.

But now, snatching up a heavy club which lay close to my hand, I rushed out of the tent. Others were thronging out too, hut, first of them all, I burst in among the dogs, striking, kicking, and shouting. I stooped and raised the head of the stranger.

Mutely he thanked me, with half-closed eyes. A choking sound issued from his throat, and he clutched with his hands and pointed to his mouth.

An earthenware jar, containing cool water, stood beside a tent but a few yards away. Hurling my club at the most furious of the dogs, which, with bared fangs, still threatened to attack the recumbent man, I ran and seized the *dorak*, regained his side, and poured water between his parched lips.

The throng about me was strangely silent, until, as the poor old man staggered again to his feet, supported by my arm, a chorus arose about me—one long, vowelled word, wholly unfamiliar, although my Arabic was good. But I noted that all kept a respectful distance from myself and the man whom I had succored.

Then, pressing his way through the throng came the Sheikh Saïd Mohammed. Saluting the ragged stranger with a sort of grim respect, he asked him if he desired entertainment for the night.

The other shook his head, mumbling, pointed to the water jar, and by dint of gnashing his yellow and pointed teeth, intimated that he required food.

Food was brought to him hurriedly. He tied it up in a dirty cloth, grasped the water jar, and, with never a glance at the Arabs, turned to me. With his hand he touched his brow, his lips, and his breast in salute; then, although tottering with weakness, he made off again with that queer, loping gait.

The camp dogs began to howl, and a strange silence fell upon the Arabs about me. All stood watching the departing figure until it was lost in a dip of the desert, when the watchers began to return again to their tents.

Saïd Mohammed took my hand, and in a few direct and impressive words thanked me for having spared him and his tribe from a grave dishonor. Need I say that I was flattered? Had you met him, my friends, that fine Bedouin gentleman, polished as any noble of old France, fearless as a lion, yet gentle as a woman, you would know that I rejoiced in being able to serve him even so slightly.

Two of the dogs, unperceived by us, had followed the weird old man from the camp; for suddenly in the distance I heard their savage growls. Then, these growls were drowned in such a chorus of howling—the howling of jackals—as I had never before heard in all my desert wanderings. The howling suddenly subsided ... but the dogs did not return.

I glanced around, meaning to address the Sheikh, but the Sheikh was gone.

Filled with wonder, then, respecting this singular incident, I entered the tent—it was at the farther end of the camp—which had been placed at my disposal, and lay down, rather to reflect than to sleep. With my mind confused in thoughts of yellow-eyed wanderers, of dogs, and of jackals, sleep came.

How long I slept I cannot say; but I was awakened as the cool fingers of dawn were touching the crests of the sand billows. A gray and dismal light filled the tent, and something was scratching at the flap.

I sat up immediately, quite wide awake, and taking my revolver, ran to the entrance and looked out.

A slinking shape melted into the shadows of the tent adjoining mine, and I concluded that a camp dog had aroused me. Then, in the early morning silence, I heard a faint call, and peering through the gloom to the east saw, in black silhouette, a solitary figure standing near the extremity of the camp.

In those days, my friends, I was a brave fellow—we are all brave at nineteen—and throwing a cloak over my shoulders I strode intrepidly towards this figure. I was within ten paces when a hand was raised to beckon me.

It was the mysterious stranger! Again he beckoned to me, and I approached yet nearer, asking him if it was he who had aroused me.

He nodded, and by means of a grotesque kind of pantomime ultimately made me understand that he had caused me to be aroused in order to communicate something to me. He turned, and indicated that we were to walk away from the camp. I accompanied him without hesitation.

Although the camp was never left unguarded, no one had challenged us; and, a hundred yards beyond the outermost tent, this strange old man stopped and turned to me.

First, he pointed back to the camp, then to myself, then out along the caravan road towards the Nile.

"Do you mean," I asked him—for I perceived that he was dumb or vowed to silence— "that I am to leave the camp!"

He nodded rapidly, his strange yellow eyes gleaming.

"Immediately?" I demanded.

Again he nodded.

"Why?"

Pantomimically he made me understand that death threatened me if I remained—that I must leave the Bedouins before sunrise.

I cannot convey to you any idea of the mad earnestness of the man. But, alas! youth regards the counsels of age with nothing but contempt; moreover, I thought this man mad, and I was unable to choke down a sort of loathing which he inspired in me.

I shook my head then, but not unkindly; and, waving my hand, prepared to leave him. At that, with a sorrow in his strange eyes which did not fail to impress me, he saluted me with gravity, turned, and passed out of sight.

Although I did not know it at the time, I had chosen of two paths the one that led through fire.

I slept little after this interview—if it was a real interview and not a dream—and feeling tired and unrefreshed, I saw the sun rise purple and angry over the distant hills.

You know what *khamsîn* is like, my friends? But you cannot know what *simoom* is like—*simoom* in the heart of the desert! It came that morning—a wall of sand so high as to shut out the sunlight, so dense as to turn the day into night, so suffocating that I thought I should never live through it!

It was apparent to me that the Bedouins were prepared for the storm. The horses, the camels and the asses were tethered in an enclosure specially strengthened to exclude the choking dust, and with their cloaks about their heads the men prepared for the oncoming of this terror of the desert.

My God! it was a demon which sought to blind me, to suffocate me, and which clutched at my throat with strangling fingers of sand! This, I told myself, was the danger which I might have avoided by quitting the camp before sunrise.

Indeed, it was apparent to me that if I had taken the advice so strangely offered, I might now have been safe in the village of the Great Oasis for which I was bound. But I have since seen that the *simoom* was a minor danger, and not the real one to which this weird being had referred.

The storm passed, and every man in the encampment praised the merciful God who had spared us all. It was in the disturbance attendant upon putting the camp in order once more than I saw her.

She came out from the tent of Saïd Mohammed, to shake the sand from a carpet; the newly come sunlight twinkled upon the bracelets which clasped her smooth brown arms as she shook the gaily colored mat at the tent door. The sunlight shone upon her braided hair, upon her slight robe, upon her silver anklets, and upon her tiny feet. Transfixed I stood watching—indeed, my friends, almost holding my breath. Then the sunlight shone upon her eyes, two pools of mysterious darkness into which I found myself suddenly looking.

The face of this lovely Arab maiden flushed, and drawing the corner of her robe across those bewitching eyes, she turned and ran back into the tent.

One glance—just one glance, my friends! But never had Ulysses' bow propelled an arrow more sure, more deadly. I was nineteen, remember, and of Provence. What do you foresee! You who have been through the world, you who once were nineteen. I feigned a sickness, a sickness brought about by the sandstorm, and taking base advantage of that desert hospitality which is unbounded, which knows no suspicion, and takes no count of cost, I remained in the tent which had been vacated for me.

In this voluntary confinement I learned little of the doings of the camp. All day I lay dreaming of two dark eyes, and at night when the jackals howled I thought of the wanderer who had counseled me to leave. One day, I lay so; a second; a third again; and the women of Saïd Mohammed's household tended me, closely veiled of course. But in vain I waited for that attendant whose absence was rendering my feigned fever a real one—whose eyes burned like torches in my dreams and for the coming of whose little bare feet across the sand to my tent door I listened hour by hour, day by day, in vain—always in vain.

But at nineteen there is no such thing as despair, and hope has strength to defy death itself. It was in the violet dusk of the fourth day, as I lay there with a sort of shame of my deception struggling for birth in my heart, that she came.

She came through the tent door bearing a bowl of soup, and the rays of the setting sun outlined her fairy shape through the gossamer robe as she entered.

At that my poor weak little conscience troubled me no more. How my heart leaped, leaped so that it threatened to choke me, who had come safe through a great sandstorm.

There is fire in the Southern blood at nineteen, my friends, which leaps into flame beneath the glances of bright eyes.

With her face modestly veiled, the Bedouin maid knelt beside me, placing the wooden bowl upon the ground. My eager gaze pierced the *yashmak*, but her black lashes were laid upon her cheek, her glorious eyes averted. My heart—or was it my vanity?—told me that she regarded me at least with interest, that she was not at ease in my company; and as, having spoken no word, having ventured no glance, she rose again to depart, I was emboldened to touch her hand.

Like a startled gazelle she gave me one rapid glance, and was gone!

She was gone—and my very soul gone with her!

For hours I lay, not so much as thinking of the food beside me—dreaming of her eyes. What were my plans? Faith! Does one have plans at nineteen where two bright eyes are concerned?

Alas, my friends, I dare not tell you of my hopes, yet upon those hopes I lived. Oh, it is glorious to be nineteen and of Provence; it is glorious when all the world is young, when the fruit is ripe upon the trees and the plucking seems no sin. Yet, as we look back, we perceive that at nineteen we were scoundrels.

The Bedouin girl is a woman when a European woman is but a child, and Sakîna, whose eyes could search a man's soul, was but twelve years of age—twelve! Can you picture that child of twelve squeezing a lover's heart between her tiny hands, entwining his imagination in the coils of her hair?

You, my friend, may perhaps be able to conceive this thing, for you know the East, and the women of the East. At ten or eleven years of age many of them are adorable; at twenty-one most of them are *passé*; at twenty-six all of them—with rare exceptions—are shrieking hags.

But to you, my other friends, who are strangers to our Oriental ways, who know not that the peach only attains to perfect ripeness for one short hour, it may be strange, it may be horrifying, that I loved, with all the ardor which was mine, this little Arab maiden, who, had she been born in France, would not yet have escaped from the nursery. But I digress.

The Arabs were encamped, of course, in the neighborhood of a spring. It lay in a slight depression amid the tiny palm-grove. Here, at sunset, came the women with their pitchers on their heads, graceful of carriage, veiled, mysterious.

Many peaches have ripened and have rotted since those days of which I speak, but now—even now—I am still enslaved by the mystery of Egypt's veiled women. Untidy, bedraggled, dirty, she may be, but the real Egyptian woman when she bears her pitcher upon her head and glides, stately, sinuously, through the dusk to the well, is a figure to enchain the imagination.

Very soon, then, the barrier of reserve which, like the screen of the *harêm*, stands between Eastern women and love, was broken. My trivial scruples I had cast to the winds, and feigning weakness, I would sally forth to take the air in the cool of the evening; this two days later.

My steps, be assured, led me to the spring; and you who are men of the world will know that Sakîna, braving the reproaches of the Sheikh's household, neglectful of her duties, was last of all the women who came to the well for water.

I taught her to say my name—René! How sweet it sounded from her lips, as she strove in vain to roll the 'R' in our Provencal fashion. Some *ginnee* most certainly presided over this enchanted fountain, for despite the nearness of the camp our rendezvous was never discovered, our meetings were never detected.

With her pitcher upon the ground beside her, she would sit with those wistful, wonderful eyes upraised to mine, and sway before the ardor of my impassioned words as a young and tender reed sways in the Nile breeze. Her budding soul was a love lute upon which I played in ecstasy; and when she raised her red lips to mine.... Ah! those nights in the boundless desert! God is good to youth, and harsh to old age!

Next to Saïd Mohammed, her father, Sakîna's brother was the finest horseman of the tribe, and his white mare their fleetest steed. I had cast covetous eyes upon this glorious creature, my friends, and secretly had made such overtures as were calculated to win her confidence.

Within two weeks, then, my plans were complete—up to a point. Since they were doomed to failure, like my great scheme, I shall not trouble you with their details, but an hour before dawn on a certain night I cut the camel-hair tethering of the white mare, and, undetected, led the beautiful creature over the silent sands to a cup-like depression, a thousand yards distant from the camp.

The Bedouin who was upon guard that night had with him a gourd of *'erksoos*. This was customary, and I had chosen an occasion when the duty of filling the sentinel's gourd had fallen upon Sakîna; to his *'erksoos* I had added four drops of dark brown fluid from my medicine chest.

It was an hour before dawn, then, when I stood beside the white mare, watching and listening; it was an hour before dawn when she for whom my great scheme was forgotten, for whom I was about to risk the anger, the just anger, of men amongst the most fierce in the known world, came running fleetly over the hillocks down into the little valley, and threw herself into my arms....

When dawn burst in gloomy splendor over the desert, we were still five hours' ride from the spot where I had proposed temporarily to conceal myself, with perhaps an hour's start of the Arabs. I knew the desert ways well enough, but the ghostly and desolate place in which I now found myself nevertheless filled me with foreboding.

A seam of black volcanic rock split the sands for a great distance, forming a kind of natural wall of forbidding aspect. In places this wall was pierced by tunnel-like openings; I think they may have been prehistoric tombs. There was no scrap of verdure visible, north, south, east or west; only desolation, sand, grayness, and this place, ghostly and wan with that ancient sorrow, that odor of remote mortality which is called "the dust of Egypt." Seated before me in the saddle, Sakîna looked up into my face with a never-changing confidence, having her little brown fingers interlocked about my neck. But her strength was failing. A short rest was imperative.

Thus far I had detected no evidence of pursuit and, descending from the saddle, I placed my weary companion upon a rock over which I had laid a rug, and poured out for her a draught of cool water.

Bread and dates were our breakfast fare; but bread and dates and water are nectar and ambrosia when they are sweetened with kisses. Oh! the glorious madness of youth! Sometimes, my friends, I am almost tempted to believe that the man who has never been wicked has never been happy!

Picture us, then, if you can, set amid that desolation, which for us was a rose-garden, eating of that unpalatable food—which for us was the food of the gods!

So we remained awhile, deliriously happy, though death might terminate our joys ere we again saw the sun, when something ... *something* spoke to me...

Understand me, I did not say that *someone* spoke, I did not say that anything *audible* spoke. But I know that, unlocking those velvet arms which clung to me, I stood up slowly—and, still slowly, turned and looked back at the frowning black rocks.

Merciful God! My heart beats wildly now when I recall that moment.

Motionless as a statue, but in a crouching attitude, as if about to leap down, he who had warned me so truly stood upon the highest point of the rocks watching us!

How long did I remain thus?

I cannot pretend to say; but when I turned to Sakîna—she lay trembling on the ground, with her face hidden in her hands.

Then, down over the piled-up rocks, this mysterious and ominous being came leaping. Old man though he was, he descended with the agility of a mountain goat—and sometimes, in the difficult places, *he went on all fours.*

Crossing the intervening strip of sand, he stood before me. You have seen the reproach in the eyes of a faithful dog whose master has struck him unjustly? Such a reproach shone out from the yellow eyes of this desert wanderer. I cannot account for it; I can say no more....

It was impossible for me to speak; I trembled violently; such a fear and such a madness of sorrow possessed me that I would have welcomed any death—to have freed me from that intolerable reproach.

He suddenly pointed towards the horizon where against the curtain of the dawn black figures appeared.

I fell upon my knees beside Sakîna. I was a poor, pitiable thing; the madness of my passion had left me, and already I was within the great Shadow; I could not even weep; I knew that I had brought Sakîna out into that desolate place—to die.

And now the man whose ways were unlike human ways began to babble insanely, gesticulating and plucking at me. I cannot hope to make you feel one little part of the emotion with which those instants were laden. Sakîna clung to me trembling in a way I can never forget—never, never forget.

And the look in her eyes! even now I cannot bear to think of it, I cannot bear—

Those almost colorless lizards which dart about in the desert places with incredible swiftness were now coming forth from their nests; and all the while the black figures, unheard as yet, were approaching along the path of the sun.

My mad folly grew more apparent to me every moment. I realized that this which so rapidly was overtaking me had been inevitable from the first. The strange wild man stood watching me with that intolerable glare, so that my trembling companion shrank from him in horror.

But evidently he was seeking to convey some idea to me. He gesticulated constantly, pointing to the approaching Arabs and then over his shoulder to the frowning rock behind. Since it was too late for flight—for I knew that the white mare with a double burden could never outpace our pursuers—it occurred to me at the moment when the muffled beat of hoofs first became audible, that this hermit of the rocks was endeavoring to induce me to seek some hiding-place with which no doubt he was acquainted.

How I cursed the delay which had enabled the Arabs to come up with us! I know, now, of course, that even had I not delayed, our ultimate capture was certain. But at the moment, in my despair, I thought otherwise.

And now I cursed the stupidity which had prevented me from following this weid guide; I even thought wrathfully of the poor frightened child, whose weakness had necessitated the delay and whose fears had contributed considerably to this later misunderstanding.

The pursuing party, numbering four, and led by Saïd Mohammed, was no more than five hundred yards away when I came to my senses. The hermit now was tugging at my arm with frightful insistence; his eyes were glaring insanely, and he chattered in an almost pitiable manner.

"Quick!" I cried, throwing my arm about Sakîna, "up to the rocks. This man can hide us!"

"No, no!" she whispered, "I dare not—"

But I lifted her, and signing to the singular being to lead the way, staggered forward despairingly.

The distance was greater than it appeared, the climb incredibly difficult. My guide held out his hand to me to assist me to mount the slippery rocks; but I had much ado to proceed and also to support Sakîna.

Her terror of the man and of the place to which he was leading us momentarily increased. Indeed, it seemed that she was becoming mad with fear. When the man paused before an opening in the rocks not more than fifteen or sixteen inches in height, and wildly waving his arms in the air, his elfin locks flying about his shoulder, his eyes glassy, intimated that we were to crawl in—Sakîna writhed free of my grasp and bounded back some three or four paces down the slope.

"Not in there!" she cried, holding out her little hands to me pitifully. "I dare not! He would devour us!"

At the foot of the slope, Said Mohammed, who had dismounted from his horse, and who, far ahead of the others, was advancing towards us, at that moment raised his gun and fired....

Can I go on?

It is more years ago than I care to count, but it is fresher in my mind than the things of yesterday. A lonely old age is before me, my friends—for I have been a solitary man since that shot was fired.

For me it changed the face of the world, for me it ended youth, revealing me to myself for what I was.

Something more nearly resembling human speech than any sound he had yet uttered burst from the lips of the wild man as the report of Saïd Mohammed's shot whispered in echoes through the mysterious labyrinths beneath us.

Fate had stood at the Sheikh's elbow as he pulled the trigger.

With a little soft cry—I hear it now, gentle, but having in it a world of agony—Sakîna sank at my feet ... and her blood began to trickle over the black rocks on which she lay.

The man who professes to describe to you his emotions at such a frightful moment is an impostor. The world grew black before my eyes; every emotion of which my being was capable became paralysed.

I heard nothing, I saw nothing but the little huddled figure, that red stream upon the black rock, and the agonized love in the blazing eyes of Sakîna. Groaning, I threw myself down beside her, and as she sighed out her life upon my breast, I knew—God help me—that what had been but a youthful amour, was now a life's tragedy; that for me the light of the world had gone out, that I should never again know the warmth of the sun and the gladness of the morning....

The cave man, with a dog-like fidelity, sought now to drag me from my dead love, to drag me into that gloomy lair which she had shrunk from entering. His incoherent mutterings broke in upon my semi-coma; but I shook him off, I shrieked curses at him....

Now the Bedouins were mounting the slope, not less than a hundred yards below me. In the growing light I could see the face of Saïd Mohammed....

The man beside me exerted all his strength to drag me back into the gallery or cave—I know not what it was; but with my arms locked about Sakîna I lay watching the pursuers coming closer and closer.

Then, those persistent efforts suddenly ceased, and dully I told myself that this weird being, having done his best to save me, had fled in order to save himself.

I was wrong.

You have asked me for a story of the magic of Egypt, and although, as you see, it has cost me tears—oh! I am not ashamed of those tears, my friends!— I have recounted this story to you. You say, where is the magic? and I might reply: the magic was in the changing of my false love to a true. But there was another magic as well, and it grew up around me now at this moment when I lay inert, waiting for death.

From behind me, from above me, arose a cry—a cry. You may have heard of the Bedouin song, the 'Mizmûne':

"*Ya men melek ana dêri waat sa jebb,*
Id el' ish hoos' a beb hatsa azât ta lebb."

You may have heard how when it is sung in a certain fashion, flowers drop from their stalks? Also, you may have doubted this, never having heard a magical cry.

I do not doubt it, my friends! For I have heard a magical cry—this cry which arose from behind me! It started some chord in my dulled consciousness which had never spoken before. I turned my head—and there upon the highest point of the rocks stood the cave man. He suddenly stretched forth his hands.

Again he uttered that uncanny, that indescribable cry. It was not human. It was not animal. Yet it was nearer to the cry of an animal than to any sound made by the human species. His eyes gleamed with an awful light, his spare body had assumed a strange significance; he was transfigured.

A third time he uttered the cry, and out from one of those openings in the rock which I have mentioned, crept a jackal. You know how a jackal avoids the day, how furtive, how nocturnal a creature it is? but there in the golden glory which proclaimed the coming of the sun, black silhouettes moved.

A great wonder possessed me, as the first jackal was followed by a second, by a third, by a fourth, by a fifth. Did I say a fifth! ... By five hundred—by five thousand!

From every visible hole in the rocks, jackals poured forth in packs. Wonder left me, fear left me; I forgot my sorrow, I became a numbed intelligence amid a desert of jackals. Over a sea of moving furry backs, I saw that upstanding crag and the weird crouching figure upon it. Right and left, above and below, jackals moved ... and all turned their heads towards the approaching Bedouins!

Again—again I heard that dreadful cry. The jackals, in a pack, thousands strong, began to advance upon the Bedouins! ...

Not east or west, north or south, could you hope to find a braver man than was the Sheikh Saïd Mohammed; but—he fled!

I saw the four horsemen riding like furies into the morning sun. The white mare, riderless, galloped with them—and the desert behind was yellow with jackals! For the last time I heard the cry.

The jackals began to return!

Forgive me, dear friends, if I seem an emotional fool. But when I recovered from the swoon which blotted out that unnatural spectacle, the wizard—for now I knew him for nothing less—had dug a deep trench—and had left me, alone.

Not a jackal was in sight; the sun blazed cruelly upon the desert. With my own hands I laid my love to rest in the sands. No cross, no crescent marks her resting-place; but I left my youth upon her grave, as a last offering.

You may say that, since I had sinned so grievously, since I had betrayed the noble confidence of Saïd Mohammed, my host, I escaped lightly.

Ah! you do not know!

And what of the strange being whose gratitude I had done so little to merit but yet which knew no bounds? It is of him that I will tell you.

Years later—how many it does not matter, but I was a man with no illusions—my restless wanderings (I being still a desert bird-of-passage) brought me one night to a certain well but rarely visited. It lay in a depression, like another well that I am fated often to see in my dreams, and, as one approached, the crowns of the palm trees which grew there appeared above the mounds of sand.

I was alone and tired out; the next possible camping-place—for I had no water—was many miles away. Yet it was written that I should press on to that other distant well, weary though I was.

First, then, as I came up, I perceived numbers of vultures in the air; and I began to fear that someone near to his end lay at the well. But when, from the top of a mound, I obtained a closer view, I saw a sight that, after one quick glance, caused me to spur up my tired horse and to fly—fly, with panic in my heart.

Even from where I sat I knew him; but, had I doubted, other evidence was there of his identity.

As I mounted the slope, thousands of fiery eyes were turned upon me. God! that arena all about was alive with jackals—jackals, my friends, eaters of carrion—which, silent, watchful, guarded the wizard dead, who, living, had been their lord!

The Ape

E. F. Benson

Hugh Marsham had spent the day, as a good tourist should, in visiting the temples and the tombs of kings across the river, and the magic of the hour of sunset flamed over earth and heaven as he crossed the Nile again to Luxor in his felucca. It seemed as if the whole world had been suddenly transferred into the heart of an opal, and burned with a myriad fiery colours. The river itself was of the green that beech trees are clad in at spring-time; the columns of the temple that stood close to its banks glowed as if lit from within by the flame of some perpetual evening sacrifice; the cloudless sky was dusky blue in the east, the blue of turquoise overhead, and melted into aquamarine above the line of desert where the sun had just sunk. All along the bank which he was fast approaching under the press of the cool wind from the north were crowds of Arabs, padding softly home in the dust from their work, and chattering as sparrows chatter among the bushes in the long English twilights. Even the dust that hovered and hung and was dispersed again by the wind was rainbowed; it caught the hues from the river and the sky, and the orange-flaming temple, and those who walked in it were clad in brightness.

Here in the South no long English twilight lingered, and as he walked up the dusky fragrant tunnel of mimosa that led to the hotel, night thickened, and in the sky a million stars leaped into being, while the soft gathering darkness sponged out the glories of the flaming hour. On the hotel steps the vendors of carpets and Arabian hangings, of incense and filigree work, of suspicious turquoises and more than suspicious scarabs were already packing up their wares, and probably recounting to each other in their shrill incomprehensible gabble the iniquitous bargains they had made with the gullible Americans and English, who so innocently purchased the wares of Manchester. Only in his accustomed corner old Abdul Hamid still squatted, for he was of a class above the ordinary vendors, a substantial dealer in antiques, who had a shop in the village, where archaeologists resorted, and brought, *sub rosa*, pieces that eventually found their way into European museums. He was in his shop all day, but evening found him, when serious business hours were over, on the steps of the hotel, where he sold undoubted antiquities to tourists who wanted something genuine.

The day had been very hot, and Hugh felt himself disposed to linger outside the hotel in this cool dusk, and turn over the tray of scarabs which Abdul Hamid presented to his notice. He was a wrinkled, dried-up husk of a man, loquacious and ingratiating in manner, and welcomed Hugh as an old customer.

"See, sir," he said, "here are two more scroll-scarabs like those you bought from me before the week. You should have these; they are very fine and very cheap, because I do no business this year. Mr. Rankin, you know him?, of the British Museum, he give me two pounds each last year for scroll-scarabs not so fine, and today I sell them at a pound and a half each. Take them; they are yours. Scroll-scarabs of the twelfth dynasty; if Mr. Rankin was here he pay me two pounds each, and be sorry I not ask more."

Hugh laughed.

"You may sell them to Mr. Rankin then," he said. "He comes here tomorrow."

The old man, utterly unabashed, grinned and shook his head.

"No; I promised you them for pound and a half," he said. "I am not cheat-dealer. They are yours—pound and a half. Take them, take them."

Hugh resisted this unparalleled offer, and, turning over the contents of the tray, picked out of it and examined carefully a broken fragment of blue glaze, about an inch in height. This represented the head and shoulders of an ape, and the fracture had occurred half-way down the back, so that the lower part of the trunk, the forearms which apparently hung by its side, and the hind legs were missing. On the back there was an inscription in hieroglyphics, also broken. Presumably the missing pieces contained the remainder of the letters. It was modelled with extreme care and minuteness, and the face wore an expression of grotesque malevolence.

"What's this broken bit of a monkey?" asked Hugh carelessly.

Abdul Hamid, looking much like a monkey himself, put his eyes close to it.

"Ah, that's the rarest thing in Egypt," he said, "so Mr. Rankin he tell me, if only the monkey not broken. See the back? There it says: 'He of whom this is, let him call on me thrice'—and then some son of a dog broke it. If the rest was here, I would no take a hundred pounds for it; but now ten years have I kept half-monkey, and never comes half-monkey to it. It is yours, sir, for a pound it is yours. Half-monkey nothing to me; it is fool-monkey only being half monkey. I let it go—I give it you, and you give me pound."

Hugh Marsham felt in one pocket, then in another, with no appearance of hurry or eagerness.

"There's your pound," he said casually.

Abdul Hamid peered at him in the dusk. It was very odd that Hugh did not offer him half what he asked, instead of paying up without bargaining. He regretted extremely that he had not asked more. But the little blue fragment was now in Hugh's pocket, and the sovereign glistened very pleasantly in his own palm.

"And what was the rest of the hieroglyphic, do you think?" Hugh asked.

"Eh, Allah only knows the wickedness and the power of the monkeys," said Abdul Hamid. "Once there were such in Egypt, and in the temple of Mut in Karnak, which the English dug up, you shall see a chamber with just such monkeys sitting round it, four of them, all carved in sandstone. But on them there is no writing; I have looked at them behind and before; they not master-monkeys. Perhaps the monkey promised that whoso called on him thrice, if he were owner of the blue image of which gentleman has the half, would be his master and that monkey would do his bidding. Who knows? It is of the old wickedness of the world, the old Egyptian blackness."

Hugh got up. He had been out in the sun all day, and felt at this moment a little intimate shiver, which warned him that it was wiser to go indoors till the chill of sunset had passed. "I expect you've tried it on with the half-monkey, haven't you?" he said.

Abdul Hamid burst out into a toothless cackle of laughter.

"Yes, effendi," he said. "I have tried it a hundred times, and nothing happens. Else I would no have sold it you. Half-monkey is no monkey at all. I have tried to make boy with the ink-mirror see something about monkeys, but nothing comes, except the clouds and the man who sweeps. No monkey."

Hugh nodded to him.

"Goodnight, you old sorcerer," he said pleasantly.

As he walked up the broad flagged passage to his room, carrying the half-monkey in his hand, Hugh felt with a disengaged thumb in his waistcoat pocket for something he had picked up that day in the valley of the tombs of the kings. He had eaten his lunch there, after an inspection of the carved and reeking corridors, and, as he sat idly smoking had reached out a lazy hand to where the thing had glittered among the pebbles. Now, entering his room, he turned up the electric light, and, standing under it with his back to the window, that opened, door fashion, on to the three steps that led into the hotel garden, he fitted the fragment he had found to the fragment he had just purchased. They joined on to each other with the most absolute accuracy, not a chip was missing. There was the complete ape, and down its back ran the complete legend.

The window was open, and at this moment he heard a sudden noise as of some scampering beast in the garden outside. His light streamed out in an oblong on to the sandy path, and, laying the two pieces of the image on the table, he looked out. But there was nothing irregular to be seen; the palm trees waved and clashed in the wind, and the rose bushes stirred and scattered their fragrance. Only right down in the middle of the sandy path that ran between the beds, the ground was curiously disturbed, as by some animal, heavily frolicking, scooping and spurning the light soil as it ran.

The evening train from Cairo next day brought Mr. Rankin, the eminent Egyptologist and student of occult law, a huge red man with a complete mastery of colloquial Arabic. He had but a day to spend in Luxor, for he was en route for Merawi, where lately some important finds had been made, but Hugh took occasion to show him the figure of the ape as they sat over their coffee in the garden just outside his bedroom after lunch.

"I found the lower half yesterday, outside one of the tombs of the kings," he said, "and the top half by the utmost luck among old Abdul Hamid's things. He told me you said that if it was complete it would be of the greatest rarity. He lied, I suppose?"

Rankin gave one gasp of amazed surprise as he looked at it and read the inscription on the back. Marsham thought that his great red face suddenly paled.

"Good Lord!" he said. "Here, take it!" And he held out the two pieces to him.

Hugh laughed.

"Why in such a hurry?" he said.

"Because there comes a breaking point to every man's honesty, and I might keep it, and swear that I had given it back to you. My dear fellow, do you know what you've got?"

"Indeed I don't. I want to be told," said Hugh.

"And to think that it was you who only a couple of months ago asked me what a scarab was! Well, you've got there what all Egyptologists, and even more keenly than Egyptologists all students of folklore and magic black and white—especially black—would give their eyes to have found. Good Lord! what's that?"

Hugh was sitting by his side in a deck-chair, idly fitting together the two halves of the broken image. He too heard what had startled Rankin, for it was the same noise as had startled him last night, namely the scampering of some great frolicsome animal, somewhere close to them. As he jumped up, severing his hands, the noise ceased.

"Funny," he said, "I heard that last night. There's nothing; it's some stray dog in the bushes. Do tell me what it is that I've got."

Rankin, who had surged to his feet also, stood listening a moment. But there was nothing to be heard but the buzzing of bees in the bushes and the chiding of the remote kites overhead. He sat down again.

"Well, give me two minutes," he said, "and I can tell you all I know. Once upon a time, when this wonderful and secret land was alive and not dead—oh, we have killed it with our board schools and our steamers and our religion—there was a whole hierarchy of gods—Isis, Osiris, and the rest, of whom we know a good deal. But below them there was a company of semi-divinities, demons if you will, of whom we know precisely nothing. The cat was one, certain dwarfish creatures were others, but most potent of all were the Cynocephali, the dog-faced apes. They were not divine, rather they were demons, of hideous power, but"—and he pointed a great hand at Hugh— "they could be controlled. Men could control them—men could turn them into terrific servants—much as the genii in the 'Arabian Nights' were controlled. But to do that you had to know the secret name of the demon, and had yourself to make an image of him, with the secret name inscribed therein, and by that you could summon him and all the incarnate creatures of his species. So much we know from certain very guarded allusions in the Book of the Dead and other sources, for it was one of the great mysteries never openly spoken of. Here and there a priest in Karnak, or Abydos, or in Hieropolis, had had handed down to him one of these secret names, but in nine cases out of ten the knowledge died with him, for there was something dangerous and terrible about it all. Old Abdul Hamid here, for instance, believes that Moses had the secret names of frogs and lice, and made images of them with the secret name inscribed on them, and by those produced the plagues of Egypt. Think what you could do, think what he did, if infinite power over frog-nature were given you, so that the King's chamber swarmed with frogs at your word. Usually, as I said, the secret name was but sparingly passed on, but occasionally some very bold advanced spirit, such as Moses, made his image, and controlled—"

He paused a moment, and Hugh wondered if he was in some delirious dream. Here they were, taking coffee and cigarettes underneath the shadow of a modern hotel in the year AD 1912, and this great savant was talking to him about the spell that controlled the whole frog-nature in the universe. The gist, the moral of his discourse, was already perfectly clear.

"That's a good joke," Hugh said. "You told your story with extraordinary gravity. And what you mean is that those two blue bits I hold in my hand control the whole ape-nature of the world? Bravo, Rankin! For a moment, you and your impressiveness almost made me take it all seriously. Lord! You do tell a story well! And what's the secret name of the ape?"

Rankin turned to him with the shake of an impressive forefinger.

"My dear boy," he said, "you should never be disrespectful towards the things you know nothing of. Never say a thing is moonshine till you know what you are talking about. I know, at this moment, exactly as much as you do about your ape-image, except that I can translate its inscription, which I will do for you. On the top-half is written, 'He, of whom this is, let him call on me thrice—'"

Hugh interrupted.

"That's what Abdul Hamid read to me," he said.

"Of course. Abdul Hamid knows hieroglyphics. But on the lower half is what nobody but you and I know. 'Let him call on me thrice,' says the top-half, and then there speaks what you picked up in the valley of the tombs, 'and I, Tahu-met, obey the order of the Master.'"

"Tahu-met?" asked Hugh.

"Yes. Now in ten minutes I must be off to catch my train. What I have told you is all that is known about this particular affair by those who have studied folklore and magic, and Egyptology. If anything—if anything happens, do be kind enough to let me know. If you were not so abominably rich I would offer you what you liked for that little broken statue. But there's the way of the world!"

"Oh, it's not for sale," said Hugh gaily. "It's too interesting to sell. But what am I to do next with it? Tahu-met. Shall I say Tahu-met three times?"

Rankin leaned forward very hurriedly, and laid his fat hand on the young man's knee.

"No, for Heaven's sake! Just keep it by you," he said. "Be patient with it. See what happens. You might mend it, perhaps. Put a drop of gum arabic on the break and make it whole. By the way, if it interests you at all, my niece Julia Draycott arrives this evening, and will wait for me here till my return from Merawi. You met her in Cairo, I think."

"By Jove, is she really?" he said. "That's splendid. She told me she might be coming up, but didn't feel at all sure. Must you really be off? I shall come down to the station with you."

While Rankin went to gather up such small luggage as he had brought with him, Hugh wandered into the hotel bureau to ask for letters, and seeing there a gum-bottle, dabbed with gum the fractured edges of Tahu-met. The two pieces joined with absolute exactitude, and wrapping a piece of paper round them to keep the edges together, he went through the garden with Rankin. At the hotel gate was the usual crowd of donkey-boys and beggars, and presently they were ambling down the village street on bored white donkeys. It was almost deserted at this hottest hour of the afternoon, but along it there moved an Arab leading a large grey ape, that tramped surlily in the dust. But just before they overtook it, the beast looked round, saw Hugh, and with chatterings of delight strained at his leash. Its owner cursed and pulled it away, for Hugh nearly rode over it, but it paid no attention to him, and fairly towed him along the road after the donkeys.

Rankin looked at his companion.

"That's odd," he said. "That's one of your servants. I've still a couple of minutes to spare. Do you mind stopping a moment?"

He shouted something in the vernacular to the Arab, who ran after them, with the beast still towing him on. When they came close the ape stopped and bent his head to the ground in front of Hugh.

"And that's odd," said Rankin.

Hugh suddenly felt rather uncomfortable.

"Nonsense!" he said. "That's just one of his tricks. He's been taught to get baksheesh for his master. Look, there's your train coming in. We must get on."

He threw a couple of piastres to the man, and they rode on. But when they got to the station, glancing down the road, he saw that the ape was still looking after them.

Julia Draycott's arrival that evening speedily put suck antique imaginings as the lordship of apes out of Hugh's head. He chucked Tahu-met into the box where he kept his scarabs and *ushapti* figures, and devoted himself to this heartless and exquisite girl, whose mission in life appeared to be to make as miserable as possible the largest possible number of young men. Hugh had already been selected by her in Cairo as a decent victim, and now she proceeded to torture him. She had no intention whatever of marrying him, for poor Hugh was certainly ugly, with his broad, heavy face, and though rich, he was not nearly rich enough. But he had a couple of delightful Arab horses, and so, since there was no one else on hand to experiment with, she let him buy her a side-saddle, and be, with his horses, always at her disposal. She did not propose to use him for very long, for she expected young Lord Paterson (whom she did intend to marry) to follow her from Cairo within a week. She had beat a Parthian retreat from him, being convinced that he would soon find Cairo intolerable without her; and in the meantime Hugh was excellent practice. Besides, she adored riding.

They sat together one afternoon on the edge of the river opposite Karnak. She had treated him like a brute beast all morning, and had watched his capability of wretchedness with all the purring egoism that distinguished her; and now, as a change, she was seeing how happy she could make him.

"You are such a dear," she said. "I don't know how I could have endured Luxor without you; and, thanks to you, it has been the loveliest week."

She looked at him from below her long lashes, through which there gleamed the divinest violet, smiling like a child at her friend. "The loveliest week," she said. "And tonight? You made some delicious plan for tonight."

"Yes; it's full moon tonight," said he. "We are going to ride out to Karnak after dinner."

"That will be heavenly. And, Mr. Marsham, do let us go alone. There's sure to be a mob from the hotel, so let's start late, when they've all cleared out. Karnak in the moonlight, just with you."

That completely made Hugh's mind up. For the last three days he had been on the look out for a moment that would furnish the great occasion; and now (all unconsciously, of course) she indicated it to him. This evening, then. And his heart leaped.

"Yes, yes," he said. "But why have I become Mr. Marsham again?"

Again she looked at him, now with a penitent mouth.

"Oh, I was such a beast to you this morning," she said. "That was why. I didn't deserve that you should be Hugh. But will you be Hugh again? Do you forgive me?"

In spite of Hugh's fixing the great occasion for this evening, it might have come then, so bewitching was her penitence, had not the rest of their party on donkeys, whom they had outpaced, come streaming along the river bank at this moment.

"Ah, those tiresome people," she said. "Hughie, what a bore everybody else is except you and me."

They got back to the hotel about sunset, and as they passed into the hall the porter handed Julia a telegram which had been waiting some couple of hours. She gave a little exclamation of pleasure and surprise, and turned to Hugh.

"Come and have a turn in the garden, Hughie," she said, "and then I must go down for the arrival of the boat. When does it come in?"

"I should think it would be here immediately," he said. "Let's go down to the river."

Even as he spoke the whistle of the approaching steamer was heard. The girl hesitated for a moment.

"It's a shame to take up all your time in the way I'm doing," she said. "You told me you had letters to write. Write them now, then—then you'll be free after dinner."

"Tomorrow will do," he said. "I'll come down with you to the boat."

"No, you dear. I absolutely forbid it," she said. "Oh, do be good; run indoors and write your letters. I ask you to."

Rather puzzled and vaguely uncomfortable, Hugh went into the hotel. It was true that he had told her he had letters that should have been written a week ago, but something at the back of his mind insisted that this was not the girl's real reason for wanting him to do his task now. She wanted to go and meet the boat alone, and on the moment an unfounded jealousy stirred like a coiled snake in him. He told himself that it might be some inconvenient aunt whom she was going to meet, but such a suggestion did not in the least satisfy him when he remembered the obvious pleasure with which she had read the telegram that no doubt announced this arrival. But he nailed himself to his writing-table till a couple of very tepid letters were finished, and then, with growing restlessness, went out through the hall into the warm, still night. Most of the hotel had gone indoors to dress for dinner, but sitting on the veranda with her back to him was Julia. A chair was drawn in front of her, and facing her was a young man, on whose face the light shone. He was looking eagerly at her, and his hand rested on her knee. Hugh turned abruptly and went back into the hotel.

He and Julia for these last three days had, with two other friends, made a very pleasant party of four at lunch and dinner. Tonight, when he entered the dining-room, he found that places were laid here for three only, and that at a far-distant table in the window were sitting Julia and the young man whom he had seen with her on the veranda. His identity was casually disclosed as dinner went on; one of his companions had seen Lord Paterson in Cairo. Hugh had only a wandering ear for table-talk, but a quick glancing eye, ever growing more sombre, for those in the window, and his heavy face, as he noted the tokens and signs of their intimacy, grew sullen and savage. Then, before dinner was over, they rose and passed out into the garden.

Jealousy can no more bear to lose sight of those to whom it owes its miseries than love can bear to be parted from its adoration, and presently Hugh and his two friends went and sat, as was usual with them, on the veranda outside. Here and there about the garden were wandering couples, and in the light of the full moon, which was to be their lamp at Karnak tonight when the "tiresome people" had gone, he soon identified Julia and Lord Paterson. They passed and repassed down a rose-embowered alley, hidden sometimes behind bushes and then appearing again for a few paces, and each sight of them, each vanishing of them again served but to confirm that which already needed no confirmation. And as his jealousy grew every moment more bitter, so every moment Hugh grew more and more dangerously enraged. Apparently Lord Paterson was not one of the "tiresome people" whom Julia longed to get away from.

Presently his two companions left him, for they were starting now to ride out to Karnak, and Hugh sat on, smoking, and throwing away half-consumed, an endless series of cigarettes. He had ordered that his two horses, one with side-saddle, should be ready at ten, and at ten he meant to go to the girl and remind her of her engagement. Till then he would wait here, wait and watch. If the veranda had been on fire he felt he could not have left it to seek safety in some place where he was unable to see the bushy path where the two strolled. Then they emerged from that on to the broader walk that led straight to where he was sitting, and after a few whispered words, Lord Paterson left her there, and came quickly towards the hotel. He passed close by Hugh, gave him (so Hugh thought) a glance of amused derision, and went into the hotel.

Julia came quickly towards him when Lord Paterson had gone.

"Oh, Hughie," she said. "Will you be a tremendous angel? Lord Paterson—yes, he's just gone in, such a dear, you would delight in him—Lord Paterson's only here for one night, and he's dying to see Karnak by moonlight. So will you lend us your horses? He absolutely insists I should go out there with him.

The amazing effrontery of this took Hugh's breath away, and in that moment's pause his rage flamed within him.

"I thought you were going out with me?" he said.

"I was. But, well, you see—"

She made the penitent mouth again, which had seemed so enchanting to him this afternoon.

"Oh, Hughie, don't you understand?" she said.

Hugh got up, feeling himself to be one shaking black jelly of wounded anger.

"I'm not sure if I do," he said. "But no doubt I soon shall. Anyhow, I want to ask you something. I want you to promise to marry me."

She opened her great childlike eyes to their widest. Then they closed into mere slits again as she broke out into a laugh.

"Marry you?" she said. "You silly, darling fellow! That is a good joke."

Suddenly from the garden there sounded the jubilant scamper of running feet, and next moment a great grey ape sprang on to the veranda beside them, and looked eagerly, with keen dog's eyes, at Hugh, as if intent on obeying some yet unspoken command. Julia gave a little shriek of fright and clung to him.

"Oh, that horrible animal!" she cried. "Hughie, take care of me!"

Some sudden ray of illumination came to Hugh. All the extraordinary fantastic things that Rankin had said to him became sober and real. And simultaneously the girl's clinging fingers on his arm became like the touch of some poisonous, preying thing, snake-coil, or suckers of an octopus, or hooked wings of a vampire shook and trembled like a quicksand, but his conscious mind was quite clear and collected.

"Go away," he said to the ape, and pointed into the garden, and it scampered off still gleefully spurning and kicking the soft sandy path. Then he quietly turned to the girl.

"There, it's gone," he said. "It was just some tame thing escaped. I saw it, or one like it, the other day on the end of a string. As for the horses, I shall be delighted to let you and Lord Paterson have them. It is ten now; they will be round."

The girl had quite recovered from her fright. "Ah, Hughie, you are a dear," she said. "And you do understand?"

"Yes, perfectly," he said.

Julia went to dress herself for riding, and presently Hugh saw them off from the gate, with courteous wishes for a pleasant ride. Then he went back to his bedroom and opened the little box where he kept his scarabs.

An hour later he was walking out alone on the road to Karnak, and in his pocket was the image of Tahu-met. He had formed no clear idea of what he was going to do; the immediate reason for his expedition was that once again he could not bear to lose sight of Julia and her companion. The moon was high, the feathery outline of palm-groves was clearly and delicately etched on the dark velvet of the heavens, and stars sat among their branches like specks of golden fruit. The caressing scent of bean-flowers was weighted over the road, and often he had to stand aside to let pass a troop of noisy tourists mounted on white donkeys, coming riotously home from the show-piece of Karnak by moonlight. Then, striking off the road, he passed beside the horse-shoe lake, in the depths of whose black waters the stars burned unwaveringly, and came by the entrance of the ruined temple of Mut. And then, with a stab of jealousy that screamed for its revenge, he saw, tied up to a pillar just within, his own horses. So they were here.

He gave the beasts a wide berth, lest, recognizing him, they should whinny and perhaps betray his presence, and, creeping in the shadow of the walls behind the row of great cat-headed statues, he stole into the inner court of the temple. Here for the first time he caught sight of the two at the far end of the enclosure, and as they turned, white-faced in the moonlight, he saw Paterson kiss the girl, and they stood there with neck and arms interlaced. Then they began walking towards him again, and he stepped into a dark chamber on his right to avoid meeting them.

It had that strange stale animal odour about it that hangs in Egyptian temples, and with a thrill of glee he saw, by a ray of moonlight that streamed in through the door, that by chance he had stepped into the shrine round which sit the dog-faced apes, whose secret name he knew, and whose controlling spell lay in his breast-pocket. Often he had felt the underworld horror that dwelt here, as a thing petrified and corpse-like; tonight it was petrified no longer, for the images seemed tense and quivering with the life that at any moment he could put into them. Their faces leered and hated and lusted, and all that demonic power, which seemed to be flowing into him from them, was his to use as he wished. Rankin's fantastic tales were bursting with reality; he knew with the certainty with which the night-watcher waits for the day, that the lordship of the spirit of apes, incarnate and discarnate, would descend on him as on some anointed king the moment he thrice pronounced the secret name. He was going to do it too; he knew that also, all he hesitated for now was to determine what orders the lord should give. It seemed that the image in his breast-pocket was aware, for it throbbed and vibrated against his chest like a boiling kettle.

He could not make up his mind what to do; but fed as with fuel by jealousy, and love, and hate, and revenge, suddenly his sense of the magical control he wielded could be resisted no longer, but boiled over, and he drew from his pocket the image where was engraven the secret name.

"Tahu-met, Tahu-met, Tahu-met," he shouted aloud.

There was a moment's absolute stillness; then came a wild scream of fright from his horses, and he heard them gallop off madly into the night. Slowly, like a lamp turned down and then finally turned out, the blaze of the moon faded into utter darkness, and in that darkness, which whispered with a gradually increasing noise of scratchings and scamperings, he felt that the walls of the narrow chamber where he stood were, as in a dream, going farther and farther away from him, until, though still the darkness was impenetrable, he knew that he was standing in some immense space. One wall, he fancied, was still near him, close behind him, but the space which was full of he knew not what unseen presences, extended away and away to both sides of him and in front of him. Then he was aware that he was not standing, but sitting, for beneath his hands he could feel the arms as of some throne, of which the seat's edge pressed him just below his knees. The animal odour he had noticed before increased enormously in pungency, and he sniffed it in ecstatically, as if it had been the scent of beanfields, and mixed with it was the sweetness of incense and the savour as of roast meat. And at that the withdrawn light began to glow once more, only now it was not the whiteness of the moon, but a redder glow as of flames that aspired and sank again.

He saw where he was now. He was seated on a chair of pink granite, and a little in front of him was a huge altar, on which limbs smoked. Overhead was a low roof supported at intervals by painted pillars, and the whole of the vast floor was full of great grey apes, squatting in dense rows. Sometimes they all bowed their heads to the ground, sometimes, as by a signal, they raised them again, and myriads of obscene expectant eyes faced him. They glowed from within, as cats' eyes glow in the dusk, but with an infinity of hellish power. All that power was his to command, and he gloried in it.

"Bring them in," he said, and no more. Indeed, he was not sure if he said it; it was just his thought.

But as if he spoke the soundless language of animals they understood, and they clambered and leaped over each other to do his bidding. Then a huddled wave of them surged up in front of where he sat, and as it broke in a foam of evil eyes and paws and switching tails, it disclosed the two whom he had ordered to be brought before him.

"And what shall I do with them?" he asked himself, cudgelling his monkey-brain for some infamous invention.

"Kiss each other," he said at length, in order to inflame the brutality of his jealousy further, and he laughed chatteringly, as their white trembling lips met. He felt that all remnants of humanity were draining from him; there was but a little in his whole nature that could be deemed to belong to a man. A hundred awful schemes ran about through his brain, as sparks of fire run through the charred ashes of burnt paper.

And then Julia turned her face towards him. In the hideous entry that she had made in that wave of apes her hair had fallen down and streamed over her shoulders. And at that, the sight of a woman's hair unbound, the remnant of his manhood, all that was not submerged in the foulness of his supreme apehood, made one tremendous appeal to him, like some final convulsion of the dying, and at the bidding of that impulse his hands came together and snapped the image in two.

Something screamed; the whole temple yelled with it, and mixed with it was a roaring in his ears as of great waters or hurricane winds. He stamped on the broken image, grinding it to powder below his heel, and felt the ground and the temple walls rocking round him.

Then he heard someone not far off speaking in human voice again, and no music could be so sweet.

"Let's get out of the place, darling," it said. "That was an earthquake, and the horses have bolted."

He heard running steps outside, which gradually grew fainter. The moon shone whitely into the little chamber with the grotesque stone apes, and at his feet was the powdered blue glaze and baked white clay of the image he had ground to dust.

Black Coffee

Jeffery Farnol

I

Professor Jarvis sat among piles of reference-books, and stacks of notes and jottings, the silence about him unbroken save for the ceaseless scratching of his pen.

Professor Jarvis hated bustle and noise of all sorts, for they destroyed that continuity of thought, that following out of proved facts to their primary hypotheses, which was to him the chief end and aim of existence; therefore he inhabited the thirtieth storey.

He had seen none but John, his valet, for nearly a month, sitting night after night, perched high above the great city, busied upon the work of which he had dreamed for years, his treatise upon "The Higher Ethics of Philosophy," and already it neared completion. A spirit of work had come upon him these last few weeks, a spirit that was a devil, cruel, relentless, allowing of no respite from the strain of intricate thought and nerve-racking effort; hence the Professor sat writing night after night, and had of late done with little sleep and much black coffee.

To-night, however, he felt strangely tired, he laid down his pen, and, resting his throbbing temples between his hands, stared down vacantly at the sheets of manuscript before him.

As he leaned thus, striving against a feeling of nausea that had recurred frequently the last few days, the long, close-written lines became to him "things" endowed with sinuous life, that moved, squirming a thousand legs across the white paper.

Professor Jarvis closed his eyes and sighed wearily. "I really must get some sleep," he said to himself, "I wonder when it was I slept last?" As he spoke he tried unsuccessfully to yawn and stretch himself. His glance, wandering aimlessly, paused at the lamp upon the desk before him, and as he stared at it, he noticed that the "things" had got from the paper and were writhing and creeping up the green shade. He sighed again, and his fingers fumbled among the papers beside him for the electric bell. Almost immediately, it seemed to him, he heard John's voice rather faint and far-away, responding from the shadow that lay beyond the light of the lamp.

"John, if you are really there, be so good as to switch on the light," said the Professor. "John," he continued, blinking at his valet in the sudden glare, "when did I sleep last?"

"Why, sir, you haven't rightly slept for a week now, just a doze now and then on the couch, sir, but that's nothing; if you'll allow me to advise you, sir, the best thing you could do would be to go to bed at once."

"Humph!" said the Professor. "Thank you, John, but your advice, though excellent, is impracticable. I am engaged upon my last chapter, and sleep is impossible until it is finished."

"Begging your pardon, sir," began John, "but if you were to try undressing and going to bed properly—"

"Don't be a fool, John!" cried the Professor, with a sudden access of anger that was strangely at variance with his usual placid manner, "do you think I wouldn't sleep if I could? Can't you see I'm sick for sleep? I tell you I'd sleep if I could, but I can't—there can be no rest for me I know now, until I've finished my book, and that will be somewhere about dawn," and the Professor glared up at John, his thick brows twitching, and his eyes glowing within the pale oval of his face with an unpleasant light.

"If you would only give up drinking so much black coffee, sir; they do say it's very bad for the nerves—"

"And I think they are right," put in the Professor, and his voice was as gentle as ever. "Yes, I think they are right. For instance, John, at this precise moment I have a feeling that there is a hand groping behind the curtains yonder. Yet this mental attitude harmonises in a manner with the subject of this last chapter, which deals with the psychic forces of nature. I allude, John, more especially to the following passage:

"'That mysterious power which some call the soul, if sufficiently educated, may cast off for a time this bodily flesh, and precipitate itself into illimitable spaces, riding upon the winds, walking upon the beds of seas and rivers, and indeed may even re-inhabit the bodies of those that have been long dead, provided they could be kept from corruption.'" The Professor leaned back in his chair, and continued in the voice of one thinking aloud:

"All this was known centuries ago, notably to the priests of Isis and the early Chaldeans, and is practised to-day in some small part by the fakirs of India and the lamas of Tibet, and yet is looked upon by the ignorant world as little more than cheap trickery. By the way," he broke off, becoming suddenly aware of John's presence, "didn't you ask for leave of absence until to-morrow?"

"Well, yes, sir, I did," admitted John, "but I thought I'd put it off, seeing you are so—so busy, sir."

"Nonsense, John, don't waste the evening, it must be getting late, just brew some more coffee in the samovar, and then you can go." John hesitated, but meeting the Professor's eye, obeyed; and having set the steaming samovar on a small table at his master's elbow and put the room in order, he turned to the door.

"I shall be back in the morning at eight o'clock, sir."

"Very good, John," said the Professor, sipping his coffee. "Good-night, John."

"Good-night, sir," returned John, and, closing the door behind him, stood for a moment to shake his head. "He isn't fit to be left alone," he muttered, "but I'll get back before eight to-morrow morning, yes, I'll take good care to be back before eight." So saying, he turned, and went softly along the passage.

II

For a long time the Professor had sat crouched above his desk, yet in the last half-hour he had not added a single word to the page before him, for somewhere beneath his brain a small hammer seemed tap-tapping, soft and slow and regular, rendering the stillness about him but the more profound. Slowly and gradually a feeling of expectation grew upon him, a foolishly persistent expectation of something that was drawing near and nearer to him with every stroke of the hammer—something that he could neither guess at, nor hope to arrest, only, he knew that it was coming, coming, and he waited with straining ears, listening for the unknown.

Suddenly, from somewhere in the world far below, a clock chimed midnight, and as the last strokes died there was a hurry of footsteps along the corridor without, a knock, and a fumbling at the handle. As the Professor rose, the door opened, and a shortish, stoutish individual, chiefly remarkable for a round, red face, and a bristle of grey hair, trotted in, and was shaking him by the hand—talking meanwhile in that quick jerky style that was characteristic of Magnus McManus, whose researches in Lower Egypt and along the Nile during the last ten years had made his name famous.

"My dear Dick," he began, "good God, how ill you look!—frightful—overwork as usual, eh?"

"Why, Magnus!" exclaimed the Professor, "I thought you were in Egypt?"

"Exactly—so I was—came back last week with a specimen—been in New York three days—must get back to the Nile at once—booked passage yesterday—sail to-morrow—noon. You see, Dick," continued Magnus, trotting up and down the room, "I received a cable from Tarrant—overseer of the excavations, you know—to say they've come upon a monolith—Coptic inscriptions—curious—may be important—very."

"Yes," nodded the Professor.

"So just looked you up, Dick—to ask you to take charge of this specimen I brought over—thought you wouldn't mind keeping it until I got back."

"Certainly, of course," said the Professor rather absently.

"Undoubtedly the greatest find of the age," pursued Magnus, "stupendous—will throw a new light on Egyptian history—there is not in the whole world, so far as is known, such another mummy."

"A what?" exclaimed the Professor, "did you say 'mummy'?"

"To be sure," nodded Magnus, "though the term is inapt—this is something more than your ordinary dried-up mummy."

"And have you—have you brought it with you, Magnus?"

"Certainly—it's waiting outside in the corridor."

For no apparent reason the Professor shivered violently, and the nausea came upon him again.

"The deuce of a time getting it here—awkward to handle, you know," and as he spoke Magnus turned and trotted from the room. There came a murmur of voices outside, a shuffle and stagger of approaching footsteps as of men who bore a heavy burden, and above all the excited tones of Magnus.

"Easy there—mind that corner—steady, steady, don't jar it; now, gently—so." And Magnus reappeared, followed by four men who bent beneath something in shape between a packing-case and a coffin, which by the direction of Magnus they sat carefully down in a convenient corner.

"Now," cried he, as soon as they were alone, drawing a small screwdriver from his pocket, "I'm going to show you something that will make you doubt the evidence of your eyes—as I did myself at first—a wonder, Dick—that will set all the societies gaping—open-mouthed—like fools."

One by one Magnus extracted the screws that held down the lid, while the Professor watched, wide-eyed, waiting—waiting.

"This specimen will be a revelation on the art of embalming," continued Magnus, busy upon the last screw. "Here is no stuffed and withered, dried-up wisp of humanity. Whoever did this was a genius—positively—there has been no disembowelling here—deuce take this screw—body is as perfect as when life first left it—and mark me, Dick—it can't be less than six thousand years old at the very least—probably older. I tell you it's beyond all wonder, but there—judge for yourself!" and with these words, Magnus laid down the screwdriver, lifted off the heavy lid and stood aside.

The Professor drew a deep breath, his fingers clutching convulsively at his chair-arms, as he stared at that which lay, or rather stood, within the glass-fronted shell or coffin.

And what he saw was an oval face framed in black hair, a face full and unshrunken, yet of a hideous ashen-grey, a high, thin, aquiline nose with delicate proud-curving nostrils, and below, a mouth, blue-lipped, yet in whose full, cruel lines lurked a ghastly mockery that carried with it a nameless horror.

"Must have been handsome at one time," said Magnus. "Very much so indeed—regular features and all that—pure Egyptian type, but—"

"It's—the—the face of a devil," muttered the Professor thickly. "I wonder what—what lies behind those eyelids, they seem as if they might lift at any moment, and if they did—Oh, I tell you it is horrible."

Magnus laughed. "Thought she'd astonish you—will knock science deaf and dumb—not a doubt. The setting of these stones," he continued with a complacent air, "round her neck—uncut emeralds they are—dates quite back to the Fifth Dynasty—yet that scarab on her breast seems even earlier still—the gold embroidery on her gown beats me—quite—and the thumb-ring by its shape would almost seem to belong to the Fifteenth Dynasty. Altogether she's a puzzle. Another peculiar thing was that—mouth and nostrils had been—plugged by a kind of cement—deuce of a time getting it out.

"The inscription upon her sarcophagus," he ran on, "describes her as: 'Ahasuera, Princess of the House of Ra, in the reign of Raman Kau Ra,' possibly another title for Seti The Second. I also came upon a papyrus—very important—and three tablets, have only had time to dip into them hastily—but from what I gather, Ahasuera appears to have been of a very evil reputation—combination of Semiramis, Cleopatra, and Messalina, multiplied by three! One of her lovers was a certain Ptomes, High Priest of the Temple of Osiris, who is spoken of as 'one greatly versed in the arts and mysteries of Isis and the high Gods.' When I first opened her sarcophagus, from the strange disorder of the wrappings—almost seemed as if she must have moved—also the golden death-mask that had covered her face had fallen off—which was curious—very. Upon examining this mask—found an inscription across the forehead—puzzled me for days—meaning came to me all at once—in bed—might be translated by a line of doggerel verse something like this:

'Isis awhile hath stayed my breath,
Whoso wakes me shall find death.'

which is also curious, eh? Why, Great heavens, man! What ails you?" Magnus broke off, for he had turned and looked at his friend for the first time.

"Nothing," returned the Professor in the same thick voice. "Nothing—only cover it up—cover it up in God's name."

"Certainly—to be sure," said Magnus, staring. "Had no idea it would affect you like that, nerves must be at sixes and sevens, should take more care of yourself, Dick, and stop that confounded black coffee."

As the last screw was driven home, the Professor laughed, a little wildly. "There are eighteen screws, about two and a half inches long, eh, Magnus?"

"Yes," said Magnus and turned to stare again.

"Good," the Professor rejoined with the same strange laugh. Magnus forced a smile.

"Why, Dick," he began, "you almost talk as though you imagined—"

"Those eyes," the Professor broke in, "they haunt me, they are the eyes of one who waits to take you unawares, they are eyes that watch and follow you behind your back—"

"Pooh! nonsense, Dick," cried Magnus, rather hastily. "This is nothing but imagination—sheer imagination. You ought to take a holiday or you will be suffering from hallucinations next."

"Sit still and listen," said the Professor, and he began to read from the manuscript before him:

"'That mysterious power which some call the soul, if sufficiently educated, may cast off for a time this bodily flesh and precipitate itself into illimitable spaces, riding upon the winds, walking upon the beds of seas and rivers, and indeed may even re-inhabit the bodies of those that have been long dead, provided that body could be kept free from corruption.'"

"Humph!" said Magnus, crossing his legs. "Well?"

"'Provided that body could be kept free from corruption,'" repeated the Professor, then, raising his arm with a sudden gesture, he pointed at the thing in the corner: "That is not death," he said.

Magnus leaped to his feet. "Man, are you mad," he cried, "what do you mean?"

"Suspended animation!" said the Professor.

For a long moment there was silence, during which the two men stared into each other's eyes; the face of Magnus had lost some of its colour, and the Professor's fingers moved nervously upon his chair-arms. Suddenly Magnus laughed, though perhaps a trifle too boisterously.

"Bosh!" he exclaimed, "what folly are you talking, Dick? What you require is a good stiff glass of brandy and bed afterwards," and with the knowledge and freedom of an old friend, he crossed to a corner cabinet, and took thence a decanter and glasses, pouring out a stiff peg into each.

"So you don't agree with me, Magnus?"

"Agree, no," said Magnus, swallowing his brandy at a gulp, "it's all nerves—damn 'em."

The Professor shook his head. "There are more things in heaven and earth—"

"Yes—yes, I know—I have cursed Shakespeare frequently for that same quotation."

"But you yourself wrote a paper, Magnus, only a few years ago, on the hypnotic trances practised by the Egyptians."

"Now, Dick," expostulated Magnus, "be reasonable, for heaven's sake! Is it possible that any trance could extend into six or seven thousand years? Preposterous, utterly. Come, get to bed, man, like a sensible chap—where's John?"

"I gave him leave of absence until to-morrow."

"The deuce you did?" exclaimed Magnus, glancing round the room with an uneasy feeling. "Well, I'll take his place—see you into bed and all that."

"Thanks, Magnus, but it's no good," returned the Professor, shaking his head. "I couldn't sleep until I've finished this last chapter, and it won't take long."

"One o'clock, by Gad!" exclaimed Magnus, glancing at his watch. "Must hurry off, Dick—hotel—sail to-morrow, you know."

The Professor shivered, and rose to his feet. "Good-bye, Magnus," he said as they shook hands. "I hope your monolith will turn out a good find. Good-bye!"

"Thanks, old fellow," said Magnus, returning the pressure. "Now, no more poisonous coffee, mind." So saying he trotted to the door, nodded, and was gone.

The Professor sat for a moment with puckered brows, then, rising hastily, crossed to the door, turned the handle, and peered out into the dim light of the corridor.

"Magnus," he called in a hoarse whisper. "Magnus."

"Well?" came the answer.

"Then you don't think It will open Its eyes, do you, Magnus?"

"Good God—no!"

"Ah!" said the Professor, and closed the door.

III

"I wish," said the Professor, as he took up his pen, "I wish that I had not let John go, I feel strangely lonely to-night, and John is so very matter of fact," so saying he bent to his writing again. His brain had grown singularly bright and clear, all his faculties seemed strung to their highest pitch, a feeling of exaltation had taken possession of him. His ideas grew luminous, intricate thoughts became coherent, the words shaping themselves beneath his pen with a subtle power and eloquence.

Yet all at once, and for no apparent reason, in the very middle of a sentence, a desire seized upon him to turn his head and look back over his shoulder at that which stood in the corner. He checked it with an effort, and his pen resumed its scratching; though all the time he was conscious that the desire was growing, and that sooner or later it would master him. Not that he expected to see anything unusual, that was absurd, of course. He began trying to remember how many screws there were holding down the lid upon that Thing, whose lips had mocked at God and man through centuries and whose eyes—ah, whose eyes— The Professor turned suddenly, and with his pen extended before him, began counting the glinting screw-heads to himself in an undertone.

"One, two three, four, five, six—six along each side, and three along the top and bottom—eighteen in all. And they were steel screws, too, a quarter of an inch thick, and two and a half inches in length; they ought to be strong enough, and yet eighteen after all was not many; why hasn't Magnus used more of them, it would have been so much—"

The Professor checked himself, and turned back to his work; but he tried vainly to write, for now the impulse held him without respite, growing more insistent each moment, an impulse that had fear beneath it, fear born of things that move behind one. Ah, yes, behind one—why had he let It be placed in the corner that was directly behind his chair? He rose and began pulling and dragging at his desk, but it was heavy, and defied his efforts; yet the physical exertion, futile though it was, seemed to calm him, but though he bent resolutely above his task—the finishing of his great book—his mind was absent, and the pen between his fingers traced idle patterns and meaningless scribbles upon the sheet before him, so he tossed it aside, and buried his face in his hands.

Could it be possible that in the darkness behind the lid with the eighteen screws the eyes were still shut, or were they—? The Professor shivered. Ah, if he could but know, if he could only be certain—he wished John was here—John was so very matter of fact—he might have sat and watched It—yes, he had been foolish to let John go. The Professor sighed, and, opening his eyes, remained motionless—staring down at the sheet of foolscap before him—staring at the two uneven lines scrawled across it in ragged capitals that were none of his:

"Isis awhile hath stayed my breath,
Whoso wakes me shall find death."

A sudden piping, high-pitched laugh startled him—Could it really be issuing from his own lips? he asked himself, and indeed he knew it must be so. He sat with every nerve tingling—hoping, praying for something to break the heavy silence—the creak of a footstep—

a shout—a scream—anything rather than that horrible laugh; and as he waited it came again, louder, wilder than before. And now he felt it quivering between his teeth, rattling in his throat, shaking him to and fro in its grip, then, swift as it had come it was gone, and the Professor was looking down at a litter of torn paper at his feet. He reached out a trembling hand to the rack upon his desk and taking down a pipe already filled, lighted it. The tobacco seemed to soothe him, and he inhaled it deeply, watching it rise in blue, curling spirals above his head, watched it roll in thin clouds across the room, until he noticed that it always drifted in the same direction, to hang like a curtain above one point, an ever-moving curtain behind which were shadowy "somethings" that moved and writhed.

The Professor got unsteadily to his legs.

"Magnus was right," he muttered, "I am ill, I must try to sleep—I must—I must." But as he stood there, leaning his shaking hands upon the table-edge, the blind fear, the unreasoning dread against which he had battled so vainly all night swept over him in an irresistible wave; his breath choked, a loathing horror shook him from head to foot, yet all the time his gaze never left the great white box, with its narrow screw-heads that stared at him like little searching eyes. Something glittered upon the floor beside it, and almost before he knew he had snatched up the screwdriver. He worked feverishly until but one screw remained, and as he stopped to wipe the sweat from his cheek he was surprised to find himself singing a song he had heard at a music-hall years before, in his college days; then he held his breath as the last screw gave.

... The oval face framed in a mist of black hair, the long voluptuous eyes with their heavy lids, the aquiline nose, the cruel curve of the nostrils, and the full-lipped sensual mouth, with its everlasting mockery; he had seen it all before, and yet as he gazed he was conscious of a change, subtle and horrible, a change that he could not define, yet which held him as one entranced. With an effort he turned away his eyes, and tried to replace the lid, but could not; he looked about him wildly, then snatching up a heavily fringed rug, covered the horror from sight.

"Magnus was right," he repeated, "I must sleep," and crossing to the couch, he sank upon it and hid his face among the cushions.

A long time he lay there, but sleep was impossible, for the sound of the hammers was in his ears again, but louder now and seeming to beat upon his very brain. What was that other sound—that came to him beneath the hammer-strokes—could it be a footstep? He sat up listening, and then he noticed that the fringe upon the rug was moving. He rubbed his eyes, disbelieving, until all at once it was shaken by another movement that ran up it with a strange rippling motion. He rose, trembling, and creeping forward, tore away the rug. Then he saw and understood the change that had baffled him before; and with the knowledge, the might of his learning, the strength of his manhood, deserted him, and covering his face, Professor Jarvis rocked his body to and fro making a strange whimpering noise, like a little child; for the ashen grey was gone from the face, and the lips which had been black were blood-red. For a while the Professor continued to rock to and fro, whimpering behind his hands, till with a sudden gesture, wild and passionate, he tossed his arms above his head.

"My God!" he cried, "I'm going mad—I am mad, oh, anything but that—not mad, no, not mad—I am not mad—no." Chancing to catch sight of himself in a mirror, he shook his head and chuckled. "Not mad," he whispered to his reflection, "oh, no," then he turned to the case once more, and began patting and stroking the glass.

"Oh, Eyes of Death, lift thy lashes, for I am fain to know the mystery beyond. What though I be the Priest Ptomes, even he that put this magic upon thee, yet am I come back to thee, Beloved, and my soul calleth unto thine even as in Thebes of old. Oh, Eyes of Death, lift thy lashes, for I am fain to know the mystery beyond. While thy soul slept, mine hath hungered for thee through countless ages, and now is the time of waiting accomplished. Oh, Eyes of Death, lift thy lashes, for I am fain to know the mystery beyond. Ah, God," he broke out suddenly, "she will not wake—I cannot wake her." And he writhed his fingers together. All at once his aspect changed, his mouth curved with a smile of cunning, he crept to where a small mirror hung upon the wall, and, with a swift movement, hid it beneath his coat, and, crossing to his desk, propped it up before him.

"They will not open while I look and wait for it," he said, nodding and smiling to himself. "They are the eyes of one who waits to take you unawares, that watch and follow you behind your back, yet I shall see them, yes, I shall see them."

From the world below came the long-drawn tooting of a steamer on the river, and with the sound, faint and far-away though it was, reason reasserted itself.

"Good heavens!" he exclaimed, trying to laugh. "What a fool I am to let a pitiful bit of dead humanity drive me half-wild with fear, and in New York too, it seems inconceivable." So saying the Professor crossed to the brandy, and, with his back turned resolutely, slowly drained his glass, yet even then he was vaguely conscious of eyes that watched him, followed his every movement, and with difficulty he forbore from swinging round on his heel. With the same iron will crushing down his rebellious nerves, he arranged his papers and took up his pen.

The human body after all has certain attributes of the cur, for let that master, the mind, chastise it, and it will cringe, let him command and it will obey. So the Professor sat, his eye clear, his hand firm, scarcely noticing the mirror beside him, even when he paused to take a fresh sheet.

The sickly grey of dawn was at the windows as he paused to glance at his watch. "Another half-hour," he muttered, "and my work is done, ended, *fin*—" The word died upon his lips, for his glance by accident had fallen upon the mirror, and the eyes were wide open. For a long moment they looked into his ere their lids fluttered and fell.

"I am suffering from hallucinations," he groaned. "It is one of the results of loss of sleep, but I wish John was back, John is such a matter-of-fact—"

There was a sound behind him, a sound soft and gentle like the whisper of wind in trees, or the brushing of drapery against a wall—and it was moving across the floor behind him. A chill as of death shuddered through him, and he knew the terror that is dumb.

Scarcely daring to look, full of a dread of expectation, he lifted his eyes to the mirror. The case behind him was empty; he turned swiftly, and there, so close that he might almost touch it was, the "Thing" he had called a pitiful bit of dead humanity. Slowly, inch by inch, it moved towards him, with a scrape and rustle of stiff draperies:

"Isis awhile hath stayed my breath,
Whoso wakes me, shall find—death!"

With a cry that was something between a scream and a laugh he leaped to his feet and hurled himself upon It; there was the sound of a dull blow, a gasp, and Professor Jarvis was lying upon the floor, his arms wide-tossed, and his face hidden in the folds of a rug.

Next day there was a paragraph in the papers, which read as follows:

"*Strange Death.*

"Yesterday at his chambers in — Street, Professor Jarvis, the famous Scientist, was found dead, presumably of heart-failure. A curious feature of the case was that a mummy which had stood in a rough travelling-case in a corner on the opposite side of the room was found lying across the Professor's dead body."

Coachwhip Publications

CoachwhipBooks.com

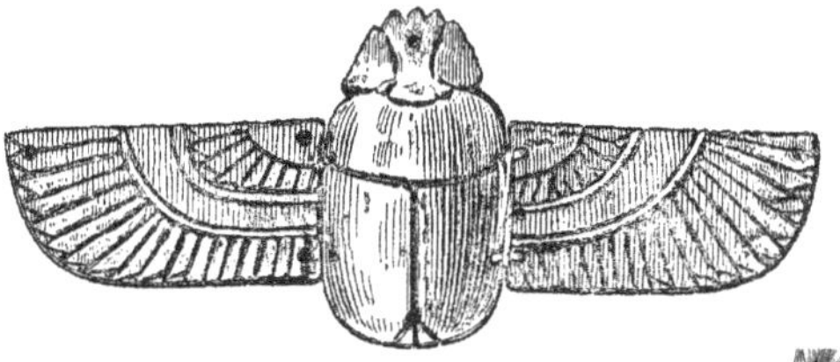

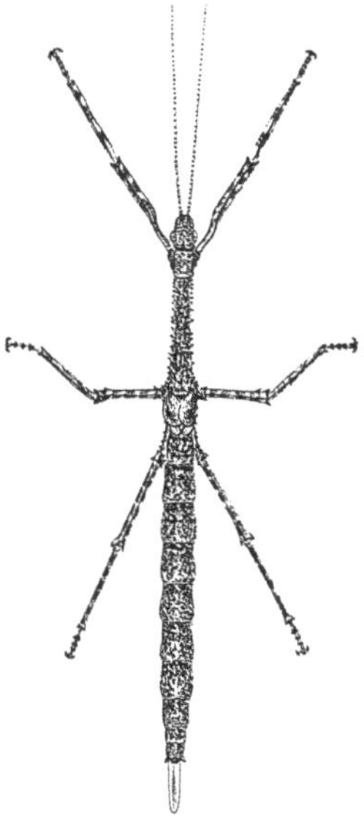

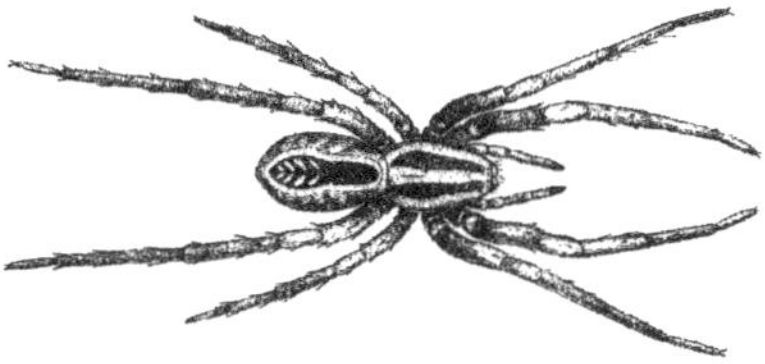

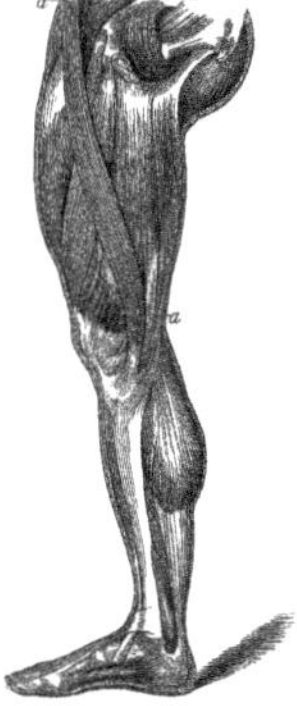

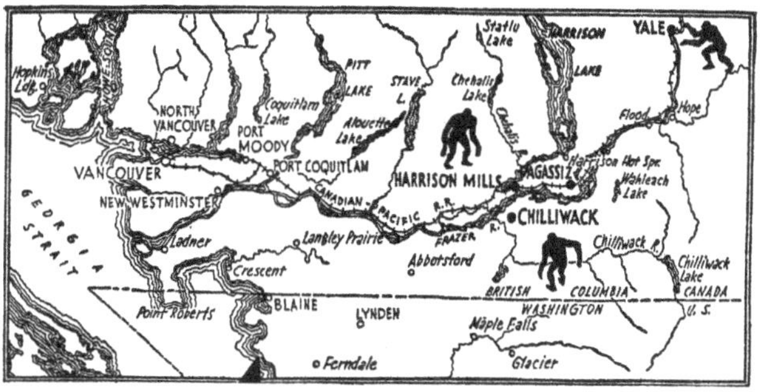

Also Available

About Time:
The Forerunners of Time Travel and Temporal Anomalies in Science Fiction and Fantasy

ISBN 1-930585-55-1

15 classic stories, from Rip Van Winkle and Peter Rugg to tales by Rudyard Kipling, H. G. Wells, and Algernon Blackwood.

Flora Curiosa:
Cryptobotany, Mysterious Fungi, Sentient Trees, and Deadly Plants in Classic Science Fiction and Fantasy

ISBN 1-930585-56-0

20 early stories of weird plants from ballooning trees and strangling vines to dangerous orchids and absorbing fungi.

Also Available

Pym

ISBN 1-930585-57-8

Two novels by Edgar Allan Poe (The Narrative of Arthur Gordon Pym of Nantucket) and Jules Verne (An Antarctic Mystery) tell a story of adventure, horror, and mystery in Antarctica.

Shadow from a Veiled Creation: Classic Tales of Supernatural Fiction in the Christian Tradition

ISBN 1-930585-26-8

Classic stories by authors who wrote from a Christian perspective of the world around them, both visible and invisible.

www.ingramcontent.com/pod-product-compliance
Lightning Source LLC
Chambersburg PA
CBHW020924020726
47495CB00002B/337
* 9 7 8 1 9 3 0 5 8 5 5 8 4 *